The Complete Screech Owls

Volume 4

D1482480

Roy MacGregor

McCLELLAND & STEWART

Copyright © 2006 by Roy MacGregor

This omnibus edition published in 2006 by McClelland & Stewart

Sudden Death in New York City copyright © 2000 by Roy MacGregor
Horror on River Road copyright © 2000 by Roy MacGregor
Death Down Under copyright © 2001 by Roy MacGregor
Power Play in Washington copyright © 2001 by Roy MacGregor

Library and Archives Canada Cataloguing in Publication

MacGregor, Roy, 1948-
The complete Screech Owls / written by Roy MacGregor.

Contents: v. 1. Mystery at Lake Placid – The night they stole the Stanley Cup – The Screech Owls' northern adventure – Murder at hockey camp – v. 2 Kidnapped in Sweden – Terror in Florida – The Quebec City crisis – The Screech Owls' home loss – v. 3. Nightmare in Nagano – Danger in Dinosaur Valley – The ghosts of the Stanley Cup – The West Coast murders – v. 4. Sudden death in New York City – Horror on River Road – Death Down Under – Power play in Washington.

ISBN 13: 978-0-7710-5491-4 (v. 4)
ISBN 10: 0-7710-5484-X (v. 1).– ISBN 10: 0-7710-5486-6 (v. 2). –
ISBN 10: 0-7710-5489-0 (v. 3).– ISBN 10: 0-7710-5491-2 (v. 4)

I. Title.

PS8575.G84C64 2005   jc813'.54   C2005-903880-2

We acknowledge the financial support of the Government of Canada through the Book Publishing Industry Development Program and that of the Government of Ontario through the Ontario Media Development Corporation's Ontario Book Initiative. We further acknowledge the support of the Canada Council for the Arts and the Ontario Arts Council for our publishing program.

Typeset in Bembo by M&S, Toronto
Printed and bound in Canada
Cover illustration by Sue Todd

This book is printed on acid-free paper that is 100% recycled, ancient-forest friendly (100% post-consumer recycled).

McClelland & Stewart Ltd.
75 Sherbourne Street
Toronto, Ontario
M5A 2P9
www.mcclelland.com

1 2 3 4 5   10 09 08 07 06

Contents

Sudden Death in New York City

ingernails?" Fahd suggested.

"For-*get* it!" Nish snorted. "I *chew* mine."

"It would take too long, anyway," mumbled Fahd, his head almost buried in the large book he held open over his shinpads. "World record for the longest fingernail . . ." Fahd looked up, his eyes widening, ". . . is four feet, one-and-a-half inches!"

"How the heck would you pick your nose?" Nish asked.

Most of the Screech Owls laughed. Travis Lindsay just shook his head. Wayne Nishikawa had always been, at one and the same time, the person he knew best and the person he knew least.

They had gone to kindergarten together, taken karate lessons together, played on the same soccer, baseball, and, of course, hockey teams. They had been in the same class every year but one. Weekends, when Travis wasn't sleeping over at Nish's house, Nish was usually sleeping over at Travis's. And yet, despite all those years, despite all those opportunities to see Nish's mind at work, Travis never had any idea what was going to come out of his best friend's mouth. Only that it would be crazy – and that someone had better laugh or else Nish would come out with something even more insane.

It was getting stuffy in the dressing room at the Tamarack Memorial Arena. The Owls were ready for practice, but the local junior team had run overtime, and the big players had left the ice so choppy and rutted that Mr. Dillinger, the Owls' manager, had begged the arena staff for a double flood. The Zamboni was only now beginning its second round.

Fahd had his *Guinness Book of World Records* out while they waited. Even though they were just days away from setting out by bus for New York City and the Big Apple International Peewee Tournament, every one of them was thinking about Nish and his New Year's resolution instead of the practice ahead.

How does Nish do it? Travis wondered. How does he pull everyone into his crazy little world? How does one chubby, goofy-looking twelve-year-old manage to be the centre of attention, no matter what?

They were leaving Tamarack on December 27, the day after Boxing Day. They would be in New York for New Year's Eve, and their coach, Muck Munro, and the team manager, Mr. Dillinger, had promised they could stay up until midnight and attend the celebrations in Times Square – *so long as they behaved themselves*.

Where Nish got the idea of getting his name into the *Guinness Book of World Records*, Travis couldn't be sure. It hadn't come from reading, he was pretty certain of that. If something wasn't on television, if it wasn't on the Internet or in a new video game or the latest movie, Nish didn't even know it existed.

But somewhere he had come up with this hare-brained notion that he could get himself into the *Guinness Book of World Records*. He'd almost driven the team crazy with it.

He'd started out thinking he'd score more goals than any minor-hockey player in history. But Willie Granger, the team's hockey trivia expert, had put a quick end to that ambition. "Wayne Gretzky had 378 one year as a novice," Willie had pointed out.

"I'm peewee," Nish had protested.

Willie had shaken his head. "He had 196 goals the year he was twelve, same age as you. I don't think you could score 170 goals between now and the end of the season – not even in practice."

Now, with the New York tournament less than a week off, Nish had almost the entire team searching out ideas for him. Fahd had offered up a dozen or more from the *Guinness Book of World Records*, including the ridiculous one of Nish, the nail biter, growing the world's longest fingernails.

"Here's a guy in Kentucky who ate sixty-eight dew worms in thirty seconds," said Fahd.

"*And then hurled for three hours!*" laughed Nish.

"How about stupid penalties?" Sarah shouted from the far side of the room. "You take enough of them, that's for sure."

Nish paused only for a quick flick of his tongue in her direction. Then he turned to Data. "What's the NHL record?"

Data had his *National Hockey League Official Guide and Record Book* on his lap, the cover resting on an arm of his wheelchair as he flipped through the thick volume with one hand. "Dave Williams," Data announced. "That's 'Tiger' Williams. Three thousand, nine hundred and sixty-six minutes . . . That's, let me see . . . just over sixty-six hours in the penalty box . . . six hours short of three full days."

Nish winced. "How about for one season?"

Data read again. "Dave Schultz – the 'Hammer.' Four hundred and seventy-two minutes . . . That's just short of eight hours."

"Muck'd kill you," shouted Sam, sitting beside Sarah.

Nish slumped unhappily in his seat. "I gotta find *something!*"

The team was well used to Nish's little funks, and they completely ignored him as talk turned to other matters. Lars Johansson wouldn't be coming, as he was spending the holidays with his grandparents in Sweden. Mario Terziano, who'd played several previous tournaments with the Owls, was being brought in to replace Lars. Everyone else was coming. Jesse Highboy was hoping for one of Mr. Dillinger's famous Stupid Stops on the bus trip to New York, when Mr. Dillinger would hand out dollars and insist that they "buy something absolutely useless with it." Derek Dillinger made a joke about "wedgies," and Dmitri Yakushev wondered if they'd be seeing the Statue of Liberty.

"Times Square is going to be the big thing," said Jenny Staples, the backup goaltender. "There might be a million people there."

"And more than a *billion* watching on TV," added Fahd.

"They'll have the countdown on that big screen in Times Square," said Derek. "I think it might be the biggest in the world."

Nish came suddenly alert. He sat up sharply, his face flushing with excitement. "How many?" he asked Fahd.

"A *billion*, I think."

"It's televised?"

"All over the world. You've seen it. Everybody's seen the countdown."

"Live?" Nish asked, his face gleaming.

"Of course live, you idiot," shouted Sam, looking up from retying her skates. "It's the countdown for the New Year. You think they tape it and play it the next day?"

Everyone laughed, but not Nish.

"Live? One *billion* people watching?"

"Yeah," said Sarah. "So?"

"So," Nish said triumphantly, turning on Fahd. "Is there anything in the *Guinness Book of World Records* on 'mooning'?"

Fahd looked up, incredulous. "*What?*"

"*Mooning* – what's the world's record for mooning? If I mooned a billion people at once, would I get in?"

Travis looked across the room at Sarah, who rolled her eyes and sighed.

Travis tried to cut off his imagination, but it had already raced ahead of him. He could see the crowd at Times Square. He could see the big video monitor and hear the countdown: *Ten! . . . Nine! . . . Eight! . . . Seven! . . . Six! . . . Five! . . . Four! . . . Three! . . . Two! . . . One!* And then, instead of the fireworks and balloons, the big screen filling with the bare-naked butt of the world's craziest peewee hockey player. Travis shook his head hard, hoping to shake off the thought the way a wet dog throws off water.

"Would I get in?" Nish repeated.

"Well, I guess," said Fahd. "But you'd get in big trouble, wouldn't you?"

"How?" Nish laughed, as if Fahd had just asked the dumbest question ever. "It's not as if I'd be sticking my *face* on the screen, is it?"

2

They drove down to New York in a light, wet snow that turned the pavement ahead black and glistening. Mr. Dillinger drove the old bus, sticking to the turnpikes and stopping only for bathroom breaks and lunch. He kept the music low, the heavy beat of the windshield wipers droning over everything, and soon most of the bus was asleep. Muck dozed in the seat closest to the door, a big book slipping off his lap several times as he fell into a deep slumber. Sam and Sarah slept with their heads tilted together. Fahd and Data played games on Data's new laptop computer until the battery ran down, and then they too slept. All up and down the old bus there were legs sticking out in the aisle, pillows jammed against windows, jackets over heads.

Travis got up at one point to stretch his legs. He looked towards the back of the bus, where much of the Screech Owls' equipment had been piled in the empty seats. There was a window on the safety door at the back, and he thought he might just stand there awhile and watch the traffic.

Unfortunately, someone was already there.

Nish. His back to the window. Bent over almost double. His belt undone and pants down around his ankles.

"*What are you doing?*" Travis hissed.

Nish looked up, blinked a couple of times as if the answer were obvious. "Practising."

"*Practising?*" Travis asked, incredulous.

"You practise hockey, don't you?" Nish said as he hiked up his pants. "Why wouldn't you practise mooning?"

Buckling up his belt, Nish stepped away from the wet, snow-streaked window. Travis half expected to see a line of police cars following them, lights flashing and sirens wailing. But there was only a van several hundred feet behind, its wipers beating furiously back and forth to fight the spray of the bus, the grey-haired driver staring straight ahead as if hypnotized by the road. He hadn't seen a thing.

But Travis had. He had seen his best friend, Mrs. Nishikawa's darling son, regular churchgoer and Boy Scout, *practising* mooning the entire world.

Travis had never experienced anything like New York City. The noise as they pulled off the turnpike ramp into the first streets of Manhattan was incredible, a city that hummed and howled in your ears. It seemed as if total panic had struck, as if around the next corner there must be a building on fire, a volcano erupting, or an invasion from outer space. Yellow taxis everywhere, everyone honking, pedestrians racing across streets as if they were being shot at rather than driven at. Police everywhere, too, laughing one minute and yelling the next as they directed the charging traffic. Vendors on every corner – roasted nuts, bagels, fresh fruit, newspapers, hot dogs, videos, books. And people, people, people. More people than Travis had ever seen.

Nish was first to discover that New York itself was a constant, moving Stupid Stop. The team was just checking into a small hotel on the corner of Lexington and East 52nd Street, about ten blocks from Times Square, when Nish wandered back from a nearby variety store with the first of his New York discoveries: a brand-new pair of sunglasses.

"They're Oakleys," he announced, naming one of the most expensive brands of wraparound glasses. "Five bucks," he added.

"Impossible," declared Sam. "You can't buy Oakleys for under a hundred."

"*I* can," Nish bragged. "And what about my watch?"

He held up his left arm and drew back the sleeve of his Screech Owls jacket with a dramatic flourish. A brand-new, heavy watch, hanging from Nish's wrist on a chunky gold wristband, flashed in the lobby lights.

Simon Milliken yanked Nish's wrist close and examined the watch like a jeweller. "It's a *Rolex*!" he gasped.

"Of course," agreed Nish. "Ten bucks."

"A Rolex costs two or three thousand!" Wilson shouted.

"Where'd you get 'em?" demanded Andy.

"Guy around the corner," Nish said. "He's got a whole briefcase full of them."

"Show me," said Andy. "I want to get a pair of sunglasses, too."

"So do I!" shouted Jesse.

"I want a Rolex!" said Simon.

Off they ran, with Nish leading the way – Oakley sunglasses perched high on his head, Rolex held out like he expected people to kiss his hand.

"That's stolen goods," said Derek. "They're going to get caught."

"They're not *real*," said Sarah. "They're knock-offs – phonies. They just look like the real thing. You wait: the logo on those sunglasses will rub off in a day and the watches won't be working by the time we leave."

"How do you know?" asked Fahd.

"My dad comes to New York all the time. He brought my mom back a fake Rolex and the hands fell off as she was putting it on. He thought it was a joke – she didn't think it was so funny, though."

"Aren't they illegal anyway?" asked Fahd.

"Of course. Illegal to sell, but not to buy. My dad says everybody buys them, either as souvenirs or to play a joke when they get back home."

Travis's curiosity was getting the better of him. He had resisted the urge to go along with the others, but now he worried that his teammates might run into trouble or get lost.

Worrying was in Travis's nature. He put it down to having been lifelong buddies with Nish, who usually gave him a good reason to worry. Ever since he'd become team captain, Travis worried even more. He wanted everyone to get along. He wanted no trouble. Sometimes he thought if he ever stopped worrying, he would start worrying about *why* he was no longer worrying.

Travis slipped out the revolving door of the hotel. Nish had said he'd gone to the little store up Lexington and bought the watch and glasses just around the corner. Travis turned quickly and headed in that direction.

He couldn't see anyone, but then he clearly heard Nish's loud voice somewhere up ahead. He was bragging, showing off in front of his friends. He was talking about how much he could get for Oakley sunglasses and Rolex watches back home.

"I could *retire* at thirteen!" he shouted.

Travis turned a corner. His teammates were huddled into a narrow alleyway that ran between a dry cleaner's and the variety store. Andy was holding a shiny new watch, rolling it over and over in his palm. Simon was trying on a pair of sunglasses.

They had made their selections from a brown briefcase, the array of watches sparkling like buried treasure. The briefcase was being held open on the forearm of a very tall bearded man. He wore a long dark overcoat that reached almost to his feet. He had on brand-new Nike sneakers that looked as if they'd never before been tried on, let alone walked in. And he wore a strange, multicoloured hat pulled tight over his ears. Standing there in the shadows of the alley, he was hard to make out, apart from coat, shoes, hat, and beard – almost as if the clothes stood there empty, a clever dummy rigged to look like a very bad character.

The man peered out from below the brim of his odd hat, and Travis shivered as his icy gaze fell on him. The man then looked at Nish, who nodded as if to say Travis was all right.

Andy was fumbling in his wallet for money. The man held his hand out to take it.

Then, suddenly, without warning, he shoved the money back at Andy, grabbed the watch from him, and slammed the briefcase shut.

The boys jumped back, startled.

The man snarled once, turned, and began running farther down the alley.

"*I'll find you later!*" he called back over his shoulder.

"*Okay, Big!*" Nish shouted after him.

'Big'? Where did *that* come from, Travis wondered. Nish was already on a first-name basis?

Big?

"What happened?" Andy asked. He was staring into his empty palm, where moments ago the fake Rolex had glittered.

Nish said nothing, just nodded towards the opening of the alley onto Lexington Avenue.

A blue New York police car was idling on the street, a stocky policeman with dark glasses staring past them after the retreating Big.

Nish started cleaning his sunglasses on his shirt. He seemed so worldly all of a sudden. He was acting as if he'd lived and done business in New York all his life.

"Big don't like cops," Nish said, putting his sunglasses on again and heading out onto Lexington. He sounded like someone in a gangster movie.

More like "Cops don't like Big," Travis thought.

He didn't like Big either. He didn't like *anything* about this, not at all.

3

They had no game and no practice that first day in New York City. Mr. Dillinger had arranged a terrific introduction to the Big Apple for them. They toured the city in a double-decker bus, stopping at the Empire State Building and then taking the ferry to the Statue of Liberty.

"What's wit' dis city and heights?" Nish asked the tour guide at the statue. "You wanna see me hurl, or what?"

Travis could hardly believe his ears. Ever since the back-alley meeting with the mysterious Big, Nish had been talking like he was the twelve-year-old head of the Mob.

They drove through Central Park and saw the outdoor rink where, Muck said, they might be holding one of their practices. Muck seemed genuinely excited by the prospect of getting out in the open air. Travis liked the idea, too. He could see skaters from the bus window, and none of them could skate very well. The Owls would be like an NHL team coming in to this little outdoor rink.

They journeyed through the theatre district and then, just off Times Square, Mr. Dillinger pointed out an old building called the Ed Sullivan Theatre where, he said, "The Late Show with David Letterman" was produced every night. Some of the Owls had seen the program, and they scrambled to the windows hoping to catch a glimpse of Letterman, the host. But all they could see were people walking fast with umbrellas held up to keep off the snow. No one in Tamarack ever used an umbrella against anything but rain. Travis thought it looked silly.

"I'm gonna be on dat show," New York Nish announced from the back of the bus.

The rest of the Owls turned to stare questioningly.

Fahd asked the obvious: "How?"

"I'll be famous – day after New Year's Eve."

"You won't be famous, " said Sam, "you'll be in jail!"

"This is the United States," Nish said, as if he was explaining something difficult to a child, "not Canada. In America, you get in the *Guinness Book of World Records*, you're an automatic star."

"Your *butt* will be the star, not you!" laughed Sarah.

"Laugh now – I'll be the one laughing later," Nish said with a sneer. "I've even worked out my own Top Ten list for when I'm on."

Most of them knew about Letterman's Top Ten list. Each school-day morning back in Tamarack, the local radio station played a tape of the previous night's list just before the eight o'clock news.

"What is it?" Fahd asked. Fahd always asked, even when others knew better than to play along with Nish's mad schemes.

"'The Top Ten Reasons Why Nish Should Be Captain,'" Nish announced.

Sarah's eyes went wide. As far as she or anyone else knew, Nish had never been considered for captain. Except, of course, by Nish.

Nish was in his glory, a deep red colour moving up into his face and making him all but glow as he began his countdown.

"Number ten," he began, "because he's won more most-valuable-player medals than anyone else on the Screech Owls."

Travis's first instinct was to try to figure out if that was so. He didn't think so. Surely it was Sarah.

Sam held up her hands to form a trumpet around her mouth and booed.

Everyone laughed.

"Number nine," Nish continued, "because he's got the best shot."

"*Boo!*" several Owls called at once.

"Number eight, because he's Muck's favourite."

"*Boooo!*" more Owls joined in.

"Number seven, because he's the fan favourite."

"*Booooooo!*"

"Number six, because he's the only Screech Owl who will ever make the NHL."

"*Booooooo!*"

"Number five, because he's the best-looking of the Owls."

"*Booooooo!*"

"Number four, because he's Paul Kariya's cousin!"

"*Booooooooooo!*"

"Number three, because his equipment smells the best."

"*Boooooooooooo!*"

"Number two, because if he doesn't get it he's gonna hurl!"

"*Boooooooooooo!*"

"And number one," Nish announced, his eyes closed in private delight, "because he's the only peewee hockey player in the entire world listed in the *Guinness Book of World Records!*"

"*BOOOOOOOOOOOOOOOOOOOOOOO!!*"

Travis had to cover his ears. The Owls were all booing and laughing at the same time. Nish was crimson, his natural colour whenever he was the centre of attention – which was almost always.

It was already an incredible trip.

4

It had snowed all through the night. Travis woke to the sound of the television blaring and Nish and Fahd battling over whether they watched "Simpsons" reruns (Nish's choice) or the New York City news (Fahd's choice). Fahd thought the traffic snarls were hilarious: the reporters and desk anchors were all talking about the snowfall in such worried voices that it seemed the city was being invaded.

In Tamarack, the snowploughs would have been out all night. The streets would be cleared, the roads sanded and salted. And every driver was as sure on snow in winter as they were on dry pavement in summer. A big snowfall was nothing.

But here the ploughs couldn't cope. Some broke down and others skidded off the road. The rest worked in vain to clear the roads for the more than a million commuters trying to get into the city. They had to close schools, cancel buses and trains, and all but shut down the city core. The snow was still falling, and the newscasters said city authorities were getting very worried, since there were only two days to go before New Year's Eve and the traditional Times Square celebrations.

Muck and Mr. Dillinger called an early-morning meeting in the lobby. The Owls stood around drinking orange juice and munching on doughnuts while Mr. Dillinger made some calls on his cellphone and then consulted with Muck.

"Our practice has been cancelled," Muck finally announced.

"The rink rats can't get to work," said Mr. Dillinger, shaking his head. "And the bus that was supposed to take us out isn't running."

The Owls groaned – but several of them, led by Nish, were faking their disappointment. Missing a practice, to Nish, was roughly equivalent to cancelling a dentist appointment.

"*Tooooooooo baaaad*," Nish bawled, pretending to wipe tears from his eyes.

"The good news is, we got another one lined up," said Mr. Dillinger. "We're going to Central Park – the outside rink."

"YES!" shouted Sarah.

"ALL RIGHT!" yelled Sam, pumping her fist in the air.

It was fabulous news. The Owls loved nothing better than to skate on an outdoor rink. Ever since the day when all of Tamarack had frozen over and Muck Munro had joined his team for a game of shinny in the field, the Owls had begged for more chances to play on the hard natural ice of an outdoor rink. They'd loved the feel. They'd loved the way Muck had let them practise any silly thing they wanted. And they'd loved, most of all, the joyous look in Muck's face as he joined in, bad leg and all.

"Gather your equipment and be down here in five minutes," said Muck.

Muck wouldn't want it to show, but Travis was certain he detected the flicker of a smile on his old coach's face.

They walked to Central Park – a long line of peewee hockey players, each wearing a team jacket, equipment bags and sticks slung over their shoulders, leaning into the snow that was still falling hard along Lexington. They turned left at 59th Street, the buildings on the north side suddenly shielding them from the blowing snow, and they headed for the opening in the distance that signalled the beginning of the park.

They weren't alone. When the Owls arrived, there was already another team there. They had partially cleared off the ice, but the snow continued to build up fast. The team had fancy new jackets – "Burlington Bears" stitched across the back – and almost a half-dozen coaches were on the ice. The coach in charge – his jacket screamed "HEAD COACH" in capital letters – held a binder and clipboard and was setting out pylons all along one side.

He blew his whistle to call the team to attention. They gathered in the corner that offered the best shelter from the falling snow. As the Screech Owls filed by, Travis could see the head coach writing down a complicated drill on his clipboard. The ink was running in the melting snowflakes.

Travis laughed to himself, but he felt sorry for the team. He could see some faces through the masks and visors, and they didn't look particularly happy. The head coach seemed far more like a drill sergeant than anything.

Muck and Mr. Dillinger had the Owls dress quietly. There was a protected area where they could store their boots and jackets. Most of the Owls put their equipment on over their track suits for extra warmth, and some of them even squeezed their winter gloves into their hockey gloves for more insulation.

But not Nish. He kicked some snow out of the way, cleared off his seat, and dumped his equipment out at his feet, just as he would if they were back in the rink at home or in the fanciest dressing room in the National Hockey League.

"What's that *smell*?" Sarah asked.

"You have to ask?" Sam said. "It's Rolex Boy's equipment."

"Spread it around," Simon called. "It could melt the snow!"

"Very funny," Nish said, carefully removing his treasured fake Rolex and laying it on the bench.

"Watch still running?" Andy asked.

Nish didn't even check. "Of course it is. A Rolex has a life-time guarantee."

"I suppose Mr. Big stands behind it," Sarah said.

"As a matter of fact, he does."

"What time is it, then?" Sam asked.

Nish wasn't about to get fooled. He checked the time on his watch. "You tell me," he said.

Sam made an elaborate show of checking her wristwatch: "Ten-fifteen."

Blood rushed to Nish's face. He checked his fake Rolex again, flashed a vicious look in Sam's direction, then practically pulled Fahd's arm out of its socket as he checked Fahd's wrist.

"Don't mess with me," Nish growled. "Nine-forty-six – same as I've got."

But no one was listening. The Owls were all laughing at the way Sam had tricked Nish into thinking his fancy new Rolex had already gone bad. He finished dressing in silence, periodically flashing a stare of pure evil in Sam's direction.

The team on the ice was still going through drills when the Screech Owls came out.

The head coach looked up, shrugged in what appeared to be disappointment, then blew hard on his whistle. All the Bears stopped instantly. He skated over to Muck.

They seemed such a contrast: the Bears' coach with the "HEAD COACH" lettering on his new jacket, his team track suit, team cap, big shiny whistle around his neck, clipboard under his arm; Muck in his ragged old sweats, his old junior jacket badly faded, his old hockey gloves and stick. No clipboard. Not even a whistle.

"You Muck Munro from Canada?" the head coach asked.

Muck nodded.

"Head coach Rod Peters from Burlington, Vermont. I understand we're to share this facility today."

"So they tell me," said Muck.

"I've already run my gang through some basic drills. You can either join in or we can split up – or, if you want, you can run some drills of your own."

"I wouldn't mind," said Muck.

The head coach seemed to be looking for a binder under Muck's arm. But there was none there.

"You want to borrow some of our pylons?" the head coach asked.

Muck shook his head.

"I have some U.S. hockey drills here – you want to borrow one or two?" the head coach said, pushing his clipboard towards Muck.

Muck shook his head.

"You got everything you need, then?" the head coach asked.

Muck held up the puck he was holding. "Everything," he said.

"Well," the head coach said impatiently, "what's the drill, then?"

Muck smiled at him. "You go sit over there. Five on at a time. Six, counting goalies. No whistles. One hour of good old shinny."

The head coach looked at Muck as if he had just walked out of a past century. "*Shinny?*" he said, as if it were a swear word. "You want these kids to play *shinny?*"

"Not just them," Muck said. "I plan to play, too. You're welcome to join in if you like."

"YESSS!" shouted Sarah.

"YAAY, MUCK!" shouted Sam, pounding her stick on the ice.

The head coach looked dumbfounded. He could not believe what Muck was proposing. Nor could he believe the reaction of the Screech Owls. Nor could he cope with his own team, who began shouting and pounding their sticks on the ice the same as the Owls. Disgusted, he skated away, calling his several assistants over to join him.

Muck held the first faceoff – and that was it: from that point on, no whistles or faceoffs or coaching. He skated off to wait his own turn, and as soon as Nish took his first break Muck stepped into the lineup himself at defence.

Travis couldn't have been happier. He loved the way his skates cut into natural ice, almost as if he were shaping it rather than simply sliding over it. He loved the raspy sound his blades made in the hard ice and the way the chips flew when he came to a quick stop.

Sarah was in her element, too. She was the best skater on the Owls, and by far the best skater on the outdoor rink. There were a few people walking through the park, a few even on cross-country skis, and when they stopped to watch the game, Travis knew it was Sarah who had caught their eye. Not just because she was a girl – the Owls had several girl players, and the Bears had a couple as well – but because of the extraordinary grace she showed moving up and down the ice, whether she had the puck or not.

Nish had realized almost instantly that the Owls had far more talent than the Bears, and so he began showing off. He tried to skate through the Bears backwards carrying the puck, and almost scored on a backhand as he slipped by their net, howling like a wolf.

Travis felt a tap on his shin.

It was Muck, sweat pouring off his face, snow melting in his hair. "You, me 'n' Sarah," he said. "We're switching sides."

Travis watched in amazement as Muck went over and talked to the one Bears assistant coach who'd come out to play. The head coach was still standing back, shaking his head as if some crime had been committed by the Owls and their stubborn coach. Muck switched jackets with the assistant coach, and Travis and Sarah switched sweaters with two of the weaker Bears players.

Muck rapped his stick on the ice. "Now we got us a game."

Travis's heart almost jumped through his jersey. It was no big deal, a game of shinny on an outdoor rink, but it felt as if he was playing in Madison Square Garden. He could see that more and more people were stopping to watch. He supposed with so many offices and businesses closed for the storm, there were a lot of people around with nothing to do. They'd gone out for a walk in the snow, and ended up at a hockey game.

It was wonderful playing with Muck. He couldn't skate all that well with his bad leg, but his passes were what the Owls called "NHL passes," so hard they almost snapped the stick out of your hand. And always, always on the tape.

The people who had gathered to watch were starting to cheer the better plays. And a television crew had appeared, the cameraman hurrying to get shots from ice level, and then of the small crowd that had formed to watch this pick-up hockey game in the heart of Central Park.

Muck sent Travis up left wing, and Travis danced around the one defenceman, leaving just Nish backing up between Travis and Sarah and the Owls' goal. Travis cut one way and Sarah cut the other way, the two of them criss-crossing right in front of Nish. Travis faked a drop pass to Sarah, but Nish was too smart and wouldn't go for it.

Travis held, and looked back over his shoulder. Muck was charging up ice, moving as fast as his bad leg would permit. He was rapping the ice hard for a pass.

Travis zipped it back to Muck.

Nish read the play perfectly, and dove to cut off Muck.

Then Muck did something astonishing. He flicked the puck

so it flew just over Nish's sprawling body and then leaped off his good leg and took flight himself, right over the spinning defenceman.

Muck and the puck landed in the clear. Travis could hear Muck laughing and whooping. Muck faked a pass to Travis, backhanded one to Sarah, and Sarah ripped the puck high into the net behind Jeremy.

The three of them – Muck, Sarah, and Travis – crashed together into the corner and fell into the soft snow that had built up along the boards. They were all laughing. Their new teammates from the Bears also ploughed in on them, everyone tapping their shins and patting them on the back of their pants.

The television cameraman was right in there with them. Travis looked back. No, there were two cameras now. *No, make that three!*

Sarah skated back, passing Nish, still sprawled on the ice, hands and legs out, red face beaming as he licked the melting snow that fell through his mask and onto his hot face.

"Get the time of that goal, Rolex Boy?" Sarah asked as she passed.

"Very funny," Nish snorted. But he was laughing. One of the cameramen moved in tight to Nish, and Nish obliged by flicking his chin strap and sending his helmet flying along the ice.

Everyone was laughing.

Even the head coach was smiling. He, too, was coming out to join in the game. He seemed a bit sheepish at first, but there was no doubt he wanted to play.

Perhaps he'd never known that hockey could be such fun.

5

"That's me! It's me! Me! Me!"

Nish was screaming and pointing, though there was no need for either. They were in their hotel room – Travis, Nish, Andy, Simon, Jesse, and Derek – and no one had trouble recognizing their friend. Of course it was him: *who else?* Nish, flat on his back, his helmet rolling along the ice, snow falling and melting over his hot, beet-red face.

The neat thing was, this was NBC Television, the nightly New York City newscast, and after nearly twenty minutes of traffic accidents and closed schools, the anchor had turned to a "lighter side of the storm." Suddenly there were shots of people cross-country skiing in Central Park and of the great shinny game between the Burlington Bears of Vermont and the Screech Owls from some small town in far-off Canada.

"It's Tamarack, idiot," Jesse shouted at the screen. "Tamarack! And we don't live in igloos, and we don't eat snow, and we weren't all born with skates on!"

"Speak for yourself," Nish said. "I could skate before I was toilet-trained."

Andy held his nose. "And when did you get toilet-trained? We must have missed it."

They were all laughing when there was a knock at the door. Andy jumped up, peeped out the spy glass, and announced, "Fahd."

"Let him in," said Derek.

"See me on da news?" Nish called to Fahd in his stupid New York accent.

Fahd shook his head. He looked excited.

"We've got something far more interesting to see," he announced.

"*What?*" several of the boys asked at once.

"You want to talk to Lars?" Fahd asked.

"He's *here*?" said Simon.

"Kind of – come on!"

The room Fahd was sharing with Data was on a lower floor, and everything was spaced out a little more to allow easy passage for Data's wheelchair. There was even a closet with the shelves and rails set low so that Data could arrange his clothes without having to stand. No closet, of course, was ever as low as Nish's; his closet was the floor, where he dumped all the clothes he'd need at the start of every tournament.

Data and Fahd had been busy. Fahd had brought along his father's digital video camera, which was now connected to Data's new laptop, which in turn was connected to the phone. Somehow, Fahd and Data had figured out how to hook up to the Internet, dial free of charge to Sweden, and connect with Lars, who had a similar setup at his uncle's place in Stockholm.

Data was on-line with Lars as they came in. Fahd's camera was set up to take in the room, and as they entered, they saw Lars on Data's computer screen. He was smiling and waving.

"Hey, guys!" a disembodied voice said from the computer. It sounded a little tinny, a bit hollow, a bit scratchy – but it was Lars's voice, no doubt. "Yo! Nish!" the voice crackled over the computer. "How's it going? You moon the world yet?"

"I'm working on it," Nish said. He looked slightly confused, almost as if he suspected this was some sort of weird trick Fahd and Data were pulling on him.

"Hi, Trav," Lars said, waving.

Travis waved back, uncertainly. Lars seemed both there and *not* there. His movements weren't as fluid as they would be on a video. It was as if a new picture of Lars was being received every microsecond, which, Travis figured, is probably precisely how it worked.

"Hey, Lars!" Travis called back. "You playing any hockey?"

"I'm in a tournament," Lars's voice crackled back. "Same as you guys. It's with my old team. I can hardly remember how to play the game the way it's played over here," he laughed.

"Simple," said Nish. "Never shoot, pass backwards, take a dive whenever anyone comes near you."

"*Thank you, Don Cherry!*" Lars shouted, sending Nish a raspberry across seven time zones.

They talked a while longer. Data used the mouse to control the camera, zooming in and out and focusing on whichever Owl happened to be talking to Lars.

Nish took very little part in the conversation. He seemed too interested in how the whole video-telephone call was happening. Travis had never before seen his friend so keenly interested in anything to do with computers. If it was a computer game, in which Nish could destroy the world with bombs and flame-throwers, then he was interested. But never before in how a computer actually worked.

Nish came back to life after they'd all said goodbye to Lars and promised to check in on him each day. They'd tell him how they were doing in the Big Apple tournament; he'd bring them up to date in how the peewee tournament in Stockholm was going.

But Nish had other ideas. "How's this work?"

Data explained. He talked about Internet long-distance calls and video transmission and how the cameras sent images so quickly it was almost as good as television reception.

"Television, eh?" Nish said.

Travis had seen that look before. He half expected to hear Nish's little brain shift gears, grinding and whining like a truck attempting to break free of a snowbank.

"Tell me, Data," Nish began, "when they broadcast the New Year's Eve countdown, how do they do that?"

"It's live television," Data said. "It's simple. They have cameras on the guy doing the countdown and project it onto the big screen. They'll have a temporary studio set up at Times Square."

"As simple as this?" Nish asked, nodding at Data's laptop.

"No. But not much more complicated."

"Can you 'bump' a broadcast?"

"I don't follow," Data said, turning his chair around to stare at Nish. He clearly had no idea where Nish was going with this. Unlike Travis, who was cringing at the thought.

"You know, can you cut in? Could you run your own broadcast and bump the one they're showing?"

Data thought about it a moment. "I suppose so. There'd be two or three cameras and a director controlling the shots. You'd have to break into their feed."

Nish sat, silently working his mouth.

If a brain could chew gum, his was blowing bubbles.

ravis understood his crazy friend's scheme instantly. It hadn't taken Nish long to put the camera and the computer together in his imagination and end up with his own big bare butt staring into the faces of a billion New Year's Eve celebrants.

"Don't even think about it," Travis warned his friend.

"Too late," Nish advised.

It was always "too late" with Nish. Travis was well used to that by now.

Fahd and Data, unfortunately, were intrigued. They hadn't any burning desire to see Nish's bare butt exposed for the entire world to enjoy, but they were computer nuts and endlessly fascinated by how things worked. Nish had posed a puzzle, and they just couldn't resist the challenge.

"Frighteningly simple," said Data after he and Fahd had consulted. "Production feeds are done by telephone lines. If you could call into the studio somehow, all you'd have to do is override their broadcast with yours. You'd need numbers and passwords, but if you had that you could bump them for a bit. I don't know how long, though."

"*Long enough for my butt!*" Nish shouted triumphantly.

"You'll get caught," Travis warned. He couldn't help himself. He was captain, after all. He was responsible.

Nish shot him a withering look. He looked as if Travis had just suggested he might get in trouble for talking in class – which, for Nish, was pretty much a daily ritual back in Tamarack.

"If the world was filled with people like you," Nish sneered, "there'd be no *Guinness Book of World Records*."

Travis said nothing, but he couldn't help thinking, If the world was filled with people like you, Nish, there'd be no world!

The snow continued to fall. One of the weather reporters called it "The Storm of the Century," which made the Screech Owls chuckle. If this was the worst storm New York City had ever seen, they ought to come to Tamarack for a week in January. Back home, every storm was "The Storm of the Century" by New York standards.

Still, it was coming down hard. The streets were filled with snow. The ploughs couldn't cope, and even when they did get down one of the jam-packed New York streets, they seemed to be ploughing the wrong way, pushing huge mounds of snow into the centre instead of to the side. They had front-end loaders out to fill the snow trucks, but the snow trucks kept getting stuck, which only made matters worse.

The mayor declared a city emergency. The governor declared a state emergency. About the only thing that remained was for the president of the United States to declare war on the storm. What would he do? wondered Travis. Blast the cloud cover off with a missile?

Mr. Dillinger organized a walk to check out the huge Christmas tree at Rockefeller Center. Everyone came along, even Muck. They threw snowballs and sang Christmas carols as they strolled.

It was, in its own way, an extraordinarily beautiful day: the snow falling in huge, damp clumps, the streets white and glowing with Christmas lights, the people wandering about as if they'd never seen anything like it. The Big Apple was turning into the Big Marshmallow.

At Rockefeller Center a crew was struggling to keep the small ice surface clear, but it was almost impossible. There were a few skaters, and they left trails behind them in the snow.

The Owls were standing around the huge, twinkling Christmas tree when suddenly a familiar sound ripped through the silence of the falling snow.

"KA-WA-BUN-GA!"

Travis and Sarah raced over to the railings to stare down onto the rink, which was well below street level.

It was Nish! He had rented a pair of odd-looking, black-booted skates and was heading out onto the ice all by himself.

Only he wasn't skating, he was sailing – swooping about in the exaggerated style of a figure skater. He turned quickly backwards and, with his arms still flying dance-style, picked up speed as he rounded the rink. Suddenly he stabbed one toe

down and leaped into the air in a ridiculous attempt at a
Salchow – only to slip and land flat on his rear end, spinning
across the ice.

The Owls, now all gathered around the railings, howled
with laughter.

Travis noticed a television crew over by the Christmas tree.
They were gathering up their equipment and racing towards
the rink.

"KA–WA–BUN–GA!"

Same call, different voice. It was *Sam* – same rented skates,
same silly exaggerated drift out onto the ice. She skated over to
where Nish lay and stopped suddenly, deliberately shooting
snow into his face.

Nish laughed. He got up, bowed deeply, and held out his
arms.

"*What are they doing?*" Sarah shouted, laughing.

Sam bowed in return, like an old-fashioned lady accepting
a dance, and then, with her nose stuck high in the air, she linked
arms with Nish and the two of them began skating around in
perfect rhythm, noses aloft, eyes practically shut, each kick long
and exaggerated.

If Travis didn't know better, he'd swear he was watching the
dance competition at the Olympics.

The people standing around began to clap and cheer. The
Owls were shouting down – KA-WA-BUN-GA!" called Fahd
in a voice that didn't seem to fit – and Muck and Mr. Dillinger
were leaning over the railing, laughing. Mr. Dillinger was
wiping away tears.

The camera moved in tight, following the two Olympic

"ice-dancers" until, on one corner, Sam decided to turn the tables on poor Nish and lift him over her head.

Sam was strong. There wasn't a member of the team who didn't marvel at her strength, but Nish was still Nish. Sam grunted and tried to hoist him high. For a moment Travis's imagination got the better of him and he could see Sam skating triumphantly about the ice surface, one hand waving free while the other held Nish high in the air, her partner's arms swaying to the music and a rose between his teeth.

Sadly, the truth was not so elegant. Sam tried, and Nish lost his balance. For a second he left the ice – screamed, "I'M GONNA HURL!" – and then, with the crowd gasping, the two of them crashed in a pile and flew into the corner. They lay on their backs, laughing and letting the snow fall into their open mouths.

The camera caught it all.

The Screech Owls raced down the wide steps, turned onto the ice surface, and ran, sliding, across to the fallen Olympic heroes.

Nish blinked up towards the camera zooming in on him. "Which newscast?" he asked, as if being filmed had become a daily experience for him.

The cameraman continued to shoot. A woman – the producer? – leaned over from behind the camera and smiled.

"Not news," she said. "'Letterman.'"

Nish's eyes went wide. "'Letterman?'"

"'The Late Show,'" she said. "You know."

"This is for 'Letterman'?" Nish said.

"We're just doing shots of the storm," she said. "This was great. Thanks a lot."

"When?" Nish asked.

"Tonight," the woman said.

Nish closed his eyes, huge flakes falling onto his face and melting instantly on his hot, sweating flesh. He looked as if he had died and gone to heaven.

"I'm gonna be on 'Letterman,'" he kept saying to himself. *"I'm gonna be on 'Letterman'!"*

7

ish walked back towards the hotel as if the air was filled with falling ticker tape, not snow. Travis had rarely seen his puffed-up pal so full of himself.

"*I'm gonna be on 'Letterman'! I'm gonna be on 'Letterman'!*"

Not *we're* going to be on 'Letterman'! Not *Sam and I* are going to be on 'Letterman'! *I'm* gonna be on 'Letterman'! If I hear that one more time, thought Travis, I'm – I'm gonna hurl!

They passed Lexington on their way to the little hotel. They were tired, and Mr. Dillinger and Muck had suggested they get back and rest up for the evening game. The two men saw them back to within sight of the hotel and then turned in the other direction. Muck wanted to see the New York Public Library, which might have struck the Owls as a bit odd if it had been anyone but Muck. But they knew him only too well; he'd rather read a book than go to a movie, rather visit an old Civil War battleground than go to Disney World.

Nish and Travis and several of the boys were lagging behind
the rest when a strange sound cut through the falling snow.

"*Pssssst!*"

Travis wasn't sure it was a voice at first. But then it came
again, sharp and fast: "*Psssst – Nish!*"

They were just passing by a small alley, so narrow a car
couldn't get through. There was a large, dark figure looming
there, covered from head to toe in heavy winter clothing.

It was Big!

"*Yo! Big!*" shouted Nish as if he'd just bumped into a long-
lost friend. "*Whazzup?*"

The New York accent was back.

Big waved them into the shadowed alleyway. "You still want
them watches 'n' things?" he asked.

"Sure do, man," said Nish. "Right, boys?"

Andy, Fahd, and Wilson all agreed. They pressed closer as
Big opened up his "treasure chest."

Travis couldn't help himself. It seemed as if the watches and
sunglasses had a magnetic quality. They were *pulling* him into
the alleyway.

This time there were no police passing by. Travis supposed
they were all tied up with traffic problems. Big didn't seem at all
worried as he showed his fake Rolexes and sunglasses.

Andy, Wilson, Fahd, Jesse, and Derek all bought stuff.
Even Travis found his hand reaching for his wallet as he rolled
a fancy-looking Swiss Army watch around in the palm of his
hand.

"I'm gonna be on 'Letterman,'" Nish told Big.

Big blinked. He clearly didn't believe it. A man who dealt in fooling people wasn't going to be easily fooled himself. "How so, man?"

Nish grinned from ear to ear. "They filmed me skating up at Rockefeller Center."

"True?"

"True – and I'll be on again, too, right after I moon 'em all New Year's Eve."

Big, who'd been taking money from the other boys, turned with a perplexed look on his face. "You what?"

"We got a plan," Nish went on. "Fahd here, and Data, he's back at the hotel, they got it all figured out how we can bump the live broadcast and get my bare butt on the big TV screen over on Times Square."

Travis wished Nish would just shut up. This was a stupid thing to imagine, let alone tell a total stranger.

But Big was interested. For the first time, he smiled, flashing a gold tooth. Travis did a double take. He hadn't seen a gold tooth since Sweden, when the Russian mob had kidnapped him and several other peewee hockey players.

He wondered for a moment if Big's gold tooth was a knock-off, too – maybe made of plastic and painted gold.

"Tell me more," said Big.

"Fahd and Data are computer geniuses," said Nish. "We got a video camera and we got a system all figured out where we can bump off the regular programming and get me on for a minute – it's gonna get me in da *Guinness Book of World Records*, Big."

"I'm sure it will," said Big. "If it doesn't get you busted."

"Not a chance," said Nish. "We got it all figured out – they won't even know what happened until it's too late."

Travis couldn't help himself. He poked Nish in the ribs. Nish turned slightly and swatted at Travis as if he were a pesky mosquito.

The boys had all the fake watches and sunglasses they could afford. Big rolled up his loot and closed the half-empty brief-case. Travis wondered how much of a killing he'd made. What were the ten-dollar watches really worth? Five? Two?

"See you around, eh, Big?" Nish said as they departed.

"You bet, Nish," said Big with another flash of his gold tooth. "I'll watch for you on 'Letterman.'"

8

he Screech Owls played their first game in the Big Apple International Peewee Tournament that evening. It was, for the Owls, little more than a warm-up. The team they were up against, the Long Island Selects, weren't much better than the Burlington Bears. The main difference was that this game would count in the standings; the shinny game against the Bears mattered only as a memory.

Sam and Sarah both played exceptional games. Sam was back on defence, and she blocked shots and carried the puck and helped Jeremy clear away rebounds so easily it seemed she might keep the Selects off the scoreboard all on her own.

Sarah was in one of her playmaking moods. It didn't matter how many times Travis or Dmitri set her up, she would pass the puck off. She simply refused to take an easy shot on goal, dropping the puck back to the point instead, or spinning around to try to set up Dmitri or Travis. By the third period, Dmitri and

Travis had two goals each, and Nish also had two pinching in from the point.

"Slow it down," Muck instructed during a brief break.

He didn't need to say any more. Every one of the Screech Owls knew how Muck refused to embarrass another team or coach in a tournament. Even in a tournament where it was possible the standings might be decided by the number of goals scored, Muck would refuse to let the Owls run up the score.

An instruction of no more scoring was like an invitation to Nish. If a game truly mattered, if the Owls absolutely *had* to have a goal, there was no one they'd want on the ice more than Nish. Nish, even more than Sarah, had the knack of scoring when it counted. But take away a reason to get serious, and Nish would try anything, no matter how crazy. His big ambition, he'd told Travis, was to score a "Pavel Bure goal": taking the puck behind the opposition cage, flipping it high into the air so it floated back over the goal, and then skating out in front quickly enough to be there in time to baseball the puck into the net. He must have tried it a hundred times in practice, without a single success.

But Nish was nothing if not determined. He picked up the puck behind his own net, skated out slowly, and faked a pass up to Liz on the left, then broke with the puck into the open space.

Travis was sitting on the bench when Nish began his charge. He lowered his head, almost wishing he weren't in the same building.

"The show's on," said Sarah, sitting beside him.

"I know," said Travis.

And what a show it was. Nish skated up and cut diagonally across centre, stickhandling beautifully. He had his head up, and Travis wondered if it was to see if there were any cameras on him.

Nish worked his way across the Selects' blueline and down into the corner. He then faked a pass to Sam, who was charging in from the far point. Sam angrily slammed her stick onto the ice when Nish hung on. He had other ideas. He kept stick-handling behind the net, watching.

"Here comes his 'Bure,'" Travis announced on the bench.

"Such a surprise!" said Sarah.

Nish tapped the puck so it stood on edge, then lifted it high so it floated, spinning, over the net and over the head of the little Long Island goaltender.

Nish dug in hard, churning round to the front. He flew out from the boards and passed the left post moving backwards, away from the net, the puck still in the air.

He swung mightily, the play perfect – except for one small detail. He missed the puck, and fell with the effort.

A huge laugh went up from the sparse crowd watching in this little rink down by the East River.

Nish got up and chased hard back down the ice as the Selects managed a three-on-one break and scored on a good screen shot that ripped into Jeremy's glove and then trickled into the Owls' net.

"He's benched," Sarah said, as she shifted over to make room for the players coming off.

"Guaranteed," agreed Travis.

Nish came off, his face beet red, and didn't even bother
looking over at Muck. What was the point? He plopped down
beside Travis, ripped his helmet off, picked up the water bottle,
and sprayed his face, hair and, a bit, into his open mouth. He
swallowed, spat, and turned to Travis.

"What's with Muck?" he asked.

"You have to ask?" Travis said.

"I'm benched," Nish said as if it were an announcement.

"You're surprised?"

"Hey," Nish grinned. "He told us not to score, didn't he?
What more can I do for this team?"

Travis grabbed the water bottle and sprayed it as hard as he
could directly into his own face.

It did no good. When he opened his eyes Nish was still
sitting there, smiling at him.

"*It's time!*" called Fahd, as if they didn't know.

It was also way past bedtime. Mr. Dillinger had said there
was a 10:30 curfew – "Lights out and no portable CD players!"
It was now 11:30, and while the lights were out, no one was
asleep. The television was on, flickering like a ghost at the foot
of the beds where six of the Owls lay, watching and waiting.

"Think they'll open with me?" Nish asked no one in particular.

The "Late Show" was just coming on. Letterman was doing
his stand-up act, an endless string of jokes about the storm,
half of which the Owls didn't get, and then came an interview

with a giggling, gum-chewing actress about being stranded in a taxi and missing her opening-night act at one of the New York theatres.

"*Bor-ring!*" Nish moaned.

"We've got some footage from around the city," Letterman said to the still-giggling actress. "Would you like to see what the storm did to a few other New Yorkers?"

"Yeah, sure," she said, snapping her gum.

"Here we go," announced Fahd.

With David Letterman cracking more jokes in the background, they showed dozens of clips of the city coping with the Storm of the Century.

There was a rhinoceros at the zoo pawing the snow like he'd never seen it before. Letterman cracked a joke about Africa.

There was a beggar lying on the street, cup held out and brimming with snow. Letterman cracked a joke about being poor that Travis didn't like.

There were shots of cross-country skiers in Central Park, a dozen shots of people trying to push or pull their cars free of snowdrifts, several shots of people falling on the street – all accompanied by more cracks by Letterman.

But nothing about Rockefeller Center. Nothing about the outdoor skating rink.

Nothing about the two "Olympic ice-dancers."

Nothing about Nish.

"*What kind of rip-off is this?*" Nish howled when the footage stopped and the show returned to the host and his guest, now with a full-blown bubble hiding her face.

"Maybe they're saving you?" Fahd suggested.

Nish liked the suggestion. "Yeah, they're saving the best for last," he said.

But there was nothing more. Travis grew sleepy, turned around, and tucked himself into his bed. He heard Fahd do the same, and eventually the television was clicked off and the odd colours stopped dancing around the room. It was pitch black, and very, very late.

It grew quiet, very quiet, and then Travis heard Nish clear his throat.

"It means I *have* to moon now," Nish said.

No one said anything back to him.

"I've *no* choice."

9

"We lost."

Lars's voice was shaky coming over the line. But whether it was the transmission or Lars himself, Travis couldn't tell. Lars always took losses hard. There was no reason why he wouldn't take a loss with his old team in Sweden just as badly.

"We won – easily!" Nish practically shouted into the small microphone Fahd had set up so they could all speak more easily to Lars.

They talked for about fifteen minutes. Lars was finding it difficult readjusting to European-style hockey. He partly blamed himself for losing the game. They talked a bit more about everything the Owls had been doing in New York and then Lars signed off. He had a game to go to.

"Fahd and I have been thinking about this," Data said as he turned off his laptop. He turned towards Nish. "And I e-mailed a couple of computer buddies back in Canada. There's no way you can do that thing you want to do live."

"I can't?" said Nish, suddenly distraught.

"We'll film it on this camera and save it on the computer," Data explained. "That way, if we can actually jump into the transmission, all I'll need to do is click the mouse a couple of times."

"And you won't have to freeze your butt off," added Fahd.

"*But it's not the same!*" Nish whined.

"What do you mean?" asked Data. "It'll still be your butt up there – no one else's – so what's it matter if you do it live or not?"

"But it's no good," Nish protested. "It's like – like the difference between a goal and an assist."

Travis couldn't believe his ears. Only Nish would think of something like that. Travis prided himself on his assists. And Sarah had once said she'd rather set up a pretty goal than score one herself.

"Take it or leave it," said Data. "It's the only way."

Nish was wringing his hands. His expression kept twisting back and forth between agony and disappointed acceptance.

Finally he said, "Okay – when do we do it?"

"Right now's as good a time as any," said Fahd.

Nish looked up in surprise. "*Here?*" he asked.

"Sure," said Fahd. "Why not? We have the camera out anyway. Data can then save it to disk."

"*Here?*" Nish practically wailed.

Data shook his head. "Here is where we are, Nish. Let's get it done."

Nish looked around the room, panicking. "Not with all *you* here!"

"What's your problem?" asked Andy.

"No way I'm mooning any camera unless you guys leave," Nish announced. "Fahd and Data can stay."

Travis couldn't help himself. He leaped up off the bed to face his best friend. "Let me get this straight," he said. "You want to moon Times Square and a billion people around the world – but no way you're dropping your pants in front of your own friends."

"*No!*" Nish almost shouted. "I need privacy."

Travis started walking towards the door. "You need a psychiatrist," he said.

Nish, looking miserable, shot out his tongue in response.

"We're outta here," Travis announced, pulling the door open. The rest of the Owls, the three plotters excluded, were right behind him.

"We'll leave you here to make an ass of yourself," Travis said.

"Very funny," Nish snarled. "Very, very funny."

They played again that afternoon. They were lucky. The continuing storm made it impossible to reach the outlying rinks in Rye and Long Island, and so more of the games had to be scheduled as close to downtown as possible.

"We've had a change of facilities," Mr. Dillinger announced at lunch.

"What rinky-dink rink are we at next?" Nish asked. He hadn't been impressed with the facility for their game against the Selects. "Or are we playing this one outdoors?"

"Not quite," said Mr. Dillinger, no longer able to hide his smile. "This one's at Madison Square Garden."

"*MSG!*" Fahd shouted.

"The one and only," said Mr. Dillinger. "Let's get going."

All Travis's worries were suddenly lifted from his shoulders. He no longer cared about the storm. He no longer even thought about Nish and his ridiculous scheme to get himself – or at least a *part* of himself – into the *Guinness Book of World Records*. All he could think about was that he was going to play at the rink where Wayne Gretzky had played his very last game.

It was a rink like no other he had ever seen. They entered at a huge side entrance, big enough to take a tractor trailer and a bus, and then walked up a long spiral ramp that left them breathless. "The ice surface is six floors up," said Mr. Dillinger.

They came out at the Zamboni entrance and then turned left into the narrow corridor leading to the dressing rooms. They would be dressing in the visitors' room, where Orr and Dryden and Paul Kariya had dressed.

After he had his shin pads and pants on, Travis went out and walked up and down the corridor in his socks. All along the walls were huge, photographs of famous people who had played Madison Square Garden. He walked along, checking the names: Elton John, Frank Sinatra, Judy Garland, the Beatles, Wayne Nishikawa . . .

Wayne Nishikawa?

Travis stopped so abruptly he slipped in his socks and almost fell.

Nish?

Taped over the photograph, with black hockey tape, was one

of Nish's hockey cards from the Quebec Peewee tournament. Nish's smiling mug was covering the face of Elvis Presley. Nish's name – cut, it seemed, from the program for the Big Apple tournament – had also been taped over Elvis Presley's name at the bottom of the framed picture. Nish's mother would have been outraged. She called Elvis Presley "The King" and had most of his records.

"Like it?" a voice called from down the corridor.

It was Nish, half-dressed, sticking his head out the dressing-room door. He was grinning.

"I'm sure Elvis would be pleased," said Travis.

"He's dead," Nish said. "I'm the new King."

"King of *what*?" Travis asked.

"King of Hockey," Nish began. "King a da Big Apple. King of the *Guinness Book of World Records* – you name it."

Okay, Travis thought, I will. He forced a grin back at his weird friend: "King of Jerks."

Nish suddenly looked hurt. "What's dat for?" he asked.

"You're acting stupid," Travis said. "You're going way overboard on everything. That stupid New York talk. That stupid mooning idea that's just going to get everybody in trouble."

"Relax," Nish said, his old grin rising back into his face. "Nobody's gonna get hurt."

"They better not," said Travis.

Nish shook his head. "Relax, pal. Enjoy the Big Apple. And don't forget – one day you'll be able to say you knew me."

"What good's that, even if you do it? It's not like anybody's going to know it's you."

"My *butt* will be world-famous," Nish said. "It'll be like saying you saw Niagara Falls being formed, or the pyramids being built – you know what I mean?"

Travis just shook his head. No, he didn't know what Nish meant. And when he tried to force his mind to work it through, it was like his brain was a computer that had suddenly crashed.

10

They were to play a team from Michigan called the Detroit Wheels, one of the top-ranked peewee teams in the United States.

Muck seemed apprehensive. "This is a smart team," he said. "Well coached and well conditioned. You make a mistake, it's in our net. So we play safe at all times – *understand, Nishikawa*?"

"Understand, Coach," Nish mumbled, his head between his shin pads, his helmet on, his stare straight down between his legs.

Sarah rolled her eyes at Travis from across the dressing room. They both knew how much Muck hated being called "Coach" – "This isn't football," he'd say, "I'm 'Muck' or, if you have to, 'Mr. Munro,' but I am *not* 'Coach'" – but they also knew that Nish was in game mode, head down, full concentration. Travis took it as a good sign.

Travis had played in a lot of wonderful rinks: the Olympic rink in Lake Placid where the Miracle On Ice game had been won, the Quebec Colisée during the Quebec Peewee, Maple Leaf Gardens in Toronto before they built the Air Canada

Centre, the Globen Rink in Stockholm, and even Big Hat Arena in Nagano, Japan. But still Madison Square Garden was special. It was as if they were skating under a huge, sprawling, golden church ceiling. And the seats somehow seemed closer to the ice, even though that was impossible. The Stanley Cup banners and retired jerseys in the rafters only made it feel all the more important, all the more special.

Travis liked the feeling of being here. He liked the way Nish had prepared for the game. He liked the way Sarah had skated during warm-up, her strides so smooth it sounded like she was cutting paper with scissors as she took the corners. He liked the fact that he hit the crossbar with his first shot of the warm-up.

The Wheels were bigger than the Owls. They were bigger and stronger and played a more physical game. First shift out, Nish got hammered into a corner on a play that Mr. Dillinger shouted should have been a penalty. No penalty was called, and Nish got right back up and into the game. No grandstanding.

"We're faster," Muck said after the first few shifts. "We can get a step on them. Speed is still the most intimidating thing in hockey – don't forget that when you're out there."

Travis felt Muck was speaking directly to him. To him and to Simon and to Jesse and to Fahd and to Liz – the smallest Owls, the ones most likely to be frightened away from the corners by the huge all-male Wheels. It felt to Travis as if they were playing against *men*, not other twelve-year-olds.

"Check out number 6," Sarah said after she and Dmitri and Travis came off from a shift. "He's got a moustache."

Travis tried to see through the other player's mask. It was difficult to say for sure, but it certainly looked like the beginnings of a moustache. He shuddered. Perhaps they *were* men. Perhaps there had been a mistake in the scheduling.

The Wheels scored first, and second, both times by essentially running over the smaller members of the Owls. Once Fahd coughed up the puck. The other time Wilson dropped it for Simon, who was simply bowled over by a larger Detroit player.

Muck showed no nervousness at all. "Use your speed," he said to Sarah at one point, laying a big hand on her shoulder for support.

Next shift, Nish made a wonderful block on a good Wheels opportunity and jumped up and moved the puck behind his own net. He fed it up along the boards to Travis, who used his skates to tick it out onto his stick blade. A large Wheels defenceman was pinching in hard on him.

Travis's original plan was to dump it out through centre and trust that Sarah could pick it up, but he didn't want to be the one who gave the puck away, so he moved it onto his backhand and put it hard off the side so it squeaked past the pinching defender and up along the boards.

Sarah read him and swept to the boards, picking up the puck behind the pinching defenceman, who was now caught up-ice.

Dmitri was on the far side. Sarah slapped a hard pass that flew over the remaining defenceman's poking stick and Dmitri knocked it down niftily with his own stick – a "Russian pass," Dimitri called these when the three of them practised high passes in practice. He kicked the falling puck onto his stick and took off, free of any checker.

Travis knew exactly what Dmitri would do – cut across the ice so he was angling into the goal. Fake a forehand to the

short side. Keep and tuck around the goalie. Then backhand a
shot high.

Sure enough, the water bottle flew off the back of the net
just as the red light came on.

Two minutes later Derek knocked down a puck at centre ice
and threw a blind pass to Nish, who was charging straight up the
middle and hammering his stick on the ice. The pass was almost
perfect. Nish reached ahead and just barely poked the puck
between the two Detroit defenders, then jumped through and
over them as they came together to block him, shooting as he
fell. The puck rose hard over the Wheels goaltender's shoulder
and Nish came right behind it, knocking the goalie flying as he
took out the net. All three – Nish, goalie and, net – crashed into
the boards.

Wheels 2, Owls 2.

"Just use your speed," Muck advised at the first break. "It's
working."

There were moments when it didn't seem to be working.
The Wheels went ahead; Andy tied it up on a great, ripping
slapper from the far circle. The Wheels went ahead by two; the
Owls tied it again, on a goal by Fahd, on a screen, and by Derek,
on a nice tip of a hard Nish screamer from the point. Nish was
all business – no showboating, no Pavel Bure moves, just Nish
working as only he could when his mind was on the game.

They finished regulation time tied 5–5. The referee
explained there would be a five-minute overtime. If nothing was
decided, then the game would go down as a tie; they couldn't go
into further overtime, as other teams were scheduled to play.

Muck wanted the win. The extra point might make the difference between the Owls making the finals or not.

They played cautiously for the first couple of minutes, each team afraid to make a mistake. Muck played all three lines evenly, hoping for a break that didn't seem to come. The Wheels seemed to be doing the same.

Travis checked the clock. One minute to go. He looked down the bench. Nish was sitting at the far end, his back heaving, his head between his legs. Not once this game had Nish done anything stupid, not once had he faked an injury, not once had he even spoken. Travis couldn't remember a single game where Nish had been this concentrated.

Muck leaned over Nish and asked him something, Nish nodded, and then Muck slapped his shoulders. Still fighting for breath, Nish bounded over the boards for what might be the final faceoff.

"Sarah," Muck called. "Your line."

Travis, too, had yet to recover his breath. But Sarah and Dmitri were already over the boards. The faceoff was in the Owls' end, and Sarah was, by far, the best at faceoffs. They needed to win this one, to keep it away from the Wheels and to give themselves one more chance to win.

In one motion Sarah plucked the falling puck from the air and turned, sticking her rear into the big Wheels centre so he couldn't get at it. Travis knew the play perfectly. She would block and he would scoop up the puck and go.

He grabbed the puck and tucked it away just as the big centre bulled his way past Sarah.

Nish was behind the net, waiting. Travis fed him the pass.

The far winger was driving in hard on Nish. Nish pretended he didn't even see him, then very gently pinged the puck off the back of the net just as the winger reached him. There was no puck for the winger to play, Nish stepped out of the way, the winger flew past, and Nish easily picked up his own pass as the puck came back to him off the net.

He swung to the far boards, looking up-ice.

Dmitri was breaking. Nish saw him and sent a high, looping pass that almost hit the clock. Dmitri straddled centre to make sure he was onside and pounced as the puck fell.

The Wheels' biggest defenceman was on him, but he was no match for Dmitri's amazing speed. Dmitri shot for the near boards and made as if to cut sharply against the defence for the net. The defence had no choice but to charge full at Dmitri, and Dmitri slipped the puck through his own legs to Sarah, coming up fast with the big centre hacking at her as he tried to keep up.

Travis saw his opening. He cut across towards Dmitri's side and headed in a long curl towards the net. His winger came with him. He could feel the player's stick hard against his shin pads, hard on his pants. He could feel the blade hooking him. The referee should have blown his whistle, but there was nothing. The officials were going to let it go.

Travis attempted to shoot, but the player chasing now had his stick blade right under Travis's arm and was pulling him off the puck. Travis tried again to snap a shot, but he missed the puck and fell. He could hear the crowd yelling for a penalty. But still no whistle.

Travis was down, the checker falling on top of him. Travis kicked at the puck with his skate and it flew back towards the blueline.

With the big Wheels player now fully on top of him, Travis struggled to see.

Nish had the puck!

Nish was in full flight. He picked up the puck at the blueline, and with one lovely little fake to the right he took out the only remaining check. He came in on the goaltender alone.

The goaltender gambled – he rushed at Nish.

Nish pulled the puck back with a perfect little tuck, stepped around the falling, flailing goalie, and, slowly, lifted the puck into the middle of the net.

Owls 6, Wheels 5. The final buzzer could barely be heard above the cheers of the crowd.

Travis scrambled to his feet and charged for Nish, already backing into corner with his stick thrown down and his gloves in the air.

Travis and Sarah and Dmitri hit Nish at the same time, with Sam coming up fast to join in and Jeremy already halfway down the ice and the rest of the Owls pouring over the boards.

"Speed!" Sarah screamed. "SPEEEEEED!"

Nish was smiling at Travis.

"King of Overtime, too," he said. "I forgot that."

r. Dillinger had a treat in store for the Owls. He'd booked a section of the new ESPN Zone restaurant just off Times Square. Travis had never seen anything like it: three floors, entirely dedicated to great hamburgers, delicious fries, and wall-to-wall sports. Everywhere he looked there were televisions tuned to sporting events across the world, hundreds of huge screens filled with basketball, football, hockey, soccer from Europe, a Formula One car race from Australia, and, best of all, in the room reserved for the Owls, three sets tuned to the World Junior Hockey Championships in Finland.

Nish strolled in like it was his own living room. He walked to the front row of fat recliner chairs, plunked himself down in the middle seat and called out, "Chips, Coke, burger – no onions, triple ketchup – and the Mighty Ducks versus Detroit, if you don't mind!" One of the waiters, laughing at Nish's nerve, flicked a remote until Nish got exactly what he wanted.

Nish pumped a fist in the air in thanks and sank so far into the big seat he all but disappeared from view.

Travis sat at a table with Sarah and Sam and Andy. They ordered onion rings and burgers and were sipping on their Cokes when Sarah, with the straw still in her mouth, nodded towards the far corner.

"Muck's enjoying himself," she muttered, the straw dropping back into the huge glass.

Muck was sitting by himself in the corner, as far removed as possible from the roar of two dozen television sets, each with the volume turned up so loud it sounded like a sports riot was in progress. He had his big arms crossed over his chest and was glowering at one of the screens tuned to the World Juniors.

"Canada losing?" Sam asked.

Sarah shook her head. "Muck hates things like this. Hates sports bars. Hates the way they broadcast games. Remember how he once told us, 'If you can't see it live, you won't see it at all'?"

Travis nodded, giggling at the memory.

"Whazzat supposed to mean?" Sam asked.

"He thinks you can only enjoy a game by seeing the whole thing," explained Travis. "He says things like, 'A camera chasing a puck is as useless as a player chasing the puck.' You know Muck – he thinks the game *away* from the puck is often more interesting than the play around the puck. So he won't watch it on television."

"He's weird," said Sam.

"He's Muck," Andy said, as if in explanation, and it seemed enough for the other three, who all giggled and nodded.

Finally, Muck could take no more. He stood up at his table, drained his Coke, and set the big glass down sharply.

Travis watched as Muck picked up his jacket and tuque and walked over to Mr. Dillinger, who was sitting with Jeremy and Jenny and Derek at another booth. Muck whispered – or perhaps shouted – something in Mr. Dillinger's ear, and Mr. Dillinger nodded and looked up sadly, as if it were somehow all his fault. Muck grinned and rapped the team manager lightly on the arm with a fist. He wasn't upset; the ESPN Zone just wasn't for him. It was perfect for the Screech Owls, though.

They stayed to the end of the Canada– Slovakia game in the World Juniors – the Screech Owls cheering wildly as Canada scored into the empty Slovak net to win 4–2 – and then, their stomachs full and their ears ringing, they paid their bills and headed out again into the street for the walk back to the hotel.

It was snowing again. Large, fat flakes drifted down like feathers between the tall buildings, sparkling as they drifted past the streetlights before joining the snow already lying along the streets and gutters of New York.

It was late, but still it looked like rush hour, the streets plugged with snow and yellow taxis and police cars and even the odd private vehicle that had failed to heed the week-long warnings to stay out of the downtown core.

The Screech Owls enjoyed the long walk back to the hotel. They tried catching the large flakes in their mouths. They threw snowballs and washed Nish's face and dumped snow down the back of Andy's jacket.

Once they got back, Travis and Sarah caught the first elevator. They held it until Fahd had wheeled Data on, then pushed the button for the second floor. The doors of the old elevator slowly closed, and they rose to the second floor, stopping with a shudder. As they waited for the doors to open, Fahd began stabbing the open button.

"Hold your horses," Travis said, thinking for a moment he must sound like his grandmother, who was always using phrases like that.

"I don't like elevators," said Fahd.

The doors caught, then opened.

Travis blinked in disbelief.

A body lay crumpled on the carpet before them, a large body, wearing a jacket with the collar turned up high so it partially covered the face. A tuque lay to one side.

There was blood oozing from a blow to the back of the man's head.

Sarah screamed.

"MUCK!"

12

"He could've been killed," Sarah said the next morning.

But Muck had been lucky. His thick tuque had softened the blow to his head. Mr. Dillinger had come back from the hospital with the news that Muck was alert and in good spirits and now had sixteen new stitches to add to his lifetime total. "That puts him over three hundred," Mr. Dillinger announced, as if Muck had set a new scoring record. These, however, were the first stitches that hadn't come from playing hockey, whether from a stick, a puck, another player's skate, or the operation Muck had after his leg was broken, putting an end to his junior playing career. What these latest stitches had come from, the police didn't know. No weapon had been found, no one was in custody, no suspects were known.

"A mugging," Mr. Dillinger explained. "Happens so often in this city they don't even bother investigating them."

Travis wasn't so sure. A mugging on the second floor of a

downtown Manhattan hotel? Why there, when it would have been so much easier to mug someone walking on the street?

By noon his suspicions had been confirmed.

Muck told the police that he'd gone out to see if he could buy a late theatre ticket, only to find out the storm had shut down the theatre district. He'd walked around a while before returning to the hotel just before the team came back from the restaurant.

Muck's room was on the second floor, same as Data and Fahd's, and when he'd gotten off the elevator and turned towards his room he'd noticed a couple of men struggling with the lock on a room down the hall in the other direction.

Something about the way the men were acting hadn't felt right to Muck, so he pretended he'd accidentally turned the wrong way and headed back in their direction, checking the room numbers. When he got there, he realized the men were standing outside the room shared by Data and Fahd, the room that contained Data's expensive laptop computer.

He figured them for hotel thieves, pretended that he'd just realized he was right the first time, and headed back to his room to call security. He'd barely reached the elevators when something hit him from behind.

The New York police, swamped with traffic problems and other disruptions from the storm, barely managed to send an officer to the hotel. The policeman, who seemed in a hurry to get going, took down what details Muck could supply and said he would file a mugging report. He advised Muck to cancel his credit cards as soon as possible.

"I don't carry any," Muck told him, and the policeman looked at Muck as if the Screech Owls coach came from another planet.

"How much cash did you lose?" the policeman asked.

"Nothing. They took nothing."

The policeman nodded as if the crime had been all but solved. "Scared off," he said knowingly. "You were lucky, mister."

"Lucky to have sixteen stitches and a concussion?" Muck asked, shaking his head. He wasn't impressed.

Travis could make no sense of it all – at least not until Mr. Dillinger happened to read out the description of the men that Muck had given the police. One of the attackers was tall, in a long, dark coat, and wore a multicoloured hat pulled well over his ears, covering much of his face.

Big?

Travis was in his room, lying on his bed watching a "Simpsons" repeat. He was almost asleep when he heard a light tap at the door. It sounded like the housekeeping knock, and he instantly wished he'd remembered to hang the "PRIVACY, PLEASE" sign on the door handle. No one called out, however, and no one tried the handle.

The knock came again, and Travis rolled off the bed and went to see who was there. He needed to get on his tiptoes to see out the spy-hole. The fish-eye lens gave a distorted image of the hall, but Travis was glad to have the wide-angle view.

Travis had never seen Fahd's head so big, his nose so long, his eyes so wide and worried. He opened the door quickly. Fahd was there, worry all over his face. Travis first thought something was wrong with Muck. But that wasn't why Fahd had come to call.

"Big was here earlier," Fahd said.

"When?"

"Yesterday. Before we went out. Nish brought him up to the room."

"Your room?"

"Yeah – Data was out with you guys. It was just the three of us. Nish had to show him."

"Show him what?"

"His butt – he wanted Big to see what he was going to do New Year's Eve."

"That's sick!"

"No, no, no, no. He showed him the *recording*. I fired up Data's computer and opened the file so he could see. That's all."

"That's all? That means he knew about the computer. That and the digital camera are worth thousands of dollars."

Fahd seemed on the verge of tears. "But that's just it," he said.

"What do you mean?" asked Travis.

"Nothing was taken. I checked. It's all still there. The computer. The camera. Data was just talking to Lars again about an hour ago."

"Then they couldn't get in the room."

Fahd looked even more upset. "They might have."

Travis was completely alert now. "How do you know? Is something else missing?"

Fahd looked down at his shoes. "My key."

"Your *room* key! How would they get it? You were out at the restaurant with us . . ."

Fahd shook his head. "I couldn't find it when we left. I think maybe someone took it off the dresser earlier in the day." He looked desperately at Travis.

Travis understood. Big had stolen the key earlier when Nish invited him up to the room.

"Then maybe they were coming *out* of the room when Muck came along," said Travis, "not trying to get *in*. We better see if anything's missing."

Fahd nodded. He looked miserable.

Data already knew about the key.

"Nothing else is missing," he announced as Travis and Fahd came in through the door.

"Nothing?" Travis asked to make sure.

"Even the pocket change I left on the dresser is still there. Even" – looking at Fahd – "your stupid fake Oakleys and the Rolex are right there on the desk where you left them."

"And nothing with the computer?" Travis asked.

"Nothing. Everything's still there, exactly as we left it."

"Then maybe Muck did come along just as they were trying to get in," suggested Fahd. "He saved the computer."

But that didn't make sense to Travis. If Muck had come along as they were trying to get in, why wouldn't they just pretend it was the wrong door and move along? Why club Muck on the head if they figured he'd seen nothing?

And if it was just a mugging, as the police contended, why hadn't they stolen his wallet?

It made no sense at all.

13

ot Big," Nish moaned. "No *way* it was him."

"Get real," Travis said. "You took him to Data's room. He knew about the computer and the camera. Fahd's room key is missing."

"*But nothing was taken!*"

"Only because Muck came along and spoiled it."

"He's a good guy," Nish protested.

"You don't even know him," Travis said, shaking his head.

"I'm a good judge of people," Nish said. "Even if it was him, he didn't take anything."

"He *hit* Muck!" Travis almost shouted. He couldn't believe Nish wouldn't face facts. But, then again, Travis wasn't at all certain exactly what the facts were in this case.

"Even if it was Big at the door," Nish repeated helplessly, "it doesn't mean he hit Muck." He stood up, reaching for his jacket. "I'm going to find him."

"Who?" Travis asked, not following.

"Big, of course. I'll ask him right to his face."

Travis opened his mouth to speak, but nothing came out. He was stunned.

"*What?*" Nish challenged.

Travis tried again. This time, even though it seemed he had no breath, he was able to speak. "If he tried to kill Muck, who's to say he won't hurt you?"

Nish looked up, not believing Travis could be so foolish as to suggest such a thing. He put his pointer and middle fingers together.

"We're like brothers," Nish said. "Brothers."

"You don't even know his real name," Travis pointed out.

"I trust him with my life," Nish argued.

"That's what I'm afraid of," Travis said, shaking his head.

But Nish wasn't listening. His boots tied and his Screech Owls tuque in hand, he was headed for the door.

"*Wait!*" Travis found himself calling.

Nish stopped at the door, turning expectantly.

"I better come with you," Travis said.

Nish smiled. "I knew you would."

It was growing dark along East 52nd and Lexington. The snow was still falling and, in a surprising way, New York City was gradually beginning to look more like Tamarack than the Big Apple. There was precious little traffic now – only a few yellow cabs and police cars, a front-end loader growling at the end of a street as it dug free an intersection – and the fresh-fallen snow was white and sparkling under the streetlights. For the first time since the Screech Owls had arrived, the city was quiet. Almost peaceful.

Nish was ploughing ahead, head down, into the lightly blowing snow. He walked with determination, each step leaving an ankle-deep hole in the snow.

Travis hurried to keep up. He was fascinated that Nish seemed to know where he was going – a twelve-year-old treating downtown New York City as if it were his own home town – but he had long ago accepted that there were some things in life that Nish understood and many things he did not. While Nish might be able to find his way around the streets of a strange city today, tomorrow he might not be able to find a clean pair of boxer shorts in the mess of clothes dumped at the foot of his bed.

They walked down Lexington and along 42nd past Grand Central Station, which was practically deserted, since no trains had been running for days.

Near Times Square Nish came to a parking lot – cars abandoned by their owners were piled so high with snow it was impossible to tell colour or make – and turned in at an alley leading off it, moving as surely as if he were in his own backyard.

"Where are we going?" Travis asked, trying, but failing, to keep the worry out of his voice.

"Big's been working the streets between Times Square and Rockefeller Center – says it's the only place there's any customers any more. Him 'n' his buds are having a rough go of it."

Travis cringed. "A rough go of it"? How could you feel sorry for a bunch of street crooks selling illegal fake watches?

Travis pointed out the obvious: "This isn't the street. This is an alley."

Nish turned and looked at Travis with contempt. "This is where they operate out of – there's cops all over the streets, in case you haven't noticed."

Nish headed deeper into the alley. It was like entering a room with the lights off. Gone were the streetlights and their warm glow off the snow. It was dark in here, and getting darker. There were footprints everywhere, dark shadows that suggested to Travis they were not alone.

He was losing sight of Nish. The alley twisted up ahead, and Travis hoped it would twist again and then come out on the next street over, but he didn't know for sure. He knew only that he felt uneasy and wished he hadn't come.

He wanted to go back. He opened his mouth to call to Nish, but no sound came out.

Travis couldn't speak for a reason – *there was a large glove clamped over his mouth!*

14

They were deep in an underground parking lot. Large pipes dripped overhead. The floor was concrete, cracked and stained with salt. The place smelled of grease and exhaust and damp. Several bare bulbs swung from the ceiling at the end of thin electrical cables, sending shadows bouncing against the walls.

Travis had been hustled here so quickly – the stinking glove clamped over his mouth, his right arm locked and pressed behind his back – that only when he was released did he realize Nish had been dragged along too.

There were only a couple of cars in sight. One may have been working; the other certainly was not. It had been stripped of its wheels, and the windshield had been smashed in. The back doors were open and it looked as if someone might have been living in it. There were dirty blankets and old newspapers everywhere.

Along the ledges of the parking garage were stacks of brief-cases, like the one Big carried his fake Rolexes in. This had to

be "head office" of the fake-watch-and-sunglasses gang, and the
two Owls were clearly considered intruders. Big was nowhere
to be seen.

The two large men who had hustled them down here said
nothing. They seemed to be waiting for something.

The larger man – heavy, unshaven, with one eye slightly off
so it was impossible to tell whether he was looking at Travis or
Nish – started at a sound that came from the down-ramp into
the garage. He seemed nervous, but at the same time expecting
someone.

"*Big!*" Nish suddenly cried out.

There was no fear in his voice. He seemed genuinely glad to
see Big walking towards them. And Big, Travis had to admit,
seemed glad to see Nish.

"You lookin' for permanent work wit' us, Hockey Man?"
Big laughed.

"I knew I'd find you somewhere around here," Nish said.
"Dese guys musta t'ought I was da heat."

Big smiled slightly. Travis wondered for a moment exactly
how Nish saw himself. Some tough guy who could hold his
own with Big and his colleagues? Not likely.

"We have to watch our merchandise, that's all," said Big.
"Lots a thieves in da Big Apple, you know."

Yeah, Travis said to himself, and three of them are standing
right here.

"What were you after?" Big asked, as if expecting a new
order for Oakley sunglasses.

Nish explained. He told about the break-in, or near break-
in, at the hotel, and how someone had knocked Muck on the

head for sixteen stitches. He said it was Data and Fahd's room, where Big had been invited only a couple of days earlier.

"That's a shame, Hockey Man. Did they get anything?"

As if you need to ask, Travis thought.

"No," Nish said. "Nothing."

"Dat's good," Big said. "Dat's good."

Travis was almost certain Big had glanced quickly at the smaller of the other two men, but he didn't catch any look back and couldn't be sure. Still, he was deeply suspicious.

"Some of da kids think one a da suspects looked like you," Nish said unexpectedly.

Big spun around — to stare at Travis, not Nish. "Peewee here?" he asked.

Nish said nothing, waiting.

Travis cleared his throat.

"M–Muck described something l–like this coat," Travis said.

Big smiled.

"Lots a coats like dis in New York, Peewee. Shadow's got one on right now."

He pointed to the heavy man dressed like himself. Travis never liked the name "Big," but "Shadow" sounded worse.

"Besides," Big continued, "I wasn't anywhere near dat place last night. Ain't that right, Shadow?"

Shadow turned, almost as if he hadn't even been listening. He blinked, then answered, "Yah, dat's right. We was at the . . . theatre."

Big nodded. He looked at Nish, waiting for him to respond.

Travis wanted to shout, *Theatre? Right! Sure! Two thugs in long dirty coats and hold-up hats watching a play?*

"Dat's good," said Nish. "I was thinking you might do something like dat."

"We was out all night," said Big. "We got witnesses."

"I'll tell dem," said Nish. "Set dem straight."

"You do dat," Big said. "You do dat."

Nish and Big then changed the topic to watches and sunglasses and how there was nobody around downtown any more to sell to. Nish seemed so sympathetic.

Travis wandered around the parking lot, waiting. He checked out the old abandoned car. Behind it he found a small cache of tinned foods and drinks and even a small cooking unit like the kind campers use. There was garbage everywhere. Opened cans. Broken beer bottles.

Why didn't they use the garbage can? Travis wondered. There was a large open drum in the corner that Travis supposed was for trash.

He wandered over and looked in. It was a firepit. There were black ashes halfway to the top, and charred broken boards, some with nails still in them. They had the camper stove for cooking, Travis knew. They must set fires here for heat. He hated to think of such a life.

Travis could tell by the sounds that Nish was getting ready to head back to the hotel. He was just about to step away from the rear of the car when he looked in on the dashboard, beneath the crumbling windshield.

A hotel-room key!

Fahd's missing key?

15

What was wrong with everyone? Travis wondered.

First, Nish had refused to listen to him on the long trudge through the snow back to the hotel. He wouldn't believe for a moment that the key was Fahd's. What proof did Travis have? he wanted to know. The key had no number on it. It didn't even have the name of the hotel on it. It could be anyone's, said Nish, even Big's.

Sure, Travis wanted to say, Big really lives in a fancy hotel and just sells fake watches and hangs around underground parking garages for fun.

Travis was disappointed in his friend, but that was nothing compared to how he felt after he got off the telephone with the New York police. He'd managed to track down the policeman who'd investigated Muck's "mugging," but the man seemed absolutely uninterested in the case. Hotel keys were a dime a dozen, he said to Travis. People lost them all the time. Seeing a key in an old car didn't mean a thing. Nor had the policeman seemed interested in Travis's description of Big and Shadow and how one of them might have been the guy who clubbed Muck.

"Son," the policeman said in a way that made Travis feel five years old, "a million people in this city might fit that description. Call me back when you get a signed confession."

Travis lay on his bed staring at the ceiling. Perhaps the police were right. Someone may or may not have been in Data's and Fahd's room, but even if they had, nothing was taken. Someone did club Muck, but nothing had been taken from him, either. Perhaps Nish was right, too. Big wasn't involved. Perhaps, for that matter, Big and Shadow *had* been at the theatre the other night – a musical, maybe, with the two of them standing at the encore to toss bouquets of flowers at the stars.

But somehow Travis didn't think so.

The Owls had a game to play. Travis was disgusted with himself; he'd become so caught up in the world of crime and police investigations that he'd almost forgotten why the Screech Owls were in New York City.

They were in the middle of a big tournament. And they'd need Travis, the captain, concentrating on hockey if they were going to have a chance of winning.

They were to play a team from Chicago, the Young Blackhawks, in the same small rink where they'd played their opener. No Madison Square Garden again until they made the final – if they made the final.

The Blackhawks were a good, smart team – well coached, big, and mean. They caught the Owls off guard early, and within a matter of minutes the score was 2–0 for the Chicago peewees on only four shots. Jenny, whose turn it was to play nets this game, was also struggling.

"You're quicker than they are," Muck said to them before the next faceoff. "Better to be fast than big. Remember the last game."

Dmitri got the Owls rolling first, with a fast dash up-ice to beat the Chicago defenceman back to a puck that just came short of icing. He pulled around the defender, scooped up the puck, and set up behind the Blackhawk net, looking for someone coming in.

Travis came in hard from the left side, Sarah down the middle. Dmitri faked to Travis and hit Sarah, who shot immediately, the puck bouncing high off the goaltender's shoulder and fluttering in the air as it fell back to the ice.

It never made it. Travis's stick flashed in front of the goal-tender and picked the puck, baseball-style, out of mid-air and sent it into the far side of the net.

"Great play!" Sarah said as they mobbed Travis in the corner.

"Lucky, lucky," Nish kidded as he poked a glove through the scrum and smacked the top of Travis's helmet.

Travis grinned. He knew Nish was closer to the truth than Sarah, but he had meant to hit the puck, and it worked. It must have looked great.

The Owls tied it in the second period when Sam made a great rush up-ice. Just as she drew the Chicago defence in to check her, she flipped a backhand across-ice that little Simon Milliken picked up and rapped off the post. The rebound went to Andy, who hammered a shot that the falling Chicago goaltender barely managed to stop, and Mario, the ultimate garbage collector, was there to pick up the loose puck and lift it into the net.

Heading into the final minute, the two teams were still tied, with four goals each. Travis knew how badly they needed the win. It would give them a perfect record, and probably put them into the finals. A tie might leave it up in the air. A loss could mean elimination.

He skated quickly by Nish as they lined up for the next faceoff. "We win, we play in MSG again," he said quietly as he brushed past.

Travis knew what those words would do to Nish. Nish would see himself back at Madison Square Garden. The championship game. A big crowd. Television. David Letterman. Nish scoring his "Pavel Bure." A Hollywood contract. Action figures of Wayne Nishikawa under every Christmas tree. Dates with supermodels. Nish so famous he'd need *real* Oakleys to hide behind so he wouldn't be mobbed – which would happen anyway, of course.

The puck dropped. Sarah took out her check and Dmitri picked up the puck and flipped it back to Sam, who was on with Nish for the final minute of play. Sam fired it cross-ice to Nish, who took the pass at full stride. He was over the blueline and headed for centre when he fired a quick, unexpected pass that flew by Travis's left shoulder.

What's he doing? Travis wondered.

But then he saw. The Blackhawk defenceman had moved up tight on Travis, setting for a turnover. He had clearly hoped to dive past Travis and knock the puck away and free, but Nish's high pass had caught the defenceman completely by surprise. He was back on his heels, and when he tried to turn he fell.

The puck pounded into the boards and dropped to the ice, bouncing out perfectly as Travis sidestepped the falling defenceman and headed in on net.

Dmitri hammered his stick on the ice, looking for the pass. Travis hit him perfectly just as the far defenceman was turning for Travis, leaving Dmitri alone. Dmitri came in, faked, and dropped a long blind pass that landed perfectly on Sarah's stick.

The Chicago centre dived, hoping to take Sarah's skates out from under her. But Sarah was ready. She dropped the puck again, just as the Blackhawks centre tackled her and took her down.

The referee's hand went up – but the whistle couldn't go until a Chicago player touched the puck.

Sam picked it up in full flight.

Dmitri rapped his stick on the side of the net.

The Chicago goalie tried to play both Dmitri and Sam at the same time.

Sam shot, a hard slapper, that blew past the goalie on the blocker side, high and in off the elbow where the post meets the crossbar.

A moment, barely, before the horn blew to end regulation play.

Screech Owls 5, Young Blackhawks 4.

The players on the ice were first to mob Sam. Then the rest of the Owls and Muck arrived, slipping and falling along the ice.

"*What a play!*" Sarah was screaming.

"*Awesome!*" shouted Dmitri. "*Great shot, Sam!*"

"I set it all up," whined Nish. "And I won't even get credit for an assist."

Block him out, Travis told himself. Just block him out.

16

It was the last day of the year. From the way the snow was still falling – huge flakes that built into drifts, the side streets of New York now impassable – it felt like it might be the last day of forever. The dawn of a new Ice Age.

The New Year's Eve celebrations had not been cancelled. They had become, instead, a bigger story than usual – the people of New York City gathering at Times Square as a kind of declaration of solidarity against the elements. It could snow all it wanted; the storm was not going to stop the countdown to midnight.

They were now predicting a record number of people in Times Square. And the occasion had become an international news story; there might be as many as *two billion* people tuning in from around the world – the largest television audience since the first moon landing back in 1969!

"How appropriate," Nish announced with delight. "Both times they'll be tuning in to see a moon."

Not only was Nish still going to proceed with his outrageous plan, but Data and Fahd had become almost as caught up in the scheme themselves.

Data had swept the Internet for information on how to hack into a broadcast line. Travis was amazed at how much information was readily available through chat lines and Web sites. Data had been able to verify that a live, on-location broadcast like this would be done through the phone lines. They already had Data's laptop computer. They had the file containing Nish's moon. They had a telephone line at the hotel and, if they really needed it, a connection to Fahd's cellphone that would allow them to do it all from Times Square itself.

But they still needed more technical information. It was one thing to know the broadcaster, Data told them, but quite another to get to the video boards that would be controlling the broadcast. It would take them hours, if it could be done at all, to hack through the broadcaster's telephone system to reach the right location to begin their work. Considering the blocks and passwords that were likely involved, the task was next to impossible.

Data, however, had found a contact in Germany who kept e-mailing new ideas for them to try, and within an hour of computer time they had their answers.

"We can get the number for the direct phone line off the broadcast truck," Data explained. "Each truck has the number listed on the outside. We need to get the number for the main truck, then we're just one password away from the control board – and passwords tend to be obvious. We can worry about that later – right now we need the number from that truck."

"Let's go!" Andy shouted.

Travis might be team captain, but he was certainly not in charge here. The idea of Nish mooning the entire world had captured everyone's imagination. All he could do was go along for the ride – and be there if he was needed.

They told Mr. Dillinger they were just slipping over to Times Square to see what the preparations were like. There were six of them altogether – Fahd, Nish, Andy, Derek, Jesse, and Travis. Mr. Dillinger told them to be careful, to stick together, and not to get in anyone's way. They promised, and set out through the drifting snow.

The stage was almost ready when they got there. This was where the host would be doing the countdown. A huge ball was going to fall down a spiral high on one of the towers precisely at midnight, and the whole ceremony would be flashed live on the big screen above the square at the same time it was broadcast across the world.

The broadcast trucks were parked up a side street just away from the stage area, but there was crowd-control fencing blocking the way, and security everywhere.

"How are we going to get it?" Andy asked.

"We'll never get past that cop," said Fahd.

"We can talk to him," Jesse said. "He looks bored anyway."

"What about?" Fahd asked.

"Nothin'," said Derek. "Just ask him some stupid questions – keep him busy while one of us slips through."

"Who'll ask him questions?" Fahd wondered.

All five of the other Owls were staring at him. They needed

stupid questions. They needed someone who could ask questions all day long if necessary. And there was only one Owl for that job: Fahd.

"Okay," Fahd said. "And who's going to get the number?"

"It'll need to be someone who won't be noticed," Andy said. "Someone smaller."

Now they all turned and stared at Travis. If it required someone small, there was only one Owl for that job.

Travis nodded okay. He didn't think he could speak.

Fahd performed brilliantly. The policeman seemed to enjoy talking to kids. He was fascinated that they had come here from Canada, and he wanted to know if any of them knew a cousin he had up there somewhere.

"In Victoria, I think," he said. "Something to do with a queen, anyway. He's got a wheat farm or something."

"Regina," Fahd offered. "You must mean Regina. It's in Saskatchewan."

"Whatever," the cop said, and switched to a subject he liked better – himself. For a long time he talked about being a policeman in New York City, while the Owls listened and kicked up mounds of snow with the toes of their boots. But slowly Fahd got him onto the topic of the upcoming show.

Fahd played him perfectly. Flattered, the policeman began talking like a television executive. He used the star's first name as if they were best of friends. He talked about rehearsals and make-up artists and how important his own job was.

"Where does the director sit?" Fahd asked.

"Well," the cop said, "it's not like the movies. There's no director's chair, and he doesn't wear a French beret and shout

through a bullhorn. In fact, there might be three or four direc-
tors. They work from that big truck back there."

Fahd and the others craned their necks to see.

"Which one?" Fahd asked.

The policeman looked back as if to make sure himself. "The
blue one. The one right dead below the portable satellite dish."

Fahd looked quickly at Travis, who understood. Travis
would need to get away now if he got the chance.

"Is that gun loaded?" Fahd asked, nodding at the policeman's open holster.

The cop laughed. "'Course it's loaded, son – you don't
think we fight bad guys with water pistols, now, do you?"

"Yeah, but," Fahd said, "in Canada they have to load them
first. And they're all holstered up practically out of sight."

"Canada ain't New York City, kid," the cop said, as if they
hadn't realized. "If I took the time to unbuckle and load up, I'd
be shot a thousand times before I was ready."

The policeman was off and running. He began to brag
about the cases he'd solved and the drug dealers he'd arrested
and the important people he'd guarded – never for a moment
aware that a bunch of twelve-year-olds had just pulled the wool
so far over his eyes he was about to flunk the one assignment he
had that day: keeping people out.

Travis slipped away and ducked under the nearest truck. He
wriggled his way through to a narrow space between one truck
with "MAKE-UP" on it and another with "MAIN FEED," all the
time keeping an eye out for security.

Someone had left deep tracks in the snow, and he kept to
them, careful not to leave his own small footprints behind.

As Travis drew closer to his goal he heard a man cough. He leaped from the footprints and scrambled under the nearest truck, rolling in the snow.

Just in time! Two television-crew members rounded the far corner and walked down the same narrow space he'd been coming through.

Travis rolled out the other side of the truck, retraced his steps, and, when the men had gone – thank heavens for coughs! – he stepped back out into the tracks and hurried the rest of the way.

"DIRECTOR" a sign read on the blue vehicle's side. The policeman had been right.

"MAIN CONTROL PANEL," it read below. And beneath that was a number: 212-555-7449.

Travis stared hard at the number. *How would he ever remember all that?* He had nothing to write it down with. He couldn't write it in the snow – what good would that do? He *had* to remember it.

The first part – 212 – was the area code. Even if he forgot that, he could easily look it up.

The second part was also a snap. 555 – he'd seen enough television shows to know that was always the number in these circumstances!

But 7449?

Easy – Travis Lindsay, Wayne Nishikawa, and Sarah Cuthbertson. Numbers 7, 44, and 9.

He raced back along the tracks through the snow, repeating the numbers out loud as he hurried to where the policeman was just winding up yet another story of a mob shootout.

17

"We have to do a dry run first," Data said. Fahd nodded. He understood. The others were not so sure. As soon as they were back in the hotel, Travis had carefully written down the numbers – mumbling as he did so, 2-1-2, 5-5-5, me-Nish-Sarah" – and though Fahd had looked at him a little oddly, he'd taken the slip of paper and handed it to Data.

"Whadya mean 'a dry run'?" Nish practically shouted. "You think I'm gonna wet my pants at a time like this?"

The others ignored him and set about hooking up the system. They connected the computer to the phone line, used a double jack to connect the telephone itself, and Fahd and Data began calling up their program.

"What's the number again?" Data asked.

Fahd spun the paper so Data could see as he typed it into the computer. There was a pause and then, quickly, a series of notes as the computer dialled.

No one dared take a breath while they waited.

There was a long, seemingly too long, hiss, then some loud clicks and buzzes, then silence.

"*We're in!*" Data said in a voice somewhere between a whisper and a hiss.

The logo of the broadcaster came up first on Data's screen, and then a small box, empty, with the cursor pulsating in the corner. "PASSWORD," it said above the box.

"Now's the tough part," said Data.

Fahd held his hands over the keyboard, his fingers dancing in the air.

"*What is it?*" Fahd kept saying. "*What is it? What is it?*"

"Probably the director's name," said Andy.

"Nah," said Data. "It would be a code word. Something they wouldn't forget."

"The date?" Jesse suggested.

"I like it," Fahd said, and immediately typed in the date.

They waited a moment while the screen faded, then bounced back.

"PASSWORD FAILURE," the screen said. "PLEASE TRY AGAIN."

"Be careful," Data said. "Probably three mistakes and it closes down. There might even be an alert on it."

"The name of the host?" Derek suggested.

"That might be it!" said Fahd. He typed the host's name in and then pressed ENTER.

The screen faded and then reappeared.

"PASSWORD FAILURE. PLEASE TRY AGAIN."

"Last chance," Data muttered. He sounded ready for defeat.

"*Happy New Year,*" said Nish miserably. He sounded as if his world had just come to an end.

Fahd turned around quickly. "What was that?"

"What was what?" Nish said, not following.

"What you just said."

"Happy New Year?"

"That could be it!" Fahd said. "That's probably it."

"Type it in," Data said.

Fahd's fingers flew over the keys. He hit ENTER, and again the page on the screen vanished. This time, however, it did not come back right away saying they had failed. When the screen returned it said something different.

"NEW YEAR'S SPECIAL."

Fahd pumped a fist over his head. "You did it, Nish! You're a *genius!*"

"It took you till now to find that out?" Nish said. But he was red-cheeked and smiling, astonished at his own lucky guess.

Files began appearing on the screen.

"What're those?" Andy asked.

"Should be everything," Data said. "Even the commercial breaks. Everything that isn't live is right here as a pre-recorded file, and all it takes is a double click to load it up onto the big screen."

"How do I get my butt up there?" Nish asked. His voice was a bit whiney, as if he resented no longer being the centre of attention, the glory going, for the moment, to Data and Fahd, who had hacked their way into the broadcast.

"Simple," explained Data. "I just insert your file into the list and double-click when we want it up. It overrides everything."

"From here?" Nish asked.

"From here," Data said.

"I get to moon the world and I don't even have to leave my hotel room to do it?"

"You got it, Einstein."

"Beauty," Nish said. "Beauty."

Just then there was a loud rap at the door.

Everyone froze.

18

For a long moment, no one dared move.

The sharp knock on the door seemed to echo through the room, though it had not been repeated.

"*Who is it?*" Fahd hissed. "Check it out!"

Andy, the tallest, crept silently to the door. He stood up straight and cautiously put his eye to the peep-hole.

He turned, smiling. "It's Sarah and Sam."

Fahd, who had already cut the connection and was in the process of turning off his computer, lifted his hand off the keys and relaxed. "Let them in," he said.

Sarah and Sam burst into the room, filling it with new energy.

"Smells like a hockey dressing room in here," Sam said. "Whatya been sweatin' over, Rolex Boy?" She poked Nish in the gut. He buckled over, pretending she'd winded him.

"What's going on?" Sarah asked. "Nish headed into the *Guinness Book of World Records* or what?"

"We're in," Fahd said. "He's almost there."

"*The entire world's gonna hurl!*" Sam shouted.

"Very funny," muttered Nish. "Very, very funny."

"I want to know how you're going to do it," Sarah said to Data and Fahd.

They were delighted to explain. They walked Sarah and Sam through all the technical details and described, with due credit to Nish, how they'd cracked the password that took them straight into the computer controls of the broadcast truck.

"Nish's butt is just a double click away from being seen around the world," said Data. "He's going to make history."

"I'll believe it when I see it," said Sam. "I don't even believe he mooned for you guys."

"*Did so!*" Nish all but shouted.

"Prove it!" Sam challenged.

She had Nish in the palm of her hand. Less than a year on the Screech Owls and Sam could work Nish better than anyone, playing him like a puppet on a string.

"Show them!" Nish commanded Data and Fahd.

"What?" Fahd asked. "The file?"

"My butt," corrected Nish.

"Show us," Sam said. "You're going to show everybody later, anyway. Surely you can give two young women a sneak preview of the Eighth Wonder of the World!"

"C'mon," said Sarah. "Give us a look so we'll know what it is when it comes up on the screen."

"Okay," Data said.

Fahd went into the directory until he found the file marked "Moonshot," then double-clicked on it. The machine whirred and hummed, stopped and started, whirred and hummed some more.

"It's a big file," Data explained.

"It's a big butt," Sam replied.

The screen flashed, then filled with a man's face.

He was wearing a ski mask, pulled down tight over his face.

"*What the hell?*" Nish shouted.

"Wrong file," Fahd said to Data.

"No," Data said. "It's the right file. Something's wrong."

The camera pulled out from the man in the ski mask. He was flanked by two other men, each dressed the same: long dark coat, gloves, ski mask over the face exposing only the eyes.

Each man was carrying an automatic rifle pointed directly at the camera.

The man in the middle began to speak. It was rough – computer data becoming sound – but it was clear and to the point.

"BE PREPARED TO DIE, NEW YORKERS!" the voice shouted slowly and deliberately. "AT MIDNIGHT WE KILL ANYONE STILL ON THE STREETS!"

The man turned his weapon and shot several rounds to the side of the camera. The shots sounded tinny over the small speakers of Data's laptop, but to Travis they sounded like exploding bombs.

"BE PREPARED TO DIE!"

Travis felt a deep, sickening chill down his spine. They were terrorists. Terrorists threatening to gun down anyone attending the New Year's Eve celebrations in Times Square.

"*Who are they?*" Sam asked, giggling slightly as if hoping it might be some elaborate practical joke.

Travis figured he knew. He had recognized the voice.

19

T. ravis hadn't been the only one to recognize the voice. As soon as he looked at Nish and saw his beet-red, sweating face, he knew that Nish, too, had realized instantly who was beneath the balaclava.

Big.

Nish took it particularly badly. Not just because the lead terrorist turned out to be his great friend, but because his ambitious plan to moon the entire world had gone up in smoke.

Travis could tell that Nish was struggling with what to do. There was little choice, however.

"We better show this to somebody," Travis said.

Nish nodded helplessly.

Travis led the little group down to Mr. Dillinger's room. Mr. Dillinger called in Muck while the Owls explained the situation. Fahd then played the recording for them both.

Mr. Dillinger called the police. A detective came and heard the story and, once again, Fahd played the recording. The police demanded that the Screech Owls take them to this man called

Big, and Nish sadly led the way to the underground garage
where he had last met with his great friend.

Travis was astonished at how quickly the police moved. In
no time, with the Owls well out of the way, they had gathered
up Big and his buddies and hauled them off to be charged.

"What for?" Nish asked.

The detective in charge looked at him as if it were one of the
stupidest questions he had ever heard. "Uttering terrorist threats,"
he said. "In this country, that's right up there with murder."

One of Big's friends had broken immediately and explained
the story.

It was all Big's idea. He'd got it when Nish had invited Big
over to the hotel room to tell him about his great scheme to
moon the world. Big had even been shown the file of Nish
mooning before the camera.

Big was smarter than Travis had imagined. He had figured
out that if he could just replace the "Moonshot" file on the
computer with another one, then instead of Nish's big butt on
the screen at Times Square the New Year's crowd would see his
own recording.

"This man claims there was no real terrorist threat," the
detective said. "The guy they all call Big figured that they
could panic the crowd who'd come down to see the show.
With everyone running for cover, and with the snowstorm still
blowing, they'd paralyze the city and empty the downtown
core, leaving them free to loot wherever they wanted – even
along Fifth Avenue.

"They filmed their own recording and saved it on disk. It
took them less than five minutes to break into the hotel room,

replace your file with theirs, and give it the same name. That way, you would load their file thinking it was yours. It was pretty ingenious – and it might have worked if you hadn't checked it out first."

"So it *was* them who hit Muck!" Sarah said.

The detective nodded. "There's also going to be assault charges," he said. "These guys are in deep trouble, believe me."

"But–but–but," Nish began, "what happened to my file?"

"It's gone," the detective said. "Outer space, I guess. But count yourself lucky, son."

"W–why's that?"

"If your file had gone up on that screen, I might be here charging you instead."

Nish stuck out his chin, challenging. "No way you'd have recognized me."

The policeman blew out his cheeks and shook his head. "We'd have checked every butt in New York," he said. "A butt like that is pretty distinctive, wouldn't you say?" He pointed at Nish's rear end.

Nish blazed red – for once speechless.

20

ew Year's Eve in Times Square was wonderful. The snow stopped falling, the ploughs came out and cleared off the main streets, and downtown New York filled with hundreds of thousands of New Year's revellers. The noise was deafening, the countdown and the fireworks spectacular. The broadcast went off without a hitch. No terrorist threats. No bare bum.

Nish was shattered. He walked around with his hands deep in his pockets and his face so sad you'd think his life was coming to an end. When the great ball dropped and the New Year arrived, he would have nothing to do with noisemakers. He wouldn't dance. He wouldn't cheer. He wouldn't look at the big screen.

"My one chance to make the *Guinness Book of World Records*," he kept muttering. "And I blew it."

"Get into the spirit, Rolex Boy," Sarah told him. "It's a whole new year – *anything* can happen."

"Nothin' that good," Nish said despondently. "That was the single greatest idea I ever had in my life. It's all downhill from here for me."

Sarah spun her finger by her temple and rolled her eyes at Travis. Travis shrugged. Nish was just being Nish. By tomorrow he'd have forgotten all about it and have a brand-new idea.

"Better get to bed," Mr. Dillinger said as he came up behind them. "We're on at noon tomorrow. Madison Square Garden. Championship game."

"Who are we playing?" asked Derek.

"The Detroit Wheels," Mr. Dillinger said. "We came first, they were right behind us in the standings."

"The Wheels?" Nish asked. "Was that the team I scored the winner against?"

Mr. Dillinger frowned and looked over his glasses at Nish. How could he have forgotten? But Travis knew Nish hadn't forgotten for a second. He just wanted to remind everyone he had scored the winner.

Nish was back in the real world.

21

verything had changed. No one was talking any more about hacking into a broadcast. Nish wasn't going on about his butt or the *Guinness Book of World Records*. He was, instead, sitting fully dressed in the visitors' dressing room of Madison Square Garden, his head resting on his shin pads, deep in concentration. He hadn't even bothered to check out the photographs in the hallway. He had come to do one thing – play hockey.

"You know what you need to do," Muck said just before he opened the door that led to the ice surface. "Go to it."

Travis smiled to himself as he strapped on his helmet. For Muck, that almost amounted to a major speech. Nothing about how far they'd come together, nothing about armies fighting glorious battles, no fancy quotes that no one could understand – just good old Muck, telling them to get out there and "Go to it."

They headed onto the ice, Jeremy first, spinning at the blue-line so he skated backwards into the net, where he immediately began scraping the ice so he could rough up his crease. He seemed oblivious to his surroundings. How Jeremy could fail to notice there were several thousand people in the stands, Travis didn't know.

Travis skated around on the new ice, feeling his legs. Sarah was up ahead, gliding smoothly as she took her turn around the back of the net. Nish was pounding Jeremy's pads like they were some horrible animal that had to be killed before the game could begin. Everything was in order for the Screech Owls. Travis even hit the crossbar during warm-up. He felt great. He knew that this game, this championship match in the Big Apple International Peewee Tournament, was going to be a great one.

The people had come out of curiosity. The snowstorm was over, and the downtown streets were slowly returning to normal, but the people of New York were still essentially stranded in their city. There was little else to do but go for a walk, ski in the park, or find something like a minor-hockey tournament to take in. Madison Square Garden had opened its doors and was charging nothing. This and the television coverage the various teams had been given during the storm combined to bring thousands out to see the final match.

Muck was right. There was nothing he needed to say about the Wheels. They were big, and seemingly older than the Owls. They had great shots, and could score goals. The two teams were almost perfectly matched, with the Screech Owls' speed and skill at playmaking roughly equalled by the Wheels' strength and shots. The two teams had already played once to sudden-death overtime. It was going to be a great final.

Sarah's line started, with Nish and Fahd back on defence. Sarah took the opening faceoff easily and sent Dmitri flying down the wing so fast he caught a slow Detroit defender off guard, set him back on his heels, and tore past him for a quick snap shot that ticked off the post – and then off the glass.

It might have been 1–0 for the Owls but for a fraction of an inch. The puck bounced off the glass, jumped over Nish's stick as he pinched in, and immediately the Wheels were off on a two-on-one with only Fahd back.

Travis knew what he had to do. Sarah and Dmitri were both caught up-ice. He was behind the play, but he had the angle on the puck carrier and had better speed. He dug down so hard he felt his lungs burn with the effort. He tucked low to the ice and tried to flick his ankles with every push off, anything for more speed.

The two Wheels were over the blueline with Fahd between them. Travis noticed the puck carrier look for his partner.

Travis gambled that he would pass.

Jumping with one final push, Travis flew through the air and landed flat on his chest, with his stick held out in front of him in one hand.

The pass was already on the way, hard and perfectly aimed at the tape of the second Wheel, who pulled his stick back to one-time it.

Travis reached as far as he could, his arm seeming almost to unhinge. He felt the puck just tick the toe of his stick blade, then heard the whistle as the puck flew over the boards and out of play. He kept sliding, right through the circle and into the boards.

The other Owls on the ice raced to him as if he'd scored.

"*Great play, Trav!*" Sarah called.

"*You saved a goal!*" Fahd shouted.

Nish said nothing. But when Travis got to his knees, he felt a quick, light tap on the seat of his hockey pants. His old friend, being grateful.

The game surged end to end, with great attacks and even greater defensive plays. Sam blocked a shot from the slot that would have gone in had she not thrown herself in front of it. Nish broke up rush after rush. Andy checked the top Detroit centre to a standstill. Jeremy was brilliant, making glove saves and pad saves, dropping down into the butterfly to prevent wraparounds, and once stopping a hard shot from the point with his mask, a shot so hard it ripped the mask clean off.

At the other end, Travis hit the crossbar – only this time it didn't make him smile. The Wheels goalie stopped Dmitri on a clean break and stopped Wilson on a great pinch from the point.

"It's coming," Muck said at the first break. "It's coming."

In the second period, both teams scored early, the Wheels on a lucky tip that went off Wilson's skate, the Owls when Mario picked up one of his specialties, a garbage goal, after Nish had sent a hard drive into the crease and the goaltender let the rebound slip away.

Sarah scored on a pretty play where she slipped the puck through a Detroit defender's feet and then pulled out the goalie. The Wheels came back on a breakaway when Fahd let his man beat him to the outside. Derek scored on a hard blast from the top of the circle. The Wheels scored on the power play after Andy had been sent off for tripping.

It was a tie game, Wheels 3, Owls 3, with one period left to play.

They flooded the ice between the second and third periods, and the Owls returned to their dressing room to wait. Nish threw a towel over his head and hid his face beneath it. He was fully concentrating now.

Travis was glad Nish hadn't noticed the camera crew walking through the crowd and shooting the action on the ice. He knew if Nish saw a TV camera, he'd become a different player from the one they so desperately needed right now.

Muck and Mr. Dillinger came into the room, Muck holding a single sheet of paper in both hands, low, and staring at it as if he could not quite believe what he was reading.

"Different rules for the championship game," Muck announced. "Five minutes of sudden-death overtime if it's still tied after three. Then a shootout. You know what I think about shootouts."

Muck hated them. Hockey, he always said, was a *team* game, not an exhibition of individual skills. But then, he didn't like the designated hitter in baseball, either. The Owls, on the other hand, dreamed of shootouts, and the glory that would come from scoring a spectacular goal.

Late in the third, Muck's fears looked as if they might be coming true. The Owls had scored on a lucky tip by Simon Milliken, but the Wheels had tied it 4–4 on another power play.

Travis could sense the game slowing. He had to admit, Muck had a point. If teams knew there would be a shootout, they tended to play *for* the shootout, counting on their best players to win it when no one was checking them.

Travis had never been checked so tightly. It was almost as if another player was inside his sweater with him, pulling him here and pushing him there. Every time he tried to escape into open ice, he felt an arm across his chest, a hook inside his elbow, a stick between his legs.

It was the same for everyone. Sarah couldn't find the space she needed for plays, Dmitri couldn't find the open ice he needed for his speed.

The Wheels checked frantically, but when they had the puck, they made no effort to carry it up-ice towards the Screech Owls' goal. Instead, they dumped it deep into the Owls' end – forcing Jeremy to leave his net to play it – then ran for the bench and a change rather than chase the puck in and try to cause a turnover.

They were in the dying minutes of a championship, and Travis had never seen the game played so methodically, so predictably. Muck was right about shootouts.

The buzzer sounded to signal the end of regulation time, and the players gathered at the bench, Nish flicking the cap off a water bottle and dumping it all down the back of his neck. They were exhausted, and now they had to face five minutes of sudden-death hockey. There would be no flood. They would play the five minutes on the same ice surface, rutted and snowy, very much to the advantage of the slower, larger Detroit team.

"Try to end it early," Muck said to Sarah's line. "I don't want us in a shootout."

Sarah won the faceoff, but the Detroit centre all but tackled her when she tried for the loose puck. Travis found himself wrestling with the opposite winger and couldn't get to it either.

Sarah tried to slip around her check and was pitchforked over, crashing and sliding towards the far boards.

Travis caught Sarah's expression as she turned. She was staring icicles at the referee, but the ref, who had been standing right beside the two centres when the big Detroit player had dumped her, was acting as if nothing at all had happened.

If Muck hated shootouts, Travis hated officials who treated third periods and overtimes as if they were different from the rest of the game.

"I can't move out there!" Sarah said when they came off.

"I know," Travis said. "It's crazy."

Travis felt a knock on the side of his shin pad. It was Nish, reaching for him down the bench with his stick.

"If I get a chance," Nish said, his face soaked with sweat and beaming red, "I'm carrying. You cover."

Travis nodded.

Next shift Sarah tried a new tactic. Instead of going for the puck as usual, she ignored it and took out the big Detroit centre, very nearly pitchforking him back as she used her strength to leverage him off the puck.

Holding off the centre with her back, Sarah kicked the puck towards Travis, who darted in under his own check to sweep it away and against the boards.

Finally, a little space!

Travis turned, picked up the puck, and headed for the back of the Owls' net. The far winger was coming hard at him, and Travis faked a shot against the boards and simply left the puck behind the net, throwing his shoulder into the checker and sending him off balance out into the slot area.

Nish was there to pick up the drop. He stickhandled easily, checking both sides.

Sarah cut straight across the ice towards the middle. Two Wheels stuck to her, both hooking.

Nish held, and when the free Detroit forward came at him, he tapped it off the back of the net so it bounced right back to him as the checker flew by.

Nish had the open left side, and took it. He moved up-ice quickly. Travis bumped the player closest to him to give Nish more room, and Sarah, the cleanest player on the team, used her stick to hold back the big Detroit centre.

Nish kept over the Wheels' blueline. Travis remembered what he had been told – "You cover!" – and dropped back into Nish's spot to be in position to defend against any turnover.

Nish faked a pass to Dmitri and still held. There was no lane to the net. He stayed along the boards and stopped abruptly as a Detroit defenceman came in hard with his shoulder. The checker missed, crashed into the boards and crumpled to the ice.

Nish was still looking to pass. The big centre had Sarah tied up. Dmitri was stapled to the far boards by an interfering backchecker. Travis was back, just outside the blueline to cover a quick break the other way, so Nish couldn't risk a pass to him that might go offside. Fahd was on the far side, but a cross-ice pass would be too risky.

Nish worked back of the Wheels' net, stickhandling easily as he tried to read the situation.

Everywhere he looked, Screech Owls players were tied up. He, however, was free; the player who'd slammed into the boards was still trying to pick up his stick with his big, clumsy gloves on.

Travis could not believe what he was seeing. It was almost as if he saw it all happen even before Nish pulled back the puck so it flipped up onto the blade of his stick.

He's not!

But he was. The puck cradled flat on his blade, Nish casually tossed it high so that it sailed over the top of the net like a golf ball lobbed out of a sand trap.

With no one on him, Nish furiously moved his legs so he came spinning around the front of the net just as the puck landed, flat, in the slot. He was still unchecked, the player who'd lost his stick only now diving, stick in hand, in the hopes of blocking the shot.

He was too late. Nish picked the top corner, blew it over the goaltender's glove, and punched the water bottle so hard off the back of the net it hit the glass and sprayed all over it, right in front of the goal judge.

The red light came on.

The Screech Owls had won in sudden-death overtime!

And Nish had scored his Pavel Bure goal!

22

Travis wasn't exactly sure when Nish had first noticed the cameras. He couldn't have missed the crews running onto the ice to film the Owls piling on top of him. But it seemed to Travis that Nish must have seen them earlier; why else would he have tried his crazy play? Travis didn't much care. It had worked. Nish had his Pavel Bure goal – and the Owls had the championship.

Nish put on a humble act when the cameras closed around him and the reporters began peppering him with questions. He called it a "lucky play" and gave credit to his teammates, but Travis didn't believe it for a moment. Nish was in his glory.

"Maybe Letterman will call," Sam said sarcastically as the rest of the Owls stood around watching Nish fielding questions.

"Guinness won't be," said Sarah, giggling.

She was right. Nish might have come to New York to moon – but instead he'd ended up a star.

After Travis had accepted the trophy, and medals were being presented to both teams, he noticed the camera crews talking with the organizers. Then just when it seemed he should pick up the trophy and hold it over his head for a victory lap of Madison Square Garden, the organizers, with the Wheels' coach in tow, hurried over to Muck.

They talked briefly, Muck scowling but eventually giving one quick nod of his head. He came back to the Owls and called them all in around him.

"They've a chance to get on the network news apparently," Muck said, unimpressed. "But the television people want to shoot a shootout. You willing to do that?"

It was clear from Muck's expression that he himself didn't want to. But Muck was Muck, never one to force his opinions on others. He was leaving it up to the team.

"You betcha!" said Nish, still beaming from his moment of glory. He couldn't get enough.

"Sure," said Andy.

"Why not?" said Sam.

Muck nodded once, curtly. "Fine, then," he said. "I'll let them know."

The organizers seemed delighted. They immediately cleared the ice of everyone but two camera crews, one on each side of the slot area where the shooters would be coming in. Jeremy and the Wheels' goaltender both took their positions.

The players all went back to their benches while the coaches made up their lists.

Sarah would shoot first.

Travis second.

Nish third.

Muck read down through the entire list. Travis was thrilled. He could feel his heart pounding. He hoped he scored.

Sarah scored easily, a beautiful tuck play as the goalie shot out his stick to poke-check her, and she simply let the puck slide into the net off her backhand.

The big Detroit centre scored on a hard slapshot that blew right through Jeremy's pads.

The Owls were still congratulating Sarah when Travis, looking down the bench, noticed something very unusual.

Sam, who was far down the list, had her helmet and gloves off and was very carefully pickpocketing Mr. Dillinger's first-aid belt.

She was taking out the scissors.

Muck tapped him on the shoulder. "You're up," he said.

Travis came out onto the ice to a nice round of applause for the winning captain. He loved it. If only the ice surface had been flooded so he could feel that glorious snap and sizzle when he made his turn.

He picked up the puck and wished there was no heavy snow on the ice. He was afraid of losing the puck, and he couldn't stickhandle very quickly. His legs felt funny, like rubber one stride, like lead the next.

Travis came in, faked, went to his backhand, and lifted the puck as hard as he could.

Ping! Off the crossbar.

Travis heard the crowd groan. He slammed his stick in disappointment, but in truth he wasn't that upset. It was just a shootout for fun, after all. It didn't count. And as only hockey players understand, if you're going to miss, the best way is off the crossbar.

As Travis skated back to the bench and his teammates shouted his name, Nish came over the boards.

Right behind Nish, giggling, sat Sam. She held up the scissors in one hand, and raised a thumb with the other.

Sarah was doubled over, laughing so hard tears were coming down her cheeks.

What was going on?

Nish made a grand circle before picking up the puck. It was as if he was on parade. He did some fancy stickhandling and took lots of time.

Both cameras were on him as he came over the blueline. They knew who this was – the kid who had scored the spectacular goal and won the game in overtime – and it was pretty obvious that if any footage made the network news, it was going to be of Nish.

But wait, there was something wrong with Nish's pants! They seemed impossibly low!

Nish tried a fancy sidestep, and his hockey pants dropped right down over his skates.

He tripped and slid helplessly along the ice.

Travis heard two wild squeals of laughter down the bench. Sarah was high-fiving Sam, and Sam was furiously snipping the air with the scissors.

She had cut Nish's suspenders!

Nish was still down, his pants around his ankles, both camera crews zooming in on the overtime hero.

He was going to be on network television.

And only a sweaty pair of boxers had kept him from setting a world record for mooning.

THE END

Horror on River Road

1

"T. hanks a lot, pal!"

Travis Lindsay's voice shook. He could feel the blood rising in his face, his throat stinging from the sharp rasp of his own words. He couldn't remember ever being so angry at his best friend, Wayne Nishikawa.

They were standing outside the Bluebird Theatre, Tamarack's only movie house, and Travis had his fists stabbed down as far as possible in the pockets of his Screech Owls team jacket. He was surprised at how tightly clenched they felt, like they needed to be contained before something terrible happened.

Travis had never hit anyone in his life – not even in a hockey game – but he knew, in an instant, how easily it could happen. If Nish had been standing there in his full hockey equipment, helmet included, instead of in a T-shirt and shorts with that stupid sheepish look on his face, Travis might have tried to hammer him into the ground to make his point. But all he could do was yell.

"You stupid idiot! What were you thinking?"

Travis knew he was headed down a useless road with that question. Nish didn't think. Nish just acted. And he had acted the perfect fool this evening.

Travis had waited all week for this movie. He and Nish had seen parts I, II, III, IV, V, VI, and VII of *The Blood Children* – *"Most Frightening Hollywood Sequels Ever Made!" "Two Stumps Up!"* – and finally Part VIII had arrived in Tamarack on a Saturday night in early June. They were determined to be there for the very first showing of what was sure to be a long run.

The two friends – make that *former* friends – had watched the first seven movies in the blood-curdling series in the comfort of Nish's living room. Nish had somehow convinced his long-suffering mother that there was something "educational" in movies that featured one-eyed, slimy aliens from outer space, haunted graveyards, flashing blood-stained scythes, rolling heads, exploding eyes, hideous zombies, and spine-tingling, horrific screams.

"Trav and I believe," Nish had told his poor mother, all the while winking behind her back at Travis, "that all such movies should be banned."

Mrs. Nishikawa, one of the sweetest, most naive human beings Travis had ever known, had nodded slowly as she stacked the dishes, a small smile on her face showing how proud she was of her well-meaning son.

"What we want to do," Nish had continued, as if making a speech, "is work on a school project on how harmful horror movies can be to kids." He neglected to mention that the movies were all rated AA.

Mrs. Nishikawa had thought it an excellent idea and congratulated Nish on showing such maturity. But Travis knew differently. He couldn't believe how trusting Mrs. Nishikawa could be. Did she not realize school was almost out for the summer holidays and that no one would be doing school work? He wondered if she would ever ask to see their project after they had supposedly written it up.

But Mrs. Nishikawa had never asked to see anything. She even made them popcorn and brought in cold pop as Nish and Travis happily watched one rented *Blood Children* movie after the other – something the Lindsays would never permit Travis to do – until they had enjoyed all seven.

Travis could never decide whether he really liked horror movies. He liked to be frightened, but not terrified. He liked being scared, so long as he was certain it would quickly pass. At Nish's house, Travis was able to make sure he had every safety device at his disposal: the pause button on the remote control, the washroom, bright lights in the Nishikawa living room, and, if necessary, Mrs. Nishikawa's happy, comforting face seeing him to the front door before the frantic race home – preferably before dark.

Never, however, had the boys seen a horror movie in a real theatre. It was something Travis had often imagined, with a shudder. The lights would be down. The screen would be huge. Other viewers – *strangers, their faces hidden in the dark* – would be screaming. Travis wanted desperately to go, but didn't know for sure if he could handle it.

"We'll get cigars," Nish said. "Light 'em up before we hit the box office and they'll figure we're adults."

Sure, Travis thought, a couple of miniature adults wearing peewee hockey jackets and smoking huge cigars. That'll fool them for sure.

Nish pushed, but Travis refused to detour past his grandparents' so they could "borrow" a couple of his grandfather's big, stinking old Corona cigars. Travis didn't steal. He didn't smoke. And he had no intention of looking like an idiot. What next? he wondered. False beards? Canes? Hearing aids? The two of them in walkers and wearing adult diapers?

In the end, they tagged along with Mario Terziano's older brother, who was taking his date to the new movie and thought it a lark to pay for the boys' tickets and sneak them in, as long as Nish and Travis didn't actually sit with them.

Passing for fourteen seemed to do something to Nish. He was even more outrageous than usual. Instead of sitting quietly in a corner of the theatre where they might go unnoticed, Nish insisted they sit dead centre. While they waited for the previews to begin, he made animal sounds, shouted out "KAW-WA-BUNGA!" and "EEE-AWWW-KEEE!" and once even passed wind loudly before holding his nose with one hand and raising the other high to point straight down at Travis.

Travis slid lower and lower in his seat.

The previews did nothing to settle Nish down. He whistled and stomped and clapped his hands. He began cracking jokes about the action on screen, and when some of the audience laughed, he got even louder.

Travis hoped desperately that Nish would settle down once the main feature began, but he was out of luck. *The Blood*

Children: Part VIII started, and as Travis sank ever lower into his seat, Nish seemed to grow in his.

First head that got lopped off, Nish shouted out, "*That was a no-brainer!*"

First alien that popped out of a graveyard, Nish blew a bugle charge as if the cavalry were coming.

The aliens moved on some sort of jet boots that enabled them to float just above ground, and they carried vicious scythe-type weapons that twisted at the end like an illegally curved hockey stick.

It was too much for Nish to resist. When the aliens moved in for their first civilian massacre, he leaped to his feet, cupped his hands around his mouth, and yelled, "*Go Leafs Go!*"

Once he hit on this hockey theme, Nish was lost. In the movie's very first "romantic" scene – a long, passionate kiss between a gorgeous blonde actress and a handsome soldier who turned out to be a vampire – he shouted, "*Two minutes for no neck protector!*"

Instead of screaming in terror, the theatre was howling with laughter. Nish had become part of the entertainment.

But not everyone was delighted by his contribution. At one point the theatre manager, Mr. Dinsmore, had walked slowly up and down the aisles, flashing his light along the seats. But when he passed by Nish, Mr. Dinsmore saw only what every adult in a position of authority saw: Wayne Nishikawa sitting up straight, innocent as a choirboy, hands politely folded in his lap.

The Blood Children: Part VIII was particularly gross. Severed heads flew about the screen. Arms and legs were chopped off by a madman with a chainsaw. Aliens blew up. Blood splattered against the camera, dripping down the screen.

"*Where's Tie Domi when you need him?*" Nish shouted.

When the movie slowed for some dull romantic development, Nish scooted out of his seat and made for the refreshment counter. He came back with two tall drinks and handed one to Travis, who took it and sighed deep into his seat. Perhaps the drink would shut Nish up; at least he wouldn't be able to shout with his mouth wrapped around a straw.

But Nish had no intention of drinking his huge pop. He pulled out the straw and dropped it on the floor. He twisted off the plastic lid and dropped that, too. Then, to Travis's astonishment, Nish began spilling out his drink. Travis cringed, hearing the liquid splash onto the floor.

The theatre floor, made of polished concrete, slanted downward towards the screen, so the liquid immediately ran away under the rows of seats in front.

Is he nuts? Travis wondered.

Nish began splashing in the liquid with his feet, picking up his sneakers and slapping them down hard. It sounded like he was running through a deep puddle.

"*Gross!*" Nish called out.

A couple sitting up ahead turned and stared. Nish splashed again, faking that he was disgusted. He turned around and angrily faced an innocent-looking young man sitting alone about three seats directly behind.

"*What's the matter with you?*" Nish called. "*Can't you use the bathroom?*"

The young man blinked, not comprehending. Up ahead, the young couple began scrambling. The pop had washed up as far as their feet now, and they made squishy sounds as they left their seats and hurried for the safety of the aisle. The young man reached for his girlfriend's hand and pulled her. She slipped and went down, screaming. Her boyfriend raised his fist at the startled young man sitting behind Nish.

"*You pig!*" he screamed. "*Use the washroom!*"

Travis sank even lower in his seat. He could feel the body beside him shaking: Nish, in full giggle. The young man up front, after helping his girlfriend to her feet, charged up the aisle.

Not knowing what was going on, but sure something bad was about to happen, the man behind Nish scurried out of his seat as the boyfriend came at him. There was the sound of clothes ripping.

"Fight!" Nish shouted. "FIGHT! FIGHT!"

The theatre erupted in whistles and shouts. The movie ground to a halt, the lights came on, and Mr. Dinsmore and several attendants hurried down the aisle closest to Travis and Nish. It took only a few moments to break up the fight. It took slightly longer, with the lights full on, to find out that the whole thing was a misunderstanding, that the disgusting liquid was nothing more than Sprite.

Nish's Sprite.

"*Get out!*" Mr. Dinsmore shouted at Travis and Nish. "*Get out of my theatre – both of you!*"

2

"**T**hanks a lot!"

Travis was shaking, but only partly from the terror of *The Blood Children*. More than anything, he shook with fury.

Here he was, finally seeing the movie he had been looking forward to for weeks, finally, for the first time, getting into a movie without adult accompaniment, and now, with the movie not even half over, he was out on the street. Not only that, but Mr. Dinsmore, pointing a long, bony finger at Travis and Nish, had threatened to call their parents to tell them what had happened. They could consider themselves "banned for life," he said.

"Banned for *life*?" Nish had snorted as Mr. Dinsmore pulled the door shut behind them. "Banned till the next movie comes to town would be more like it. He needs our business. And he won't be telling any parents on us; he'd be the one in trouble for us being in there, not us."

Travis wasn't going to waste any more breath arguing. There was no sense trying to talk to Nish now. It didn't matter to Nish that they had missed the end of the show. For Nish, the show had simply moved out into the streets, where he was still the star and the plot was whatever he decided to do next.

Travis figured the least he could do was throw him an unexpected twist, so he turned on his heel and walked away.

"Where're you going?" Nish asked.

Travis said nothing, did not even turn to acknowledge the question.

"What's wrong with you?" Nish called after him.

Travis ignored him. Leaving Nish staring after him, he struck out for home, his sneakers sticking and snapping on the pavement from Nish's drink. He did not hear Nish's own sticky sneakers following; perhaps Nish knew better than to try to act as if nothing had happened. The two had fought a thousand times before, but this one would take longer to heal than most.

It was bright along Main Street. The lights from the stores made it feel almost like daylight. There were lots of people about, some of them carrying ice cream cones, which they licked frantically in the warm late-spring air. Travis turned his thoughts away from Nish, but he was still shaking. *The Blood Children: Part VIII* had more than lived up to its gruesome billing.

To get home, Travis had no choice but to turn off Main Street. He waited until the very last possibility, then chose what he knew would be a reasonably bright route, River Street. He looked into the cloudy sky. His father had called for a new moon – "It means good fishing," he'd said over breakfast that morning – but if there was a moon it was nowhere to be seen. How Travis wished it could be a clear and cloudless night.

River Street had good lighting, but the posts were far apart and there were no storefronts here to wash their friendly light into the street. There were more shadows than bright spots, and unlike Main Street there were no people out walking with their dripping ice cream cones.

The wind rattled the new leaves overhead, almost as if it were trying to get his attention. Travis wished Nish was with him, but he knew he couldn't go back. Besides, Nish wouldn't be there anyway. He would have headed down McGee Street and cut back across King to get home.

Travis also knew that after a horror movie Nish would stay as far away as possible from the cemetery that ran along River up from Cedar Street. No way would Nish walk past a grave-yard after watching *The Blood Children*.

Travis, on the other hand, had no choice. He had to walk past the cemetery to get onto Cedar and home.

He shoved his fists deeper in his jacket pockets. He wished he could wrap his right hand around a big, weighty stone. When he was younger and afraid of large dogs, he would often secretly carry a rock in his jacket pocket, though he'd never actually had to throw one. Its heft had given him an odd comfort.

What good a rock might be against ghouls and zombies, he didn't know. No rock at all to weigh him down might be a better idea. He could run faster then. He wondered if he should be running.

The wind was picking up, moaning now in the high tree-tops. Up ahead, shadows flickered. A cat yowled behind one of the houses.

In another few steps Travis would be beside the Tamarack

Cemetery. He swallowed hard. His throat felt dry and his tongue swollen – strange, since he, unlike Nish, had just finished drinking a huge pop. He wondered if he could scream, if he *had* to scream. He could feel his heart pounding as if Muck had just put the Owls through a hard series of stops and starts.

Someone was crying!

It was impossible to tell exactly where the sound was coming from. It was so faint, barely audible above the rustle of the leaves. For a moment Travis thought it must be the cat, or the wind through a different type of tree – but then he heard a quick choke and the sharp intake of breath.

He stopped, afraid to make a sound.

He forced himself to turn to his right and look into the cemetery. It took a moment for his eyes to adjust. There were no streetlights here and no lighting from the graveyard. The cemetery was bordered with dense lilacs, some still in bloom, and their sickly sweet smell was thick in the night air. The smell of a funeral parlour.

Something was moving! He couldn't be sure what. He thought he glimpsed a light bouncing through the branches.

Travis felt frozen. If he ran, he would only draw attention to himself. If he stayed, his wildly pounding heart might burst. He forced himself to think: he could either bolt for the other side of the street and then double back when he came to Cedar, or he could move silently along the cemetery fence until he came to the gate, and a break in the trees, where he could see in.

He closed his eyes and took a deep breath. He let it out and took a second, and held it.

He began moving, each step as cautious as if he were walking along the ridge of a high roof.

Again, the wet choking sound of someone crying!

Travis was almost to the gate. The light was moving rapidly now, seemingly dancing on the end of a string as it moved through the branches.

He was at the gate, free of the branches and leaves of the lilac.

The light suddenly snapped off.

It was dark again, pitch-black.

It's nothing, Travis told himself. Nothing at all. He let go the deep breath he'd been holding and gulped fresh air.

Of course it had been nothing. It *had* to have been nothing. Just the sound of the wind and a flash of the moon through the branches. Or distant car lights, maybe. Or that "swamp gas" Mr. Dillinger had told them about, which people mistook for UFOs. Or just a reflection. Nothing really. Nothing at all.

Travis turned to walk away, and felt every drop of blood and every ounce of oxygen leave his body.

A boy was standing by the gate.

A boy, about twelve years old.

As pale as the sliver of the new moon just now cutting through the clouds.

Weeping.

Travis stared, his mouth open, unable to speak.

The boy wiped away the tears with the back of a thin, pale hand. He smiled, weakly.

"*Help meee,*" the boy said.

And then he was gone.

3

I f you think of the stick as an extension of your arm," Muck was saying, "you'll get the knack of it a lot easier."

Muck was standing at centre ice in the Tamarack Memorial Arena, only it wouldn't be quite accurate to refer to it as "centre ice," because below his feet was concrete. The ice had been taken out weeks before. Nor was Muck in his usual track suit. Instead, he wore a torn T-shirt, worn sneakers with no socks and no laces, and an old pair of sagging white shorts with a green stripe down the sides. The long scar from the operation that had ended his dream of playing NHL hockey was clearly visible to the sixteen kids standing around him, listening.

"And don't aim. *Think* your shots in. If you picture it happening, nine times out of ten it *will* happen."

It *sounded* like hockey. Five a side; goalies, defence, and forwards; centres and wingers; passing, shooting, and checking; practices, scrimmages, and games. But at this time of year, with Muck Munro standing there, it could never be hockey. Muck

133

had few rules about hockey, and the Screech Owls knew them by heart. Hockey is a game of mistakes. Keep your head up. Speed wins. They call it a game because it's supposed to be fun. And no summer hockey, not ever – not with Muck Munro coaching.

Yet here was Muck, at centre "ice," surrounded by the Screech Owls.

Several of the Screech Owls players – Nish and Travis included – had asked Muck to reconsider his rule against playing summer hockey. They wanted to spend the summer together as a team. And several of the parents had volunteered to set up car pools to get the team to the few rinks in the area that kept ice going all summer.

"No," Muck had replied.

The Owls had been disappointed, and it showed on their faces.

"But you can stick together as a team," he'd added. "And I'll coach."

The Owls now looked confused.

"But–but," Fahd began, "you said, 'No summer hockey.'"

"That's correct," Muck said. "Summer is for other games, other skills."

"What other skills?" Sarah had asked.

Muck smiled. "We'll play lacrosse."

Travis had been amazed at how quickly it all came together. Some of the Owls barely knew what lacrosse was, but after Muck told them how, in some places, lacrosse was even more popular than hockey, and how almost every hockey player he'd ever known – himself included – who had tried the game had fallen completely in love with it, they began to change their minds.

What convinced them was Muck's point that the skills learned playing lacrosse would pay off later on the ice. Wayne Gretzky was a great promoter of the game, and said it was in playing lacrosse that he learned how to use the area behind the net so brilliantly to set up passing plays. Joe Nieuwendyk, who once won the Conn Smythe Trophy as the MVP of the Stanley Cup playoffs, said his astonishing ability to tip pucks out of the air and into the goal came from playing lacrosse. Bobby Orr loved lacrosse; Adam Oates, the great playmaker, loved lacrosse; and even Nish's idol – his "cousin" Paul Kariya – had played it while growing up in British Columbia.

The Owls were sold.

A few of the Screech Owls had played the game before, but never together as a team. Jesse Highboy, who pointed out the game had been invented by Natives, had an uncle who'd played on a Mann Cup championship team – "Lacrosse's equivalent of the Stanley Cup," Jesse had boasted – and Andy Higgins, who had moved to Tamarack from another town, had played two years of atom lacrosse before he turned peewee age.

In a surprisingly short period, the Screech Owls peewee hockey team, one of the best peewee hockey teams around, became a passable lacrosse team. So much of the winter game translated perfectly to the summer game, and the differences, for the most part, were obvious. Concrete instead of ice. Sneakers instead of skates. A stick with a pocket for catching and carrying the ball instead of a stick with a curved blade for taking passes and shooting a puck. Yet so many of the passing and checking patterns remained the same. And the idea of both games was exactly the same: put the round object in the other team's net more often than they can put it in yours.

"Goaltenders are a big difference," Muck explained at the Owls' second practice. "More goals are scored in lacrosse. Lots more goals."

"*Yes!*" shouted Nish, who lived to score goals.

"And the goalie has no protection," said Muck. "Once he leaves his crease, he's fair game."

"*Yes!*" shouted Nish, who was forever picking up penalties for "accidentally" running over goalies.

"Now, we need a very, very special player for this position," Muck continued. "We need someone who's big – someone with a great big butt that's going to fill our net so there's no room for anything else to get in."

"*Yes!*" shouted Sarah and Sam, both of them pointing at the only Screech Owl who could possibly fill Muck's requirements.

"*No way!*" Nish shouted. "I'm an 'out' player – I don't do goal!"

"You're sure?" Muck asked, both eyebrows arching.

"I *score* goals," Nish protested, his face reddening and twisting. "I don't *stop* goals."

"Well," said Muck, "what if I told you that lacrosse goalies can carry the ball all they like."

"*Who cares?*" Nish whined.

"What if I told you that lacrosse goalies can cross centre,

unlike hockey goalies, and that they can even try to score if they
have a chance."

"*Big deal*," Nish groaned.

"What if I told you that, in lacrosse, the goalie is the glory
position?"

Nish's big face twisted so tight it seemed to Travis it might
soon start dripping water. No one said a word. Nish opened his
mouth as if to speak, then closed it again as if suddenly unsure.

Muck waited patiently, flicking the new white lacrosse ball
up and down in his stick pocket and staring at Nish, a small
smile on his face.

Nish twisted and sputtered and finally gave in.

"I'll think about it."

Nish turned out to be a wonderful goaltender. With his double
chest pad on, his big shoulder pads and pants, his flopping shin
pads, and his heavy helmet and cage, he seemed two or three
times larger than when he was dressed for hockey. He was large,
but also quick, and he took so easily to the game that even Muck
appeared surprised.

Travis knew for certain it was Nish deep inside all that
padding when, during a scrimmage, Nish blocked a shot and
scooped it up in the big, wide goalie stick and headed straight
up the floor towards the far net.

At the far end, Jeremy Weathers was still trying to get used
to the thicker, heavier equipment of the lacrosse goaltender.
Only little Simon Milliken was back, and Nish used his weight
and bulky equipment to run right over him as if he were a pile

of earth and Nish a bulldozer. He came in, faked once, and ripped a hard sidearm shot that clicked in off the far post behind Jeremy.

Anyone else would have turned and trotted back down the floor, but not Nish. He dove into Jeremy's net, knocking the smaller goaltender aside, and grabbed the still-bouncing India rubber ball. Once he had it, he wiggled back out and, holding the ball over his head as if it were the Stanley Cup, raced around the rink boards, tipping his helmet at an imaginary, cheering crowd.

Nish had found his natural position.

4

ravis loved lacrosse. It took a while to get used to the new equipment – the thick pads over his lower back, the loose gloves – but nearly half of what he wore was from his hockey bag: the same helmet, the same shoulder pads with a plastic extension tied on to give his arms more protection, the same elbow pads, even the same Screech Owls sweater, which he continued to kiss for good luck as he pulled it over his head.

The stick was another matter. Tamarack Sports had brought in a shipment of Brines – wooden shafts, plastic heads, and nylon braid pockets – and all the Owls had been outfitted with them, each shaft carefully cut to length by Mr. Dillinger. Unlike in hockey, sticks in lacrosse were expected to last several seasons, not a few games.

Travis's new stick had a nice weight, but at first it seemed awkward in his hands. He could scoop up the ball so it skipped into the pocket, but as soon as he tried any of the fancy twirls or fakes that Jesse was so good at, the ball would drop or go flying off in the wrong direction.

But he kept working at it, sometimes alone against the back wall of the house – the steady thumping almost driving his parents crazy – sometimes against the wall of the school gymnasium, and more often than not, now that they were best friends again, out in the street with Nish.

Nish had shown up the very next morning after *The Blood Children: Part VIII*, behaving as if nothing at all had happened. The way Nish acted, he and Travis might have been to see the latest Walt Disney with a church group, after which they'd had a pleasant discussion and then walked home to say their prayers before bed. Not a word about the spilled Sprite, or the fight, or the two of them getting banned for life from the Bluebird Theatre by Mr. Dinsmore.

Travis found he could not say anything about the graveyard. By the time he'd made it home that night, his heart was back in his chest and his brain was refusing to accept what he had seen. Mr. and Mrs. Lindsay had still been up when he arrived home. They had no idea what movie the two boys had gone to see. Travis's mother had put out chewy chocolate chip cookies for him, and he found a cold root beer in the refrigerator. By the time he had started on his third cookie he'd convinced himself there had been no boy and no light and no one crying and no reason whatsoever to think that anything had happened as he passed by the graveyard. It was all his imagination, triggered by the horror movie, the shadows, and the wind.

By morning, when his mother tapped on his bedroom door

to let him know that Nish was outside, waiting for him, he'd practically forgotten about it.

They'd tossed the ball around a bit in the yard, then walked up Church Street towards the school, where Nish began to chalk out a net on the brick wall of the gym.

Travis knew he was starting to get a feel for the game. While Nish worked on the net, Travis fired the ball again and again against the wall, the solid *thump . . . thump . . . thump* so comforting in its steady repetition. He loved the way the India rubber ball smacked against the brick wall, seeming to bounce back faster than it had flown into it, and whispered to a stop in the leather cushion of his stick.

Whip . . . smack . . . hiss . . .

Whip . . . smack . . . hiss . . .

Nish had almost finished drawing his net. It seemed small to Travis. He knew that the net was not as wide in lacrosse as in hockey, but this seemed narrower still, and not nearly as tall as it should be.

Nish was, of course, giving himself every possible advantage. He stepped back, considering his art.

"You know what I've decided?" Nish asked, not even looking towards Travis.

Travis caught the ball and held, his rhythm broken, and waited for Nish to continue. "What?" he prodded.

Nish stared at the wall, almost as if he hadn't yet decided anything.

"I don't think *The Blood Children: Part VIII* was a very good movie."

"How would you know?" Travis asked. "You never even saw it."

"I saw enough to know it sucked," Nish said, as if he was the world's number-one movie critic.

"It wasn't bad," argued Travis, who still resented not seeing the ending.

"It wasn't scary at all," Nish said.

Travis said nothing. He couldn't tell Nish about the boy and the graveyard. Nish would not only laugh at him, he'd tell everybody in town.

"I could do better than that myself," Nish continued.

Travis dropped the ball out of his stick. "What's that supposed to mean?"

"I'm gonna make my own horror flick, that's what."

5

ravis often wondered where Nish got his ideas. Was there a closet somewhere in the Nishikawa home that held every stupid, ridiculous, impossible thought every twelve-year-old kid had ever dared think?

No, Travis thought, it wouldn't be a closet. It would have to be a toilet.

But what amazed Travis most was Nish's ability to get other people caught up in his dumb schemes. Even people with common sense, like Data, who'd figured out how to get Nish's bare butt up on the big Times Square television screen at New Year's.

The horror-flick idea proved even more popular than most.

Fahd, of course, had the camera. Simon and Sarah thought they could write a script. Data could edit the movie on his computer. Everyone – even Travis, he finally had to admit to himself – wanted to play a part in it. Any part at all.

Nish couldn't decide whether he wanted to direct or be the star – and finally settled it by saying he would do both.

"That's not fair," Sam had protested.

"Lots of big stars direct themselves," Nish had said. "Sylvester Stallone, Clint Eastwood."

Fahd and Data, who knew a lot more about movies than Nish did, said the whole idea wasn't nearly as far-fetched as some of the others thought. Fahd knew about all sorts of cheap productions that had gone on to huge success. "*The Blair Witch Project* was a horror movie made by a bunch of students," he told them. "It cost sixty thousand dollars to make and pulled in 140 million – so it's not impossible."

Nish instantly decided that 140 million dollars would be the *minimum* they would make with their movie. A movie that, at the moment, had one used camera, no script, no plot – not even a title.

No matter, Nish was already spending his millions. A new bus for the Screech Owls, of course, with complete stereo and video controls at every plush leather seat. Perhaps even a team plane to take them around the world. "I want to play in Australia," he said, "and in China and in Africa and, for my good buddy, Wilson, in Jamaica."

Wilson laughed. "There's no rinks in Jamaica."

"So?" Nish asked with a shrug. "I'll build one."

"Shouldn't you think about the movie first?" Sam asked. "You're spending the profits and you don't even know what the movie's going to be about."

"I have *people* to do that," Nish said, with a wave of the hand towards the rest of the Owls.

And so the debate began. They gathered around a picnic table in the park, and for more than an hour talked about possible plots.

Simon and Fahd wanted to make a movie about aliens who land in Tamarack but make the mistake of dropping their flying saucer through the arena roof in the midst of a Screech Owls hockey game and are sliced to tiny, bloody bits by the skates of the hockey players.

"Stupid," said Nish.

Andy wanted to make a vampire film, with plenty of blood-sucking and graveyard scenes and open caskets and people walking around town with garlic bulbs hanging around their necks.

"Can't stand garlic," Nish decided.

"Frankenstein!" Jenny shouted. "Someone builds a monster in science class and it wakes up at night and terrorizes the town."

"Been done too many times," said Nish.

"The flesh-eating Windigo!" Jesse offered. "It comes out on snowy nights and scares people half to death."

"Where would we get snow?" Nish asked.

"Good point," Jesse said, disheartened.

They talked about invasions of deadly bacteria, about how they'd stage exploding bodies, about how they'd film spaceships. Every suggestion seemed to have a huge strike against it. Too expensive. Too difficult. Too corny. Too *un*-scary.

Nish slammed his meaty hand down on the picnic table. "We need something original. A story no one has ever done before."

Travis found himself speaking even before he knew what he was saying. He couldn't believe it. Here he was, the one who knew best how impossible Nish's schemes could be, the one who had seen a thousand Nish brainstorms wash out in their execution.

"There is one," he said, quietly.

A silence fell around the picnic table. Travis could almost hear the heads turning towards him, the eyes all waiting.

"And that is . . . ?" Sarah prodded.

"Tamarack has its own horror story," Travis said, "only I'm not that sure about it."

"What do you mean, not sure about it?" Sam asked.

"I just remember my grandfather and one of his friends once discussing something terrible that happened out on the River Road – something really awful that my grandfather said was the worst thing that ever happened here."

"Well," Nish said impatiently, "*what was it?*"

"I don't know. They stopped talking about it when I came in the room."

"Well," Sam said, "*find out.*"

t was the day of the Screech Owls' first lacrosse game ever. They were scheduled to play the Toronto Mini-Rock, a peewee version of the Toronto Rock professional lacrosse team, with identical sweaters, their own team bus – and an *attitude*.

Some of the Owls had gone over to the rink that morning to catch the arrival of the Toronto team. They seemed, to the Owls, much bigger, much older, and much more arrogant than their own little team. They got off the bus with a cocky, know-it-all swagger, all decked out in team sweats with the Rock logo, and all with equipment bags that looked so professional Travis was glad none of the Owls had bothered to cart along their own equipment.

Several of the Mini-Rock players took out their sticks – each one a brand-new, top-of-the-line Brine with the loose strings carefully braided – and they whipped the ball around so quickly Travis could hardly follow it.

They never missed a pass. The ball never struck the sides of their sticks. The Mini-Rock players whipped back passes and underarm passes and sidearm passes. They even played a game in which the player making the catch had to hold his stick up perfectly steady, without moving it no matter what the throw, and each time the ball flew directly in without so much as a tick against the side.

"I think I just came down with an injury," Nish said.

"Me, too," said Andy.

Muck held a brief warm-up practice shortly after noon. To give them a feel for the upcoming game, Muck had the Owls simply run in two different circles, the players in each circle lobbing the ball between each other. They took a few shots at Nish – none of which he stopped – and then Muck sent them out on laps while he headed off in the direction of the coach's dressing room.

"What's with Muck?" Nish shouted at Travis as he puffed up from behind him.

"Looks like he's quitting!" shouted Fahd from the other side.

"Muck doesn't quit," said Travis.

They ran until they could feel the sweat rolling out of their helmets and all the way down to the small of their backs. They ran until the balls of their feet stung. They ran, and ran, until the rink filled with a sound far more familiar from winter: Muck's whistle.

Muck was in the home players' box, and he was no longer alone. Standing at his side was a very old man with white, white hair and the thickest glasses Travis had ever seen. It looked as if he was staring out at the Owls through those little shot glasses Mr. Lindsay kept in the locked liquor cabinet.

The Screech Owls looped over towards the players' bench and the cool relief of the water bottles. Most didn't even bother to drink, just tilted their masks back on their heads, grabbed the plastic bottles, raised them high, and sprayed.

Lacrosse sweat, Travis decided, was different from hockey sweat. Twice as much and twice as warm. It always amazed him how, in a hockey game, a good sweat could almost cool him at the end of a hard shift. Not so in this game. This sweat was like scalding water on the skin. *Salted* scalding water.

Muck opened the door and stepped aside for the old man to step out onto the floor.

Travis could hardly believe what he was seeing through his stinging, blinking, sweat-filled eyes.

The old man had sneakers on. And white shorts with green stripes identical to Muck's. And he was carrying a lacrosse stick unlike any other on the floor.

The old man's stick was made from a single piece of wood, and wood so polished from use, the shaft seemed to shine in his hands. It curved at the end like a shepherd's crook, and the loop was completed by something that looked like hard leather. The pocket itself was leather while the pockets of the kids' sticks were nylon string. And the loose leather strands at the end of his stick were perfectly braided and each one tied off with a different colour of bright cloth.

Travis had never seen such a stick before. It was . . . well . . . *beautiful*, but he couldn't see how it would be good for anything, unless you hung it on a rec-room wall and called it an antique.

Muck cleared his throat, a signal for them all to pay careful attention. "This is Mr. Fontaine," he said.

"Hello, boys," Mr. Fontaine said.

How bad are his eyes? Travis wondered. Can't he see there are girls on this team?

"And girls," Sam corrected.

Mr. Fontaine blinked, looked around several times. "Yes, yes," he said. "Sorry about that. Muck told me there were girls on this team – something we sure didn't have in our day."

"Mr. Fontaine was my coach when I played lacrosse," said Muck. "He knows more about this game than anyone standing here knows about hockey – so listen to everything he says. He'll be working with us this summer."

Travis couldn't help looking over at Nish, who was rolling his eyes. Nish usually didn't have time for anyone even a few years older than he was, let alone several decades. And he was a firm believer in modern equipment – the best new skates, the best pants, top-of-the-line sneakers, the right logo on his T-shirt and baseball cap, the tiniest cellphone, the number-one video game, CD, or movie.

There was only one kind of antique Nish liked, he once told Travis. Leftovers in the refrigerator!

Muck picked up his whistle and blew it lightly. "Let's work on some drills."

Travis had been working at the far end of the floor with Sarah and Dmitri – Muck was keeping them to their hockey lines for the time being – and he was trying to get around Sam and Fahd for a clean shot on Nish.

His size was hurting him. In hockey he had his speed to take him around defence, but in lacrosse you either went right through the defence or else you tucked the ball in tight to your body and tried to roll through. Cross-checking was perfectly legal in lacrosse, and Sam, with her great strength, was almost flicking Travis away like a pesky mosquito every time he tried to break through for a shot.

"You're having trouble, eh, son?" Mr. Fontaine said, noting the obvious.

"I guess," Travis said.

"You know," Mr. Fontaine continued, "it's not necessary for you and the ball to travel together – so long as you both reach your destination at the same time."

Travis had no idea what the old man meant.

Mr. Fontaine took the ball from Travis and dropped it into his own old stick. It made absolutely no sound as it fell, cradled deep inside the leather.

Mr. Fontaine moved the stick to his shoulder, then whipped it hard in a shot aimed straight at Nish's head. Nish hit the concrete – but the ball was still in Mr. Fontaine's stick!

"You okay, son?" the old man called to Nish. "Slip on something?"

Nish mumbled something in response and scrambled back to his feet.

The rest of the Owls had gathered to watch. Those who had seen the fake were in shock. They had never seen a stick move so quickly, almost like a frog's tongue flicking a passing fly out of mid-air.

"Now," Mr. Fontaine said to Sam, "you try to stop me – okay?"

Sam seemed unsure. "O-kay," she said.

The old man looked at her hard. "I mean *stop* me, understand?"

Sam still seemed uncertain. "I guess," she said.

The old man flicked a few fakes. It seemed, to Travis, as if he were playing with a huge Yo-Yo instead of a lacrosse stick. Once, he even turned the stick upside-down and swung it in a perfect 360-degree circle, handing it off behind his back, and *still* the ball held its position snug in the pocket.

The old man began running at Sam. Travis had never seen such skinny, blue-veined legs. They were white as the lacrosse ball. And they also seemed unsteady, as if he shouldn't even be walking, let alone running on an arena floor.

Sam was red with embarrassment for the old man. She made a half-hearted effort. Mr. Fontaine snapped out a fake that sent her screaming to the floor, convinced he had just sliced her ear off.

The old man flicked his stick so that it lobbed the ball slowly back and over his head, then without looking he stabbed the stick behind his back, catching the ball again perfectly. He seemed to know, instinctively, where the ball would be.

Mr. Fontaine helped Sam up.

"I mean *stop* me, my dear, don't pity me."

"Y-y-yes, sir," Sam said.

He circled back, bouncing the ball and picking it up again without so much as a glance as he turned on those spindly, weak legs and charged again.

This time Sam came out hard, her stick held up to block the old man.

He faked ever so gently with one shoulder. Sam spread her feet, prepared for any turn he might take.

Quick as a snap, Mr. Fontaine bounced the ball between her legs as she turned to go the other way with him. He slipped around the other side, caught the ball on its way up, faked once to put Nish into a sliding block, and then whipped the stick around his back to drop an unbelievable backhander into the net.

"*My God!*" Andy said beside Travis.

"*Unbelievable!*" added Jesse.

Mr. Fontaine reached into the net, spun his stick effortlessly against the ball as it rolled about the concrete floor, and pulled his stick away with the ball once again nestled perfectly in the pocket.

I would die happy, Travis thought, if only once I could pick up the ball like that.

The old man came trotting back to Travis. He held out his stick, turned it over, and deposited the ball in Travis's hand.

"Now you try it," he said.

7

our hours later, the Screech Owls were losing
17–5 to the Toronto Mini-Rock. The score
was hardly unexpected; they were only just
beginning and the Toronto team had been around for years.
What was important, Muck told them, was not who won, but
how the Screech Owls developed as a team. The game would
give them a sense of how far they had yet to go before they
could call themselves a lacrosse team.

Nish had played well. He had blocked dozens of shots, some
of them while lying on his stomach in his crease and kicking up
his legs. Balls had hit him on the head, on the chest, on his toes,
and once even on his butt when he got so confused he forgot
which way he was facing.

Sarah, too, had played well, though she was up against a
huge centre who at first kept bowling her over whenever they
fought for a loose ball. Her opponent was the Mini-Rock's top
player, but she didn't let him overwhelm her. Her playmaking
skills in hockey were all evident in lacrosse, and she had good

enough speed to keep up with and even beat the Mini-Rock forwards. She had scored three of the Owls' goals, and twice sent Dmitri in on breakaways. Dmitri was easily the fastest player on the floor, but he kept dropping the ball before he could get a shot away.

Travis had his own troubles. He kept getting knocked away from the play. He couldn't win the corners, and he couldn't break through the defence to give Sarah another target apart from Dmitri.

Late in the third Sarah cleanly won a draw and broke up-floor quickly. She threw the ball to Dmitri, who caught it and began racing down the far boards.

A large Mini-Rock defenceman came out and drilled him with a hard cross-check, spilling the ball along the boards, bouncing crazily from sidespin.

Sarah moved past her check and scooped the ball on the run. She set along the far boards, faked a pass to Sam on defence, then threw completely cross-floor to Travis.

Travis felt the ball rattle against his pocket, but it stayed. It felt heavy. He was panicking, and he couldn't stop it. The other defender was charging right at him, stick held out like he was coming to take Travis's head off.

His first instinct was to duck, but he knew that would only make the situation worse.

He stepped towards the defenceman, faked, and the defender stopped, setting. Travis dropped his shoulder, forcing the defender to spread his feet. He bounced the ball through and darted quickly by the surprised defenceman just in time to lunge ahead and catch the ball, barely, before it spun off into the corner.

There was only the goaltender between Travis and the net. The goaltender puffed out his chest pad and came at him. Travis faked again and raced towards the corner, breaking the goalie's angle.

He fired blind. All he saw was the red light flash. All he heard was Sarah's scream.

"YYYYYYYYEEESSSSSSS!"

He had scored the first lacrosse goal of his life – and on Mr. Fontaine's magic play!

Travis loved the feel of his linemates piling on. It had been a meaningless goal – no way could they win – but it had been a beautiful one.

At the bench even Muck was smiling. Travis came off, and Data tossed a towel around his neck as he took his seat on the bench.

Travis felt a pair of hands on his shoulders. They were the oldest-looking hands he had ever seen. Pure white where they weren't freckled or liver-spotted. Gnarled, bony fingers. Huge, swollen knuckles. They looked as if they might shatter if someone squeezed them. But then *they* squeezed – quickly, and with surprising strength.

And then they were gone.

he final score was 19−8 for the Toronto Mini-Rock. It had been a clean game, and the two teams shook hands. Mr. Dillinger had ice-cold Cokes waiting for them in the dressing room, and Muck took the unusual step of making a very short post-game speech.

"By the end of the season we'll be even with them," Muck said. "Just wait and see."

Travis doubted it, but he still felt very good. Lacrosse was fun, almost as much fun as hockey, and he had to wonder if he'd ever scored a sweeter goal in winter than the one he'd scored just now.

"Where's Mr. Fontaine?" Travis asked as the dressing room emptied.

"He never came in," said Derek.

"Went straight from the bench to the front door," said Sam.

Travis shrugged. Perhaps he had to be somewhere. Too bad, though, because Travis had wanted to thank him for the lesson.

He drove home with his parents. Mr. Lindsay, who had played a little lacrosse when he was growing up, was delighted with the game and said he hoped this signalled the return of a sport that had simply faded away for lack of interest.

"Who was the old man on the bench with Muck?" Mr. Lindsay asked after a while.

"Mr. Fontaine," Travis said.

"Zeke Fontaine?" Mr. Lindsay asked.

Zeke? Travis wondered. What kind of name is that?

"Just Mr. Fontaine," he said from the back seat. "That's what Muck called him. He's going to help Muck coach."

They drove in silence after that. Mr. Lindsay seemed to be thinking about something else.

Finally, Mrs. Lindsay asked her husband, "Do you know him?"

"I don't know if it's who I think it is," said Mr. Lindsay.

"And who do you think it is?" Mrs. Lindsay asked.

"I'd rather not say until I know for sure."

Nish was at Travis's door early the next morning. He'd already forgotten about the loss to the Toronto Mini-Rock and had turned his attention completely to the horror movie that was going to make them millions and show Mr. Dinsmore down at the Bluebird Theatre that he had made a terrible mistake kicking out next year's Oscar winners.

"If we can't find anything local to do it on," Nish was saying,

as he helped himself to a huge bowl of Froot Loops and poured
on maple syrup instead of milk, "don't worry about it. Fahd and
I have been kicking around a few new ideas."

"Like what?" Travis said, busy buttering his toast.

Nish stopped chewing long enough to explain. "Fahd's got
this great idea of a humungous ball of gas coming out of space
and crashing into Earth and killing everybody. He wants to call
it *Fart Wars*."

"Sounds stupid to me," said Travis as he reached for the raspberry jam.

"Me too," Nish said, Froot Loops exploding from his mouth
as he talked. "I mean, you can't even *see* a fart. You can't scare
anybody unless you can show something that stinks so bad
people fall over dead from it."

Travis couldn't resist. "Make the movie about your hockey
bag – or better yet, your lacrosse bag. Just unzip it on Main
Street and watch people drop like flies!"

"*Very* funny."

"I thought it was."

They set off early to see Travis's grandfather. He and Travis's
grandmother lived in the lower part of town where the river
widened slightly and Lookout Hill cut off the morning sun.

Old Mr. Lindsay, a retired policeman, had lived his entire
life in Tamarack. His father had been a logger in the days when
the magnificent white pine in the hills around town had been
shipped all over the world. His grandfather had been a trapper
and had built the first cabin ever on the banks of the river. Travis

sometimes thought the town should have been named after his family, not after an old tree that grew only in swamps and couldn't hang onto its needles.

They found old Mr. Lindsay in his garage workshop, puttering. His workbench was covered in the old alarm clocks and radios and toasters – pickings from the garbage, favours for neighbours – that he loved to spend his spare time figuring out and fixing. There was a cup of coffee steaming beside the vise and, hanging off the edge of the workbench, a large smouldering Corona cigar sending smoke twisting towards the fluorescent light. Old Mr. Lindsay was not allowed to smoke in the house, which made Travis wonder if he really enjoyed fixing the neighbours' broken appliances or whether he simply needed an excuse to get out of the house and light up.

"Good mornin', boys," the old man said as he set down his glasses and reached for his coffee. "Radio says you came up short last night. Sorry I couldn't make the game."

"You didn't miss much," said Nish.

"Said on the radio you scored one, Trav. Good on you. What about you, Mr. Nishikawa? Pretty unusual for you to be kept off the scoresheet."

"I'm playing goal," Nish muttered. "Biggest mistake I ever made in my life."

Old Mr. Lindsay stared at Nish a moment, his eyes twinkling and a little smile growing. "I doubt that – I doubt that very much."

A small radio lay in pieces before the old man. He was checking the circuits with a tiny screwdriver that had a light bulb at the end which flashed whenever he touched a live wire.

He put his glasses back on and returned to the task at hand, well used to having the two boys drop in and watch.

Nish nudged Travis with his elbow.

"Grandpa . . . ?" Travis began.

"Yes, sir?" the old man answered without looking up.

"What's the *worst* thing that ever happened in Tamarack?"

"That new traffic light on Church and Main. Why?"

"No, I mean a long, long time ago – back when you were young."

The old man looked up and grinned. He tilted his glasses onto the top of his head. Travis now had his full attention.

"Well, that would have to be the meteor that killed off all the dinosaurs, wouldn't it?"

Travis shook his head. He liked his grandfather's strange sense of humour, even if he rarely got the joke.

"No, when you were a cop – a policeman, I mean."

"You mean a cop. That's what we called ourselves, and nothing wrong with it, either."

The old man paused, sipped his coffee, and picked up the smouldering cigar and shoved it into his mouth. "I handled a murder investigation all by myself once," he finally said, puffing on the cigar, his eyes almost closed. "But that was two crazy drunken brothers arguing about whose turn it was to go out to the woodpile. It wasn't a nice thing, but hardly the worst."

"What about that thing out on River Road you and Mr. Donahue were talking about one day when I was over?"

The cigar came out and old Mr. Lindsay set it down, hard. He was no longer smiling. He pushed his glasses back into place on his nose, and turned back to his work.

"I don't remember," he said.

Travis was taken aback. His grandfather suddenly seemed so cold and uninterested. Perhaps he really didn't remember. Travis's grandmother was always going on about how his grandfather could lose his glasses on the top of his head, and how he had to write down everything he intended to do each day – and then usually lost the note.

"River Road," Travis repeated. "Something about –"

But Travis's grandfather cut him off with a curt "*No.*" End of topic. No further discussion.

They stayed around and watched the old man work, but there was hardly any more talk. Travis's grandfather seemed almost in another world, and they were not going to be invited in. After a while they said they had to go and together they walked down towards the river wondering what they could do now.

"Far as I'm concerned," said Nish, "I'm more curious than ever to know what the story is."

"So am I," said Travis.

"You got any ideas?"

Travis didn't. They could search through the library files to see what the local newspaper might have written, but they didn't even know what the topic was. Besides, a little newspaper whose front page featured ribbon-cutting ceremonies wasn't likely to contain a story that even the police wouldn't discuss.

"What about this Mr. Donahue you mentioned?" asked Nish.

"He's in the retirement home," Travis said. "My grand-parents go and visit him sometimes, but Grandma says it's hardly worthwhile. He lives in the past."

Nish turned and stared at Travis, his eyes growing wide. "Well?" he said. "Could we ask for anything better than that?"

utumn Leaves Retirement Home lay just
beyond the arena on the bank of the river
where a small rapids ran along one side of the
waterway and a large, deep pool lay along the other. Across the
water, the sidewalks and lights of River Street came to an end
and River Road, a gravel road now heavily oiled to keep down
the dust, began. Beyond that lay the marina, the town dump, a
few farms, the lake, and the seemingly never-ending bush.

It wasn't Travis's first time at the home. He'd come with his
parents to visit a great-aunt who had died a year earlier. Nish,
however, had never been, and didn't have a clue how to behave
once he got there.

"Where do you think *you're* going, young man?" a turtle-
faced woman demanded as he sauntered past the reception desk
without so much as a nod in her direction.

"To see Mr. Donahue," Nish answered, barely breaking
stride.

"You'll have to sign in," she snapped.

Nish stopped, heading to the visitors' book and grabbing for the pen that dangled off the end of a string attached to the desk.

"Are you family?" she demanded.

"That's right," Nish answered.

She stared at him over the tops of her glasses. Travis could hardly blame her; Nish looked as likely a relative of old Mr. Donahue as the retirement home looked like the hockey rink.

Nish never missed a beat. Catching her suspicion before it had time to go anywhere, he turned and pointed at Travis. "*He* is."

"I see," said the turtle. "What family, exactly?"

Travis had to think fast. "Nephew," he said. It wasn't exactly a lie; there had been a time when he was told to call Mr. Donahue "Uncle Ralph" because Travis's grandfather and the old man were best friends together on the police force.

The turtle looked dubious, but let them pass after they'd signed in.

"He's in 228," she shouted after them.

They found the room at the far end of the second floor, but getting there was a bit unnerving. An old man in a wheelchair had been singing songs without words as they passed. An old woman, her stockings fallen down around her ankles, had sworn at them and swung at Nish with her cane.

"Remind me not to get old," Nish whispered behind his hand as they headed down the corridor.

Travis said nothing. He felt sorry for these people and was glad that his own grandparents were still healthy and living in their own house. He tried to imagine Nish as an old man living here, but couldn't. Would he be mooning everyone who passed?

Would he be wearing X-ray glasses to see through the nurses' uniforms? Would he lie in bed screaming "I'M GONNA HURL!" every time a doctor came close?

They knocked at the partially open door.

"*Get in out of the rain!*" an old voice cried out from the other side.

Nish turned to Travis and made a face. Was that a joke? Or did the person inside really think it was raining in the hallway?

Travis recognized Mr. Donahue at once. He was sitting in a chair beside his bed and was just pushing away his food tray after the noon meal. He was completely bald, his head as polished as the top of the cane Travis's grandmother sometimes used. Mr. Donahue was fully dressed, wearing a tie and navy blazer with a police crest on the breast pocket, but his shirt seemed to belong to someone twice his size. The collar looked like two or three of Mr. Donahue's bird-like neck could have fit inside it.

It was almost as if he had shrunk since Travis had last seen his grandfather's old police friend. Travis couldn't remember how long ago that had been, but at this rate, he thought, in another couple of years Mr. Donahue's neck could fit through one of his blazer buttonholes.

"*Mr. Lindsay!*" the old man shouted. "How kind of you to come."

Travis was amazed the old man remembered him. It took a couple of minutes before he realized Mr. Donahue had not recognized Travis at all. He had mistaken him for his father.

It was soon clear that Mr. Donahue was about thirty years behind the real world. He was still a policeman in his mind. He was talking with his partner's young boy.

Nish understood this faster than Travis. And instead of trying to correct the old man, he let the conversation proceed as if they really were more than thirty years in the past.

Mr. Donahue complained about draft dodgers. He bragged about the Montreal Canadiens – who did he think was playing for them, Travis wondered, Jean Béliveau? And he complained about the boring lunches his wife was packing for him. Travis had never even known there *was* a Mrs. Donahue.

"What's the biggest crime you ever solved?" Nish suddenly asked.

Mr. Donahue looked up, surprised. His pale blue eyes were astonishingly clear, the whites as pure as snow.

"Biggest crime I was ever involved in," he almost shouted, "was *never* solved – and you two boys know that as well as I know myself."

Travis took a gamble. "River Road," he said mildly.

"*Exactly!*" Mr. Donahue said, shaking a long finger in Travis's direction. "Most terrifying thing I've ever seen in my life."

Nish took a much larger gamble. "What happened?"

Mr. Donahue looked down again. At first the boys wondered if he'd heard. Then they wondered if he'd drifted off to sleep on them. When he finally looked up, the eyes had reddened, and the pale blue glistened under the ceiling lights.

"I don't know, boys. Only one person can answer that question, as far as I'm concerned."

"Who's that?" Nish asked.

Old Mr. Donahue hammered his fist in fury on the arm of his chair. It glanced off and struck the food tray, sending it clattering to the floor.

"*Fontaine!*" he shouted. "*Zeke Fontaine!*"

Travis swallowed hard. He had heard this name only the night before, when his father mentioned it on the way home from the lacrosse game. "Zeke" had sounded funny. Now it struck terror in him.

Sweat had broken out on Nish's forehead. He was leaning towards Mr. Donahue, working so hard to get him to talk that he didn't even see the shadow looming in the doorway and the face of the turtle appear, looking like it was about to bite the handle off a rake.

"*What* is going on in here?" she demanded.

Travis was already picking up the spilled tray. "Nothing – he just dropped his tray, that's all."

"What was all the shouting for?" she snapped. "There's to be *no* shouting at Autumn Leaves."

"*I'll shout when I damn well feel like shouting!*" Mr. Donahue bellowed. Travis realized there was no love lost between the turtle and Mr. Donahue.

"Who are these young men, Mr. Donahue?" she asked.

"I have no idea!" Mr. Donahue snapped back.

"He's one of my grandfather's closest friends," Travis tried to explain as the turtle pushed the two boys towards the front door. He was surprised she didn't twist their ears to hustle them out. "I've known him all my life!"

"Well," the turtle said when they got to the door, "he doesn't know you any more. He doesn't even know who *he* is any more."

With that, she shoved them through the revolving doors and out onto the front steps of Autumn Leaves.

"Who the hell is Zeke Fontaine?" Nish asked as they headed down the driveway towards the river.

"I think I know," said Travis.

"Well," Nish demanded, "*who?*"

"Our lacrosse coach."

10

"Zeke Fontaine . . . ," Mr. Lindsay said. "I thought he had died years ago."

Travis had gone to the source of the coach's strange first name, and Mr. Lindsay had at last seemed willing to talk about the mysterious old man, even if, as he said, neither he nor anyone else knew the whole story.

"Zeke Fontaine was once a great lacrosse star," Mr. Lindsay said. "Played out west on a couple of Mann Cup teams, I think. He came here in the 1960s and set up the town's minor lacrosse system. At one point lacrosse was as big as hockey around here, you know, but it eventually faded and then vanished altogether – at least until this year, when Muck came along and revived it."

Mr. Lindsay sipped at his coffee and stared out the window. "I should have seen the connection right away," he said, almost to himself.

"What connection?" asked Travis.

"Muck Munro. He was a heck of a hockey player," his father said. "You know that. Probably would have played in the

NHL if he hadn't got hurt. But he was an even more talented lacrosse player.

"Zeke Fontaine had two young stars," he continued, "Muck and his own son, Liam. Liam was probably better than Muck. In less than three years Zeke built his team into a national contender. Hadn't lost a single game all year when the bad stuff happened . . ."

"What bad stuff?"

"Liam got killed. At least people *think* Liam got killed – they never found the body. The lacrosse team was headed for the provincial championships, but they never played another game. And Zeke Fontaine never coached another game."

Travis's father was speaking almost dreamily now, as if Travis wasn't even there. He would take his time – Travis knew his father well – but he would tell whatever he knew. Travis would just have to sit. Patiently.

"Zeke Fontaine claimed his son was attacked by a rogue bear. They lived out River Road – I guess he still lives out there – and the old man said his son was walking home from the rink when he got attacked.

"It made some sense. Farmers had been complaining about this huge black bear with a streak of white along one flank that had been attacking their stock – Silvertip, they called it. Some sheep had been killed and eaten, and even some cattle were slaughtered and, I think, a horse. It was pretty ugly.

"There was a huge hunt for the bear. They brought in rangers and even a couple of army snipers and killed every black bear they could track down. Soon as they killed them, they cut open their stomachs and analyzed the contents, but they couldn't find any evidence whatsoever that any of them had attacked the boy."

Mr. Lindsay fell silent.

"What about the bear, Silvertip?" Travis asked. "Did they shoot it?"

Mr. Lindsay took a long sip, remembering. "They did. Two local policeman, Darby Fenwick and Constable Rodgers – I forget his first name – cornered it back of Lookout Hill and one of them emptied his service revolver into it. But that wasn't enough to stop Silvertip. He charged them both. Tore them to ribbons. Rodgers was killed straight away, but Fenwick took three days to die. Only time I ever saw your grandfather fall down on his knees and bawl. It was the worst thing that ever happened in this town."

"Did they find the bear?"

"No. Never."

"What about the boy?"

"Never found him, either. And that's when the story turned really ugly.

"One of the other kids on the team claimed that Zeke and Liam had had a big fight at the rink, which was why the boy happened to be walking home that day. It's a long haul out to where they lived, you know.

"Anyway, that got the police looking more closely at Zeke. They found a rifle at the house that had been fired recently. They found old clothes burned in a backyard barrel. They found a shovel with fresh dirt on it. Zeke had an answer for everything: he'd been shooting groundhogs; he'd been burning old oil rags; he'd been working in the garden.

"I know your grandfather, for one, never believed him. The police were convinced he'd done his own son in and sent the police on a wild goose chase – I guess you could say wild *bear* chase – that had cost the force two good men. They blamed Fontaine for their deaths."

"Did they charge him?"

Mr. Lindsay shook his head. "Couldn't. Never found the boy's body. Never had any evidence apart from their own suspicions."

"Wasn't that enough?"

"Never stand up for a minute in court."

"So what happened?"

"Nothing. The town turned against Fontaine. He left town. I thought he moved back to the West Coast, where he'd played. I guess he moved back here after he retired. No one ever bought the Fontaine property even though it was listed for sale – people thought it was cursed after the three deaths, I guess. Only person who stood by Zeke was Muck Munro."

"Muck?"

"Yep. And Muck, you'd think, would have reasons of his own to blame the old man. He'd lost his lacrosse team. He'd lost his chance at the provincial championship. He'd lost his best friend on the team. But unlike practically everyone else in Tamarack, he never once blamed Zeke for what had happened."

"How did Muck get him to coach again?"

"Who knows? Maybe he thinks getting him back in lacrosse will do him good. Maybe he sees in you Owls what the two of them lost after Liam went missing – a chance to win the provincial championship."

"*Our* team? Not very likely."

"You never know," said Mr. Lindsay, finally smiling again. "Who's to say Nish isn't the greatest goaltending prospect in lacrosse history?"

"*Get real*," said Travis.

An hour later the Screech Owls knew all about Liam Fontaine, Silvertip, the two dead policemen, and the great mystery of Zeke Fontaine, their new coach.

"It makes my skin crawl," said Sarah.

"Fantastic," said Nish.

Sarah turned on Nish, appalled. "Why would you say something like *that?*"

"It's *exactly* what we want for our movie!"

ravis was getting a feel for lacrosse. The Owls practised daily – Muck handling the drills, Zeke Fontaine teaching individual skills – and it seemed when they weren't officially practising or working on Nish's crazy horror movie, two or three or more of the Screech Owls were gathering at the school to toss the ball around and try pick-ups and fakes and back passes.

Three games into the season, Sarah had emerged as the team's number-one star, just as she was in hockey. She moved down the floor with the same easy grace that she had always shown on skates. And if she read the game well in hockey, it was nothing compared to how she could read plays in lacrosse: tossing balls to seemingly empty spaces, only to have her passes arrive perfectly on time; finding openings for shots and setting up from behind the opposition net in a way that might have made even Wayne Gretzky applaud.

The oddest thing about Sarah, Travis noticed, was that she made no noise as she ran. Her sneakers barely whispered as they met the floor. No huffing and puffing. Nothing. Like a film without sound. Travis, on the other hand, slapped up and down the concrete. But he was barely audible compared to Nish.

Nish, too, was growing into his role. When he moved, it was like an old train starting up. His sneakers squeaked and screeched and flapped. The foot guards of his big shin pads snapped against the tops of his sneakers. And he grunted with every effort as he moved about in the big, bulky goaltending equipment.

Nish was challenging more, coming out and chasing balls into the corners, then using his good throwing ability to send long breakaway passes down the floor. Dmitri, finally getting a feel for his stick, had become a major scoring threat with his speed, and Nish was starting to look for him more and more. Sam, with her strength, was turning into an excellent defence player, tough, determined, her cross-checks leaving opposing players wincing even before she struck.

Travis was quickly becoming the team's most skilled stick-handler. He found he had the *touch* in lacrosse. He could tell, instinctively, which way and how high a spinning loose ball would bounce. He was able to pick up rolling balls on the run, using a wonderful spin of the pocket over the ball that Mr. Fontaine had taught him.

"This way," the old man had said, "you won't have to run straight at a ball the way players who scoop balls need to. You become like a cat with this move, able to strike from anywhere – even pluck a ball right out of another player's stick."

For whatever reason, Mr. Fontaine had decided Travis was his "project." He told him he was passing on his secrets, and as soon as Travis mastered one of them the other Screech Owls would be demanding he teach it to them after practice.

Mr. Fontaine taught him how to "steal" a ball from a player foolish enough to hold the ball out front as he looked for a play. "You have your pocket upside-down," he said, "and you come down hard on his pocket with your stick, spinning just when the two pockets hit."

It took Travis the better part of a morning to master that one, but eventually he could do it. It happened so fast it reminded Travis of the magician's cup-and-pea trick. There really were things that could happen faster than the eye can see.

"You're good with that stick, boy," the old man said one morning after practice. "But I think you'd be even better with a *real* stick."

By "real" Mr. Fontaine meant "wooden." He said to Travis he thought the Owls' fancy new Brine sticks were flashy but useless. He himself used a very old but perfectly preserved Logan – a legendary lacrosse stick, Muck told them, once made on the Six Nations Reserve in southwestern Ontario. And true enough, it seemed that Mr. Fontaine could fake far better than they ever could, and even shoot harder than any of them, with the possible exception of Sam.

They put it down to experience.

"I want you to try mine," the old man said to Travis one day as practice was breaking up. He handed Travis the Logan; Travis handed him the Brine.

He weighed the old stick in his hands. It felt awkward and unbalanced. It was heavier than his Brine. And it smelled.

Mr. Fontaine noticed Travis sniffing the pocket area. He smiled. "Linseed oil," he said. "Keeps the catgut flexible."

"Catgut?" Travis asked.

"The edge of the pocket opposite the wood," the old man explained. "It's called catgut."

Travis looked hard at the edge. It was yellowed and stringy and hard, but flexible at the same time. Strung together as it was, it formed a "fence" between the soft pocket and the outside of the stick, and allowed a player to keep the ball tucked safely in the pocket. Travis's stick, of course, was hard plastic on both sides.

He was afraid to ask where the catgut came from.

He was, in fact, afraid of Mr. Fontaine. *Terrified* of him. The old man never looked directly at the kids as he talked to them. Perhaps it was just the thick glasses, but the effect was a little creepy. And he never spoke to them all as a group. Always one on one. He didn't learn their last names – a blessing, Travis figured, since he was a Lindsay and the old man might connect it to the policeman who tried to nail him for murder so many years ago – and he didn't hang about after practice the way Muck sometimes did just to talk or throw the ball around for fun.

"Like it?" Mr. Fontaine said after Travis had picked up a few loose balls and tried a few throws with the Logan.

In a way he did; in a way he didn't. He didn't have a feel for it yet, but he could tell, when he threw, that there was a wonderful *power* in the old man's wooden stick. When Travis shot with his Brine, there was no feeling apart from the thrust. When he shot with the Logan, it was as if he could feel every roll of the ball as it came out of the pocket, almost as if, when the ball was released, it got an extra kick from the laces that Mr. Fontaine so carefully worked through the upper portion of the pocket.

"Yeah, sure," Travis said.

"You come out to my place this afternoon. I've got something for you."

Travis looked up. For the first time that he noticed, Mr. Fontaine was looking directly at him. He could see pain in his old eyes – almost as if they were on the verge of tears – and Travis knew that he couldn't say what he so desperately wanted to say. *No, thanks.*

Instead, he said what he felt he *had* to say: "O-kay."

He felt a shiver go down his spine. It was probably the hottest day of summer. He was covered in sweat from the practice. But it still felt as if an icicle had just slid down to the small of his back.

Muck's whistle blew at centre floor. Travis handed the wooden stick back, took his Brine, and ran, feet slapping on the floor, to join the scrum.

Muck had a piece of paper in his hands. "I have here a letter from the Lacrosse Association," he began, before starting to read. "'Dear Mr. Munro . . . etc., etc., etc. . . . We are pleased to announce that your application to have Tamarack host this year's provincial championship for peewee has been accepted. The dates suggested by your committee are also approved, and invitations have been issued this week to fourteen teams.'"

"YYESSSS!" shouted Sarah.

Muck folded the paper and stuck it into the back pocket of his old shorts. "We have a lot of work still to do," he said.

12

The moviemakers had a lot of work to do, too. Fahd and Data had organized the cameras — they already had Fahd's video and had borrowed another from Mr. Dillinger — and Data was even helping Sarah work out a plot outline on his laptop computer, but they still needed to know more.

Simon was worried about how they would ever get film of bears around Tamarack.

"There are always bears out at the dump," Jesse said.

"That's hardly what we're looking for," Nish, the Hollywood director, argued. "You're talking about bears ripping apart green garbage bags. I'm looking for bears that rip apart *people!*"

"How are you going to arrange that, Movie Boy?" asked Sarah. "Or are you going to *volunteer?*"

"Very funny," Nish said. "We find the bear – then we worry about how we make it look like it's attacking two policemen. Maybe we use dummies. With a lot of blood and guts and quick cuts, no one will be able to tell the difference."

"There's only one dummy in this movie," Sarah shot back.

The team meeting about the horror movie did not go well. Some of the Owls were beginning to lose interest in Nish's project. Others wanted to abandon the idea of a local story in favour of another crazy idea from Fahd. Fahd wanted to use one camera to film closeups of frogs and toads and salamanders and snakes and spiders, then use the other camera to take shots of downtown Tamarack, and run the two together and call it *Invasion of the Creepy Crawlies*.

"Brilliant," Nish said with all the sarcasm he could muster. "Positively *brilliant*, my dear Fahd."

"Thanks," Fahd said.

"C'mon, Trav," Nish said, scooping up the notes he was making in an unused school exercise book, of which he seemed to have dozens. "We're wasting our time here."

Travis and Nish headed out River Road on their mountain bikes. Both carried their lacrosse sticks carefully tied along the crossbar and hanging out in front. Travis had a ball stuffed deep in his pocket. Nish had his backpack, and in the pack he had Mr. Dillinger's video camera. They were going, Travis had told him, on a "scouting" mission.

"Fontaine invited you out?" Nish had asked Travis.

"Yeah," Travis said. "He said he had something for me."

"Maybe a bullet!" Nish said, giggling.

"That's not funny."

Travis didn't really think he had anything to worry about, going to old man Fontaine's place in the bush, but he was

nervous enough not to want to do it alone. He'd convinced
Nish to come by saying they'd be able to gain a better sense of
setting, and if they took the camera they could stop in at the
dump on the way and maybe get some footage of bears.

"Fine with me," said Nish. "Mr. Dillinger's camera has an
unbelievable zoom – it'll be like you're close enough to reach
out and touch them."

It was now mid-July, the roadside filled with white daisies
and orange devil's paintbrushes and yellow buttercups. The
farmers along River Road were in the fields, and the air was ripe
with the smell of the fresh-cut hay. It was a wonderful day for a
bike ride, and Travis only wished he could enjoy it more. His
stomach was jumping. He had no idea what Mr. Fontaine
wanted him out here for.

They came first to the town dump. It had changed dramatically from when Travis was younger. Sometimes, on a cool
summer evening, his family used to drive out to sit in the car
and watch the bears pick through the garbage. Occasionally,
bear cubs would walk right up to the cars – there might be six
or seven bears in all – and sometimes a mother bear would race
over and scold her offspring for getting so close.

No cars came out in the evening any more. The dump was
fenced off now, and the entrance gate was chained at the end of
each day. An attendant was always on hand to ensure that no one
dumped toxic materials or paint cans or old tires, and there were
recycling bins for everything from glass and plastic to egg
cartons and newspapers.

"Still open!" Nish shouted back as he neared the gate.

They pedalled inside and over to the attendant's shed. Travis and Nish both knew the man on duty – an older brother of Ty Barrett, who sometimes helped Muck out with the Owls' hockey practices.

"Looking for 'garbage' goals, boys?" he asked.

"Good one!" Nish said, though Travis could tell he didn't really mean it.

"Any bears?" Travis asked.

"A couple, now and then," the attendant said. "Not like before, though. The ministry came in and shot a few of them this spring, you know. Called them 'nuisance' bears – but who they were bothering is beyond me."

"Damn!" shouted Nish. "We could've filmed that!"

The attendant looked at Nish, waiting for him to explain.

"School project," Nish said. "Trav 'n' me are working on a film about area bears, good or bad."

The attendant lifted his cap and scratched his balding head. "Isn't school out?" he asked.

"This is for next term," Nish explained.

"Would it be all right if we filmed one, if there's one around?" Travis asked.

The attendant took his cap off entirely. His thin wisps of hair were tightly curled and greasy. Travis was struck by how the man's cap left a line that split his face into two distinct parts: one that had seen too much sun, one that had seen no sun at all.

He looked about, almost as if expecting to find a surveillance camera hidden in the pines that bordered the pit where the garbage was thrown.

"Come with me," he said finally.

Nish hauled Mr. Dillinger's camera out of his backpack and the two boys leaned their bikes against the shed as the attendant set off for a far corner of the pit.

Travis's nose felt like it might burst with so many smells, most of them foul and sour. There was only one sound, however, the ill-tempered screeching and calling of hundreds of seagulls. They were everywhere, fighting over the garbage, rising in waves as the attendant kicked a loose green garbage bag down and into the pit, then falling back like a soft blanket of white feathers as the bag settled.

They came to a small stand of pines with cedars growing below. The attendant held his finger to his lips to hush them, then pushed through ahead of the boys.

The branches were in Travis's face. He was hot, and sweating, and the garbage dump stank beyond belief – but then, in an instant, he forgot everything but what he saw before him.

Two black bears were standing over a half-torn garbage bag!

Travis's heart pounded. Sweat dripped down his nose and into the corners of his mouth. A mosquito landed on his cheek and he couldn't even bring himself to slap it for fear of scaring off the two bears.

Scaring them off or, worse, attracting their attention!

Nish was already filming. "Man-oh-man-oh-man," he muttered. "This is just what the director ordered."

Travis worried that Nish might be making too much noise. But the bears seemed to be paying no attention. Travis stared at them, fascinated. At first they seemed smaller than he expected, but then one of them stood on its hind legs and sniffed the air, and Travis knew if he were beside it the animal would tower over him, easily.

The other bear poked his nose at the bag, grunted, and then swiped at it casually with one paw. The paw seemed to move in slow motion, yet despite the lack of effort the bag exploded into a shower of paper and empty containers and plate scrapings.

Travis imagined those same claws hitting a human head. He shuddered.

Nish was filming furiously. "Why-oh-why-oh-why does that have to be a stupid green garbage bag?"

"You'd prefer a body?" the attendant whispered, amused.

"Can you arrange one?" Nish answered.

"Sure," the attendant smiled. "Just walk out there and try to pet one of them."

"*L-look!*" Travis suddenly found himself saying. He pointed beyond the two bears. Up the hill, stopping every now and then to raise a long, pointed nose to test the air, came the largest bear Travis had ever seen. It was at least *twice* the size of the two bears who had just given Travis shivers and shudders with one casual blow of an open paw.

The bear paused, rose onto its haunches, sniffed the air, and turned. It had white hair along the far flank – almost as if someone had spilled bleach along him.

"Silvertip," the attendant said.

Travis's mind raced. *The* Silvertip? Impossible! He would have to be forty or fifty years old.

"Not the one they wanted to kill?" Travis asked.

The attendant shook his head. "Naw. The old guy who works here with me says there was another Silvertip back sometime in the seventies that they hunted but never caught. This one's young – but I still call him Silvertip. Maybe he's a grandson or great-grandson or something. He's a mean beggar anyway. I think maybe we'd be smart to head back."

Travis and Nish didn't need much convincing. The big bear – Silvertip – was now up to the garbage bag the other two bears had been fighting over. The smaller bears had scattered like seagulls on his arrival, both of them scooting back down the bank with their tiny tails between their legs. The boys would have laughed except they had no desire to attract Silvertip's attention.

The big bear stood on his back legs, sniffed, and seemed to stare towards the boys.

Travis's heart stopped. *He's twice as tall as I am!*

But the bear must not have seen them. He half-flicked a paw at a bag and, again, the garbage flew. He buried his head in the trash, grunting and pushing with his nose.

The three spectators backed away through the low cedar.

"Great footage!" Nish kept saying. "*Great* footage!"

But Travis wasn't thinking about movies. They still had one more stop to make on this journey.

13

ravis had known there was a house out here in the deep bush – several times his family had driven this far out River Road to picnic at a nearby widening of the river that everyone in town called "The Lake" – but he had always believed the old place to be abandoned. The entrance was badly overgrown and the old black wood-frame building was barely visible from the gravel road.

There was, however, a mailbox. "B. D. Fo tai e," it read. Both the *n*'s were missing, but Travis had no trouble recognizing the name. Where, he wondered, did they get "Zeke" from?

There was also a sign, worn and fading: "BEWARE OF DOG."

"You're on your own, pal," Nish said as he brought his bike to a gravel-spewing stop. "No way I'm goin' in there."

"I went to see the bears with you," Travis answered. "You can come here with me."

Reluctantly, Nish dismounted. "Personally," he muttered, "I'd rather take my chances with the bears."

They pushed their bikes up the long, overgrown laneway, the grass in the middle so high it was a wonder anyone could drive through. Travis listened for the first bark of the dog, but there was no sound.

He looked around for a car, or a half-ton truck, but could find none. Perhaps he was out. More likely, however, he had no car and Muck was picking him up and dropping him off. That would be just like Muck.

There were orange irises growing on one side of the laneway, but they had never been tended to – or at least not for years. They weren't at all like the irises in Travis's grandmother's garden, and yet in their own way they were spectacular, almost as if their survival here gave them a doubled beauty. A few of the irises had recently been cut, the stems sliced off as neatly as if a razor blade had swept through them.

All around were rusted metal bars, old bedsprings, tires, car engines, a fishing boat with the bottom rotted clean through and, surprisingly, an old homemade lacrosse net made out of galvanized steel plumbing pipes and covered with burlap instead of netting. The burlap was rotting off. The net hadn't been used for years.

Travis edged his way up to the rickety porch that hung off the main building. It looked like it was held in place by old Scotch tape rather than nails. The boards were soft and gave. He wondered if he might fall through.

"*I'm outta here!*" hissed Nish.

"You're not going anywhere," Travis whispered quickly.

Nish was sweating as heavily as if he were in full goal-tender's equipment and playing the third period of a lacrosse game. His face was beet-red and twisted in a grimace. Travis would have expected nothing less.

Travis arrived at the door. It was open a crack. There were flies – bluebottles, mosquitoes, horseflies, deerflies – all around the opening, but it was impossible to tell whether they were trying to get in or out. From what little Travis could make out in the dark, he wouldn't blame them for trying to escape. The floor was filthy and littered with junk. It was dark and it smelled of greasy cooking and kerosene and something else, something familiar.

Travis took one look back at his sweating pal and realized what the odour was: stale human sweat, worse than a lacrosse dressing room.

His heart pounding, Travis swallowed, took one deep breath, and knocked.

The boys waited. No movement. No barking. Nothing.

Travis knocked again, this time rapping his knuckles a little harder on the old door, which swung open slightly. He jumped back, afraid he'd be accused of just walking in.

But there was nothing.

"Thank God," breathed Nish. "He's not home."

Travis stepped back. "I guess not," he said. He didn't know if he was disappointed or not. He didn't like the idea of having to come out here again.

"But he specifically said this afternoon," Travis said.

"I guess he forgot," Nish said, seeming greatly relieved. "Let's go."

"Let's just check around back first," Travis suggested.

He caught Nish's look. It was as if he'd suggested they both do a little extra math homework or stay after school to help. A look of absolute, disbelieving disgust. But Travis knew Nish would be too afraid – both of Mr. Fontaine and the bears – to strike out on his own for home. He would have to wait for Travis, no matter what.

"Hurry it up, then," Nish hissed. "I haven't got all day. I'm a busy man."

Travis led the way around the side, shaking his head. What on earth could Nish mean, "I'm a busy man"? Was his cellphone ringing? Did he have to take a private jet to Hollywood? This movie stuff had gone to his head – and all they had was a little footage of three bears fighting over a garbage bag.

"It won't take long," Travis said in a whisper over his shoulder. He was still listening for the dog, once again wishing that instead of the lacrosse ball he had thought to stash a rock in his pocket, just in case. But still there was nothing. Not a sound anywhere but for the buzzing flies.

They turned around the side of the building, following a well-worn track. There were sheds out here, machine sheds and hay sheds and what must once have been animal sheds. He could still, faintly, smell the distinct odour of chicken and horse manure. But it seemed old. Very old. Decades old, for all Travis knew.

He checked each shed, but found no one. He dipped his head into what was obviously the tool shed and noticed a lamp burning – a coal-oil lamp, its wick flickering in the slight breeze that slipped in through the door. Travis knew that Mr. Fontaine must be around, or must have been around not long ago.

He turned to tell Nish that the shed was empty, that they

could go home now. But Nish, moments ago as red as the bell on his mountain bike, was now as white as a sheet. His mouth seemed frozen open. He was pointing off into the bushes.

There, in the distance, someone was kneeling beneath a tall hemlock. Travis could tell from the man's back, the long grey-white hair, the thick eyeglasses, the old grey shirt, that it was Zeke Fontaine. He seemed to be picking at something on the ground. He was flicking off pebbles and small branches, carefully arranging something on the earth. Something orange.

Irises!

Travis quickly looked at Nish again. His friend was still white, but his mouth had become unfrozen, and he was carefully mouthing something to him.

A grave!

Zeke Fontaine was arranging flowers over a grave. The ground had been cleared under the hemlock and carefully swept. A rough rectangle of earth rose slightly above the surrounding ground, the space not quite as large as a plot at the local cemetery. But big enough for a boy.

Liam Fontaine's grave?

Travis shuddered. Was this the secret burial place of little Liam Fontaine? Was this what the father had done with the body after he had murdered his own son?

Travis and Nish exchanged a look of terror. It was time to get out of there. Travis turned quickly, and stepped onto a dry, dead twig.

SNAP!

"*We're dead meat!*" Nish hissed.

Travis felt what little blood there was left in his face drain to his feet. He nearly went down with it, instantly dizzy, in full panic.

"*Hey!*" a voice called out. "*Just stay right where you are!*"

14

The yell from under the high hemlock froze both boys in their path. Neither dared move.

Travis could almost hear the rifle go off, feel the bullet finally quiet his heart, smell the earth as it was shovelled in on him as he and Nish joined Liam in the shallow grave, feel the weight of the irises crushing down on his shattered, bleeding chest.

"*Hey!*" the voice called again. "*That you, Travis?*"

Zeke Fontaine was up and walking towards them, moving surprisingly quickly for an old man. He wasn't going to shoot them, he would strangle them!

"*Travis?*" the old man called.

"Y-y-yes," Travis answered.

"I don't see too well no more," the old man said as he neared them. "But I could pick out your buddy at a hundred paces – goalie equipment or no goalie equipment."

"H-hi M-Mister F-F-Fontaine," stammered Nish.

"Glad you came," Mr. Fontaine said, clipping both boys lightly on the shoulder. "I was just out fixing up the grave."

Travis and Nish exchanged the quickest of glances, but Zeke Fontaine's eyesight was not so poor that he didn't catch them. "Dog died two weeks ago," he explained. "He was seventeen years old. You know how old that is in our years, Nishikawa?"

"N-no sir."

"One hundred and nineteen, that's what. Seventeen years old and blind as a bat and even fewer teeth than me."

Zeke Fontaine peeled back his lips so the boys could see his teeth. The three or four that still stood were dark from cavities, his gums red and sore-looking. Travis had to look away.

"Wh-what about the sign?" Nish asked.

"The sign? Oh, yes, 'Beware of dog.' I put that up to inspire him. Sparky wouldn't have hurt a fly, which may explain why there are so many of the damn things around here."

Sparky, thought Travis. Sparky, not Liam. An old dog, not a boy. An old dog with fresh-cut irises on his carefully tended grave.

How could he have been so wrong?

They stayed more than an hour at Zeke Fontaine's. He went into the house and returned with chocolate bars and glasses – remarkably clean glasses – and as they ate their chocolate he took them over to the well. He lowered the bucket and drew up water so cold and fresh and delicious that Travis thought if they could ever bottle it and sell it they would make millions.

"Glad you came along," Mr. Fontaine said to Nish. "I've been thinking about teaching you boys the 'Muck Munro.'"

"The 'Muck Munro'?" they said at once.

"He's never told you about it?"

Both boys shook their heads.

"He'd perfected it just before the championship, you know. Never got a chance to show it."

Travis nodded, afraid to say anything. What, after all, could he say? *Oh yes, never got to play in the championship because you murdered your son and it was all called off.*

"Muck and my boy . . . ," Mr. Fontaine began.

Travis and Nish both flinched. They hadn't expected the old man to mention Liam.

"Muck and my boy worked on this play until they could do it in their sleep. You want me to show it to you?"

"Yeah!" Nish said enthusiastically.

"You got your sticks here?" the old man asked.

"They're on our bikes," said Travis.

"Well, go get 'em. I'll get mine."

Travis and Nish hurried back to where they had laid down their bikes.

"He's not such a bad old guy," Nish offered.

"No," said Travis, a bit ashamed of the surprise in his voice.

Mr. Fontaine was walking back from the house with his old Logan stick in his hand. Travis was getting used to the sight of the wooden stick now, and in fact had decided it was beautiful compared to his own with its plastic head.

"You remember that bounce play I taught you?" Zeke Fontaine said to Travis.

"Sure," Travis said. "Use it all the time."

"Well, Muck Munro had that one mastered, too. My God, but he was a fine young player – one of the two best I ever saw."

Travis bit his tongue, hoping that Nish wouldn't dare ask who the other great prospect was. They both knew the answer: Liam Fontaine.

"Muck would use the bounce play a few times a game. Then I taught him this little trick we used to call the 'Muck Munro.'"

Mr. Fontaine was already wrestling the old net out of the mess of rusting metal scrap in the yard. He placed it in front of the tool shed, where the ground was trampled smooth and hard, nearly as hard as a concrete floor.

"You're our goaltender," Mr. Fontaine said to Nish. "So get in here.

"Now, Travis," he continued, "you're last man back and I'm coming in. Give me that ball."

Travis threw the ball, and the old man plucked it out of the air like a cat playing with a floating milkweed seed. It made absolutely no sound, but when the stick ceased to spin, there was the ball, nestled in the pocket as neatly as if it had been placed there by hand. It was something Travis never tired of seeing.

The old man felt the heft of the ball, threw a few fakes, and ran out in a short loop before coming in on Travis. He feinted once, then forced Travis's feet apart with the shoulder fake and bounced the ball clean between Travis's legs, floating effortlessly around him to catch it coming up, fake a backhand, and then slip a slow underhand behind the sprawling Nish.

"*Nice goal!*" Nish shouted.

"But I wouldn't be able to do it all the time," the old man said, twirling the ball out of the net and back into his old Logan. He came up and stood side by side with Travis, acting as if both were defenders on the same play. "You'd learn to expect it. You'd fall for it once or twice, maybe three times, and next time you'd keep your feet together and block the bounce, wouldn't you?"

"I guess I would," said Travis.

"Sure you would," said Mr. Fontaine. "So you need to come up with a new trick. Keep your feet together this time and I'll show you the 'Muck Munro,' okay?"

Again the old man set out in his easy loop. He turned, smiled once, and then came in on Travis.

Travis saw the shoulder fake, but refused to move his feet, watching for the bounce pass so he could block it.

But there was nothing, only a gentle whisper high over Travis's head. As he looked up he caught sight of the old man, still smiling, nothing whatsoever in his hands, peeling by him on the outside.

Travis was so surprised, he lost his balance. He slipped on the hard earth and fell backwards, jarring his tailbone as he hit the ground. Behind him he could see, upside down, the old man reach up and catch his floating stick. He faked once, twice, then worked a gentle sidearm past Nish on the short side.

Nish was laughing so hard he couldn't even try for it. He fell in a heap on the earth, howling and holding his sides.

Travis, too, began to laugh.

"Wh-what happened?" he asked.

"Nothing," the old man said. "Just the 'Muck Munro,' that's all."

The old man had the ball back in his stick. He was smiling. "This time just watch," he said.

Both boys took up their positions. The old man did his lazy loop again, and as he turned, Travis noticed how he took one hand off his stick and wedged the ball down hard into the pocket.

He came in, tried the shoulder fake, and then threw the stick high over Travis's head so that it stayed upright, seeming to float through the air as he moved around Travis, reached up and grabbed the handle again.

The old man shook the stick hard, once, and the jammed ball popped free, ready for the fake and an easy goal.

Never had they imagined anything so magical, never had they seen anything quite so lovely as the upright stick, spinning through the air like a long, skinny top that didn't even need a surface over which to dance.

Zeke Fontaine threw Travis the ball. "Your turn," he commanded.

The old man took up Travis's place on defence, Nish resumed his spot in the net, and Travis set out on his own lazy loop before turning.

Travis tried, discreetly, to jam the ball into the bottom of his pocket. But it wouldn't stick. He came in on the old man, faked, and then, when Mr. Fontaine went to block the bounce play, he tossed the stick high. The ball spun out the moment he let go of the stick.

Nish caught the lost ball.

The old man turned, his face puzzled.

"Let me see that," the old man said, as Travis picked up his stick.

Travis was confused. "See what?"

"Your stick," Mr. Fontaine said. "Let me have a look at it."

Travis handed it over and the old man examined it carefully. He jammed the ball down into the pocket, then tossed the stick high with a spin. But the ball flew free. Travis felt a little better; at least it hadn't been just him.

The old man took his own stick in one hand and Travis's in the other and glanced back and forth between the two. Finally he dropped Travis's Brine.

"Damn modern sticks," the old man said. "Sorry, boys, didn't mean to swear, but look at this."

The two boys drew closer. Mr. Fontaine jammed the ball into his own stick. It pushed aside the catgut at the bottom and wedged tight to the wood. He spun the stick and the ball stayed locked in the pocket. Then he picked up Travis's stick and tried the same thing. Since the head was entirely hard plastic there was no flexibility. He couldn't wedge the ball into place.

"You got to have the catgut," the old man said, as if confirming something he already knew. "You can't do it with these plastic jobbies. You got to have the real thing – a Logan."

He turned back to Travis. "Would you play with a Logan if you had one?"

Travis swallowed hard. "Yes, sir," he said, "I would."

For a moment Travis thought he was about to be given Mr. Fontaine's own stick, but Mr. Fontaine clearly had something else in mind. "There's a Logan in the house that's practically brand new," the old man said. "Used one summer only." He paused, to correct himself. "Used *part* of one summer."

Travis felt a tremor in his back. Used part of one summer? A Logan, practically new?

"Come in here a minute," Mr. Fontaine said. He turned and headed towards the house, obviously expecting the boys to follow. Travis looked at Nish. Nish looked at Travis. Then both turned and followed him into the house, as they had been asked.

The flies buzzed around them. Travis swatted a mosquito. The old man was rooting about in what seemed to be a shed tacked on to the back of the main house. An open doorway to one side led to what looked like it might be the living room. There were papers all over the place.

Mr. Fontaine grunted with satisfaction and stepped back, pulling a lacrosse stick out from a pile of shovels and rakes that were leaning against the wall. He turned, punching the pocket, wiping a hand up and down the handle to clear away the dust.

Dust or not, Travis could tell it was a Logan. Barely used. Still as good as the day it was bought, thirty or forty years before.

"You think you can take good care of this?" the old man asked as he handed it over to Travis.

"Yes, sir," Travis said. "It's beautiful."

"It belonged to my boy," Zeke Fontaine said. "He was Muck's best friend. And as good a lacrosse player as I've ever seen in my life."

The old man sounded so sad as he said this. Travis had no idea what to say to him.

"He sounds like a neat kid," Nish said, filling in the gap.

The old man nodded. He looked up, his old eyes glistening in the dim light. "There's a picture of him there on that table," he said, pointing a slightly shaking finger.

It was an old school picture, now badly faded, but it showed a handsome young man with light blond hair and a wide, confident smile.

"Looks about our age," Nish said.

The old man nodded.

Travis could say nothing. He was dumbstruck. He stood, his mouth wide open, staring at the photograph of Liam Fontaine.

He felt he had seen the boy before . . . somewhere.

At the graveyard?

15

or the entire ride back to town Travis wondered how to tell Nish that he thought he had seen Liam Fontaine before. He had no idea how he could say *anything* without making a complete fool of himself. What could he say? That he had seen the boy at the cemetery the night they had gone to *The Blood Children: Part VIII*. Nish wouldn't believe him. And who would blame him? Travis couldn't believe it himself.

It made no sense.

Nish, however, was thinking only about his movie. He babbled all the way about the "great setting" Old Man Fontaine's place would make for a horror flick. Nish loved the dark, spooky house. Loved the dog's grave. Loved Zeke Fontaine's face – so much in fact that he was even toying with asking the old man if he'd like a part in his film.

Get real! Travis wanted to say. But he said nothing. He let Nish dream on. And he tried to force his own thoughts back to something more down-to-earth.

The Screech Owls were due to play the following evening in Brantford, home of the second-best team in the league, the Warriors. It was going to be a tough test for the Owls. If they could compete against the Warriors, they were a real lacrosse team.

Travis wondered if he had enough courage to try the stick Mr. Fontaine had given him.

The Warriors were everything Muck had warned them they would be. Big and tough and extremely skilled, if a bit slow on their feet. Mr. Dillinger seemed particularly worried and fidgeted terribly, almost as if he wished he had something useful to do – like sharpen skates. But Mr. Dillinger only had water bottles to fill and laces to worry about, and the lack of work just seemed to make him more nervous.

Travis, too, was nervous. He took the new – or was it old? – Logan out for warm-up and one of the referees came running over to check it out. Not because it might be illegal, as Travis first feared, but because he had recognized the make and wanted a closer look.

"You're a lucky young man," he said to Travis as he handed it back.

Travis wasn't so sure.

The game began. Sarah won the draw easily, but was instantly flattened by a hard check from behind. The ball squirted to Travis's side and he tried to scoop it up but lost it when it ticked off the catgut. A Warrior scooped it free, tossed it cross-floor, and sent in his winger on a break. He rolled right off

Fahd's check and scored easily on a bounce shot that Nish misjudged.

One shot, one goal.

The Warriors built the score to 5–0 by the time of the first intermission. Travis and the other Owls sagged against the boards, spraying water directly onto their faces and munching on orange sections that Mr. Dillinger had cut up when he ran out of other things to do.

Travis was disheartened. The Owls looked weak and disorganized and unskilled.

"Your speed," Muck said. "Use your speed."

Sarah got them rolling with a great rush up-floor in which she turned her back on the defence as they came together, crashed into them, and dropped off to Dmitri, who stepped around the falling defenders and beat the Brantford goalie on a sidearm.

Andy scored on a long shot that took an odd bounce.

Simon scored on a shot that tipped in off a Warrior's stick.

The Warriors scored two more, and the Owls answered with two, one by Sam and the other by Travis on a low underhand that skimmed the floor and slipped right in between the Brantford goalie's feet.

They were into the third frame, the Owls still down by two goals, when Wilson scored on a wonderful solo effort that took him up-floor and around the opposition net, sending in a high overhand lob that just cleared the goaltender's shoulder before the clock ran out.

There was only a minute left in the game.

Sarah had the ball in her own corner. Two Warriors were on

her. She huddled down and popped the ball free to Nish, who'd left his crease to help out.

Travis cut towards centre. "NISH!" he screamed.

Nish saw him and hit him perfectly. Travis took the ball, turned, and headed in.

One defender back.

Travis reached up and wedged the ball down hard into the pocket. He had tried the bounce play twice already. Once it had worked. Once it hadn't. They might be expecting it again.

He dropped his shoulder.

The defender didn't go for it, keeping his legs together to block any bounce.

Travis tossed his stick, high and spinning through the air, and stepped around the surprised defenceman. The stick seemed to move in slow motion. It hung suspended in the air. Travis could hear gasps from the crowd. He could hear his own feet slapping on the floor.

Moving in under the stick, he reached up with one hand and caught it. He jammed the stick down so the bottom of the handle rapped off the arena floor, jiggling the ball free.

A fake, a fake backhander, and he slipped an underhand shot in the short side.

The arena erupted.

The players on the floor mobbed Travis. The players on the bench bolted as the clock ran out and the buzzer sounded.

Travis had scored a thousand goals in hockey, including practices, exhibition games, and road games, but it was never like this.

Even Nish was on top of him, weighing about fifty extra pounds in his sweat-filled, stinking equipment. He had never smelled so sweet!

Now there were other hands pulling him free. Strong, big hands. It was Muck. He was smiling and shaking his head. "I guess I know where you got that."

Travis smiled back. He looked for Mr. Fontaine, but the old man was already at the gate leading off the floor and away.

There was no use chasing him. The players were all holding each other and half dancing in the corner of the rink. They had only tied the game, but they had tied the *Warriors*.

They were a team.

A competitive team.

With only the championship now to go.

16

 t's no good."

Travis didn't like what he was hearing, but wasn't surprised. Data and Fahd and Sarah and Sam were delivering the verdict on the video he and Nish had brought back from the dump.

"You can see too much of the dump," said Fahd.

"No one's going to be scared out of their wits by a bear ripping apart a garbage bag," said Data.

"We're going to have to try again," said Sarah.

Travis let out a long breath. "Okay," he said. "What can we do?"

Sam had some ideas. They would set up in the deep woods just behind the dump and try to film one of the bears in the wild. They could then combine this with the better shots of the bears taking swipes and runs at each other in the dump, but only the ones that didn't show the garbage.

Fahd jumped in: "And we can do a third series of shots showing dummies being ripped apart or blowing up or whatever.

If we edit them in, people will think the bears are ripping people up. We just need to find a few dummies."

"No problem there," Sam said, looking right at him.

Fahd had heard the joke before, but still didn't get it.

"Fine!" Nish interrupted. "There's only one problem. How do we find a bear in the woods?"

"He comes to us," Sam said. "You have to *attract* them – that's what hunters do."

"We're not going to *shoot* them!" said Data.

"Yes we are," said Sam, "with a camera."

"Hunters bait them," said Simon. "They put out rotting meat."

"*Gross!*" said several of the Owls together.

"The bears are attracted by the smell," Simon continued. "It has to be a strong smell, that's why they use meat that's gone bad."

"Where are we going to find a smell *that* powerful?" wailed Fahd.

"Think about it," said Sam.

There was a pause. No one understood.

Sam slowly raised her hand and very deliberately pointed, as if she were taking aim, at the source of a smell powerful enough to attract the attention of wild bears.

Nish!

Travis thought to himself, It's a good thing that we're capturing this on film, otherwise no one would ever believe it!

They were deep in the bush behind the garbage dump. They knew they were in the right area when Jesse found a large beech tree with sharp, regularly spaced scrapings across the bark. "A bear has scratched here to sharpen his claws," he announced.

Travis looked up, way up. For a bear to reach that high, it would have to be twice the height of Travis. At least. He shuddered.

"*What's this?*" Nish called from farther up the trail.

The others hurried along. Nish was standing over a huge black mound of what looked, on first glance, like mud.

"Bear dropping," said Jesse.

Nish giggled. "How come *we* don't call it 'dropping'?"

"Because most of us have the decency to use a toilet," said Sam.

"At least this proves a bear has been here recently," said Simon.

"Time to get ready, Stinker Boy," said Sarah.

All eyes were now on Nish. He was, already sweating. His face was twisted like an old sock.

"We're *not* going to do this," he wailed.

"We are so," said Sam. "Now get your stuff on!"

17

nd that was how Wayne Nishikawa came to be walking down a bush trail in full lacrosse goalie equipment. He looked a bit like a bear himself, the heavy equipment nearly doubling his bulk and making him waddle as he walked.

Sam's idea had been ingenious, Travis thought. They needed a terrific, horrific smell that no bear on earth could help but notice. What better than Nish's lacrosse equipment?

Nish had been outraged. He was furious when Sam suggested it and fought the idea tooth and nail. But the Owls had thought about it and decided. In the end, he had no choice. The horror movie, after all, was his idea. If it was going to work, they all had to pitch in – and this time it was his turn.

"*I'm the director!*" he'd whined. "*Not bear bait!*"

Jesse and Simon, who knew more about the bush than the others, had taken over the rest of the planning. Jesse knew, from experience, that nothing gets rid of a black bear better than a sudden sound, so they were carrying whistles, and Jesse even had an old pot and a wooden spoon to smack together if they needed to drive one off.

"*What if one of them starts to eat me?*" Nish had whined.

"What's '*I'm gonna hurl!*' in bear language?" laughed Sarah.

"Don't worry about it," said Jesse. "Bears are a lot more scared of people than people should be of them."

Nish had dressed, reluctantly, at the side of the road and then walked in with the rest to take up their positions. He would waddle along the trails in his stinking equipment; Jesse and Simon would be right behind him in case some sudden noise was needed; and the Owls would set up with their cameras in two strategic places, hoping to get some good footage of a black bear rambling through the woods. With luck, they'd even have one of them rise on its haunches to sniff the air for some stinking Nishikawa.

Travis and Sarah and Sam were to take the far end of the path. Fahd and Andy were among the Owls at the near end.

Travis found a perfect stand of cedar to wriggle into. The branches were soft and smelled wonderful, and the skirt of the cedar was so low and dense that, once he was inside, he could not be seen from the trail.

Sarah and Sam hunkered down on the other side of the trail. Sam had the video camera. If either Travis or Sarah saw signs of a bear coming, their job was to alert Sam to be ready.

It was a hot, lazy day. There were still mosquitoes in the woods, and Travis wished he'd remembered to bring along a bottle of bug repellent. He felt he was being eaten alive.

The wind was still. The only sounds were the occasional songbird flitting through the trees, the grating call of a crow high in the maples, and as the air grew hotter, the deep, long buzz of cicadas that seemed to come from nowhere and everywhere at the same time.

Travis thought he heard a whistle!

It could mean one of only two things: a bear had been spotted, or a bear had to be frightened off.

He listened hard, wondering if he put his ear to the ground whether he could hear the sound better, the way a railway track is supposed to let you know a train is coming long before it can be seen.

He could hear breathing now! Heavy breathing, puffing!

Travis pushed out a little from under the apron of cedar branches. He looked down the trail, the sunlight dancing as it played through the high branches and spotted the path with occasional bright patches.

The sound was closer now! And he could hear branches being pushed aside and then swishing back into place.

He could hear grunting! The telltale sound of Nish working hard.

Travis looked across at Sarah and Sam. Sam was readying the camera. Sarah was leaning down, staring towards the sound of the oncoming Nish.

The branch of a spruce was thrust aside, and Nish pushed through, breathing very heavily now. He wasn't running, but he seemed anxious, frightened.

Travis suddenly felt sorry for his friend.

Nish kept going, past Sam, past Sarah, past Travis, completely unaware that they were hidden there in the bush.

The spruce bough swung again, this time more slowly.

Travis felt his breath catch.

The head of a bear pushed through, swinging its nose from side to side, sniffing for Nish!

Travis could see Sam already filming. She was well out of sight and downwind from the bear. It hadn't noticed her.

The bear pushed the rest of the way through. It was huge!

It paused, sniffed the air again, then rose on its haunches.

Travis caught the briefest flash of white.

Silvertip!

18

here were Jesse and Simon?

Travis frantically searched the dark shadows beyond the bear. There was neither sight nor sound of them.

Perhaps the whistle had been a warning to scare off the big bear, but hadn't worked! Perhaps the two boys had become separated from Nish or taken a wrong turn.

Maybe Nish *was* running! Maybe that was as fast as he could go with all that equipment on!

Travis instantly regretted this whole wild scheme. They should never have agreed to send Nish out in his equipment. It might have seemed funny at the time – but no longer.

The bear settled on all fours again, sniffed and grunted loudly.

"HHHELLLLLP!"

The call came from ahead on the path. Travis swung around and saw that Nish had turned and seen the bear up on his hind legs. Nish was still wearing his goaltender's mask, but the cage over his face couldn't hide the pure, absolute terror in his eyes.

"HHHELLLLLP MMMMEEEE!"

Travis acted at once. His friend had called and he had to respond. He leaped free of his cover and jumped up and down, waving his arms.

"SHOOOO!" he shouted. "GET AWAY, BEAR!"

The bear stopped, rose again on his haunches.

Travis knew at once he'd made a mistake. He'd have had better luck against mosquitoes with that silly shout than against the biggest bear in the woods.

"SCRAMMMM!" he shouted with more force. He picked up a branch and threw it, spinning and crashing through the air. He wished he'd had a rock in his pocket. He looked around but could see none on the soft, needle-covered earth.

Silvertip stared at Travis, then raised his nose, sniffing. Sniffing for me? Travis wondered. Or sniffing for Nish?

Silvertip settled, then turned, his huge shoulders snapping dead twigs as he changed direction and headed off the path.

Straight for Travis.

"TRAVISSS!" Sarah shouted. "GET OUT OF HERE, QUICK!"

Travis was running before he could even think. He was pushing through spruce and cedar, the branches whipping into his face, and he was stumbling and sliding and slipping up and down hills.

He knew it was wrong. He knew that one thing you were never supposed to do around a black bear was turn tail and run. Back away slowly, the park rangers always said. Make noise, show no fear, and back away slowly. Don't panic, don't show them you're petrified – and never run away screaming.

But that's just what Travis Lindsay did.

Silvertip sniffed the air again and then picked up his pace, heading straight in the direction Travis had just taken.

"GO, TRAVISSSS!" Sam called.

Travis thought he was in good shape from lacrosse, but he had never tired so quickly in his life. He was covered in sweat. It was stinging the scrapes from the branches and raspberry bushes. He had dirt in his eyes. But he was still moving.

He crashed through the bush, down a dried-up creek, and up a small hill. He leaped over rocks, used roots to pull himself higher, swung onto a bluff and kept on running.

Travis's lungs were killing him. He stopped, just for a moment, to catch his breath and look back.

Silvertip was still coming!

Travis hurdled logs and crashed through bogs and stumbled over stones, but he kept going.

He no longer needed to look back to see if the bear was following.

He could hear it behind him.

The big bear grunted like a pig. He crashed through the bush as if it were made of paper, not hardwood and rock. He snapped branches and ripped aside logs and sent rocks churning down slopes.

Travis leaped up a small hill and over a fallen tree and came – suddenly – to a dead end.

He could go no farther.

Ahead was open air, and thirty feet straight down was a tangle of rock and stumps and dead branches.

Silvertip was already on the hill, grunting heavily, crashing through everything in his path.

Travis had no choice. He had to jump. There was a soft ledge about halfway down. If he could land on that he might roll safely to a stop. He might even be able to stay there, out of reach of the bear.

He had no time to think. No time to cry or pray. He just leaped.

He felt the air cool on his face, welcome on his scrapes. He felt himself floating through the air, moving so slowly he almost believed he was taking flight.

Then he crashed into the ledge.

It no longer looked, or felt, so soft.

He hit hard and rolled, paused for a moment on the edge, then dropped again, heading for the bottom.

19

Travis had no idea how long he had lain there. He knew he was hurt. His left hand was throbbing. He felt his legs, moved them both, flexed his feet. They were fine.

He looked up to the top of the bluff.

Silvertip was standing there, staring down!

Travis had no more strength left to run. Something sticky was on his face and dripping down onto his lips. He tested it with his tongue. *Blood!*

Instinctively, with his right hand, he fumbled for a stone to protect himself. He stared up at the bear, and the bear stared back, sniffing the air.

Travis felt a large, round rock and tucked it in tight to his chest. If the bear comes down, he thought, I might be able to scare him off with one good throw. But I'll only have one chance.

Silvertip backed off.

He's looking for a way down! Travis thought.

He was crying. He was crying for his parents and his grand-parents and for Muck and Mr. Dillinger. Crying for Nish and Sarah and all his teammates. Crying because they'd been so foolish.

He could hear the bear grunting, hear the slide of gravel and stone as the huge beast began coming down the side.

He drew the rock back, ready to throw.

CLANG! CLANG! CLANG! CLANG! CLANG!

What was that sound?

Travis shook his head, trying to get a fix on it.

CLANG! CLANG! CLANG! CLANG! CLANG!

Jesse's pot! The wooden spoon on the old pot!

Now there was a whistle. Then another. Loud and shrill.

There was movement in the cedars. First Jesse pushed through, still banging, then Simon with his whistle blasting, then Sarah and Sam, with the camera still filming, and finally Nish, his helmet off and his face redder and wetter than Travis had ever seen it.

"*He's over to your right!*" Travis called.

They looked to where Travis thought he had heard the bear coming down.

"*He's long gone!*" Jesse shouted down to him.

"*Stay there, Travis,*" shouted Sarah. "*We're coming to get you!*"

Travis felt his first full breath enter his lungs. He could feel his hand hurting now, his skin was stinging, but he felt absolutely wonderful.

Silvertip was gone!

He set his rock down, already smiling at his own foolishness. *As if this would have stopped Silvertip!* he said to himself, looking at it.

It was an oddly shaped thing, perfectly round on one side, jagged on the other, and not all that heavy for its size. He almost threw it away before catching himself.

It wasn't a rock at all!

Travis stared at it, not believing what he held in his hand.

A human skull!

20

"The remains have been identified as those of Liam Fontaine, a twelve-year-old Tamarack boy who disappeared under mysterious circumstances more than thirty years ago."

Travis was not surprised to hear the newscast confirm what everyone in town already knew. The provincial police had called in the forensic investigation unit from Toronto, and more bones had been found in the rubble and rotting branches where Travis had landed when he fell down the bluff.

It was not a shallow grave. It was typical of a black bear cache, a kill hidden under branches and leaves and partially covered with earth. Teeth marks on the skull and several bones clearly indicated that the youngster had been killed by a rogue bear.

Zeke Fontaine had not, as so many had believed, killed his son.

Travis was taken to the hospital, cleaned up, checked over, X-rayed, and released. His left hand still hurt, but the doctors

said he could play lacrosse if he wanted, so long as he was careful
not to use his hand too much.

There was no more talk about a movie. No one wanted to
make the ninth episode of *The Blood Children* or even the first
episode of *The Killer Bears of Tamarack*. Now that they knew the
truth, it seemed wrong to think about Liam Fontaine's fate as a
plot for a made-up story, and none of the Owls ever again mentioned it – not even Nish, the director.

All the Owls wanted to do now was concentrate on lacrosse,
and they were happy to have a practice to go to the next day.
Even so, they had trouble concentrating on breakouts and
defence patterns and the like. Travis, in particular, found it hard
to keep his thoughts on the game.

Two newspapers from Toronto had sent reporters to talk to
him and the other Owls involved in the find. No one, merci-
fully, had mentioned Nish's ridiculous movie or how he came
to be wandering through the deep woods dressed in his lacrosse
goaltending equipment. That would have been just too hard to
explain.

And now there was a television camera at the practice. Travis
was wondering what effect the camera might have on Nish
when he noticed a couple of familiar figures standing behind
the seats, watching.

One was his grandfather, who rarely came to games and had
never, ever been to a practice.

The other was old Mr. Donahue from the Autumn Leaves
Retirement Home.

Muck ended the practice with a team run around the boards, first clockwise, then counter-clockwise, then in a long figure-eight pattern with the players crossing at centre floor lobbing a ball back and forth to the nearest passing teammate.

Travis was exhausted. After Muck blew the whistle to signal practice was finished, Travis loped over to where Mr. Fontaine was hauling the water bottles out of the players' box. He picked one up and sprayed the water directly into his face. Travis had come over deliberately. He still hadn't said anything to Mr. Fontaine.

"How's the Logan?" Mr. Fontaine asked, smiling.

"Fine," Travis said. "I love it." He didn't know what else to say.

Mr. Fontaine looked younger. He no longer seemed so white, so stooped. No longer seemed as if he were trying to disappear as he walked.

Mr. Dillinger was holding the door open for them to leave the floor and head for the dressing rooms. Mr. Fontaine went first, Travis right behind him.

His grandfather and Mr. Donahue were waiting.

Mr. Fontaine kept his head down, though Travis knew he must have recognized the two former policemen.

"Do you have a moment, Zeke?" Travis's grandfather said.

The old lacrosse coach stopped, fidgeting with the water bottles he was carrying. He seemed to have trouble looking at the two men.

"Ed and I just want to say how sorry we are," old Mr. Lindsay was saying. He had his hand out, waiting.

Slowly, old Mr. Fontaine reached for the hand of the former policeman who had always believed something else had happened to little Liam Fontaine.

Muck wanted to speak to them.

He had never done this before. Muck speaking to them before a game was rare. Muck speaking to them after a game was almost unheard-of. Muck speaking to them after a practice was unimaginable.

Nish was lying flat on his back on the floor. He had his mask off and was holding a water bottle directly over his head, spraying hard. Sam and Sarah were also on their backs on the floor, their legs resting on the bench. Mr. Fontaine had said it was a great way to get the blood flowing right again.

"Saturday morning we start the tournament," Muck said. "We're the hosts and, naturally, we don't want to let the town down. That means you're expected to behave well in addition to playing well. Got that, Mr. Nishikawa?"

"Got it, Coach!" Nish called from the floor, still spraying water in his face.

Muck frowned. He hated being called "Coach," which only made Nish do it all the more.

"When we began the season we didn't know much about this game," Muck said. "I think we owe Mr. Fontaine here a vote of thanks for helping us out."

The dressing room erupted with cheers.

"Our aim is to provide some real competition," Muck said, "and when we played against Brantford, we proved we can do it. Mr. Fontaine has another thought, though, and I'd like you to hear it from him, if you don't mind."

Mr. Fontaine swallowed hard and stepped to the centre of the floor.

Even Nish was paying attention now, his empty water bottle held to his chest like a newborn baby.

Mr. Fontaine cleared his throat. He rapped his old Logan stick once on the floor.

"We can win it," he said.

Nothing more. And certainly nothing less.

We can win it.

21

T. he provincial peewee championship began in Tamarack on a Saturday morning so hot there was some concern Nish might melt entirely away. He sweated so much in game one against the Niagara Falls Thunder that several times the officials had to blow down play and get the arena staff to come out with squeegees and clear off the water around the Screech Owls' crease.

Nish had good cause to sweat. The Thunder was a good team, fast rushing and smart with the ball. But for Nish's extraordinary play the Owls would have fallen out of contention right from the opening whistle. Sarah and Travis and Dmitri also played their best game yet. Sarah ended the game with eight assists and a goal, Dmitri with seven goals and three assists, and Travis with four goals and four assists. The Owls won 14–9.

In game two they were up against a team from upstate New York, the Watertown Seaway. They won easily, 22–5, with Jesse Highboy leading the charge with four goals and four assists.

Sarah had another four goals and three assists, and Travis and Dmitri both had two of each.

"You're leading the tournament in scoring," Jenny shouted back to Sarah as she scanned the results in the lobby. Sarah said nothing. She blushed and headed outside with Dmitri to toss the ball around between matches. Travis joined them, blinking as his eyes adjusted to the incredible brightness of the sun.

Mr. Fontaine was already out there. "C'mere for a moment, son," he said when he noticed Travis. "Let me see that stick again."

Travis handed over the precious Logan. Mr. Fontaine ran his bony hands up and down the shaft and over the pocket and along the catgut. He punched the pocket and felt the heft of the ball in it and punched the pocket again.

"You're shooting slightly high, you know," the old man said, adjusting his glasses on his nose.

Travis knew instantly that Mr. Fontaine was right. One of his goals had looked spectacular, the ball tipping in off the cross-bar, but in fact he had intended to skip the ball in off the floor.

Mr. Fontaine's hands were fast at work. He was undoing the braiding and pulling and yanking the lines left and right. He put the heel of his foot in the pocket and pushed down hard, using the ground for leverage. He tried the ball again, adjusted the pocket again, then declared himself satisfied and rebraided the stick.

He handed it back to Travis. "Try an overhand fake."

The ball seemed to sag in the pocket. It felt odd, and for a moment Travis wished Mr. Fontaine had left the stick alone.

He tried the fake and was amazed at how it held in the pocket. He giggled. The old man giggled along with him.

"Try a full forehand fake," the old man said, "and let it become an underhand shot."

Travis didn't follow.

"Here," the old man said. "Watch me."

Mr. Fontaine took the ball and faked a couple of times to get the feel of it. Then he fired what looked like a hard overhand against the arena wall, but the ball held perfectly in the pocket. Mr. Fontaine let the stick swing almost in a full arc, past his left knee and towards his back, but at the last second it changed direction and he ripped a hard underhand that slapped off the wall and jumped back into his stick so fast it seemed he couldn't possibly have had time to catch it.

"*Wow!*" said Travis.

"Try it," Mr. Fontaine said with a grin.

Travis did, and lost the ball on the fake. He made a second attempt, and lost the ball when he tried to stop the arc and turn the stick. He lost it a third time on the shot.

But the fourth time he got it.

"It's yours now," the old man said. "You own that play."

22

Jenny Staples was again at the round-robin chart pasted up in the lobby. The Owls had won three games and tied one, and a tournament official was just now pencilling in the two teams that would meet in the championship game.

He wrote "SCREECH OWLS" above one line.

Then he began writing on the opposite side: "T-O-R . . ."

"Oh no!" wailed Jenny. "Not the Toronto Mini-Rock!"

But it was indeed. The Owls against the Mini-Rock, the team they had lost to 19–8 earlier in the summer. The biggest, meanest, toughest, nastiest, and *best* peewee team in the province.

The game was set for Saturday night at eight o'clock. "Prime time!" Nish called it. The local cable station was going to carry it live, and Nish was acting as if ESPN, TSN, Sportsnet, and Eurosport were all going to broadcast it.

"*Sports Illustrated* called," Nish told them as they dressed. "I got next week's cover."

It was as if the Owls had never before played a *real* lacrosse game. Travis had never felt the game move so quickly, never felt *himself* move so quickly. There was no time to think, no time to plan, only time to react – and right from the start the Mini-Rock were reacting quicker than the Screech Owls.

The big Toronto centre was again dominating Sarah. He used his strength and size to bowl her over on draws. He crushed her in the corners. He hassled her when she wasn't even in the play, and twice tripped her when she tried to break free. Not once did the referee call a penalty, which angered the Screech Owls' bench so much some of the players shouted at the referee.

"Enough of that!" Muck said, once.

Once was enough. Every player on the bench knew that Muck disapproved of catcalls. He always said, "Players win and lose games, officials don't."

The Mini-Rock went ahead 4–1 early in the match, the Owls' sole mark coming from little, skinny Fahd, who whipped a sidearm shot blind from the point and let it fly like a laser for an open corner of the net.

Muck kept pushing the Owls to use their speed, and it began to make a difference. Dmitri was sent in alone by Sarah, and double-faked the goalie flat onto his back before scoring the Screech Owls' second. Sam scored on a hard overhand that ticked off a Mini-Rock player's shoulder pads.

By the start of the third, the game was tied 9–9. The squeegee patrol was working overtime to keep Nish's crease clear of water, but it seemed the more he sweated the better he played. Several of Nish's stops had been unbelievable. He was clearing shots away with his stick to prevent rebounds and had

developed a trick of falling backwards when he stopped a ball,
flipping his stick high as he went down and sending the ball up
into the rafters. A couple of times it even went over the netting
at the back of the goal and sailed into the stands.

"He's showing off," Sarah said to Travis as they sat a shift.

"He's going to score on himself if he isn't careful," said
Travis.

"He's brilliant," said Dmitri.

Both Sarah and Travis looked oddly at Dmitri.

"He's *Nish!*" both corrected at once.

Yet Travis had to admit that Nish *was* brilliant. He was
playing the game of his life.

The Mini-Rock went ahead 13−11 on a string of goals and
assists by the big centre.

"Speed," Muck kept saying. "Use your speed!"

Dmitri broke free and ran almost the entire length of the
floor to score.

The officials called a time-out so the arena staff could mop
up around Nish's crease. It was beginning to look like they
needed a pump, as well as the squeegees.

Travis felt hands on his shoulders. He looked down. Long,
bony fingers, white and wrinkled.

"Time for a little creativity, son," Mr. Fontaine said in Travis's
ear.

Travis had tried his bounce pass, but he'd been knocked
flying before he could step around the defence. His left hand
was still a bit sore from the fall, so he'd been afraid to try the
"Muck Munro"; if he botched it, the Mini-Rock would end up
with the ball and he'd be lost, without his stick, at the other end.

But he still had the overhand fake.

Travis checked the clock.

Ninety seconds.

"*Sarah!*" Muck called out.

Sarah's line spilled over the boards. Travis punched his stick pocket a couple of times and lined up while Sarah took the draw.

"Get a *real* stick!" the winger opposite him called out.

Travis said nothing. It was to his advantage if the other side dismissed his Logan. The more he and his stick were underestimated, the better chance they'd have.

Sarah won the draw cleanly. She fired the ball back to Sam, who ran behind Nish's net and stood, using the goal as a guard.

The clock behind her was running down.

Sarah broke cross-floor and Sam hit her perfectly with a pass. Sarah passed – *backhand* – to Dmitri, who broke up the far boards and then cut for centre floor, slowing down the play.

Travis was coming up his wing. Dmitri backed into his check, protecting the ball, and looked for Travis. He flicked the ball quickly, straight into Travis's pocket.

The second defender rushed at Travis. He faked overhand as hard as he could.

It looked like a panic shot. The defender moved to block it. But Travis held the shot, turning his stick as it swung so it seemed impossible that the ball had stayed.

The Mini-Rock goaltender, convinced he'd missed it, looked quickly behind him to see if the shot had been so fast it was already in the net.

Travis held the arc and turned his stick just as it swung past his knee.

The ball was still in the pocket.

Quick as his wrists would reverse, Travis fired the ball under-hand, the shot rising as it passed the surprised defenceman and came in on the even more surprised goaltender.

Ping!

In off the crossbar!

Mini-Rock 13, Owls 13.

Travis had tied the championship game with old man Fontaine's overhand fake!

23

There was no time for celebration. Thirty-three seconds remained on the clock with a draw at centre floor.

Again, Sarah took the draw and flipped it back to Sam, who began another retreat behind Nish's net. The Mini-Rock, however, had other ideas. They put a two-player press on Sam, the two closest forwards rushing her in the hopes of causing a turnover or a panic throw.

Both forwards hit Sam at once. She buckled under their cross-checks, but just as she went down she managed to direct the ball towards Nish's crease.

Nish raced forward, scooping up the ball. He was in full stride, his leg pads clicking as he ran and his sneakers leaving faint damp spots on the floor.

Up over centre floor Nish ran.

Travis was alarmed. Nish had never come out this far before. If he lost the ball now, they were sunk.

Sarah and Dmitri were both calling for passes. One Mini-Rock defender broke off, covering Sarah, the Owls' most dangerous playmaker.

That left Travis free.

He saw that Nish could see him. He raised his stick, expecting the pass. He barely saw Nish's hand move. The thick goalie glove went up into the pocket and jammed the ball down hard into the crotch of the stick.

Nish faked to Travis, then turned on the only player back. He faked a bounce shot through the player's legs. The defenceman went down to block. Nish threw his goalie stick high in the air, so high it came within a whisker of rattling off the overhead lights that hung from the rafters.

It was as if all time had come to a stop.

Travis could sense the crowd, every eye in the place raised to the heavens as Nish's huge floating, spinning stick went up and over and began to come down.

Nish crashed right through the crouching defender, sending him flying. He reached up with one hand and caught his stick perfectly, placed his other hand up the shaft, and in one motion he shot.

A perfect "Muck Munro"!

The ball bounced once, rattled between the leg pads of the Mini-Rock goaltender, and into the net.

Screech Owls 14, Mini-Rock 13.

Travis's first instinct was to look at the clock.

Nothing left, the buzzer already going.

His second instinct was to pile on Nish, who was already down in an accommodating heap.

The Screech Owls had won the championship.

Travis was in the pile. Dmitri was on top of him. Sam, then Fahd, then Sarah.

"*You stink!*" Sarah shouted.

"*Ain't it beautiful?*" shouted Nish.

The floor was filling with players and coaches and managers and officials. Muck was running towards the Mini-Rock net, where the official was just pulling the winning goal out from the netting. Travis saw him speak to the official, who nodded and handed over the ball. Muck took it in both hands, gently kissed it, and then walked over to meet Zeke Fontaine, still heading towards the pile from the bench.

Muck held out the ball for his assistant coach.

The old man looked at it. Travis could see he was weeping.

Muck shook the ball. He, too, was in tears.

The old man took the game ball as if it were the most precious, fragile thing in the world.

In a way, it was. More than thirty years after it should have happened, Muck Munro and Zeke Fontaine had their provincial championship.

24

wo days later, the Screech Owls all went to the cemetery, where little Liam Fontaine would finally be laid to rest.

The Owls wore their team sweaters and acted as an honour guard. Muck and Mr. Dillinger acted as pallbearers.

A priest spoke, but Travis wasn't listening to what he said. He stood, staring at the freshly dug grave and the small white coffin, the air heavy with the scent of flowers, and he wept. He didn't even bother to wipe away the tears.

He had never known the boy. Liam Fontaine had been dead for decades before Travis was even born. And yet Travis couldn't get it out of his head that they were burying the same boy he had seen that night as he came home from the movie.

He knew it wasn't possible. He knew it made no sense at all. But that was how he felt.

After the priest stopped speaking, they lowered the coffin, and old Mr. Fontaine leaned over, placing something down into the grave.

Mrs. Lindsay and Mrs. Nishikawa came along with armfuls of roses, handing one each to the Screech Owls for them to place in the grave.

This was what old Mr. Fontaine had done, thought Travis, maybe leaving an orange lily, and he stood behind Nish and Sarah to take his turn.

Sarah dropped her rose and moved on. She, too, was weeping openly.

Nish dropped his. His face was red, his cheeks burning with tears.

Travis bent to drop his rose on the coffin and realized that it was not a flower at all that Liam Fontaine's father had sent to be buried with the boy.

It was the ball from the championship game.

THE END

Death Down Under

1

"I s it still flushing backwards?"

"*Drop dead!*"

The first voice belonged to Fahd; the second, coming from inside the toilet bowl, belonged to Nish. The first was laughing, and the second sounded, understandably, near tears.

Nish was throwing up in the bathroom. Not *pretend* hurling for once, but really being sick.

Travis felt like he might be next. A few minutes earlier he had even scurried into the little hotel bathroom himself, the same bathroom where most of the Screech Owls had gathered earlier in the day while Nish – using the vitamin pills his mother always packed – had given a demonstration how toilets here flushed in the opposite direction.

"Only Nish would know which way they go down back home," sneered Sarah, who'd come in with Sam to watch.

It had been hilarious, with Nish red-faced and grunting as he climbed up on the sink and reached over to let the little brown pills plop loudly into the toilet bowl before he pressed the flush lever with his toes to send them swirling in what he explained was the reverse of normal, clockwise rather than counter-clockwise, down, down through the hotel waste system.

But no one was laughing now. Travis had been sure he, too, would be sick to his stomach, but all he could do was retch a couple of times and wish, more than anything else in the world, that Nish had been right.

That everything here did run backwards.

Including time.

Travis's stomach hurt. His temples hurt. The back of his neck hurt like he'd been cross-checked headfirst into the boards.

And yet the Owls still hadn't played a single hockey game in Australia. They'd been so excited about that first game Down Under, but now it was impossible even to think about playing hockey. Who could, after what had happened?

The team had never been so up for a trip. They had visited some exciting places before, but this trip was special, because it had come to them completely out of the blue and involved probably the last place on earth any of them ever thought they'd be playing their favourite game.

It all began with a letter that had arrived one day in the downtown office of Mr. Lindsay, Travis's father:

The Australian Ice Hockey Federation, in an effort to promote minor hockey development in Australia, would

like to extend an invitation to the Tamarack Screech Owls
to come to Sydney, Australia, for the first-ever "Oz Peewee
Invitational."

The trip would coincide almost exactly with the March
school break.

Travis's father had been surprised there was even ice in
Australia, let alone a national ice hockey organization. Australia,
Mr. Lindsay said, was probably the top sporting country in the
world, but the sports they played were soccer and cricket and
swimming and track-and-field and basketball. When a country
was mostly desert, when the temperature on a bright January
day could reach forty-eight degrees Celsius, well on the way to
making ice *boil*, hockey was hardly the game that came to mind.

But Mr. Lindsay, as president of the Tamarack Minor
Hockey Association, discovered that little in Australia is ever
quite what it first seems. The Australians would pick up all costs,
including airfare, for the Screech Owls peewee hockey team and
their coach and manager. All that was requested in return was
that in the future the Screech Owls invite an Australian team
to take part in a minor hockey tournament put on by the town
of Tamarack.

But there was more. The Australians were convinced they
could not really compete against the Screech Owls in the "Oz
Invitational," and so the games would be exhibition only. To
add to the competitive edge, however, the City of Sydney would
put on a "Mini-Olympics" at the same time, to be held at many
of the same facilities that had been used for the Sydney Summer
Olympics – the best Summer Games ever, many people thought.

"Can I do synchronized swimming?" Nish had asked when Muck read the letter to them in the Owls dressing room after practice.

"Better that than beach volleyball!" Sam had shouted from the other end of the room. "At least that big butt of yours would be under water."

"Imagine Nish in a *thong*!" Sarah had laughed, kicking off her skates.

"People have seen me in less," Nish shot back, his face reddening as he leaned over to loosen his laces.

"Don't remind me," Travis said, wincing at the flood of memories: Nish in the Swedish sauna, Nish and the World's Biggest Skinny Dip at summer hockey camp, Nish running nude on Vancouver's Wreck Beach, Nish planning to "moon" the entire world at Times Square . . .

From the moment Muck read that letter, the excitement had built. They were going to the land of kangaroos, koalas, platypus, crocodiles, and the deadly Great White Shark. They were going to Sydney, that magnificent city they'd all seen on television during the Olympics Games. And they were going to be in their own Mini-Olympics.

Dmitri was talking about running the 100-metre dash. Travis wanted to try the mountain bike course. Liz, who was on a swim team, couldn't believe she'd be getting a chance to try out the Olympic pool. Wilson, probably the Owls' strongest player, wanted to try weightlifting. Little Simon Milliken said he knew how to wrestle. Derek and Jesse wanted to form a team for tennis doubles. Sarah and Sam said they were going to be the Owls' official beach volleyball team, and Sarah, the team's best athlete, also wanted to enter all the races and swimming events.

"Rhythmic gymnastics," Nish had said one day at practice. "I think *that's* my new sport. You know, prancing about and throwing a ribbon up in the air and catching it."

"Get serious," Travis had told him.

"I'm also thinking about synchronized diving," Nish said, leaning back in his stall, his eyes closed dreamily.

"What?" Sam had yelled over. "You and a *boulder*!"

"Nah. Me 'n' you – how about it?"

Nish had meant it as a joke. With his eyes still closed, he hadn't seen Sam winking at Sarah.

"You're on, Big Boy – me 'n' you!"

Nish's eyes had popped open, but it was too late. The whole team loved the idea.

Sam was an excellent diver. There wasn't a player on the team who didn't remember her wild leap from the rocks high over the Ottawa River when they'd gone rafting. But neither was there an Owl who didn't know that Wayne Nishikawa, the World's Biggest Big Talker, was terrified, absolutely petrified, of heights.

Travis had smiled to himself. This was going to be interesting.

In the days that followed, Sarah Cuthbertson, more than any of the other Owls, had become consumed with the upcoming trip. She'd often said her greatest dream was to become a marine biologist, and she told them that Australia was like a dream come true. It was where the Great Barrier Reef was, and its waters offered the finest scuba diving and snorkelling in the world.

"I plan to see lots of seahorses, *and* my first Great White Shark," she said.

It would happen quicker than any of them imagined.

2

It had taken twenty-two hours to fly to Australia, and after they'd been driven to the little hotel they'd be staying in down by Sydney's famous Opera House and Nish had given his ridiculous demonstration of the way toilets flush "backwards" in Australia, the Screech Owls had set out to shake off the jet lag with a quick tour of the harbour and the famous Sydney Aquarium.

A little green-and-yellow-and-red ferry boat – Travis was convinced it was identical to one he'd played with in the tub when he was much younger – had taken them out on a cruise around the magnificent, fin-shaped Opera House and then under the massive Sydney Harbour Bridge. It was a beautiful day, the water almost as blue as the clear sky.

Their guide, Mr. Spears, had pointed way up above the water to the highest spans of the bridge, where it seemed ants were moving along slowly. But they weren't ants – they were *people*. People climbing high over the top span of the enormous bridge.

"We call 'er 'The Coathanger,' mates," Mr. Spears had announced in his strong Australian accent. "Greatest view in all of Oz from up there."

Travis smiled. He liked the way Australians called their country "Oz." They said it with such affection. Travis couldn't think of a nickname that would work for Canada. "Can" sounded, well, *stupid*. People would think you were talking about a toilet, not a country.

"You have to tie ropes around your middle to go up," Mr. Spears told them. "And they charge a good fee – but it's well worth it, mates, well worth it. You should consider it while you're here."

"*No way!*" Nish had shouted.

"We could practise our synchronized dives from there," suggested Sam.

"Practise yourself! I'm not climbing anywhere except outta this stupid boat."

Travis had looked at his old friend. Nish was a bit green. The jet lag, the rolling of the ferry, the sight of people climbing high over the water – it was all a bit much for Nish's sensitive stomach. It was the only part of his friend, Travis thought, that had ever shown any sensitivity at all.

Soon, the bridge was well behind them and the ferry had dropped them off at Darling Harbour. They walked up along the wharf to the massive glass building that housed what Data claimed was the best aquarium anywhere.

"The Sydney Aquarium has saltwater crocodiles," Data said. "Grow more than twenty feet long and will attack and eat an entire cow – or a person, if they feel like it. Most dangerous animal on earth, I think."

"I thought the Great White Shark was," said Fahd.

"Earth, Fahd," corrected Data. "I said *earth* – sharks don't walk on land, do they?"

"Actually," Sarah said, interrupting, "you're both wrong. The truly scary creatures of Australia you wouldn't even notice."

"*Sure*," Nish said sarcastically. "Like what? Killer hamsters? Vampire goldfish? Sabre-toothed bunny rabbits?"

Sarah was smiling slightly. Travis noticed it even if Nish hadn't. He knew that Sarah had Nish right where she wanted him.

"Ever hear of the Box Jellyfish?" she asked.

"*Jell-O* fish?" Nish howled. "You gotta be kidding."

"Jell-EEE fish, dummy, and I'm not kidding," said Sarah. "You swim up against one of them and, if you live, you'll wish you hadn't. It's kind of like being skinned alive and then spray-painted with acid, they say."

"No way I'm even going swimming!" shouted Lars.

"There's none in the waters around Sydney," said Sarah.

"Good!" said Lars. "There better not be."

"In Sydney you have to watch out for the funnel web spider," Sarah said, her little smile returning. She was enjoying herself. "It's the most poisonous spider in the world."

"Will it kill you?" Fahd asked.

"Yes," said Sarah, "but slowly. First you bounce off the walls for a few hours like you're about to explode, then you start shaking, turn blue and shiver until you pass out. If they don't get the antidote into you in time, you're history."

Travis winced. Australia had seemed like such a warm and welcoming country, a bit like Canada, and a bit like the United States, and a bit like England, and a whole lot like itself. The last thing it seemed was dangerous. But now he wasn't so sure.

They had a wonderful tour of the aquarium. They all stood with their noses to the glass as harbour seals swam in dazzling circles only inches away. They saw the fearsome saltwater crocodiles in the "Rivers of the Far North" display. They spent more than an hour at the "Touch Pool," picking up hermit crabs and elephant snails and nervously handing around a shark-egg case as if it might suddenly split open to reveal a miniature "Jaws."

At the Great Barrier Reef display, Sarah found her beloved seahorses. There was a special exhibit of orange Big-belly Seahorses, hundreds of the oddly elegant creatures hovering about in a glass tank. Travis stared in wonder, baffled as to how a small bony fish could look so like a real horse, the arch of the neck and the head almost identical, the big yellow eyes filled with an intelligence and concentration that seemed impossible for such a tiny little thing. Travis felt as if *he* were on display and the seahorses examining him.

He could see how they'd managed to captivate Sarah, even if certain others could not.

"What's so special about these things?" Nish asked, unimpressed.

"They're an inspiration for women," said Sarah, turning her head slightly away as that mysterious smile danced again across her lips.

Nish's face twisted into a question: "What's *that* supposed to mean?"

"What do you know about seahorses, anyway?" Sarah asked.

"That you can't ride them?" Nish answered sarcastically. "That it's tough to find little saddles for them? How the heck should I know anything about them?"

"The males have the babies," said Sarah, winking over the tank at Sam, who was giggling.

"I'm not *stupid*!" Nish shouted.

"Can we vote on that?" Sam called over.

"MEN CAN'T HAVE BABIES," Nish insisted, all but stamping his feet.

"These men do," said Sarah. "The female gives him the eggs to carry, he fertilizes them and carries them in a pouch on his belly and later gives birth to them."

Nish's face was beet-red. "*I'm gonna hurl!*"

"Some of us like the idea," said Sarah.

"Maybe *you* could do it, Nish!" called out Sam. "You've already got the gut for it!"

Nish was trying to answer back. He stammered. He spat. He turned even redder. Then he stomped off, the laughter of the rest of the Owls ringing in his scarlet ears.

Travis felt sorry for his old friend. The girls had been a bit unfair. It wasn't Nish's fault he didn't know about seahorses. It wasn't his fault he was heavy. Travis would even have come to his rescue if Nish didn't always make fun of everyone else's shortcomings.

Saving the best for last, they wandered finally into the huge Oceanarium, a fascinating, twisting series of glassed-in tunnels through the water, where eels, stingrays, sea turtles, a dozen different varieties of fish, and even several sharks swam around them so close that the Owls felt the huge creatures might brush against them – or *bite*!

"We have a special treat for you, mates," said Mr. Spears after a quick discussion with one of the aquarium staff.

"What's that?" asked Fahd. All the Screech Owls were pressing in towards Mr. Spears and the attendant.

The attendant cleared her throat and spoke. "You're about to go through a tank holding a Great White Shark!"

"*NOOOO!*" screamed Sarah.

"*YESSSS!*" screamed Sam, meaning exactly the same thing.

"Yesterday, fishermen off the south coast had a Great White get tangled up in their nets. He was cut loose and placed in a transportation pool, and we've just released him into a special compartment here. No one else has seen him yet. You'll be first."

"*ALL RIGHT!*" the Screech Owls yelled together.

"You'll have to be quiet, though. He's not used to the tanks and he's never seen a group come through before. No tapping on the glass. No sudden movements. Promise?"

"*WE PROMISE!*" the Owls shouted.

Keeping very quiet, they moved into a tunnel that Travis had earlier noticed was blocked off from the public. The barriers were down now, and the lights were on, sending an eerie glow into the glass tunnels ahead of them. It was almost as if they were walking in outer space.

They came into a huge tank where, for the first time, there were no eels or turtles or fish of any kind sliding along the glass. This pool seemed empty, except for a large shadow at the far end.

The shadow moved!

Travis felt the entire group suck in its breath and hold it. It was as if they were suddenly *in* the water, not passing through in air tunnels. No one moved. No one spoke. No one even drew breath.

The Great White turned, its dark back as huge as a boat. It rolled slightly, white belly flashing.

Still no one dared breathe.

It drifted silently across the roof of the tunnel. Then it rolled again, one beady eye scanning the group as if it might be looking for an appetizer before settling down to a main course of peewee hockey team.

It made several passes over them, each time twisting slightly to stare.

Whenever it went by, it was as if a dark cloud were moving overhead. Travis could not believe its size. It was massive.

Its mouth opened slightly, revealing dozens of long, sword-sharp teeth.

"Toss him a Clorets!" snorted Nish.

The attendant immediately hushed him. No one laughed. Even Muck seemed awestruck, his own mouth wide as he stared up.

The shark's huge mouth opened again, bubbles rolling out.

"He's *burping*!" hissed Fahd.

This time someone did laugh: Nish, of course.

The Great White opened wider, and a flush of red-and-white shreds came out.

Travis could hear a quick intake of air as everyone gasped a second time.

What is it? wondered Travis. *Fish guts? Or maybe seal?*

The shark turned and passed again, dropping so low its fins touched the top of the tunnel. Travis could hear them rubbing, almost squeaking, against the glass.

The mouth opened again, and a great burst of bubbles rolled out and raced for the surface.

"Indigestion, pal?" whispered Nish.

The mouth opened even wider, and something else came out.

It was round and very white, trailing something dark, like string.

Travis tried to see as it thumped hard on the glass above their heads, then rolled off the tunnel roof through the churning, bubbling water.

He took a step closer, staring hard.

Not string – *more like hair!*

Black hair.

Down, down the object tumbled. It landed against a rock, bounced gently, then settled back, caught between the rock and an outcrop of coral.

The Screech Owls rushed over, then stopped abruptly.

It was a human head, partially digested – one milky eye staring up at them, the other socket empty.

Travis heard a loud thud behind him.

The attendant had fainted.

3

ish was still throwing up in the bathroom. Fahd was staring blankly at the TV while he flicked through the channels without stopping. Lars was asleep, tossing and twisting under the covers and groaning every now and then as if caught in a nightmare.

Travis was lying on his bed, pressing the tips of his fingers to his throbbing temples and wishing he could just stay there until the last five or six hours somehow magically erased themselves.

There was a light rap on the door. Fahd put down the remote and stood on his tiptoes to see out the peephole.

"It's Sarah," he said. "And Jenny and Sam and Liz."

"Let 'em in," Travis said. The girls were sharing the room next door. Perhaps they'd even heard Nish retching.

Before they could say anything, there came one huge retch from the bathroom, followed by Nish coughing and choking and spitting, then the flush of the toilet and the tap turning on, hard.

They waited, no one saying a word. Fahd began flicking mindlessly once more through the channels, but no one complained and no one asked him to stop. They all stared at the flickering screen, grateful for any distraction.

The door to the bathroom opened, and Nish, a bath towel wrapped around his head, stumbled out and promptly bumped into Sam, who was sitting on the edge of the bed.

The towel unwound to reveal a shining, pink face, eyes swollen and bloodshot, black hair soaking wet. Nish must have had his head right under the tap.

"Feel better, Barf Boy?" Sam asked.

Nish flicked the towel in her direction, snapping it harmlessly in the air.

"Something I ate," he mumbled. "Food poisoning, I guess."

Sarah couldn't help laughing. "Whoever got food poisoning from chocolate bars and Coke?"

"I eat other stuff!" Nish protested.

"No one's ever seen you!" Sarah said, giggling.

"How're you guys doing?" Travis asked.

"Not good," admitted Liz. "I can't get it out of my head."

"Neither can I," said Lars, now wide awake and disentangling himself from his sweat-soaked sheets.

The telephone rang, and Lars, who was closest, picked it up.

"Hello?" Lars said uncertainly. He nodded several times. Then said, "Okay," and hung up the receiver.

The others stared, waiting.

"It was Mr. Dillinger," Lars explained. "Muck's lined up a game for us. We're on the ice in an hour."

"*In an hour!*" Sam shouted, as if it were impossible.

But in a flash everyone was in action – Lars stabbing his feet into his shoes, even Nish diving into the heap in the corner that passed for his luggage to pull out a clean T-shirt and extra socks. They weren't tired. They'd slept most of the flight and, besides, the events of the past few hours had made relaxation impossible.

Muck was doing exactly the right thing, Travis realized. He was forcing them back into the world they knew best.

The Owls needed ice time.

4

ravis knew his comfort zone. It smelled of concrete and industrial cleaner and hot dogs rolling endlessly on a stainless steel grill. It sounded like a sharpening stone running dryly across a skate blade. Like the laughter of a dressing room, and the strange silence of a rink when the Zamboni has just finished. It was the sight of shining new ice just waiting for Travis Lindsay's skate blades to draw his favourite designs over it.

And Muck Munro knew it, too. He knew what the Screech Owls liked better than anything else in the world: a game where they could *play* – a game where the stands were empty and everyone could relax and enjoy the game they loved. It was just what they needed.

"We're playing the local rep team," Muck said. "Some of them are new to hockey, and they've never played a North American team before, so go easy on them and just have some fun. Don't even think of this as a practice. It's shinny – understand?"

Travis nodded. As captain, he had to understand a little

better than the rest; it would be his job to make sure the shinny game went the way Muck wanted it to. That meant not embarrassing anyone, not running up the score if they had a chance, no rough stuff, certainly no fights, and no mouthing off.

In other words, it was Travis Lindsay's job to make sure Wayne Nishikawa was kept in line.

Travis leaned over and checked out Nish. As usual, his best friend was dressing in a far corner of the room, everyone keeping a distance from the bag of equipment the girls called "The Skunk's Armpit." Nish was burrowing away in it like a raccoon in a garbage bag, pulling out garter straps and old underwear and yellow-stained T-shirts. Travis figured if Nish could stick his head into his own hockey bag without hurling then he must be feeling better. He was back to being Nish, all-star defenceman for the Tamarack Screech Owls.

They were playing in the Macquarie Ice Rink, which was attached to a shopping centre out Waterloo Road. According to Mr. Dillinger, it was the only hockey rink in Sydney. In Canada, a city the size of Sydney would have had dozens. The building was simple but functional, with roomy dressing rooms, the lines and circles in the ice surface freshly painted for the tournament, and air-conditioning powerful enough to keep the ice hard and fast.

They were playing, appropriately, the Sydney Sharks. They had a logo almost identical to the one worn by the NHL's San Jose Sharks, their socks matched their sweaters, and, from what Travis could make out in the brief warm-up, they had first-rate equipment. Stepping out onto the ice surface, they looked like an elite peewee team from a city like Toronto or Vancouver or Detroit.

It was after they took that first step that the difference was noticeable.

Only three or four of the players could skate as well as the Owls. A couple of them were well over on their ankles. One carried his stick as if it were an alien weapon that had popped through a time warp into his puzzled hands.

Sarah drew even with Travis then spun around to face him as she skated backwards up-ice.

"Check out number 17," she said, before speeding effortlessly away.

Travis followed the direction of Sarah's pointed stick. The Sharks were circling about their own net, firing pucks at random while they waited for their goaltender to take up his position.

Travis would have known who Sarah meant even if he hadn't seen the number flash as the Shark's tallest player curled back towards the net, slapping his stick on the ice for a puck.

Number 17 was tall, with blond curly hair sticking out under the back of his helmet and his jersey tucked into his hockey pants on the right side, Wayne Gretzky style. He moved with a grace that set him apart at once from every one of his teammates. He skated with that strange, bowlegged stride that has been the trademark of so many of hockey's loveliest skaters – Bobby Orr and Gilbert Perreault from the old days, or more recently Alexander Mogilny and Pavel Bure – and he had the same quirky little shoulder shuffle that Sarah sometimes did when she was about to change pace. He was one of those players who seemed naturally at ease with everything he touched: equipment, sweater, stick, skates, ice. A little shuffle, and he shot ahead like he'd come out of a cannon – yet Travis had barely noticed the change in stride.

Number 17 shot, high and hard, ringing the puck off the crossbar and over the glass into the protective netting behind the boards. He raised his glove in a fist.

Travis liked him instantly. He didn't even know number 17's name, but if he had a thing about trying to put pucks off crossbars, Travis knew they already had much in common.

He looked across ice to where Sarah was working on her crossovers along the blueline. There was something different about her. She always did a dance of crossovers across the blueline, but always, always, she faced her own net while doing them. This time she was turned around, closely watching number 17.

Muck blew his whistle hard at centre ice. The Owls stopped immediately, shovelling the loose pucks back towards the net and heading for their coach, who was standing with the coach of the Sydney Sharks.

The players all arrived at once, most of the Owls using cute little referee stops – one skate turned sideways and tucked behind the other, body tilting back to dig in for a soft stop – while some of the Sharks were using the "snowplough" stop that Travis had last used in initiation hockey.

This wasn't going to be much of a game.

"A little mix-and-match," Muck said, using his whistle to point. "Lindsay, Cuthbertson, Noorizadeh, Staples, Nishikawa – move over and line up on this blueline."

Travis looked at Sarah, who shrugged and pushed over on one leg. Fahd and Jenny and Nish followed.

The other coach called out five names, including the Sharks goaltender, and told them to join the five Owls on the blueline.

Muck looked over, a half grin playing at the corners of his mouth.

"Okay," he said. "Change sweaters, all of you."

The five Sharks were already struggling out of their sweaters. Sarah looked once at Travis, made a quick face, and dropped her gloves to remove her helmet. Travis followed suit, kissing the inside of his sweater as he dragged it back off. None of the Sharks players wore a "C," or even an "A" for assistant captain. He hated giving up his treasured "C" for any reason.

One of the Sharks tossed his sweater at Travis. "Here ya gow, myte," he said, smiling. At first Travis thought the kid was joking, putting on a fake Australian accent, but then he realized it was his actual way of talking – it was just that it sounded much more strange in a hockey rink than it did out in the streets of Sydney.

When the sweaters had been exchanged, the two coaches spoke to their new players.

"Evens things up," the Sydney coach said to the Screech Owls now wearing Sharks jerseys. "Muck tells me you two" – he pointed to Travis and Sarah – "should play with Wiz."

Wiz? Travis wondered. Who the heck was *Wiz*?

"*Wiz?*" Sarah asked, blinking in confusion.

"Him," the coach explained, pointing with his stick towards number 17, who was leaning on his stick, helmet up, smiling back at them.

"That's a funny name," said Sarah.

"His real name's Bruce," laughed the coach. "But the kids all call him Wiz. Short for Wizard, eh?"

"*Wizard?*" Sarah asked, still puzzled.

"Wizard of *Oz*," the coach said. "*Get it?*"

5

t didn't take them long to "get it." With Muck refereeing while Mr. Dillinger worked the Screech Owls bench, the shinny game got under way with number 17 at centre between Sarah and Travis, and with Fahd and Nish going over to give the Sharks' defence a little depth and Jenny in net to give them a fighting chance.

It felt strange for Travis not to have Sarah at centre and Dmitri flying down right wing, but strange only for the first couple of shifts. By midway through the first period, it felt like he and Sarah had spent their entire lives as wingers for the Wizard of Oz.

Travis had seen talent like this rarely. Certainly Slava, Dmitri's Russian cousin, had similar skating skills, but this Aussie kid, Wiz, seemed to see the game as well as Sarah herself.

It was almost impossible to get to know anyone in the midst of a hockey game. The three sat together on the bench when their line was off, but they talked little except about plays they might try. Wiz – Travis still had trouble thinking anyone might be called that – was certainly friendly enough, but he was also all business during the game, even if it was a meaningless exhibition match.

"What's the big D's name, mate?" he asked Travis at one point.

"Wayne Nishikawa," Travis said. "Everybody calls him Nish."

"He's bloody good, eh?"

Travis nodded, a bit reluctantly. Nish was in full show-off mode, just as Travis knew he would be in an exhibition match. He was lugging the puck, keeping the puck, trying to score the fancy goals. But Jeremy was hot in the Owls' net, and no matter how much Nish pressed he wasn't able to beat him.

It was a strange game. The players' ability varied widely, but the coaches were careful to keep the weaker lines against each other – Sydney players in Owls sweaters against Sydney players on the Sharks' side – and Travis and Sarah and their new centre against the top Owls lines. Ten minutes into the game, no one had scored a single goal.

Travis couldn't believe some of the things Wiz could do. He had exceptional speed, but he wasn't a glory hog. He'd no sooner get the puck than he'd be looking for either Travis or Sarah on a break, and he used the points brilliantly, cycling pucks in the corner until he saw an opening to fire a pass out to Nish or Fahd or one of the Sydney defenders for a good shot. Wiz and Nish were clearly feeding off each other, trying to outdo each other with the perfect, unexpected pass.

Wiz also had a trick that Travis would have given anything to learn. Just like an NHLer, Wiz could scoop up a puck from the ice, bounce it a couple of times on his stick, catch it dead on the blade, and then hand it over to Muck for a faceoff. Even Muck seemed impressed.

Travis couldn't count the hours that he and Sarah had spent trying to scoop pucks the same way.

Andy Higgins scored first for the Owls on a hard slapper that beat Jenny to the five-hole. Then Simon Milliken scored. Fahd scored on a tip-in, and one of the better Sharks scored on a lucky rebound.

"Well, mates," Wiz said as they sat on the bench waiting for their next shift. "What say we put on a little show for them?"

"You're on," said Sarah, heading over the boards.

They changed on the fly, Sarah racing back to pick up a loose puck that Nish kicked up as a Shark pressed him against the boards behind his net. Sarah turned, reversed directions, and flew around the net and headed up Travis's side.

Travis instinctively crossed over.

Sarah sent a high pass to Wiz, which he knocked down easily with his glove and kicked up onto his stick. He flew up across centre, looking for Travis on the far side.

Travis rapped the ice for a pass, and Wilson, trying to read the play, dove to block the pass everyone thought was coming.

But Wiz faked the pass, dropped the puck back into his skates, and, kicking it back and forth between his blades like a kid with a soccer ball, danced around Sam and moved in alone.

He came in hard, and stopped dead, throwing Jeremy off completely. Without even a glance, he passed back to Sarah, now driving hard for the net. Sarah stickhandled quickly around Jeremy and threw it back to Wiz for the shot.

But Wiz didn't even try to take the puck with his stick. He

angled his skates so the puck hit his left blade, then his right, and rebounded perfectly across the crease onto Travis's stick.

The net was completely empty. Travis could have done a math problem he had so much time. He just tucked the puck in and turned to look at Wiz, who was grinning from ear to ear.

"Was that on purpose?" Travis asked as Wiz and the others came to slap his back.

"You'll never know, mate," Wiz answered, laughing.

They had an hour to play. The Owls went ahead, the Sharks caught up. Sarah scored a lovely goal on her usual shoulder-fake move. Dmitri scored a typical Dmitri backhander that shot the water bottle off the net.

"What's the score?" Sarah shouted as they realized time was winding down. The Zamboni driver was already starting up his machine.

"Who knows?" said Wiz.

"I think we need one to win," Travis said.

"One it is, then, mate," Wiz said as the coach called their line for the final faceoff.

Wiz won it easily. He shovelled the puck to Nish, who swung back and around his net, hitting Sarah on the far side.

Sarah passed cross-ice to Travis, who chopped the puck into the middle for Wiz, who was already at full speed.

Wiz hit the blueline in front of Sam and did a perfect "spin-nerama" move, leaving Sam on her knees while he spun like a top around her, the puck moving perfectly with him.

Wiz moved in behind the goal, holding the puck. Both Travis and Sarah raced for the sides of the net, trusting in a pass.

Wiz passed to Sarah, who rapped it back.

Wilson tried to take out Wiz, but Wiz bounced the puck off the back of the net as Wilson flew by into the boards.

Sam took out Travis. Andy, coming back hard, took out Sarah. Simon Milliken tied up Nish on the point so he couldn't break for the net and a pass.

Wiz stickhandled so loosely he might have been the only person on the ice. He looked up, smiling.

Travis tried to scramble back, but Sam had too good an angle on him and was too strong for him to break away.

Wiz did his little scoop move, and instantly the puck was lying on his stick blade as if he were about to hand it to the referee.

Is he quitting? Travis wondered. *Did the horn blow?*

But he wasn't quitting. With the puck still balanced perfectly on his blade, Wiz skated out from behind the net, looped the stick in a fake that sent Jeremy over flat on his back, and then *tossed* rather than shot the puck high in under the crossbar.

Muck's whistle and the horn blew at exactly the same time.

The Sharks – and the Owls who were temporary Sharks – mobbed Wiz, who was laughing at what he'd done.

"No fair!" Jeremy was shouting to Muck and slamming his stick on the ice at the same time. "That's illegal."

Muck just shook his head, grinning.

"Never seen a goal like it," he said. "But there's nothing in the rule books to say you can't do it."

6

Murder, however, followed no rules. There was nothing fair about it. Nothing to say who might do it, or how.

Travis wasn't even certain it was murder, though a head cut clean off certainly suggested foul play.

The facts were obvious: Great White Shark burps up human head. Obviously, someone had to die to produce the human head. But no one knew who, or how, or, for that matter, where all the other body parts were.

"GRISLY DISCOVERY FOR CANADIAN HOCKEY VISITORS," said the headline on the front page of that day's *Sydney Morning Herald*. Below the headline was a photograph of the Screech Owls being brought out of the Aquarium by first-aid workers. Sam was bawling into Sarah's shoulder. Nish looked like he'd already thrown up.

It was the first time Nish hadn't raced to see his picture in a newspaper. "Food poisoning," he kept saying. "But no one will believe me." And no one did.

By the next day, they had a little more to go on. Police pathol-
ogists had determined the head belonged to a male Asian, probably aged between twenty-five and fifty. There had apparently
been some minor dental work done on the man's teeth, but the
chances of finding the dental records of a man who could have
come from anywhere in the world, who was but one of approx-
imately a *billion* men in that age group who could be roughly
described as "Asian," were remote if not impossible.

"Who *was* he?" Data kept asking. He had used his laptop to
connect to the Internet and had scoured every Southeast Asian
newspaper he could find published in English to see if a man
had gone missing at sea, but he'd come up with nothing.

The police weren't much further ahead. Mr. Dillinger had
phoned them to ask if they had any new information. The poor
shark had been drugged so it could be examined, but an X-ray
and ultrasound had indicated no other human body parts inside,
which meant the shark had somehow scooped up the head as it
fell down through the water or else while it lay on the sea
bottom. According to the Sydney coroner, marks on the neck
area suggested the head had been severed by something other
than shark's teeth.

"Which means," Data added, "that the man was decapitated."

Mr. Dillinger grimaced. He didn't like to put it that way,
but obviously, the man's head had come off somehow. In a terrible boating accident? Struck by a propeller? Caught on an
anchor line?

"Chopped off with a machete!" Fahd offered.

Mr. Dillinger just looked at Fahd, the team manager's big, wrinkled face looking sad and anxious for a change of topic.

"But why?" Sam asked.

"And *who*?" Sarah added.

That morning, the Owls set out for Homebush Bay, the site of the Summer Olympic Games. They took the Green line train out to Lidcombe Station, then switched to the Yellow line that looped out around Olympic Park and back.

It was another beautiful day. Travis was already beginning to notice a major difference about Australians. No one here ever talked about the weather. At home it was almost a constant topic of conversation – *Will it last? Enjoy it while it's here! What's the forecast?* But in Sydney the weather seemed entirely taken for granted. If every day was bright and warm, if every sky was blue, what was the point in discussing it?

Olympic Park was fantastic. They walked along the waterways and parks around the site and saw where the Olympic Athletes Village had been. They toured the Olympic pool with its high, jagged "shark's fin" architecture. They saw the Olympic Stadium where the stunning opening ceremonies had been held and the Olympic Flame lit.

There were other peewee teams already there, all of them excitedly preparing for the Mini-Olympics part of the tournament, and if Travis thought some of the Australian players looked out of their element on ice, they certainly looked at home here.

"I think I'll try pole vault," Dmitri said.

Several of the Owls went over to the pole vault area with Dmitri to watch. He picked out a thin, flexible pole, paced off his run, walked back once to measure the height he'd need to clear the bar, walked out, paused, and then ran, dropping the tip of the pole so it caught and whipped him high, perfectly shooting his legs up and away before releasing the pole while he floated easily over the bar.

"Is there anything Dmitri can't do?" Sam asked, laughing and cheering with the rest.

They spent much of the afternoon trying out different venues and equipment. Dmitri and Sarah kept pretty much to the track. Fahd went over to the archery field with Lars. Jeremy and Gordie Griffith spent time in the basketball court pretending they were Vince Carter and trying to slam-dunk off a small trampoline that some of the workers had set up in front of one of the nets. Derek and Jesse took on Liz and Jenny in doubles tennis at the same courts where Serena and Venus Williams had won the gold medal in doubles.

Everybody was busy but one lonely Screech Owl: Wayne Nishikawa. He wouldn't join Travis at the handball courts. He wouldn't play tennis. He wouldn't go with Fahd to the archery. Sarah asked him if he wanted to swim in the Olympic pool, but he wasn't interested. Sam asked him if the two of them should work on their diving, but he said he wasn't ready.

"Look," Travis said, "if you had your choice of anything, what would you do?"

Nish didn't miss a beat. "Go to Bondi Beach."

Travis remembered that Bondi Beach, on the other side of the city, was where they had held the beach volleyball competition. But hadn't they torn down the volleyball stadium when it was over?

"There's nothing there," Travis said.

"That's what *you* think," Nish said.

Travis watched in astonishment as Nish dug deep into his wallet and produced a page torn from a Sydney guide book he must have picked up in the hotel lobby. He carefully unfolded the page and handed it over, a look of triumph on his beaming face.

Travis took the page, and saw at once what had caught his friend's eye.

BONDI BEACH CULTURE

No visit to Sydney is complete without a visit to Australia's most famous beach. But visitors be warned – Nude Sunbathing is Everywhere at Bondi!

Travis handed the crumpled page back to Nish.

"You never give up, do you?"

"Everyone has a calling in life," smiled Nish. "Some become priests. Some become doctors or teachers. I'm a natural-born nudist."

"C'mon," Travis suggested, changing the topic, "the girls are at the diving pool. Let's at least check it out."

They headed along the wide Olympic Boulevard until they came to the International Aquatic Centre. A side door was open for the visiting peewee teams, and they raced up the steps and in. The building took Travis's breath away when he saw how massive it was inside. It seemed there were as many seats as in an NHL hockey rink. The Olympic pool was at one end, with the medal podium still there beside it. At the far end of the building was the diving pool, with the one-metre and three-metre boards flanking the high tower. From where Travis stood, the tower appeared as high as a bungee jump – only with nothing but the water below to break your fall.

"*Come on up!*" a voice called.

Travis and Nish scanned high into the ceiling. It was Sarah at the very top of the tower. She was wearing a red maple leaf Canadian swimsuit, and her hair was dripping wet. *Had she already jumped?*

"KKKAAAA–WWWAAAA–BUNGAAAA!"

The jungle cry came from behind Sarah. A blur of red roared past her – red swimsuit, red hair, red face – and out onto the diving platform. It spun once in a perfect somersault and plummeted down, down, down, to crash into the water with a splash so big it reached Travis and Nish.

Sam.

"That must have stung," said Nish.

But before Travis could answer, the water broke again, wet red hair flying, fist pumping, red face defiant.

"EEEEEEE–AAWWWWWWW–KEEEEEEE!"

"She's insane," Nish said matter-of-factly. Sam, yelling the same stupid yells Nish always yelled. Sam, the centre of attention just like Nish always had to be. But according to Nish, *she* was the insane one.

Sam swam to where the two boys stood and eased out of the pool. She walked right by them and headed straight back to the tower, hands on her hips, water dripping in a trail behind her.

"You here for our practice, Big Boy?" she called over her shoulder to Nish.

"Didn't bring a bathing suit," Nish answered, flustered.

"Since when did *that* ever stop you?" Sarah yelled down from high up the tower.

Then she jumped, as graceful in mid-air as she was on the ice, as completely in control falling as she ever was skating or running. She completed a perfect jackknife, then opened up to slice into the water with hardly a ripple.

"She's good," said Sam, nodding in approval.

"She's good at everything," said Travis.

"I gotta get going," Nish said. He was already walking towards the door.

"What about our practice?" Sam yelled.

"Later," Nish said. "It'll have to be later. I'm busy right now."

Travis stared after his friend. He had seen a familiar look in Nish's eyes. It had nothing to do with being "busy." Nish was just terrified of heights – almost as much as he was afraid of being laughed at.

7

T. here was a note waiting at the front desk for Sarah and Travis when they came down for breakfast the next morning:

Dear linemates!

My dad is taking the boat out today. We've room and snorkelling equipment for the three of us and four more. Check with your coach – my dad has already called.

Wiz

"*Seahorses!*" Sarah shouted. "*Finally, I'm going to get to see real wild seahorses!*"

She ran straight back to her room to tell the other girls. Travis figured he should check first with Muck. The Screech Owls coach said he had indeed got a call, and there was no problem with it as far as he was concerned. Wiz's father, it turned out, was a former NHL player, Des Roberts, who'd ended up working in Australia helping build ice surfaces, and now lived here permanently. Muck and he had even known each other back in junior days.

"He's fully certified for diving," said Muck. "So's his wife, and she's going along, too. So off with you – and enjoy yourselves."

Wiz had said there would be room for Sarah and Travis and four more. Sarah was bringing Sam and Jenny. Travis figured he'd ask Fahd and Nish.

"*Snorkelling?*" Nish said, rolling the word around his tongue like it was something a pig wouldn't swallow.

"Yeah," Travis said. "C'mon. You took that course – here's your chance."

Nish shrugged. The previous winter Travis had talked him into signing up for scuba lessons at the local pool. Sarah had taken the lessons too, and though all had learned how to use air tanks well enough to pass the course, none of them had dived anywhere but in the pool.

"I'm up for it!" shouted Fahd.

"We have to go out in a boat?" Nish asked.

"Get real," Travis said, losing his patience. "You want us to swim out the harbour?"

But Travis knew what Nish was getting at. He really did have a weak stomach. He didn't like heights. He didn't like being at sea.

But Travis knew how to get him. "Sam's going," he said. "You wouldn't want her to think you're chicken, would you?"

Nish reddened a bit, then suddenly brightened. "What about snorkelling at Bondi Beach?" he suggested.

A horrific picture formed immediately in Travis's mind. Women out for a topless swim suddenly screaming and racing for shore, everyone convinced it must be a shark – until the big, sunburnt back of a snorkelling Nish rises from the waters, grin wider than his face mask.

"We're going farther than that," said Travis. "Grab your suit and let's get going."

Nish didn't move. He seemed undecided.

Finally, he headed over to his pile of clothes on the floor, kicked several times at the heap, reached in deep, and came up with his beloved Mighty Ducks of Anaheim swimsuit. It was a piece of clothing, Travis noticed, that Nish far preferred to throw off than pull on.

They took off from the marina at Mosman Bay, almost directly across the big harbour from the Opera House. Mr. Roberts had a beautiful boat. It was pure white, with sleeping quarters below for eight, a small galley for cooking, and even a tiny washroom. The boat was outfitted for deep-sea fishing and cruising, with an elevated bridge for the controls and a high antenna for radio communication and navigation. It was called *Puck*, a name that Travis figured would have been lost on every person who had ever seen the boat – right up until the moment the Screech Owls came aboard.

Wiz and his parents were great hosts. They had hamburgers and hot dogs cooking on the barbecue on deck, and a cooler full of ice-cold Cokes ready to go the moment they left the marina. The kids ate and drank as the Robertses took turns showing off the various sights. They passed by the Taronga Zoo – Nish claimed he could see giraffes staring out above the trees – and saw where the prime minister and the governor-general lived. Then, with the towering Sydney Harbour Bridge growing smaller in their wake, they headed out through the mouth of the harbour into the open sea, where they turned right – *starboard*, Travis reminded himself – to travel due south along the high rocks of the oceanside bluffs.

The ocean was rolling. The big boat rode the swells nicely and moved at a good pace. Travis checked Nish, who seemed in fine spirits. He was standing at the bow, the wind blowing his black hair straight back, and he was smiling as he watched the shoreline.

Finally he pointed. "*Bondi Beach?*" he called up to Mr. Roberts, who was standing on the bridge with Wiz, the two of them consulting a chart.

Mr. Roberts – a big man with large hands and a crooked nose he said proved he'd once played in the NHL – looked up, stared hard towards shore, and then nodded back at Nish.

"*You got binoculars?*" Nish shouted.

Wiz hurried down from the bridge with the binoculars, holding them out for Nish.

"How powerful are they?" Nish asked. He seemed almost frantic.

"Real good, mate," said Wiz. "What d'ya want 'em for?"

"*Topless sunbathers!*" Sam shouted from the other side of the boat.

"*You have a mental case on your boat, you know!*" added Sarah.

"You're sure he's not an Aussie?" Wiz laughed. "He sure acts like an Aussie bloke!"

Nish almost yanked the binoculars away from Wiz. He put them to his eyes, adjusted the focus, and leaned out in a desperate effort to get closer to the fabled beach.

Wiz held on to Nish's shoulder to make sure he didn't end up as shark bait.

Nish scanned the shoreline back and forth.

"*See anything?*" Sam called.

"They're not *strong* enough!" Nish whined.

"Sorry about that, mate," laughed Wiz. "You'll just have to make do with some topless seahorses, I guess."

"*And they're the men!*" Sarah and Jenny shrieked together.

"Very funny," Nish grumbled.

"Very, very funny."

hey cruised for nearly two hours, the sun warming their backs and dancing off the crests of the gentle swells. It was a beautiful day, the sky sprinkled with curious gulls riding the wind currents high above the boat and the air so warm the kids were soon stripped down to just their swimsuits and a thick layer of sunscreen.

Mr. and Mrs. Roberts were the kind of parents a kid only dreams of: rock music blared from speakers set up on either side of the bridge, the cooler was never out of cold pop, and they had enough chocolate bars and licorice to satisfy even the world's number-one sweet tooth, which belonged, of course, to Nish.

Nish was holding up well. He had his Oakley sunglasses sitting perfectly on the peak of his brand-new Billabong baseball cap. He had his Mighty Ducks swimsuit on, and he lay, stomach down, on a huge beach towel, his legs waving in the air while he pounded out the beat on the deck with one fist and held a giant half-eaten Oh Henry! chocolate bar in the other.

Nothing green about Nish's gills, Travis thought. At least not yet.

Nish, however, was not the centre of attention. That honour went to Wiz, who was entertaining the girls with a little air concert, hopping around the deck on one foot while he picked out a wild imaginary guitar solo. Sam and Sarah and Jenny were all up and dancing to the music. Fahd had a couple of wooden salad spoons out and was playing along on the drums. Mrs. Roberts must have noticed the salad spoons, but she was saying nothing. Wiz and his new friends were welcome to enjoy themselves any way they wished.

"*Up ahead!*" Mr. Roberts shouted from the bridge.

Travis got up from the towel where he was lying beside Nish and put his hand above his eyes, trying to shield them from the sun. It was almost impossible to see, the way the sun was skipping off the waves, but eventually the boat swung to the port side and Travis was able to make out what lay ahead.

It was an island out of a movie. It lay like a pearl-encircled emerald in the sparkling blue ocean. The sand looked almost white. On each side rocks rose from the sand up to a plateau, where trees seemed to wave at them in the light wind coming out of the east.

Mr. Roberts let up on the throttle and eased farther to port, as though he planned to circle the island. Travis couldn't understand why. If ever he had seen a natural landing site, it was dead ahead, on the sand.

"*There's the reef!*" Mrs. Roberts yelled out. She was leaning over the bow, straining to see, golden curls – exactly the same as Wiz's – bouncing in the wind.

Mr. Roberts nodded and swung the wheel hard, bringing the boat around in a full circle.

"*Drop anchor!*" he shouted.

Wiz immediately set to work. He called Fahd and Travis over to help him throw the anchor over the side, then pushed a button that released the anchor cable. The anchor struck the bottom, and he pushed the button again, setting it securely.

The boat slowed and stopped, rocking in the gentle waves.

"We're going to dive here!" Mr. Roberts called down to the kids. "After, we'll take the inflatable in to the beach for a little picnic. Okay?"

"*O-kay!*" the Owls shouted together.

Wiz was already hauling out the gear. There were masks, fins, snorkels, gloves, even a couple of large underwater flashlights.

"You've all snorkelled before?" Mr. Roberts asked.

"Sure."

"Yeah."

"Travis and Nish and I have our scuba diving certificates," Sarah said.

"You do?" Mrs. Roberts said, surprised.

"But we've only ever done it in a pool," added Travis.

"Well," Mr. Roberts said, pleased. "Wiz and I dive, too. And I think we've got enough equipment to go around – maybe the five of us will get out if we've time."

First, though, they snorkelled. The three girls went with Mr. Roberts, the three boys with Wiz, all of them advised not to touch a thing unless either Mr. Roberts or Wiz said it was all right. Mrs. Roberts would stay in the boat so she could help out in an emergency.

"I've a good book," she told them. "I'm perfectly happy right here."

Travis put his equipment on, sat on the ledge just above the water at the stern, and let himself fall in backwards, the same way he'd been taught to enter the water while scuba diving.

But he'd never felt water like this before. It seemed, somehow, brighter and lighter than any water he had swum in before. He'd snorkelled all over his grandparents' little lake at the cottage, but that water was dark even if you looked at it in a glass, and it was impossible to see down more than ten or twelve feet. This was more like a pool – but better. He could taste the saltwater on his lips. He could feel it stinging where he'd scraped his shin on the coffee table in the hotel room. But it also felt so clean, almost as if he were being scrubbed by the ocean as he moved through it with his head down, his arms dangling by his side, and his legs lightly kicking.

It seemed he could see forever. The light slipped and shook down through the water and bounced off the bottom. He could see plants moving, and fish – more fish than he had ever imagined possible – moving in and out of coral banks that were themselves so vibrant he could barely believe the colours.

There were pink and orange sponges, all of them moving so slowly in the water it seemed they were swaying to music. There were brilliant fire-red beds of soft coral, and dark, brainlike stands of hard coral. Wiz used a thumbs-up or thumbs-down signal to let them know what could be lightly touched and what should be avoided. It seemed to Travis that half the creatures they were seeing had stingers. He wondered how Wiz ever kept them all straight. He hoped he could.

With Wiz leading the way, they moved into shallower waters and began diving down to pick up shells and crabs and examine them. At one point Wiz grabbed a green turtle by the back legs and swam with it, aiming towards Nish, who turned suddenly, screamed a huge wall of bubbles, and headed fast for the surface. A moment later, he was back down again, as enchanted by the colours and light and sea creatures as the rest of them.

The two groups swam together for a while. Wiz dove down deep and came back up with a large orange sea star, which he handed to Sarah. She took it as if it were a flower and gently carried it back to the bottom and set it down.

A shadow moved off to the right!

Travis turned, startled. A huge ray was swimming beside him, the fin closest to Travis lifting like a huge, lazy wing as it turned away.

Mr. Roberts expertly grabbed onto the ray as it passed, a hand on each of the huge fish's "shoulders," and rode it along for a while.

He signalled Nish to come and join him.

Nish scrambled deeper, his motions rough and awkward compared to the extraordinary elegance of the big fish.

Mr. Roberts held the ray tight while Nish placed his hands where Mr. Roberts' had been. Once Nish had a grip, Mr. Roberts let go.

The big fish moved off, hauling Nish, kicking madly, with it. It saw Sarah and Sam, drifting just in front while they watched and laughed at Nish, and it turned abruptly, almost throwing him off.

But Nish held tight. The ray came straight at Travis, saw him, and banked again. Travis stared into his friend's face. He saw fear and total joy at the same time.

Nish opened his mouth wide, bubbles scattering.

Travis heard a muffled roar, Nish shouting.

"KAAAAAA-(*gulp*)-WWWAAAAAA-(*gulp*)-BUNGAAAA!"

9

"Y ou really want to see seahorses, do you?" Mr. Roberts asked after they'd all come back to the boat for a rest.

"More than anything else," said Sarah.

"There's some thick seagrass growing just off the far side of the island. I've seen them in there. I've also seen the odd seadragon there."

"*Seadragon?*" said Sarah, her brow furrowing.

"You like seahorses," said Mr. Roberts, "you'll *love* seadragons. They're very rare, and found only in these waters. Only place in the world, as a matter of fact. They're like seahorses – both are what they call pipefish – only a million times more exotic. There's two types – the Weedy Seadragon and the Leafy Seadragon, which is even weirder-looking. Think of something that's half seahorse and half Christmas tree and you'll be close. Once you see one, you'll never forget it."

"*And they're here!*" Sarah said.

"I've seen some. Can't guarantee it, but if you and the other kids want to try fitting on that scuba equipment in the hold, I'll take you down for a look."

"*YESSSS!*" Sarah shouted, then immediately blushed with embarrassment.

Travis wasn't certain it was such a good idea. Sure, they knew how to scuba dive, but their only experience had been in the town pool, where the greatest danger lay in slipping on the soap in the shower. Here, there were moray eels and poisonous jellyfish and stingrays and killer puffers and, of course, the most dangerous shark in the oceans, the Great White.

But Mr. Roberts and Wiz said they knew the reef and the island and the seaweed beds beyond as well as they knew their own backyard.

"*Better!*" said Wiz. "The only time I'm ever in the backyard is when I'm mowing the lawn!"

Mrs. Roberts and the others set off in the inflatable boat across the coral reef to the beach. Mr. Roberts, Wiz, Sarah, Nish, and Travis pulled up the anchor and took a wide, safe sweep around the island before anchoring again.

The light was different here. Instead of bouncing and rippling off the bottom, it seemed to die in a dark green ebbing and flowing mass that was the seagrass.

They suited up, checked their air, and dropped again into the water. They went down deep and stayed deep. The only sound Travis could hear was coming from his own bubbles.

Travis found the training coming back to him. The tank at first felt cumbersome on his back, but soon he grew used to it and he could slip along the bottom almost like the ray Nish had been riding. A small shift of his shoulders and he could turn; a single flick of one flipper and he could shift directions. In and out of the seaweed clumps he twisted and turned, feeling more a part of the ocean than he had imagined possible.

There were small fish everywhere, bright silvery ones that moved in huge schools, rainbow-coloured ones that slipped in and out of coral caves. Sarah and Wiz came across a school – a *herd*? – of seahorses and waved the others over, and they watched the funny little creatures almost bouncing along the currents as they moved through the seagrass.

To his far left Travis saw Mr. Roberts signalling. He had his finger up to his mouthpiece. He wanted them to move carefully.

Down into the waving grass they followed him, until he came to a stop before a large clump growing above a huge chunk of white coral.

He parted several strands and pointed.

Inside, moving along a floating blade of grass, was the strangest creature Travis had ever seen.

It looked a bit like a seahorse that had been through a wringer. Its head was miniature, its "ears" seemed like something from a space movie. It looked as if it were dressed all over in little leaves, the greenish gold fronds fluttering like humming-bird wings as the slender creature moved.

Mr. Roberts held out a finger and the seadragon cozied up to it, wrapping its odd leafy tail about his finger. He moved the exquisite little creature over directly in front of Sarah's mask.

Travis could see Sarah's eyes. They were wide and as alive as the creature itself. She was in love!

Wiz pointed off in the distance. There were more seadragons moving through the grasses. He pointed again. More still!

They split up. Wiz, Nish, and Travis followed a small group of seadragons as they moved, half swimming, half drifting, along a steep slope down into deeper waters, where more weed rippled in the distance. It seemed there were seadragons everywhere. They floated around the boys like falling snowflakes.

Wiz pointed to a huge green turtle that had been roused by the human invaders and was quickly moving away along the sandy bottom.

The boys gave chase, just able to keep pace with their flippers. He was huge, big enough for them all to hitch a ride on, and they began chasing harder.

The turtle turned sharply, vanishing under a mass of weed and through a narrow gap in the rocks.

Wiz made the turn perfectly.

Nish missed, and took the long way around.

Travis followed Wiz, reaching out to grab the rocks and propel himself through the opening.

Wiz had caught the turtle by one large fin. He was indicating that Travis should take the other.

Travis moved swiftly. He seized the large flipper and was instantly surprised by the strength of the animal. But he held fast.

The turtle kept swimming, oblivious to his two hitchhikers. They were moving quickly. Travis turned, and Wiz gave a thumbs-up with his free hand. Travis didn't have the confidence to loosen his grip, so he smiled a burst of bubbles. Wiz laughed, his face vanishing in his own bubbles.

It was like flying. Over banks of coral and down tight to the sand they sped. Through long funnels of grass and in between the rocks.

Finally Wiz let go, and Travis did the same. The turtle, without so much as a look back, vanished into the deeper, darker waters.

The two boys turned towards each other, laughing and high-fiving until they realized they were alone.

No Nish.

10

T. ravis's first instinct was to panic. He and Wiz had been so caught up in their ride they had ignored the first rule of diving: *stick together.* Travis was in unknown territory, but at least he was with Wiz.

Nish, on the other hand, was completely out of his element.

Wiz must have seen the fear in Travis's eyes. He took Travis's shoulders in his hands and squeezed tight. He indicated that Travis should follow him, and set off in the direction they had come, kicking hard.

They swam for what seemed a long time. Travis knew they had begun with at least twenty minutes of air time, probably more, but he had no idea how much they had used up. *Maybe Nish was already out of air!* He realized he was panicking, and that panic simply used up valuable air, so he forced himself to slow his breathing and concentrate on following Wiz.

Travis thought he recognized some of the rock structures and began to calm down. Nish was probably already back at the boat. He was probably already into his second cold Coke, laughing at Travis for wasting so much good pop and chocolate time by swimming around after a stupid turtle.

They reached the same tight rock formation where they had lost Nish, but no one was there.

They moved through the floating seagrass, past a scurrying school of seadragons, and on over the ledge into shallower water.

Just before the rise, Travis thought he saw something out of the corner of his eye. Then he realized that Wiz was turning abruptly in the same direction, bubbles boiling up around his head.

It was Nish!

But not alone. Another diver had Nish in a headlock and was violently twisting Nish's neck. He was trying to knock Nish's air hose out of his mouth.

Travis was confused. Another diver? Where had he come from?

Wiz was already onto the attacker. He was larger than Wiz, but not by much, and Wiz was moving so quickly he seemed to catch the diver off guard. The man must have loosened his grip, because Nish was able to break away.

Travis knew he had to tend first to his friend, who looked in total terror. His hose had popped free and he was making no effort to put it back.

Travis grabbed Nish's flailing arms and held them tight. He looked sternly into his eyes and tried to send him a message: *Settle down, do as I tell you.*

He held onto Nish with one hand and used the other to grab the air hose, which was floating freely now. He shoved it back into Nish's mouth. Nish choked, but then began gulping. He was getting air.

Travis could feel the panic letting go of his friend's body. Nish sagged immediately, and Travis realized how exhausted he must be. He must get him to the surface.

Travis began pushing his friend up. He checked down and saw that Wiz was holding his own with the attacker. They were struggling hand-to-hand, both twisting violently, but Wiz was not being thrown around.

If he can just hold on, Travis thought, *I'll come right back to help.*

He kicked as hard as he could. Nish burst through the surface first, spitting out his mouthpiece and screaming at the same time.

"HHHEEELLLLPPPPPPPP!!!"

The boat wasn't too far away. Travis saw Mr. Roberts spinning the wheel and turning in their direction. The anchor was already up. He and Sarah had probably been looking for them, worrying.

Travis left Nish and dived back down, kicking hard, his heart pounding alarmingly as he headed back.

The man was trying the same move on Wiz. He had him in a headlock and was pulling hard at Wiz's air hose, but Wiz was refusing to give in.

Travis kicked hard and drove his head as hard as he could straight into the man's gut.

The attacker doubled over, letting go of Wiz.

There was more movement in the water. Bubbles and swirling arms and legs. For a moment, Travis couldn't make out what it was.

Then he saw Mr. Roberts, wearing only his bathing suit and in his bare feet, kicking as hard as he could at the attacker.

The man pushed once at Wiz, turned, and fled, his flippers allowing him to outdistance Mr. Roberts, who was fast running out of breath and already headed for the surface.

Travis reached out and took Wiz's elbow, but Wiz shook him off and headed back down to the ocean floor.

He pulled at something that raised a cloud of sand. It was a net bag, almost covered by the sandstorm the fight had stirred up.

He held it up, shaking it so the sand washed away.

It was filled with seadragons.

Dozens of seadragons.

And most of them were already dead.

11

"I don't understand."

Mr. Roberts seemed to speak for them all. Everyone, including those who had gone to the beach to set up for the picnic, had returned to the boat. They were gathered now on the deck, the net bag had been carefully placed into the fishing boat's live well, and the last of the living seadragons had been gently lifted out by Mrs. Roberts and Sarah and returned to their natural habitat.

But most of the tiny, delicate creatures were dead. They must have been stuffed very roughly into the bag, or crushed to death as the man had hauled the bag around behind him as he searched for more of the wonderful little pipefish.

"I just don't understand," Mr. Roberts repeated. "If he was taking them to sell to collectors, why would he not be more careful? He must have known he was killing them."

"It's so cruel," Sarah said, her voice breaking.

"What exactly happened down there?" Mr. Roberts asked Nish. "Why would he attack you?"

Nish seemed near tears himself. There were huge red welts about his neck and shoulders where the man had wrestled with him. His voice was choked when he spoke, and his hands shook.

"I lost sight of Trav and Wiz," Nish said uncertainly. "I tried to catch up to them, but they were after that turtle and I lost them in the seaweed. So I just circled back, heading for the boat. And when I got into the shallow water I came up behind this guy – I thought it was you, Mr. Roberts – and when I started swimming fast towards him, he turned. He must have thought I was attacking him or something."

"Why would he think *anyone* was attacking him?" Travis asked. "He must have been doing something that he shouldn't have been doing."

"Obviously," said Mrs. Roberts. "He was killing these little things for no reason at all."

"How did he get here?" Wiz asked. "You can't swim here from the mainland."

"There was a boat on the other side of the island," Mrs. Roberts said. "We saw it from the beach."

"What kind of boat?" Mr. Roberts asked.

"I'm not sure," Mrs. Roberts said. "I think I might have a picture of it, though. I was using the video camera, and I think I might have panned it."

"I'll look later," Mr. Roberts said. He seemed dejected. What had been planned as a wonderful adventure suddenly had a sour taste to it.

Travis looked down at the tragedy the man had left behind. The little seadragons didn't look like they could ever have been real. Lifeless, they no longer contained the magic that Travis and the others had felt. They seemed like something grade-school kids might have made with pipe cleaners, a little bit of soggy green paper, scissors, and glue.

Why would the man do this? Travis wondered.

It made no sense at all.

They cruised back in silence. No rock music and very little talk, except for what was necessary. Travis grew sleepy with the growl of the engine and the steady slap of the waves on the bow of the Robertses' boat. Sarah sat with the seadragons, carefully lifting them one by one, smoothing out each one and holding it in the palm of her hand before she slipped it over the side, giving it its own private burial at sea.

Nish didn't look so good. So far, for him, Australia had been a series of stomach upsets. He had thrown up after seeing the head burped out of the Great White – "food poisoning," he still maintained – and his stomach was once again rolling like the sea. He had moved as far forward as possible, leaning directly out over the bow and trying to look far into the distance, avoiding the steady tilt and drop and tilt again of the ocean.

"You all right?" Wiz asked him.

"Fine," said Nish, with a look that said otherwise.

"I'll get my dad to pull closer to shore," Wiz said. "If you can fix on the shoreline, you'll feel better. It works for me."

Nish nodded, gathered his strength, and spoke again. "Can he get real close?" he said, pausing to let his bucking stomach settle again. "And can I have the binoculars back?"

Wiz stared a moment at the green-gilled visitor. He shook his head in amazement.

"You're not sick at all, are you?" Wiz finally said, smiling.

"You're wrong on that one," Sarah said.

Wiz hadn't seen her come up behind them. She was also checking on Nish.

"*Sick* is the only way to describe him."

ascinating."

Data had his wheelchair tight to the desk in his room and was working on his laptop computer. He and Fahd had spent hours on the Internet ever since the kids had returned from their diving trip with their incredible tale of the dead seadragons and Nish's attacker.

Data had checked out Web sites all over the world. He had sent off e-mails and already had a couple of answers. Now he had compiled his own file and was scrolling down the screen, telling the rest of the Screech Owls the essentials of what he and Fahd had found out.

"No wonder people are fascinated by seahorses," Data said.

"The only males in the world who have babies," Fahd added unnecessarily.

"There's one – they even have a name for him, James – who gave birth to 1,572 babies at once."

"Another world record for you to go after, eh, Nish?" said Sam, giggling.

"*Get a life!*" Nish snapped.

"There's a huge world trade in seahorses," Data said. "They dry them out and grind them into powder to feed to people. They're used in traditional Chinese medicine for everything from curing asthma to restoring energy to old people.

"Says here that forty-five *tonnes* of seahorses are consumed each year in Asia – that's sixteen million of them!"

"Impossible!" Sarah gasped.

"It's true," said Data. "There's all kinds of myths about them, mostly to do with the males giving birth, which some people take as proof of male superiority. Some also believe that the seahorse can heal itself spontaneously. That's probably because they can grow back their tails if an attacker snaps it off, but not instantly."

"Anyway," Fahd added, jumping in, "you can see why so many might be eaten and why they're so valuable. A little bowl of seahorse soup will cost you four hundred and fifty dollars in a restaurant in Taiwan."

"A bowl of *soup*?" Sam said. "You can't be serious?"

"I am," said Fahd. "In some places, a kilogram of seahorse powder can go for as high as fifteen thousand dollars."

"They must be nearly extinct!" said Jesse.

"No," said Data. "There are thirty-two different species, and they're found all around the world. Only one is on the endangered species list."

"What about seadragons?" Sarah asked. "That's what he had. Seadragons, not seahorses."

Fahd nodded. "We know that."

Data cleared his throat. "There's almost nothing on the Web about them. Apparently they're found only in Australia. There are two different species in the world and both exist right here. Even in Sydney Harbour. But they're quite rare, apparently, especially the Leafy Seadragon."

"That's what we saw!" Travis interrupted.

"Well, there's not much we can tell you about them. The Threatened Species Network is trying to have them put on the protected list, but so far they've had no luck."

"What about Chinese medicine?" Andy asked.

"Hardly even mentioned," said Data, scrolling down to the bottom. "One article says they're considered to have even more power than the seahorse. *Ten times* the power. Supposed to cure all the same things, but also give a person incredible courage."

"Hardly seemed a courageous thing to me," Sarah sniffed. "Grabbing them and stuffing them into a bag so they die."

"I know," Fahd agreed. "But that must have been what he was up to. Collecting them to sell on the black market."

"But why attack Nish?" Travis asked. "What did he think Nish was — a cop?"

"We'll never know," said Sarah, shaking her head. "I guess we'll just never know."

13

They played against the Brisbane bandits the following day. Fahd, of course, asked where Brisbane was, and when Muck said it was quite a ways north of Sydney, Simon jumped in to say if it was more north, then the chances were they might be better hockey players. That seemed to make sense, until Data explained that the farther north you go in Australia the hotter it gets. Darwin, in the far north of Australia, was surrounded by rain forest and had tropical weather all year round.

"That figures," said Nish, noisily wrapping clear tape around the tops of his skates. "Everything's always backwards here."

Muck couldn't resist. "Is that a request to play forward, Nishikawa?"

"No way!" said Nish, reddening. "You can't be serious?"

"Sure I am," Muck said. "Great opportunity for us all to try new things. Whatdya say? You're always racing up the ice anyway when you shouldn't be, so why not *start* out of position to save yourself a little time?"

Nish groaned, placing his face in his beefy hands.

"Tell me this isn't happening," he mumbled to himself.

But Muck was serious. He had already juggled the lineup and put their new positions down on a card, so it wasn't just a sudden idea. Travis was now on defence, paired with Dmitri. Lars was another centre, playing between Sam and Fahd. Sarah was back with Andy. Everyone else was also changed. Left wingers became right wingers. Right wingers moved left.

"This is madness," grumbled Nish.

"It'll keep you alert," said Muck. "You can fall into a rut playing all the time with the same person or in the same position. Maybe now you'll find out why so many forwards can't seem to make it back to backcheck."

They finished dressing and took to the ice. The Bandits were already out there, spinning around in their own zone. They stared in something close to awe at the Owls coming out onto the ice. Travis could sort of see why. His team looked marvellous in their matching sweaters and socks, their Screech Owls logos, and each sweater with the player's name over the number – Travis with "Lindsay, 7" and that treasured C just a bit above his pounding heart.

None of the Bandits could skate like Sarah. None had Andy's size or Nish's shot. But they were clearly a better team than the Sydney Sharks, most of whom – Wiz included – were in the stands to watch.

Travis had one of those days. He hit the crossbar on his first shot in the warm-up, and when the game got underway, he had no trouble at all on defence, in part because the Bandits were slow, and in part because Dmitri was so fast he could make it back in time to cover up if either he or Travis got caught cheating.

Muck seemed remarkably relaxed. He knew that the Owls would never meet a team as good as them over here, and he seemed determined to make it fun for everyone. This wasn't a true tournament, after all, just a series of exhibition matches. The Owls were under strict orders not to run up the scores, and Muck gave them permission to try all the things they'd be afraid to try in real games back home.

For Nish, now a centre, this was a licence to go insane. He took it upon himself to carry the puck whenever he was on the ice, no matter how thick the traffic. He spun and danced and dipsy-doodled with the puck. He tried spinneramas and even, at one point, deliberately fell onto his knee pads and slid right between the Bandits' defence while choking up on his stick and still stickhandling.

The others were less flashy. Travis tried his backpass a couple of times, and Dmitri read it perfectly. He tried his fancy puck-off-the-skates play, and it worked twice. He even tried the heel pass Bad Joe Hall had taught him, and it worked.

Sarah, on defence, put on a skating spectacular. She was up and down the ice so fast it must have seemed to the Bandits that there were two Sarahs out on the ice, one playing up and one back.

Every time Sarah made an interesting play, the Sharks erupted with cheers, led by Wiz. Sarah was obviously their favourite – or maybe, Travis couldn't help but wonder, just *Wiz's* favourite.

The Bandits took a while to adjust to the Owls' speed, and they certainly lacked their skill, but they were eager and persistent.

With the Owls up 3–0, Nish tried a foolish lob pass to himself that one of the Bandit defenders read, stepping forward and batting the puck out of the air before it could land. It flew into open ice, and the little Brisbane defenceman raced for it, picking up his own hand pass, which was legal, and then heading up-ice against Dmitri and Travis.

Dmitri had the angle to keep the defenceman cut off from the net, and Travis flew across ice to try to check the puck away from him. The little player threw a pass backhand, blind, but it landed perfectly on the tape of a scurrying Bandits forward, who now had a clear run in on Jenny.

Panicking, he shot, and Jenny kicked it out with a pad, right back onto the blade of the shooter. He shot again, and this time it hit Jenny in the side and pushed on through, dropping on the ice and rolling into the net.

Owls 3, Bandits 1.

The Brisbane bench emptied. They rushed the scorer and piled on the little defenceman as if he had scored the Stanley Cup winning goal in overtime. In any other circumstance, this would have been a delay-of-game penalty for Brisbane, but the referee let it go. Even Muck was hammering the boards in admiration, cheering on the very team he was playing against.

After that, the game dramatically improved. Brisbane seemed to find their nerve playing the big team from Canada, the land of hockey, and they scored twice more to tie the game.

Nish scored on a rather overly dramatic rush from back of his own net, fell after he'd slipped the puck in, and lay on the ice, waiting for the Owls to leave the bench and pile on. But Muck, of course, would have nothing to do with such a display.

Eventually Andy skated over and rapped his stick on Nish's knee pad, and Nish, beet-red even behind his mask, got slowly to his feet and skated back to the bench. They were laughing when he arrived, and he flung his stick down so hard it bounced off the first-aid kit and caught Mr. Dillinger on the arm.

"Far end," Muck told him.

It was all he needed to say. Nish moved down and took his familiar "benched" seat at the far end. He had played his last shift against the Bandits.

They played another twenty minutes. Travis scored on a nifty backhander, and the Bandits scored again.

In the final minute, the Bandits coach brought his goalie out as an extra attacker, and Muck answered by bringing his goalie out as well. Travis had never heard of such a thing, but he guessed it wasn't against the rules. Muck also put out the Owls' weakest players, with instructions to take it easy.

Ten seconds to go, and the little defenceman who'd scored the Bandits' first goal got a backhand on a puck that was rolling up on its edge and lobbed it hard and high down the ice. It seemed, for a moment, as if the puck might lodge in the rafters, but it came down, bounced sharp to the right, skidded, and slid, and barely nipped into the near corner of the net.

Tie game!

The buzzer sounded and both sides cleared their benches, rushing out of habit to congratulate the goalies – only this time there were no goalies on the ice.

"Ridiculous!" Nish said as he skated out, pretending to be working out kinks and stiffness from sitting so long. "Muck had no reason to pull our goalie, as well."

"He wanted a tie game," said Travis.

"You know what they say in the NHL," Nish said.

"What?"

"A tie is like kissing your sister."

Travis turned, blinking in astonishment. "What's *that* supposed to mean?"

"It means ties suck, ties are for losers, ties don't mean anything, ties are like a 50 on your report card – you passed, but your mom's mad at you and your teacher never wants to see you again."

"You'd know about that!" Travis laughed.

The Brisbane Bandits weren't taking it like a 50 on a report card. A 5–5 tie against this top peewee hockey team from Canada was, Travis thought, more like an A+, like skipping a grade, like an extra month of summer holidays.

Or would it be "winter" holidays in Australia?

14

fter the game, the Screech Owls took the train back out to the Olympic Park, where all the teams from the Oz Invitatonal had been given a full afternoon for practice.

It was beginning to sink in that the real joy of this tournament was going to be the Mini-Olympics. They'd had a good time playing the Bandits, and the Bandits had taken inspiration from their incredible tie game, but Muck had just proved that no matter how it was arranged, a competitive game was still more fun to play than a lopsided one.

The Mini-Olympics would be the real competition. Travis could sense it. The air was electric at the Olympic Park, the same high-tension, thrilling charge Travis normally felt at a top-rated hockey tournament. Everywhere they went there were competitors their own age working out and clocking themselves and trying to lift weights and hitting tennis balls and swimming and diving and dribbling basketballs. Just as the Owls

– the visiting star team – felt a special glow whenever they took to the ice in Sydney, the Aussie kids took on their own glow when they appeared on the track and in the pool and on the basketball courts.

The Wizard of Oz could easily have got his nickname from playing a half dozen different sports. He was, Travis realized, a natural athlete. He could run faster than anyone else. He could swim faster. He could come within a few inches of actually dunking a basketball.

Everywhere Wiz went, Sarah could be found. Or was it the other way around? They had become a sort of golden couple of the Mini-Olympics – Sarah the best female athlete in the entire Olympic Park, Wiz the best male.

Nish was out of sorts. He was a star at hockey. He could be something of a star at lacrosse, as well. But Travis had never known Nish to play, or even care about, a single other sport.

Nish swam, but not very well. He was strong, but not nearly as strong as Sam or Andy or Wilson. He was so slow on the track he wouldn't even consider running.

"Why don't they make Nintendo an Olympic sport?" Nish whined.

"Well, it's not," Travis said.

"Or burping? Or making your armpits fart? Something I'm good at?"

"You're out of luck," said Travis.

"Or," Nish's eyes suddenly lit up, "why not skinny-dipping as an Olympic event?"

Travis's mind recoiled with an image of a packed Olympic

pool reacting in horror as Nish, butt-naked, raced in the doors
and along the side of the pool and off the diving board – Nish,
butt-naked at attention, the gold medal for Individual Skinny-
Dipping around his neck while the Canadian flag was raised
and "O Canada" struck up by the band, a small tear rolling
down his cheek and off, bouncing off his shoulder to land on
his other cheek. . . .

Travis shook off the thought. "Don't even think about it,"
he warned his unpredictable friend.

"Well," Nish moaned, "I gotta do *something*."

"You can practise our dives!" Sam interrupted.

"I can't dive from the tower!"

"You promised," Sam reminded him. "I put us down. We're
on the list. You can't back out now – unless, of course, you're
chicken."

Travis tried the 200-metre run and then the 400 metres – he
liked the second distance better, not too short and not too long,
a good test – and after he'd warmed down he decided to check
out Nish and Sam's practice for synchronized diving.

A crowd had gathered at the pool. They were watching
Wiz and Sarah race for fun – Wiz barely winning over eight
lengths – and they were watching Liz and Sam practising their
diving.

Sam noticed Travis coming in and waved to him from the
top of the tower. She pointed down to the floor below her, and
there Travis found Nish, huddled against the rail.

"You don't have to do it," Travis told him.

"Of course I have to. She dared."

"A dare doesn't mean a thing."

"Maybe not to you, pal. It means *everything* to me."

There was no use arguing. Nish was the only human being Travis knew who came complete with buttons. You couldn't see them, but they were there. Sarah knew exactly how to push them to get the reaction she wanted. Muck knew how to push them when he needed a good game. Sam was fast learning how to push them, too.

"You ready, Big Boy?" Sam called down.

Nish nodded. Sam dived, a perfect one-and-a-half somersault before she cut neatly into the water. She surfaced, pushing her hair back, and smiled up at Travis and Nish.

"We're going to win gold, you know – Nish 'n' me."

"I'll believe it when I see it," said Travis.

They began on the one-metre boards. With Sam advising, Nish dove again and again and again. She counted out "*one-two-three*" and then they both bounced and tried to leave their boards at the same time.

It took a while, but Nish was a fast learner. He might have a large body, but he had great control over it, and it didn't take him long to perfect the somersault and back dive and even a small twist. The more they dove, the more coordinated they became. Some of the dives were horrible, and everyone watching laughed mercilessly, but an increasing number were perfectly in time. A few times they dove so perfectly in tandem the pool erupted in a smattering of admiring applause.

"You're a natural, Big Boy!" Sam shouted.

Nish said nothing. He nodded. He didn't seem even remotely comfortable.

They moved to the three-metre boards, and Nish looked, for a moment, terrified. But Sam cajoled and prodded and coaxed, and eventually he began diving from the three-metre with the same surprising grace he'd shown on the one-metre.

"*We're headed for the gold medal!*" Sam shouted, pumping a fist after one perfectly matched dive.

It was time to try the tower. Sam went up first, and stopped at the first platform to wait for Nish.

Nish mounted the steps like a convicted murderer brought to a scaffold. He moved like a sloth, both hands firmly on the handrails, his feet so reluctant to leave the steps it seemed they might be glued there.

He made it to the first level and froze. Nothing Sam could say or do could convince him to climb higher. He stayed there, eyes closed, his entire body shaking.

"Travis!" Sam called. "You better come and help him down!"

Travis scrambled up the steps and took hold of Nish's wrist. His fingers were locked solid.

"Let go," Travis said. "We're going back down."

"I . . . can't . . . move," Nish said.

"You can't stay here."

"Keep your eyes shut," Sam said, "and we'll guide you."

Slowly, they brought Nish back down. There were a few giggles from the crowd, but no open laughter. It was one thing to kid Nish about his stupid ideas, but no one wanted to humiliate him.

As soon as Nish's feet touched the floor he opened his eyes – they were brimmed red, but perhaps that was just the chlorine in the pool.

He didn't say a word. He headed straight for the door and was out, gone.

"There goes my gold medal," sighed Sam.

ost of the Screech Owls were relaxing in a small park near their hotel. It was another warm, beautiful day. They had shopped for souvenirs along Harrington and Argyle – Nish bought his traditional tournament T-shirt, this one with a kangaroo with a pouch full of ice and cold beer – and they'd all bought ice-cream cones to eat while they sat about on the iron benches.

"Well," Sam said with a snicker, "would you look at that?"

Wiz and Sarah were walking towards them, hand in hand. Sam whistled loudly. Sarah let Wiz's hand drop. She obviously hadn't expected to run into her teammates.

"Where'd you get the ice cream?" Sarah asked as they came closer. Her face was pink.

"It'd melt before you two got within a mile of it," Liz giggled. Everyone else laughed. Wiz and Sarah looked embarrassed.

"We walked over to the aquarium," Sarah said.

"Find out anything?" Andy asked, licking the drops away from the bottom of his cone.

Everyone gathered around to get the news.

"The Great White has been let go," Sarah said. "They just wanted to be sure it was all right. It's fine, so they took it out to sea and released it."

"Won't the police need it for evidence?" Fahd asked.

"Not really," said Sarah. "They know it swallowed just the head without the rest of the body."

"Apart from that, the police aren't saying anything," said Wiz. "But one of the marine scientists at the aquarium told us they think it was an execution."

"*An execution!*" shouted Sam.

"That's right," Wiz said, lifting his right hand and chopping the air. "Someone probably sliced it off with a machete. He was probably on his knees with his hands behind his back when it happened."

"I'M GONNA HURL!" groaned Sam.

"That's my job," corrected Nish.

"But why?" Wilson repeated. "Did they have any thoughts on why?"

Sarah and Wiz shook their heads. "They don't know," said Wiz. "They figure it must have happened at sea. I mean that's pretty obvious, isn't it? The shark didn't crawl up on a beach somewhere and gobble down the head. It probably happened in a boat. But only the person who did it knows where, and why."

"Creepy," said Jenny.

"We also talked to someone there about traditional Chinese medicines," Sarah said. "She knew everything about seahorses and why they're considered such powerful medicine. She says hardly anyone knows much about the seadragons, though, only that they're considered to have even stronger powers."

"She found out we were in the Mini-Olympics," laughed Wiz, "and you wouldn't believe the things some of the athletes did at the Olympic Games."

"Like what?" Wilson pressed.

"Like drinking the stomach contents of honey bees," Sarah said, laughing.

"*Disgusting!*" shouted Liz.

"If you think that's bad, how about injecting your veins with spider blood?" Wiz said. "That's what the Chinese swimmers said gave them so much energy."

"That's crazy!" said Fahd. "It makes no sense."

"Hey," Wiz interrupted. "They won gold medals, didn't they? They're the best in the world, aren't they?"

Nish was listening intently. His eyes were wide open and he was nodding up and down. Normally, he would have been the first to make a joke about spider blood or bee vomit, but instead he looked like he was sitting in a church pew nodding in agreement to a sermon.

What, Travis asked himself, *could Nish possibly be thinking?*

16

The Screech Owls were up for another game in the Oz Invitational, this time against the Perth Pirates. They went ahead 6–0 in the first period on two goals by Jesse Highboy, a breakaway marker by Simon Milliken, and a goal each by the Travis–Sarah–Dmitri line.

At the break, Muck called Sarah and Travis aside and told them to take off their sweaters and follow Mr. Dillinger. Mr. Dillinger led them to the Pirates' dressing room and knocked on the door. The Pirates' manager opened it, welcomed them with a big "G'day, mates!" and tossed a couple of fresh sweaters their direction.

"You can join your mate around the corner – we cleared some space for the three of you."

Sarah, a half step ahead of Travis, suddenly pumped a fist in the air and shouted. "*Yes!*"

Someone else was also pulling on a Pirates sweater.

Wiz!

He pulled his head through the neck hole, shook his curls, and grinned at them. "I made a special request for my old line-mates," he laughed.

Three of the Pirates' weaker players were already off to join the Owls. The coaches were mixing things up a bit again. Wiz had been invited down out of the stands, where he and some of the Sharks had come to watch the Owls play, and with the addition of Travis and Sarah the Pirates would have one line better than anything the Owls could put on the ice.

Now they had a game going.

The Pirates came to life thanks to the new line. Wiz, teamed up once more with players equal to his extraordinary talents, was getting better and better every shift. He made miraculous passes to Sarah and Travis, and always seemed to be in position whenever one of them ended up with the puck in a corner of the Pirates' end.

Wiz scored twice on hard one-timers after being set up in the slot. Sarah scored a beautiful goal on an end-to-end rush. Travis scored on a pretty tic-tac-toe play in which Sarah left a drop pass for Wiz coming in late, who worked a perfect spin-nerama around the Pirates defence before rapping a backhand pass to Travis on the open side.

They were within two goals of the Owls when Wiz picked up the puck in his own end and flew the full length of the ice with only Nish scrambling back in time. Wiz came in over the Owls' blueline, dropped the puck into his skates, and tried, once again, the spinning move that had worked so perfectly only minutes before.

This time, however, Nish was ready for him.

Nish stepped forward, bringing his gloves up into Wiz's face, and he flattened the Australian so hard Travis could hear the crack against the ice two lines away.

Wiz spun into the corner, his body limp.

Nish picked up the puck, ignoring the referee's whistle, and slapped it all the way down the ice.

The whistle went again.

Suddenly everyone was shoving. Travis had been in shoving matches before, but usually in defence of his silly friend. This time it was Travis shoving Nish, and Sarah coming in screaming at him.

"What was *that* all about?" she shouted.

Her face was red with anger. Nish's face was redder yet. He looked like a tomato about to explode.

"*He's a hot dog!*" Nish shouted back, shaking off Travis's grip.

"Who are you to call anyone a hot dog!" Sarah yelled, her voice shaking.

Wiz, who was now up on one knee in the corner, looked more puzzled than shocked. Travis figured it was probably the first time anyone had ever taken a run at him. From what he'd seen of Wiz's talents, though, it wouldn't be the last.

"*Bug off!*" Nish snarled, shaking everyone off and skating away to take his rightful place in the penalty box.

Sarah skated towards Wiz, now trying to get on his feet.

He wobbled slightly, his legs suddenly rubber.

"You better get to the bench," said Sarah.

"I'm okay," Wiz said, but he slipped and almost fell again.

Sarah took one side and Travis the other, and they skated him back to the bench, where the manager and coach reached out and helped him to a seat.

Wiz was smiling.

Travis had never seen such a reaction. In any other hockey game he'd ever been in where something stupid like this had happened, the anger would last through the rest of the game and sometimes into the next. There'd be bad feelings and talk of revenge.

"I guess I was asking for that," Wiz said. "Tell your mate I owe him one, okay, Trav?"

Travis nodded. He would certainly do that. Nish deserved whatever was coming to him.

After Nish had served his penalty, Muck sent him to the far end of the bench to sit in a spot all too familiar to him – hockey's equivalent to the desk in the far corner of the classroom.

Wiz took one more shift but was still a little unsteady from the hit and skated off early. He didn't return for another shift.

The game never regained its energy. Fahd scored on a point shot that hit a defenceman's skate and went in. Wilson scored on a long shot that bounced once and skittered between the goalie's pads. Travis scored a second on a nice breakaway pass from Sarah. Dmitri scored on his customary high backhand. Sarah set up their new winger, probably the quickest of the Pirates, for a breakaway, and he scored when he fanned on the shot.

The Owls won 9–6, but the Pirates acted as if they, in fact, had won the entire tournament. Never before had they scored so many goals – even if five of the six had come from players "on loan" to them – and they seemed delighted merely to be on the same ice surface as such skilled players from Canada and the legendary Wizard of Oz from Sydney. Several of the players even insisted on getting their photos taken with Sarah and Travis before they took off their equipment.

One of the Pirates, the quick little player who'd scored on the fanned shot, said he'd see them again in the Mini-Olympics. "We're a lot better at those sports than we are at this one, y'know," he told them.

Travis was beginning to suspect that they all were – that the Mini-Olympics were going to be the great equalizer for the Owls.

ata picked up a copy of the *Herald* on their way back to the hotel. There was a photograph of the shark that had been released by the aquarium, and an update on the mysterious head that had been burped up by the huge fish.

"He's a Filipino!" Data announced after he had scanned the article.

"How can they tell?" Fahd asked.

"Maybe that's where his shoes were made," offered Nish.

"Save your sick jokes for your friends," Sarah advised. "If you have any left."

Travis couldn't help notice that Sarah still hadn't forgiven Nish for his hit on Wiz.

Nish was in trouble with his whole team, not just Sarah. Travis had told him that Wiz had said he "owed him one," but Nish had just laughed it off as if the whole thing was no big deal.

Data laid the paper open on his lap and gave the Owls the essence of the article.

"Dental analysis," he said. "Something about the type of filling material only being available in the Philippines, anyway."

"Great," said Wilson. "Only eighty million dental records to check."

"It's a start," Data argued.

"Why don't they just look for a body that's missing a head?" Nish suggested.

There was a sharp rap at the door.

Travis, who'd been lying on his bed half watching television while Nish and Fahd napped, jumped up and went quickly to the peephole.

It was Andy, a look of concern on his face.

Travis opened the door to let him in, but Andy had other ideas. He wanted Travis to come with him. "Data's been on the Internet again," he said. "Says he thinks he might have found something."

Data was deep in thought when they walked in, staring at the screen of his laptop as if it held some enormous secret he could not quite read.

He turned his chair when he heard the door click. "Hi, Trav," he said. "I've been doing some research for us. Did you know the number-one research spot for seahorses is in Canada? Project Seahorse, at McGill University in Montreal."

Travis shook his head. Of course he didn't know.

"Project Seahorse has links to everyone. They've even

funded an experiment with fishermen in the Philippines to see if they can build a seahorse fishery that's sustainable."

Travis wondered when Data was going to get to the interesting part. But he said nothing.

"The Philippines is where almost all seahorse fishermen come from," Data continued. He clicked the mouse and a page from a scientific article popped up. "The average income in those villages is around three hundred dollars," he read. "That's for an entire year. Can you imagine?"

"I get almost that for my allowance," said Andy.

Travis shook his head. It was exactly the amount of money he'd brought on this trip, and he'd been planning to spend every penny before leaving. He felt a little guilty that a person might make no more than that in an entire year – and be expected to feed a family on it.

"That's the huge attraction of seahorse harvesting," Data continued. "Remember that bowl of seahorse soup Fahd found on the Internet – four hundred and fifty dollars for just one bowl in Taiwan?"

Travis nodded. He remembered.

"And a kilogram of dried seahorses being worth as much as fifteen thousand dollars?"

Travis nodded again.

"That's why there's such a big concern about the future of seahorses. Already one species on the endangered list and several others in trouble. Areas that used to produce lots of seahorses are now fished out around the Philippines, and now there are press reports about Philippine fishermen in Australian

waters after seahorses – apparently it's becoming a major political issue."

Travis could no longer help himself. "So?"

"So," Data said slowly, as if explaining to a very dull student,
"if seahorses are that valuable, what must a seadragon be worth?"

Travis half followed, but still couldn't figure out exactly
where Data was headed.

"Did you get a good look at that guy who attacked Nish?"
Data asked.

Travis shook his head. "I didn't see much."

"Anything?" Data asked. "Eyes? Colour of hair? Anything
at all."

"Black," Travis answered after he thought about it. "He had
black hair. Thick and fairly long. It was flowing when they
fought."

Data clicked through a few more pages. Travis waited for
him to say more, but Data seemed deep in thought.

"What?" Travis finally asked.

"Remember Wiz saying the head had been sliced off by a
machete?"

"Yeah."

"Well, that suggests he was executed. The police have said
he was Filipino. Maybe he was poaching around that island and
maybe the guy who attacked Nish – or the gang that guy
belonged to – decided they wanted him out of there so they
could have all the seadragons to themselves."

"I don't know," said Travis.

"How much do you think that sack of seadragons he had
weighed?"

Travis had no idea. They'd immediately let go the ones that were still alive, and they'd thrown overboard the ones that were dead – except, of course, for the one that Sarah had so carefully saved and that was now dried out on a dresser in the room Sarah was sharing with Liz, Sam, and Jenny.

"Wet or dry?" Travis asked. He'd noted there was quite a difference after being allowed to examine Sarah's treasure.

"Dried," Data said.

"I don't know. A couple of pounds, at least. More than a kilo."

Data gave a very slight nod of satisfaction. "Seahorses at fifteen thousand dollars a kilogram," he said slowly. "Think how much a kilogram of seadragons would be worth to a poor fisherman."

Travis tried.

He could imagine the money. He could not, however, imagine it being worth taking a machete and lopping off a person's head.

Nothing could be worth that.

18

arah and Wiz went back to the aquarium to see if they could find out where, exactly, the Great White Shark had been caught up in the fishing nets.

They came back an hour later. Their new friends had been helpful, but no one kept records like that. All the aquarium staff had was a phone number for the captain of the fishing boat that had brought the shark in. Sarah and Wiz had been able to reach him straight away, but he wasn't exactly helpful. He figured it had been in the direction of the island they were thinking of, but he pointed out with a laugh, "Sharks swim around, you know. The Pacific Ocean is a bit bigger than a holding tank at the Sydney Aquarium."

"The direction is right," said Data, who was convinced there was a connection. "Let's say they executed him the same day the shark got caught. The head hadn't been digested at all. We can *presume* the shark was at least in the vicinity of the island around that time. And we know that the seadragons are found there."

"Circumstantial evidence," said Sam. "The police would laugh in your face."

"We need more," Data said. "What about the video Wiz's mother took?"

"You can barely make it out," said Sarah. "It was shot into the sun. You can't make out anything on the boat. No name, nothing. You can barely see what shape it is. There's no flag – so we have no idea where they came from."

"What about going back?" Data asked.

"How?" Andy wondered.

"What about Wiz?" Data said. "Maybe he could ask his father?"

Somehow, Wiz had talked his father into doing it. With Sarah and Travis's help, he laid out all the evidence that the Owls had gathered – no matter how questionable it was – and asked him simply to take them back out to the island the following morning with the video camera. If the seadragon fishermen weren't there, then they'd have to admit they were beat.

Mr. Roberts had understood. He wasn't convinced there was any connection between the head and the seadragons, but he *was* convinced that his son would never forgive him if he didn't at least try.

They met at the Mosman Bay marina shortly after breakfast. They were a smaller group this time, just Mr. Roberts, Wiz, Sarah, Travis, and Nish. Travis had worked hard to convince Nish to come. He hoped Nish might apologize to Wiz so that they could make up, but it seemed that Nish agreed to come only because he had nothing else to do.

Wiz had said nothing. He'd never mentioned the hit again. Travis envied him his endlessly sunny disposition.

The seas were as calm as they had been the first day. Mr. Roberts ran at three-quarters throttle, the sleek boat clipping over the low waves in a steady machine-gun chop that cut down on the rolling and made Travis feel sleepy. He slouched down in the sun, spread on some sunscreen, and let himself doze off.

He woke up only when he sensed the engines being cut. It took several moments for his eyes to adjust to the brightness. He blinked, and blinked again. The boat was settling, rolling and rocking as it slowed. Off in the distance he could make out the island.

Mr. Roberts had the binoculars up to his eyes. He was scanning the seas on all sides. Travis was certain he had seen something when Mr. Roberts suddenly held the binoculars steady and adjusted the focus.

He handed them to Wiz. "About two o'clock," Mr. Roberts said.

Wiz looped the strap around his own neck and stared off in the direction of the 2 on a clock face.

"There's something there all right," he said after a while.

They all took turns looking. When Travis got the binoculars, it took him several moments to settle on a glimmering white object that seemed to bob and wink in the swells. It was much too far, even with the powerful binoculars, for him to make out anything on the boat. He couldn't even tell if there were any people on deck.

"Can we get closer?" Wiz asked.

"Not without them seeing us," said Mr. Roberts.

"But we need a photograph," Sarah added.

Mr. Roberts nodded. "You'd get nothing from here, even with the zoom," he said. "We've got to get closer – but we have to do it without alerting them."

"How?" asked Wiz.

Mr. Roberts smiled. "Simple. We run right at 'em full throttle. By the time they see us, we'll have your shot. Okay?"

Sarah shrieked. "*Okay!*"

"*Let's do it!*" shouted Wiz.

"Get the camera ready," Mr. Roberts said. "*And hang on for your life!*"

The big boat shuddered, reared like a horse, and bolted straight into the coming waves. As it gathered speed it rose gradually until they were planing over the waves, heading straight for the unknown boat.

Travis felt the deck shudder. He grabbed onto the handrail, the wind whipping his face as he stared straight ahead.

Nish clung to the boat's antenna, which was bolted to the port side of the cabin area. He held fast, his flesh jiggling as the boat clipped hard over the water. Travis could barely see Nish's face. He could see enough, however, to know that Nish was not liking this. Not liking it at all.

Up ahead, staring straight into the wind, Wiz and Sarah hung partly onto the railing, partly onto each other.

Mr. Roberts pushed the engine to full throttle, the boat roaring loudly as it seemed to rise even higher, all but flying over the low swells.

The strange boat was fast coming into view. It was difficult to tell – they would have to compare when they got home – but it looked like the one on Mrs. Roberts' video.

Sarah had the camera. She was trying to steady herself and focus ahead on the boat, which now seemed to be rushing towards them.

Something moved on the deck!

It was a man, and he was throwing scuba equipment into a hold. Another man emerged from the tiny cabin, stared towards them, then drew his head back in.

The water began to churn at the stern of the boat, the engines firing in a cloud of blue smoke.

"*They're running!*" Wiz called from the bow.

Travis took a quick glance at Nish. He was green, his eyes squeezed shut and his mouth in a painful grimace. He looked like he was about to be sick.

The first man on the unknown boat now ran to a wooden box on deck, reached in, and pulled out something long and dark.

"*Get down!*" Mr. Roberts yelled. "*He's got a gun!*"

Mr. Roberts turned the boat sharply, sending Travis spilling across the deck. He caught himself and looked quickly back to where Nish had been.

He was still there, glued to the antenna, his eyes still shut! Travis suddenly realized how dangerously exposed his friend was.

The man levelled the gun at the approaching boat.

"*NISH!*"

The voice belonged to Wiz.

Wiz left Sarah, who was still taking pictures, and ran towards the antenna. He dove before he got to Nish, knocking him away from the antenna and down onto the deck, and landing hard on top!

KRRRRACK!

SSSSSMACK!

The two sounds were almost simultaneous.

The first came from the boat just ahead of them. The second came from Mr. Roberts's antenna.

Travis turned just in time to see the antenna crash down over the railing and break off into the sea. The shot had struck it exactly where Nish had been clinging.

"*Hang on!*" Mr. Roberts yelled.

KRRRRACK!

Another shot, but not nearly so close.

KRRRRACK!

Again, but still farther away.

Mr. Roberts had the boat turned right around now and was racing back hard in the direction they had come.

Travis chanced a look over the railing. The other boat wasn't following. They were free.

He heard a groan and knew it was Nish.

Had he been hit?

But there was no blood. Wiz was carefully disentangling himself from Nish, who was twisting and moaning on the deck. Wiz grabbed Nish's hand and pulled him to a sitting position.

"What hit me?" Nish asked.

"It's what *didn't* hit you that you should be thinking about," Wiz said, laughing.

Nish shook his head, still not understanding.

He turned and looked back at the shattered antenna.

Exactly where he would have been standing, if Wiz hadn't taken him out.

Nish looked over at Wiz, his mouth moving helplessly.

Wiz smiled. "Hey," he said. "I owed you one – remember?"

Sarah hurried over, breathless. She was holding the camera as if she were afraid it might break, or vanish.

"I got some great shots!" she said.

Wiz laughed. "Thank God *they* didn't or we'd be one Nish short right about now!"

Nish shook his head and stared at Wiz.

He still didn't know what had just happened.

19

hey returned to Mosman Bay with no trouble. The mystery boat had not given chase, and Mr. Roberts, fortunately, knew the sea and shoreline so well he was able to find his way back even though the antenna was useless.

They'd turned over Data's theories and Sarah's photographs to the Coast Guard and told them about being fired on by the mysterious fishing boat. The Coast Guard promised they'd look into the matter immediately.

There was nothing else for the Owls to do. There was no point in just waiting around to see what the Coast Guard could find out. It might take days.

Besides, the Games were about to begin.

As soon as they were off the ice, the Screech Owls became the underdogs.

Whoever had set up the Mini-Olympics had done a wonderful job. There were roughly ten Australians for every Screech Owl, but everything was evened out by turning the first six places in each event into points, and multiplying by ten each time a Screech Owl placed in the top six.

Fahd took silver in archery. Sarah took a gold in the 200-metre, a silver in the long jump, and a bronze in both the high jump and the hurdles. Wilson took a silver in weightlifting. Derek and Jesse came fourth in tennis doubles. Andy took bronze in the javelin, and Simon took a bronze in wrestling. Travis came fourth in the 400-metre and fifth in the pole vault, an event he'd never even tried until this day.

The best story, however, was in the pool, where Sarah and Wiz seemed to be stepping onto the podium every few minutes. Wiz was a wonderful swimmer, and took three golds in different events. Sarah took two golds and a silver. Liz took a silver and a gold in the butterfly – the only Owl who could do the difficult stroke – and Jesse came fifth in the backstroke.

The final scheduled event of the day was diving. Players, parents, and competitors packed into the Olympic pool for the windup to what had already been a wonderful day. Two Aussies – a girl from Melbourne, and a teammate of Wiz's on the Sydney Sharks – dominated the events and took the top medals. Sam, diving in the individual events, took a silver and a bronze, and Sarah took a fourth in the one-metre competition.

Just before the synchronized diving event, the organizers called a time out.

"Just thought you might all like to know the running tally," a man wearing an Australian team tracksuit said over the public address system. "With the scores weighted to take into consideration our special visitors from Canada, we have the day's standings at Australia 211, Canada 209."

A huge cheer went up from the mostly Australian crowd.

"Can you believe it?" Sarah said, turning with her hands pressed to the side of her face. "We're almost tied."

"Down to the final event," Muck chuckled. "Sudden death overtime in the Olympics."

"But, but," Sam sputtered, "we only entered synchronized diving as a joke!"

"Well," said Mr. Dillinger. "Looks like the joke's on us, then. Which reminds me. Where is our other diver?"

Everyone looked around for Nish.

"He went back to the hotel around noon," Andy said.

Sarah looked stricken. "He wouldn't bail on us?"

"Sure he would," said Sam, shaking her head. "He's chicken – we all know that."

"I saw him a few minutes ago at the snack bar!" Fahd announced.

"*He's here?*" Sam shouted.

Travis jumped in. "I'll get him," he said to Sam. "You get ready."

Travis ran up through the stands, and into the corridor where the snack bars were located. He turned right, then left, following his instincts: the fancier snack bar was to the left. He ran down the corridor, past parents and young hockey players who were happily buying up souvenirs and waiting in line for ice-cream bars. Down around the corner and towards the far exit he ran, hoping, praying, that Nish would be there. The Screech Owls' Olympic hopes lay with him.

It seemed ridiculous to Travis. None of the Owls had taken the Mini-Olympics very seriously, believing that, on average, the Australian kids would be far superior to them at almost anything but hockey. But no one could have predicted how dominant Sarah would be in her events – inspired, no doubt, by Wiz's equally impressive performance. No one could have predicted that all the Owls would get so caught up in the competition. And now it was all down to one event that they had considered little more than a joke.

Nish, with his great fear of heights, diving from the high tower.

Travis turned the corner and could see the large snack bar in the distance. A bulky body was sitting at one of the tables, his back to Travis, but unmistakable all the same.

"Nish!" Travis called as he flew into the snack bar so fast his sneakers skidded and squeaked on the floor. "You're on! You're up! They're calling the diving event."

Nish appeared completely calm, but he had a disgusted look on his face. He was sitting before a bowl of soup, a small plastic bag on the table to one side, and he was slowly spooning the remainder of the soup into his mouth.

How can he eat at a time like this? Travis wondered.

"Just give me another minute," Nish said.

Travis sat, waiting, while Nish carefully finished off his soup, pulling a face for every spoonful.

"If it tastes so awful," Travis asked, "why finish it?"

Nish grimaced. "Always clean up your plate, Travis. Didn't your mother teach you any manners?"

Travis shook his head. A lecture on good manners from Wayne Nishikawa was the last thing in the world he ever expected to hear.

"Hurry up!" Travis urged.

Nish tilted the bowl, filled the spoon, and slotted it into his mouth, swallowing quickly.

He burped and set the spoon down.

"You'll have to run!" Travis warned.

Nish looked at him, then down at his table. "Clean this up for me, then," he said. "I'll go ahead."

"Sure, sure – whatever. Just hurry!"

Nish pushed himself up, the chair growling across the polished concrete, and began hurrying off in the direction Travis had come from. Travis gathered up the bowl and spoon and tray and began heading for the garbage can.

He'd forgotten the plastic bag.

He stepped back and grabbed it. It felt empty, except there was the sound of fine grains of salt or sand running inside.

He set the tray down, opened the bag, and peered in.

Whatever it was, it was very dry, and flaky.

He sniffed at the bag.

He knew that smell!

The ocean . . . the smell on the boat . . . a fishy smell . . .

Nish hadn't!

He couldn't have!

Travis sniffed again, his mind racing. There was no doubt about it. He recognized the smell now.

The seadragon. Sarah's dried-out seadragon. The little creature with the mythical ability to give a man courage.

Sarah's seadragon ground into powder and mixed in a soup.
And now in the stomach of Wayne Nishikawa, *tower diver*.

20

am was already waiting at the tower when Travis arrived back at the pool. She and everyone else seemed to be looking at exactly the same place: the doorway to the showers and change rooms.

Ten seconds later, the doors opened.

It was Nish, in his Mighty Ducks of Anaheim bathing trunks. He raised both arms to the crowd like he was the wrestling heavyweight champion of the world.

The stands erupted in cheers.

Nish bowed.

He's going to make a fool of himself, Travis thought. *He's going to panic.*

The Australian synchronized diving team was already at the top of the tower. It struck Travis, from the way they were joking around and laughing, that perhaps they had taken this particular event no more seriously than had the Owls. Surely, though, they hadn't entered any hockey players who were terrified of heights.

The two Aussies moved to the edge, high above the water, talked over their planned dive, high-fived each other for luck, and leapt off at the count of three.

One flipped frontwards, the other managed only a half-flip, and they crashed heavily into the water, bodies badly out of time.

They surfaced to a loud chorus of good-natured booing from the Australian players in the stands.

Both waved, laughing.

Thank heavens, Travis thought. *They're not taking this seriously, either. But they'll still win*, he realized. *Because Nish won't even be able to climb up, let alone jump off – and the Mini-Olympic championship will be theirs.*

Nish was at the steps. He had one hand on the railing. Sam was just ahead of him, pleading with him to hurry. From the look on her face, she seemed a lot more agitated than Nish.

Nish smiled, turned and waved again, causing a ripple of laughter to move through the crowd.

He scurried up the steps to join Sam.

He must have his eyes closed, thought Travis. *This is where he froze last time.*

But Nish didn't freeze, he didn't even pause. He took Sam's hand as he reached her and almost hauled her up the next series of steps to the top of the tower.

The Owls gasped. Nish was now ten metres above the water. He was standing on a small platform four storeys high, with nothing but air between him and the water.

And he wasn't screaming!

He wasn't screaming. He wasn't crying. He didn't have his

eyes shut. He wasn't shaking. And he wasn't hanging on to anything but Sam's hand while he waved with the other.

Sam looked as baffled as anyone else in the crowd. But she shrugged, turned to Nish, went over some quick instructions as to what they'd do, and the two of them approached the edge of the tower.

The entire pool took one breath and held it, as if they, not the divers, were about to plunge underwater.

In the eerie silence, everyone could hear Sam's soft voice doing the countdown.

"*Three . . . two . . . one!*"

At "*one!*" both left the tower. Nish held a swan dive, as did Sam, and then both, almost in perfect unison, did a quick flip before entering the water. The splash was so small it seemed more like two coins striking the water than two hockey players who'd never dived competitively in their lives.

A huge cheer went up from the crowd, the Aussies louder than the Canadians.

Sam and Nish surfaced, fists pumping.

"KAAA–WAAA–BUNGA!" they shouted together.

"KAAA–WAAA–BUNGA!" the crowd shouted back, laughing.

Twice more they dove, Nish each time racing fearlessly up the steps and onto the tower. They tried back dives that almost worked, and a double flip that worked remarkably well. The Australians pulled off a nearly perfect flip and twist, but their third dive might as well have been called "Cannonballs off the High Tower." They hit the water so hard, with such a huge splash, that the crowd gasped with relief just to see they were still alive.

"*The results of the synchronized diving event!*" the announcer's voice echoed throughout the large pool. "*Canada takes the gold medal!*"

The crowd, Aussies as well as Canadians, exploded in cheers. Nish and Sam had won the gold.

The Canadians had won the Mini-Olympics!

It seemed impossible to Travis that it was over so soon. He had looked forward to the Mini-Olympics since they'd been announced, and now they were history.

The flag had been raised, the national anthem sung, the medals strung about Nish's and Sam's necks, and everyone in the crowd had congratulated each other on such a marvellous day. Travis's back had been slapped until it burned. Wiz had given him a hug so hard he thought his ribs would break – though it seemed like half the hug Wiz had reserved for Sarah.

Everyone was asking to see Nish's medal. He had it off his neck now and was handing it about, when suddenly he stepped back from the gathering of well-wishers.

How unlike Nish, Travis thought. *He's finally got exactly what he wants, why wouldn't he revel in it?*

But then he got a better look at his friend. Nish was a little green about the gills again.

"You okay?" Travis asked his friend.

Nish burped lightly. "I don't feel so good."

"Something you ate?" Travis asked, grinning.

Nish looked hard at him, eyes narrowing. "Who told you?"

Travis shook his head. "Who's going to tell Sarah?"

"What do you mean?"

"She wanted to keep that seadragon, don't you think?"

But whatever Nish was thinking, it had nothing to do with what Sarah wanted or not. He was very green now.

He put his hand over his mouth.

With his other hand, he pushed Travis aside, running hard for the washroom.

21

here was much laughter and shouting on the train ride back to the hotel. Nish and Sam were cheered, and Fahd returned Nish's treasured gold medal to its rightful owner. Travis told the story of the plastic bag and the funny smell and how he'd finally figured out that Nish had powdered up the dried seadragon and eaten it with soup to give him the "courage" he lacked. And who could now argue that it was just a silly myth? It had worked, hadn't it?

"How much did you say a bowl of that soup cost?" Sarah asked Data.

"In Taiwan, four hundred and fifty dollars."

"Well, then, that's what Nish owes me, I guess," she said.

"That's nothing compared to what you all owe me!" protested Nish, only to be drowned out by happy boos.

When they finally got back to the hotel, Mr. Dillinger and Muck had them all gather in the lobby. There was news, and Muck wanted them all to hear it.

Mr. Roberts was there with a uniformed member of the Coast Guard.

"This is Captain Peterkin," Mr. Roberts said. The Coast Guard captain nodded. "They've made a series of arrests today and would like to talk to you."

Captain Peterkin cleared his throat. He had a finely clipped, sand-coloured beard, and a large moustache that wiggled oddly as he spoke. Some of the Owls fought off giggles as he began speaking, but when they realized what it was he was saying, they all grew quiet.

"The man whose head was discovered at the Sydney Aquarium," the Coast Guard officer said, "has been identified as a Filipino fisherman who was illegally trapping seadragons off the south coast of Australia, mostly in an area just off Sydney Harbour."

"How was he killed?" asked Fahd.

Captain Peterkin cleared his throat again. "Executed, we believe," he said. "Several different poaching operations were competing for the same ripe area for seadragons. Thanks to photographic evidence produced by" – he consulted a small index card in his hand – "Miss Sarah Cuthbertson, we were able to make a positive ID on a Philippines fishing boat in our waters and conduct a stop and seizure operation. We found several kilograms of expired seadragons. We also seized a number of weapons, including a high-powered hunting rifle and several machetes."

"I thought so," said Fahd.

"We also have a confession from one of the apprehended fishermen. There had been a battle for these particular seadragon grounds, and, it seems, our unfortunate headless man was one of the losers."

Travis couldn't stop himself. He had to know. "I don't understand something," he said.

The Coast Guard captain raised one eyebrow in Travis's direction.

"Why would that man attack Nish? He must have been trying to kill him, but all he had to do was swim away and we'd probably never have noticed."

The Coast Guard captain looked around, puzzled.

"Which one of you is Nish?" he asked.

Nish stepped forward, blushing hard.

The captain looked a long time at him. Nish grew redder and redder. Finally the captain scratched his beard and nodded, satisfied.

"Put a diving mask on this young man," Captain Peterkin said, "and put him underwater, and you'd all probably mistake him for a Filipino poacher."

"Impossible," Nish said, a smile returning to his beaming face.

"And why's that, son?"

"Because I can't *stand* seadragons – that's why."

22

T. here was one final hockey game still to play. It would be the *grand finale* of the Oz Invitational, the Screech Owls of Tamarack, Canada, against an all-star team of the best peewee hockey players in all of Australia. Wiz Roberts would captain the Aussie All-Stars against Travis Lindsay and the Screech Owls.

They played at the Macquarie Ice Rink, but so many curious spectators wanted to watch, they could almost have filled an Olympic stadium. The organizers packed in as many as could legally fit and then turned a blind eye as dozens more squeezed in. At 7:00 on a Saturday night they dropped the puck.

"*Dah, da-da-da, da-ahhhh!*" Nish sang as he lined up beside Travis before the anthems.

"Hockey Night in Australia?" Travis asked, smiling.

"You got it, *myte*," Nish answered in an Aussie accent.

This game was different. The two teams were perfectly balanced. Wiz was the equal of Sarah on the ice, and each of the

Aussie teams in the tournament had one, two, or three young-sters good enough to play for the Screech Owls. And the Aussies were so fired up by the chance to play on an all-star team in front of such a loud, boisterous crowd that they all seemed faster, smarter, and bigger than before.

"These guys are good," Travis said on the bench after his first shift.

"They're amazing!" said Dmitri.

Travis and Sarah leaned back and winked at each other behind his back. It was great to be back with Dmitri. It had been fun playing with Wiz, but the three Owls had a special connection.

Dmitri scored the first goal on a play Travis had seen so many times it seemed he was watching an old movie. Sarah won a faceoff and got the puck back to Nish behind Jenny's net. Nish moved up towards the blueline and lifted the puck so high it almost hit the rafters. Dmitri, anticipating perfectly, chased the puck down when it landed and came in on a clear breakaway. Shoulder fake, shift to backhand, a high lifter – and the Aussie water bottle was in the air, saluting Dmitri's trademark move.

Travis realized that playing against Wiz was very different from playing with him. He was astonished at how strong he was on the puck; he simply refused to be knocked off. He scored once and set up a second, and halfway through the first period Muck countered by insisting Travis's line go head-to-head with Wiz's line whenever the Aussie sensation was on the ice.

That meant Sarah against Wiz, Wiz against Sarah. They checked each other. They faced off against each other.

Travis wondered how they would handle this, but he had his answer almost at once when Sarah shouldered Wiz hard out of the faceoff circle and used her skate to kick the puck to Travis.

Travis curled back, losing his check. He looked up and down the ice. Lars was free on the far side, and he fired the puck back to him.

Lars took stock of the ice, faked a pass over to Wilson, and instead chopped the puck off the boards to Dmitri. Dmitri took off like a shot up the far wing and slipped a quick pass to Sarah, now hitting centre.

But the pass never got to her. Using his shoulder, Wiz easily knocked Sarah off the puck, grabbed it, and turned hard back the other way.

Lars and Wilson tried to take away his space by closing in on him, but Wiz saw it coming. He plucked the puck off the ice so it sailed between the two squeezing defenders and leapt into the air over them, Lars and Wilson crashing together in a tangle of sticks and skates.

Wiz was in alone. He deked out Jenny and fired the puck hard into the goal. He turned, laughing, and plucked the puck off the ice as it rebounded out of the net, twisting his stick perfectly so the puck lay on the blade, just like an NHLer, and handed it to the linesman.

Heading into the third period, the Owls were down 5–3. Muck, for the first time, seemed really into the game. He had his coach's face on, giving away nothing, but telling each and every one of the Owls that this was the time to get serious. No more shinny. No more glory plays. Just real *hockey*.

"Nothing stupid, Nishikawa," he said. "We need you on the ice, not in the penalty box."

Nish nodded and he stared straight down at his skate laces.

Nish is in the game, Travis told himself. *Nothing to worry about there.*

"We need you, Sarah," Muck said.

Sarah nodded, her face streaming with sweat. It would be up to her, both to hold off Wiz and to make sure the Owls came back.

The crowd had grown so loud Travis wondered if they were pumping in a tape of a Stanley Cup game. It seemed impossible that so few people could make so much noise. But they were all Aussies, he reminded himself, and there was no louder fan on earth than the Aussie at full volume.

Besides, they could sense a win. They could smell victory. To beat the Canadians at their own game would be something special.

Travis slapped his stick against Nish's shin pads before the faceoff. Nish never looked up. His face was as red as the helmets on the Aussie All-Stars. Sweat was rolling off him, and they hadn't even started the final period. He was in the Nish Zone – and Travis was glad to see him there.

Nish began the charge. He picked up a puck in his own end, faked a pass up to Travis, and carried out, playing a sweet give-and-go with Dmitri at centre ice.

Nish, carrying again, came across the Aussie blueline, tucked a drop pass between his legs, and left the puck for Sarah as he took out the one Aussie defender.

That left Sarah and Travis with a two-on-one. Sarah waited, faked a shot, and then slid a hard pass across the crease to Travis, standing at the corner of the net all alone.

It was one of the easiest goals of his life. He simply let the puck hit his stick and tick off into the net.

Nish would also set up the tying goal. He carried again, a few minutes later, and hit Andy with a long breakaway pass. Andy came in, rifled a slapshot off the post, and Nish, charging hard to the net, picked up the rebound and stuffed it before the goaltender could get across to block his shot.

Aussies 5, Owls 5.

With the clock ticking down, Wiz brought the crowd to its feet with a stupendous carry that began in his own end and involved stickhandling past Sarah not once, not twice, but three times.

But Sarah would not give up. She chased and chased, using her speed to cut off the twisting, turning Wiz as he worked his way up-ice.

At one point Travis could see Wiz laughing as Sarah slid in, once again, to knock the puck free. But with two blinding-fast hand movements he was past her, the puck still on his stick.

Travis had never seen anything like it. Was this how the twelve-year-olds in Brantford felt when they realized they were up against Wayne Gretzky? Was this what it was like to play against a young Mario Lemieux or a Jaromir Jagr?

Wiz still had the puck. He looked up and threw a quick, hard pass towards the net that his winger, swooping in from Travis's side, barely ticked with his stick.

Barely, but enough. The puck skipped once and dived in under Jenny's outstretched pad.

Aussies 6, Owls 5.

The roar of the crowd was so loud, Travis looked straight up, half convinced the roof was crashing down.

He checked the clock.

Thirty seconds. Probably not enough.

Sarah led their line over to the bench, but Muck held out his hand to stop them. He wanted them on for the final shift. Their best chance was with Sarah up front and Nish back. If they couldn't make something happen, no one could.

Sarah took the faceoff. She seemed furious that Wiz had so dazzled her moments before. She held the puck, stickhandled deftly around him, turned back and did it again, just for good measure, and then sent a pass back to Nish.

Nish surveyed the ice.

Twenty seconds left.

He began moving slowly up across centre. He saw Travis and flipped a quick pass.

Travis faked to go to centre ice, then turned sharply, heading down the boards.

The Aussie defenceman followed, aiming a shoulder at him.

Travis bounced ahead, the hard check missing him as the defender crashed into the boards.

Travis heard the crowd gasp.

He stopped, stickhandling. He sent the puck around the boards to Dmitri on the far side, and Dmitri clipped it back hard to Nish.

Ten seconds.

Nish moved in.

Wiz dove to block the shot.

Nish faked, danced around a spinning Wiz, aimed, and fired hard and high.

Ping! Off the crossbar!

Travis watched helplessly as the puck popped high in the air, turning over and over and over.

Sarah was already back of the net.

The puck landed and she scooped it, plucked it off the ice like an NHLer, and was about to hand it back to the referee.

But no whistle had gone!

Three seconds.

Sarah, balancing the puck on the blade of her stick, stepped around the corner of the net and had her feet taken out from under her by a sliding defenceman.

But not before she whipped the puck, lacrosse-style, high into the far corner.

The referee's whistle blew! The horn went!

Owls 6, Aussies 6.

Sarah had tied the game with the Wizard's own move!

Travis's gloves and stick were already in the air. He, too, was flying, sailing towards a mound of Owls that already included Dmitri and Nish, with Sarah on the bottom.

Nish's cage was almost locked on Sarah's, Nish's face crimson as he screamed.

"YESSSSSS! SARAH!"

"Back off, Dragon Breath!" Sarah shouted, laughing. "Before I gag!"

But no one paid any attention. More bodies arrived. The bench had emptied. Travis, twisting happily in the pile, could make out Mr. Dillinger's pant leg, then Muck's jacket sleeve, then smell Muck as the big coach himself landed smack in the middle of the pile.

23

There would be no overtime. A tie, the organizers, the coaches, the managers, even the players, all agreed was the perfect ending to the perfect tournament. Aussie All-Stars 6, Screech Owls 6. Screech Owls 6, Aussie All-Stars 6. No matter how you said it, it sounded perfect.

The players lined up and congratulated each other. The Wiz had a special rap across the shins for Nish, a headlock for smaller Travis, and a bear hug for Sarah. The two of them, Wiz and Sarah, then moved off to stand together for the closing ceremonies. Travis wasn't close enough to tell for certain, but he could have sworn that Sarah was somehow smiling and crying at the same time.

There was one more order of business: the Game Star.

"It's me," Nish hissed into Travis's ear as they stood waiting for the announcement.

"How do you know?" Travis asked, thinking that Muck might have tipped him off.

"Who else?" Nish said.

Travis winced and shook his head. Nish was back to normal.

"*The MVP of the Oz Invitational*," the announcer's voice droned over the loudspeakers.

He paused for effect, no one daring to say a word.

"*From the Screech Owls –* WAYNE NISHIKAWA!"

The arena erupted in thunderous applause. The players banged their sticks on the ice. Nish, acting as if this were an everyday experience for him, piled his stick and gloves and helmet in Travis's arms and skated off to accept his due.

Travis watched in amazement as Nish bowed to the fans and then shook hands with the organizers.

A man in a suit pulled an envelope out of his pocket and made a big display out of handing it over to Nish, who took it and stared at it. There was no announcement over the public address as to what it was.

With the man's encouragement, Nish opened the envelope and removed a piece of paper from inside.

What is it? Travis wondered. *A cheque?*

The man, beaming, reached out to shake Nish's hand. Nish must have been stunned by the amount of money, for he dropped the paper and another organizer had to pick it up for him. The first man reached out, took Nish's limp hand, shook it hard, and slapped him on the back.

Nish turned, his mouth a perfect circle, the blood draining from his face.

He skated, weakly, back to Travis while the sticks continued rapping and the rink maintained its loud standing ovation.

"*What is it?*" Travis shouted over the cheering.

Nish said nothing. He merely handed his award over.

Travis looked at his friend. Nish was white now, his eyes half shut.

Travis unfolded the paper and read: "Free Admission for One – Sydney Harbour Bridge Climb."

The Coathanger!

Nish's mouth twisted in search of words.

Finally he found them, speaking in a voice so low Travis could barely hear.

"I think I'm gonna hurl."

THE END

Power Play in Washington

Bllaaammm!!!!!!

Travis felt as if the explosion had gone off in his chest. He felt it in his lungs, in his stomach, in the three fillings of his teeth. He felt it right through his hands clapped tightly over his ears since the soldiers with machine guns — *Soldiers! Machine Guns! At a peewee hockey tournament?* — had told the Owls to lie flat on the pavement.

He could see it with his eyes closed. A sudden explosion of red — *his own blood?* — as the pavement seemed to jump.

One thundering explosion, then quiet, and then the sound of clutter falling. Something metal in the distance. Something plastic to his right.

Something soft on the back of his neck!

He opened his eyes, the daylight blinding, the air filled with dust from the explosion.

Travis took a hand off one ear and reached back to pull the object off his neck. He was stunned and repulsed by what he saw.

A filthy pair of old boxer shorts!

NISH'S!

363

2

here to begin?

The Screech Owls had left Tamarack the day before to drive down to Washington, D.C., for the International Goodwill Peewee Championship. They were one of three Canadian teams invited to this spring tournament, and one of several teams from outside the United States.

They had been working for weeks for this moment. They'd held bottle drives and bingos. They'd auctioned off a pair of tickets for a game between the Toronto Maple Leafs and the Detroit Red Wings.

Mr. Dillinger and coach Muck Munro had taken turns driving on the way down. Everyone was in a great mood, though the Owls got fed up with Nish's non-stop tapping on the window – *tap-tap . . . tap-tap-tap . . . tap-tap* – and forced him to sit on an inside seat where he couldn't bug them any longer. It was always something with Nish. A new yell, a new way of talking – and now a stupid rhythm he couldn't get out of his head and soon his teammates couldn't get out of theirs.

Mr. Dillinger had called for a "Wedgie Stop" just after the border so they could all stretch their legs and loosen up their underwear. And he'd stopped *twice* for "Stupid Stops" – Nish stocking up on plastic vomit and sponge toffee and huge cannon cracker fireworks that weren't legal at home.

He used the plastic vomit to gross out Simon Milliken and Jenny Staples, and a couple of hours later, after six straight sponge toffees, grossed out drivers passing by on Interstate 70 with his own, real-life vomit while poor Mr. Dillinger stood beside him handing over paper towels – but that's another story altogether.

The Screech Owls had made it to their very first practice at the MCI Center, the huge downtown NHL arena where the Washington Capitals played. The Owls had rarely been so excited to get to a new rink, and it wasn't just because this was the home of the Caps. Right after the Owls, the Washington Wall were scheduled to practise. And everyone knew about the Wall, the team with the most famous peewee hockey player of the moment: Chase Jordan – the twelve-year-old son of the President of the United States.

Everything had seemed fine, at first.

Nish, looking a bit green, had got off the bus first and headed up a back street for a little air. All the other Owls had gone to the back of the old bus to help Mr. Dillinger get the equipment out.

It was a ritual they could do without thinking. Derek Dillinger was up at the rear door, helping his dad and Muck toss

down the bags. Wilson and Willie and Andy, three of the bigger
Owls, were carting the equipment bags to the side and stacking
them with Fahd's help. Travis and Jesse got Sam and Sarah to
help with Mr. Dillinger's skate-sharpening machine. Jeremy and
Jenny took care of their own goaltending equipment. Simon
and Lars and Dmitri carried the sticks over to Gordie and Liz,
who stacked them and sorted them out according to players'
numbers. Data, working from his wheelchair, ticked off the
equipment on a special sheet he and Fahd had designed to keep
track of it all.

They were almost finished when a large van sped around
the back of the big rink, squealed to a halt, and four men jumped
out. They were all big, all in suits, and each had a small earplug
in his left ear with a clear plastic wire coiling down inside the
back of his shirt collar. They all wore sunglasses, Travis noticed.
He also noticed the handgun that flashed briefly in its holster
before one of the men caught his flapping jacket and buttoned
it quickly.

"*What do you think you're doing?*" the lead man had barked at
the Screech Owls.

Mr. Dillinger, sweat pouring down his face, smiled from
beneath his big moustache.

"We have the ice booked at three for a practice," he said.

The man ripped a sheet of paper out of his vest pocket and
studied it.

"Screech Owls?" the man said. It was more accusation than
question.

Mr. Dillinger nodded. "We're from Canada."

The man paid no attention. He snapped the gum he was frantically chewing and flashed his badge at Mr. Dillinger, who had no time to read it.

"Secret Service," the man said. "We have to secure the building."

"President's son?" Mr. Dillinger asked.

The man offered no answer. He turned to where the kids were stacking the equipment bags.

"*Pull those equipment bags over here and line them up!*" he shouted.

"We're on in twenty minutes!" Mr. Dillinger protested. "We have to dress!"

The man paid no attention. He signalled his three colleagues to move into action. Each one grabbed two bags and half-carried, half-dragged them over to a roped-off area at the rear of the parking area. They laid the bags out in a row.

"*Get your bags over there and put them the same way!*" the lead man barked.

Muck, who hadn't said a word so far, signalled the kids to do as the man said. Travis moved his bag over and dropped it beside Sarah's.

"This is ridiculous!" Sarah whispered as they turned back.

"It's like a movie," Travis said.

"A *stupid* movie."

"*Okay!*" the lead man shouted when Lars had dropped the last bag in line. "*Now back off against the building. And no sudden movements!*"

Sam rolled her eyes at Travis.

"*Look!*" gasped Sam.

Another van had pulled up. Its doors opened, and this time two soldiers with large dogs on leashes got out.

"Sniffer dogs," said Fahd.

"What for?" said Sam.

"Standard Secret Service procedure," explained Fahd, who always knew such things. "They secure any building first where a member of the First Family's going to be. We better get used to it."

"What a *pain*," groaned Sarah.

The dogs were frisky. One was a German shepherd, the other a black Labrador. They seemed more interested in playing with each other and their handlers, but one sharp hand signal from each handler and the dogs instantly went to work.

The dogs started at opposite ends of the long line of bags. They sniffed up and down, in the side pockets and around each bag, then moved on, with their handlers holding tight to the leashes.

Suddenly, the Labrador's tail stopped moving. The Lab crouched down. The hair on its back rose. It lay down, muzzle pointing towards one of the bags.

The lead man now shouted excitedly into his wrist, "*K-9 Four! K-9 Four!*"

"He's gone off the deep end," Lars giggled.

"It's a wrist radio," Fahd explained. "Code for something."

There were sirens now. And it seemed the temperature had suddenly risen even further.

The Secret Service men were scurrying. One shouted "*Explosives positive!*" into his own wrist radio.

"Whose bag is it?" Dmitri asked.

Travis craned his neck to catch the number stencilled on the side of the bag.

Forty-four.

Nish's bag.

The firecrackers from the Stupid Stop!

Travis shouted out to Muck and Mr. Dillinger that it was Nish's bag, and Mr. Dillinger, understanding immediately, had tried to catch the attention of the lead Secret Service man – but there was near panic now, and no one would listen to him.

Within moments the area had been cleared, blocked off, and the Owls had been told to lie flat on the pavement and not to lift their heads.

But even so, they could still see much of what was happening.

An armoured vehicle arrived almost immediately. Soldiers scurried to move away all the equipment bags the dogs had checked, leaving just the one – number 44 – in the centre of the cordoned-off area.

Another vehicle screeched to a halt and its back door opened.

A ramp extended from the doorway, and a shiny metal robot rolled out. Directly behind it walked a heavily armoured soldier fiddling with a control box.

"A bomb robot!" whispered Fahd.

"What for?" asked Wilson.

"They're checking the bag for a bomb!"

"Maybe they should be checking it for poisonous gas!" giggled Sarah.

"*Shut up over there!*" barked the lead Secret Service man. He was still furiously snapping his chewing gum.

The Owls went silent. They watched, helplessly, as the robot whirred over to the bag, seemed to take photographs of it, then backed off.

Soldiers gathered around the man with the control box, studying its screen.

Yet another armoured vehicle arrived. Two soldiers, also heavily armoured, scurried out. One held a huge, bazooka-like gun. Several other vehicles backed away quickly.

The two soldiers took up position, one holding the weapon, the other aiming it.

"*They're going to blow up Nish's bag!*" Sam said, her voice skipping between a scream of terror and one of absolute delight.

3

Blllaaammm!!!!!!

It wasn't just Nish's filthy old jockey shorts that rained down upon the cringing Owls.

Sarah got hit with a T-shirt, its armpits yellow and with what seemed like half an old pizza hanging from it. The front said, "Welcome to Lake Placid."

Half-eaten chocolate bars rained down, torn strings of red and green licorice, a broken pen with a girl in a bathing suit on it, smashed X-ray glasses, ripped comic books, torn hockey cards, once-white socks as hard as hockey pucks, smashed water bottles, tools to fix televisions, burst ketchup packs, fungus-covered French fries, old lacrosse balls, grade five, six, and seven workbooks, balls of used shin-pad tape, smashed videotapes and Nintendo games, cracked and empty CD cases, a busted fake Rolex watch, a wizened orange that had turned almost green, burst Coke tins, bent shin pads, torn shoulder pads, ripped Screech Owls home and away jerseys, a thumb from a hockey glove, and a helmet with a plastic visor smashed worse than the windshield of a car that had run into a brick wall.

"MY STUFF!"

The cry came from the far end of the parking lot. Travis didn't even have to lift his head to know who had called out.

Nish was standing at the corner of the rink staring in disbelief at the assembly of army trucks and soldiers and anti-bomb equipment. He was, if anything, looking even greener than when he'd walked off to "get some air." The air was still filled with smoke and fluttering pieces of card – Nish's precious stash of his own hockey cards from Quebec City.

"*What have you done to my equipment!*" Nish wailed.

The lead Secret Service guy was walking fast toward Nish, frantically brushing debris off his suit.

"*Who the hell are you?*" the Secret Service man demanded, his teeth ripping into his gum.

"Wayne . . . Nishikawa," Nish answered. He looked like he was about to throw up again.

"You with this team?"

"Yeah."

"Well, we had to blow up your equipment."

"Why?"

"Dog sniffed explosive. You have explosives in there, son?"

Nish put on his finest choirboy look and shook his head.

"Just my hockey stuff, sir," he said.

"Well," the Secret Service man snapped, turning on his heels. "You'll have to get new stuff now." He walked away, leaving Nish astonished.

The Owls were on their feet, dusting themselves off and picking up pieces of Nish's equipment. Lars held a skate blade high, shaking his head as he stared at it.

"*There's nothing left!*" Nish wailed.

"There's this, Big Boy!" Sam shouted.

She threw something at him. He caught it in the air and held it up.

It was yellowish-white, torn and smouldering, smoke rising from holes that had been peppered through it by the explosion.

A metal cup fell from it and clattered on the pavement.

"They even blew up my jock!" Nish moaned.

"I'VE NOTHING LEFT TO WEAR!"

4

am and Sarah were in the dressing room, kneeling at opposite ends of Nish's new equipment bag, when Nish stepped out of the washroom, his hair freshly watered down and parted for the practice. Both girls had their heads buried in the open bag, and both, at the moment he appeared, sat back and, eyes closed, made a grand display of drinking in the air from the bag.

"Ahhhhhh," Sam said, inhaling deeply. "Like a garden of flowers!"

"Like a spring shower," Sarah agreed. "We could call it 'Breeze of Nish' and sell it."

"Get outta there!" Nish shouted, blood racing to his face. "Or I'll give you a breeze that'll peel paint off the walls."

"Such a charmer," Sam giggled as she and Sarah backed away and Nish took up his usual seat in the corner farthest from the door.

The bag in front of him was an Owls equipment bag, but the number, 44, was scribbled on in grease pencil rather than stitched. Mr. Dillinger had scrambled to replace Nish's destroyed hockey equipment, and he'd done an amazing job. Carrying extra skates in the general equipment bag had paid off; there was a pair of size 8s that Andy had outgrown but which fitted Nish almost perfectly. There were extra pads and gloves and a pair of pants that Mr. Dillinger had stitched up. Mr. Dillinger even produced new team socks for Nish and a new sweater. Not his old 44, of course, which had been destroyed in the explosion, but 22. "Some people say you're only half there, anyway," Mr. Dillinger had joked, and even Nish had been forced to laugh.

But he was hardly happy now.

"This isn't me!" Nish had moaned when he was finally suited up.

"*Thank God!*" Sarah and Sam had shouted out at the same time.

"I'm missing my 'A,'" he whined.

"We can fix that," said Mr. Dillinger. He pulled out a roll of tape, cut three strips, and stuck them on to form a quick assistant captain's "A."

"And I'm missing my lucky shorts!" Nish groaned, almost in tears.

"*Lucky us!*" shouted Sam.

"I've worn them since Lake Placid!" he muttered.

"*When?*" Travis asked, eyes widening in disbelief.

"Lake Placid," Nish repeated.

Travis, like every other Owl in the room, did some rapid mental calculations. *Months* had passed since the tournament in Lake Placid. *Hundreds* of games and practices. *Surely he hadn't worn the same pair of boxer shorts in every one of them!*

"You must have washed them?" Fahd asked, equally incredulous.

Nish shook his head. "Only a fool would wash off good luck," he groaned.

"It's a wonder Washington is still standing!" laughed Sarah.

Nish said nothing. He leaned back in his stall, closed his eyes, and stuck out his tongue in the general direction of everyone in the room.

Muck threw one of his "curve balls" into the practice. After they had worked on a new break-out pattern and taken shots at Jenny and Jeremy, Muck had them all toss their sticks over the boards and onto the bench floor while Mr. Dillinger struggled out from the dressing room area with a large, open cardboard box.

"Everyone take one!" ordered Muck. "And *no* reloading!"

Travis looked at Nish, who scowled back. What was Muck up to?

Lars's hand was first into the box. He pulled out a green, clear plastic water gun, water dripping from the plug and trigger. Wilson got a blue one. Sarah got a red one. Hands plunged into the box, each one emerging with a cheap, filled-to-the-brim water gun.

"Have fun," Muck said, and stepped off the ice, hurrying up the corridor towards the Owls' dressing room before anyone could think to take a shot in his direction.

"What're we supposed to do with these?" Nish asked, holding his up like he'd never seen one before.

"*This!*" Sam shouted, squirting him straight in his open mouth.

She took off down the ice, Nish chasing. Bedlam broke out at the bench as Owls began firing at Owls. Screaming and yelling and laughing, they chased each other around the rink, trying to get a shot in.

Andy and Simon went after Travis, but he was too agile a skater for them to nail him with a good blast. He twisted behind the goal. He used the net for a shield. He scooted out and towards the blueline and then turned back so fast his skates almost lost their edge.

Everywhere, the Owls were twisting and turning and ducking and trying to cut each other off. Travis slipped back behind the net again, jockeying for position as Simon came in from the left.

Travis faked one way, then turned back on Simon, blasting him as he twisted and coiled back along the boards.

Travis realized what Muck had done. They were playing – but they were also practising! They might not have sticks or pucks, but they were still working on hockey skills. Twisting and turning along the boards was not unlike cycling in the corners. Racing for the net was not unlike looking for a scoring chance. Trying to cut off a player who'd just sprayed you and was now racing down the ice was not unlike trying to read the ice to make a check.

It made Travis laugh to think how brilliant Muck could sometimes be. The Owls would be convinced this was nothing but messing around – and yet they were probably learning far more about hockey than they were about water pistols.

Nish, naturally, ran out of water first.

When the others realized this, they turned on him as a team. Nish cowered in the corner with his hands held up helplessly to block the spray of more than a dozen water guns. Finally, the last spurt went down his neck, and Nish rose up in a rage and began blindly chasing the scattering attackers.

They were saved by a shrill whistle from the bench. Muck's whistle. Everyone stopped dead in their tracks and turned to glide towards the bench where Muck was standing, whistle still in his mouth, face red with anger.

Beside Muck was Mr. Dillinger with the box that had held the water pistols, and behind them was the Secret Service leader, earplug still in, teeth still snapping on his chewing gum. He looked stern.

"Put 'em away, kids," Mr. Dillinger said. "Security says you gotta hang 'em up."

"What's wrong?" asked Sam, as she tossed her empty pistol into the box.

"Water pistols," Muck said quietly through clenched teeth, "are apparently a 'security breach' in this rink."

"Just while the tournament's on, Coach," the gum-snapper said. "We have to confiscate them and they'll be returned to you before you head back home."

"*Water* pistols?" said Sarah.

Travis studied Muck. He knew that the quieter Muck spoke the more upset he was bound to be. He also knew that Muck hated to be called "Coach." It was an American thing, he always said. Hockey was a Canadian game, and his name was the same whether he stood behind the bench or out in the parking lot: Muck Munro.

"Any kind of pistol, miss," the man said. "Replicas, facsimiles, toys – whatever. One of my men sees one of these being pointed, and we shoot first and ask questions later, understand?"

Nish didn't. "Like what?" he asked. " 'Are you using hot or cold water?' "

"Don't be smart, mister," the man said. "I have authority to suspend any team or player from this tournament we deem to be a security risk – and you've already got one count against you, do you not?"

Nish flushed deep red. He said nothing more.

Mr. Dillinger took the last of the pistols, folded the flaps of the box, and handed it over to the security head, who tossed it to an assistant.

"Three times around," Muck said to the Owls. "Skate it out of you. Let's go now!"

Muck blew his whistle sharply three times. The man with the earplug winced, and Travis grinned to himself. Muck rarely blew his whistle, and never hard. This was just his way of taking a shot at the security head. Good for Muck!

Travis skated with Sarah, the two of them talking about the absurdity of the situation and laughing, again, at how helpless Nish had looked when the team had him down in the corner and was spraying him at will.

"Look over there," Sarah said suddenly, tilting her head towards the opposite side of the ice.

A kid their age – curly red hair, blue eyes – was standing so close to the glass at the visitors' doorway that his breath was fogging it up.

He was in full uniform, holding his helmet in one hand and a stick in the other. He stared at the Owls as they left the ice.

"Earplug's watching him," said Sarah.

Behind the youngster, studying him with fierce concentration, was the Secret Service head, the man who chewed gum like a beaver going through a branch.

Travis giggled. Earplug was a perfect nickname for him.

Beyond Earplug stood another three men, each facing in a different direction, each standing on the balls of his feet as if he might, on a moment's notice, have to tackle someone.

Travis and Sarah stared back.

"Guess who the kid is," Sarah said.

Travis knew – the President's son, the centre for the Washington Wall.

He was so close to the glass it was almost as if he were trying to push through.

Travis understood. All his life, a hockey rink and especially a clean, untouched ice surface, had been his own greatest escape. It must be worth even more, he realized, to the son of the President of the United States.

Sarah took off her glove and waved to the boy.

Unsure, the boy lifted his hand and gave a quick wave back.

Behind him, the Secret Service man snapped his gum and scowled.

5

Travis was the first to wake in the little hotel room he was sharing with Nish and Fahd and Lars. Nish was still snoring. He'd managed to turn completely around in the large double bed he was sharing with Fahd, and his toes were resting on the pillow beside Fahd's head. Poor Fahd, thought Travis. What a sight to wake up to!

Sunlight was streaming in the window. There were dust particles dancing in the air – "angels," Travis's grandmother called them – and he watched for a while, wondering how they avoided the pull of gravity that ruled everything else on earth. Perhaps his grandmother was right.

Mr. Dillinger was filled with plans for the day. They would walk around the Capitol building, down the Mall to take in the view from the top of the towering Washington Monument, and on through the park and across the bridge to Arlington Cemetery. Then they'd walk back to the Smithsonian Air and Space Museum to see the *Spirit of St. Louis* and the spacesuit worn by

Neil Armstrong, the first man on the moon, before returning to
the hotel to rest before the first game of the tournament.

The Owls had drawn team number one in the round robin
– Djurgården, from Stockholm, Sweden. Lars, who knew some
of the players, had already warned the Owls that they would be
in for a tremendous battle. Travis could hardly wait.

They set out in weather so beautiful it seemed impossible that
there were still deep snowbanks back home. Here, the cherry
trees were in full blossom as they headed out into the park, Muck
and Mr. Dillinger leading the way, Sarah helping guide Data's
chair. They walked to the huge, open-air Lincoln Memorial,
where Muck insisted on reading, out loud, Abraham Lincoln's
Gettysburg Address: "Four score and seven years ago . . ."

"I thought this was a hockey tournament," Nish whispered
in Travis's ear, "not a history class."

Travis said nothing. He knew how Muck loved his history,
and knew, as well, how much Nish hated anything to do with
school that wasn't recess, March break, or summer holidays. But
there was no point in arguing. Nish had already wandered off,
fascinated with the echoes he could produce by tapping a small
stone against the marble: *tap-tap . . . tap-tap-tap . . . tap-tap*. Where
was security when you actually needed it?

They set out across the bridge over the Potomac River and
up into the gently rolling slopes of Arlington National Cemetery,
where they walked quietly about the Tomb of the Unknown
Soldier and the graves of President John F. Kennedy and his
younger brother, Bobby. Bobby might one day have become
president too, if he hadn't been shot like his brother. Muck
seemed deeply moved. With his eyes shining, he tried to explain

to them what the Kennedys had meant to people like him and Mr. Dillinger.

"Everything seemed possible back then," he said in a quiet voice. "They were so young and so full of life. We all wonder what the world might have become if they had lived. If it hadn't been for John Kennedy, you know, the world wouldn't have reached the moon."

"If it hadn't been for Ol' Nish," Nish whispered in Travis's ear, "the world wouldn't have *seen* the moon."

Nish could never leave well enough alone. Muck was talking about space travel and as usual Nish wanted to talk about himself. Besides, he was exaggerating. Maybe Nish had planned to moon the world in New York City, but he hadn't done it. Fortunately.

"Why were they killed?" Fahd asked.

Muck shrugged. "Presidents are always in danger of being assassinated. We'll see where Abraham Lincoln was killed at Ford's Theatre. It's not far from the rink. And Ronald Reagan was shot right back there, near the Capitol and surrounded by Secret Service. There's no pattern, which is why it's so difficult to defend against. It's usually just some nut."

"What about the President's kids?" Jenny asked.

Muck furrowed his brow. "They have to be protected, too," he said. "You never know what some lunatic might try."

"Is that why there's all that Secret Service stuff around the hockey tournament," Lars asked, "because they're worried about the kid?"

"That's one reason," Muck said.

"There's another?" Data asked.

Muck nodded.

"What?" several of the Owls said at once.

Muck smiled sheepishly. "I'm not really supposed to say . . ."

"You *have* to now," Jesse shouted.

"Well," Muck said, "just don't broadcast it around."

"We won't!" shouted Fahd. "What is it?"

"The championship trophy is going to be presented by the President."

Travis swallowed hard. It felt like he was trying to push a pill the size of a puck down his throat. If the President of the United States was going to be presenting the trophy to the winning team of the championship, then he would be giving it to the captain of the winning team.

And if the Screech Owls won, that would be Travis Lindsay.

D jurgården skated out in the Swedish national team colours: beautiful yellow sweaters with the three crowns of Sweden in blue crests across their fronts. They looked intimidating, the sort of team that is so skilled, so fluid, and so organized that they can sometimes defeat the other team before the warm-up is even over.

Travis was particularly nervous. He missed the crossbar on five straight shots in warm-up. He tried to figure out what was wrong but couldn't quite put his finger on it. The first game of a big tournament? It shouldn't be that. All the security?

"This doesn't *feel* right," a voice squeaked in his ear.

He knew at once it was Nish. He was relieved to discover his friend was also uneasy.

But for different reasons.

"I need my old boxer shorts back," Nish whined.

"They're in the garbage. Go pick 'em out," Travis laughed.

"They're ruined. I should sue."

"Sue the government of the United States of America for your boxers?" Travis asked.

"They had no right to destroy them."

"They have the undying gratitude of our whole hockey team," Travis said.

"*Nothing* feels right," Nish continued, not listening to anything Travis was saying. "I've got the wrong shorts on. Wrong equipment. Everything's wrong. I don't even *smell* like me!"

"God bless America!" Travis said, and skated away from his muttering, mumbling pal.

What a difference an ocean made! When the Owls went to Sweden, they were baffled at first by the big Olympic ice surface. Now the Djurgården peewees had the same problem in reverse. To them, the ice was cramped and tight. Less space meant less time, and they were panicking with the puck. Used to being able to work the corners, they now had to fight for them, and the usual long cross-ice passes of European hockey were easy pickings for the Owls – particularly for a player as quick as Dmitri.

Dmitri scored the first two goals. He snared a lazy Swedish pass in the neutral zone, roared in on the opponents' net, faked once, went to his backhand and roofed the puck, sending the water bottle flying. On the second, he finished off a pretty tic-tac-toe play where Travis slipped the puck back to Sarah, moving in late on a rush, and Sarah snapped the puck ahead to Dmitri as he came to a spraying stop at the far goal post. Dmitri had only to redirect the puck in behind the falling goaltender.

"They'll find themselves," Muck warned at the first break. "Just like you guys had to find yourselves over there."

Muck was right. In the second period, the Swedes adjusted their game. Forwards carried less and shortened their passes. Defencemen used the boards more, pinching in on the Owls whenever they could and causing pucks to jump free. The first Djurgården goal came on a scramble, and then a fluid-skating centre scored a beautiful goal on a solo rush when he managed to slip the puck between Nish's legs and get in alone on Jenny.

"Never would have happened if I'd had my old boxers on," a red-faced Nish muttered when he plunked down on the bench.

"The puck would have *melted*!" laughed Sam, plunking down beside him and giving him a shot in the shoulder.

Both teams scored in the third, Djurgården on a tip, and Lars on a beautiful end-to-end rush with a hard backhander along the ice that just caught the corner.

Muck called a time-out with two minutes to go and hardly said a word. There was really nothing to say. Everyone knew how much a win mattered in a round robin. Travis also knew that Muck wanted his top line out for the final moments, and Sarah was gasping for breath, having just killed off a penalty.

Nothing had gone right for Travis. He had the one assist, but nothing more. The one good shot he'd had slipped off his blade and flopped off to the side of the net. He thought the other team might even be laughing at his weak shot. He needed something. Anything.

Nish and Sam were back. The most powerful five Owls had the ice, and Sarah won the faceoff by sweeping it back to Nish. Nish moved back behind his own net, checking the clock quickly and then measuring the ice for the best side to go up.

He faked a pass to Travis along the left boards and then shot it back off the boards to Sam on the other side.

Nish moved out quickly, "accidentally" brushing by the fore-checker to put him off balance and give Sam more time. Sam used it to step around the second forechecker and fire a hard pass up-centre to Sarah, who was curling just before the red line.

Dmitri was already away down the right side. Sarah dumped the puck in as she crossed centre, and Dmitri beat the Djurgården defence to it.

Dmitri danced with the puck out to the open corner. Travis cut for the slot, slapping his stick on the ice.

Dmitri hit him perfectly.

Travis tucked the puck in to himself as he drifted around the last defenceman. He had an open shot – and fired hard. The goaltender jumped, literally leaving the ice, and the puck hit him high in the chest pad and dropped back down in the crease.

Travis was still moving in. He saw the puck there, patiently waiting for him, as the goalie came back down on his skates, scraping hard and falling off to the other side.

Open net!

Travis stabbed at the free puck just as a glove lunged out of nowhere and yanked it to the side and out of harm's way.

Travis could not stop his stab. He hit air, then fell, tearing the net off its moorings as he was hit from behind.

He could see nothing. All he could hear was the referee's whistle, so close it seemed to be screaming. He rolled over, looking back to see what the call was and who had hit him. At least he had drawn a penalty, he figured. Not as good as a goal, but not bad.

But the referee was not pointing at any of the Djurgården players. He was pointing hard towards centre ice.

Travis was momentarily confused. He knew the signal from somewhere. Had he seen it in the rule book? Had he seen it on television?

Suddenly it came to him.

Penalty shot!

7

"Number seven – white!"

Travis didn't need to hear it again. He knew what the referee's call meant. He'd been closest to the puck when the Djurgården defenceman had put his hand over the puck in the crease. The penalty-shot call was automatic.

"A penalty shot has been awarded to the Screech Owls," the PA system crackled throughout the arena. "The shot will be taken by number seven, Travis Lindsay."

Travis got shakily to his feet. It wasn't because of the hit that he felt wobbly.

He skated slowly to the bench, where Muck was leaning over, a big arm open for Travis to skate into. If only the arm would open up like a cave and swallow me, thought Travis. If only they'd called out number nine for Sarah, or ninety-one for Dmitri, or even forty-four – no, *twenty-two!* – for Nish. *Anybody but me!* But outwardly Travis managed to remain calm. Muck's big arm around his shoulders helped.

So did Muck's voice, so soft and reassuring.

"There's a secret to the penalty shot, you know," Muck said.

"What?" Travis asked, desperate to know.

"Shoot," Muck said, and smiled down at him. "Some guys get so excited they forget to shoot. Just shoot the puck and see what happens."

Travis nodded. He felt like he couldn't talk.

The linesman was placing the puck at centre ice. Only the officials, the Djurgården goaltender, and Travis Lindsay were on the ice.

The referee blew his whistle and swung his arm to indicate it was time.

Travis circled back on his own side of centre. He could hear the crowd cheering. He could hear his teammates thumping their sticks against the boards.

He picked up the puck and felt it wobble at the end of his blade. He almost lost it immediately.

He dug in. He hadn't noticed how much snow was on the ice, but they'd played the entire game and there had been no flood. Now it seemed there was snow everywhere! The ice was chopped up and gouged and the snow seemed to have piled up so deep in front of him he needed a plough to get through.

He felt his legs turn to rubber, his stick to boiled spaghetti. He felt his hands weaken, his shoulders sag. He felt his brain begin to race like a motor at full throttle. He felt his eyes go out of focus, his hips stop moving, his spine collapse, his brain spring apart like the rubber in a sliced golf ball.

He was on a breakaway – a penalty shot in an international tournament – and he was screwing up!

Time had never gone so slow, and at the same moment so fast.

He looked up. The Djurgården goaltender seemed completely at ease. He had come out to cut off the angle, and now was reading Travis perfectly and wiggling his way back toward the net, always with the angle right, giving away nothing.

What do I do? Travis wanted to shout. Deke him?

Blast away?

Fake the shot and try and get the angle?

Go five hole?

Backhand?

Forehand?

He wanted to stop dead in his tracks, turn to the bench and scream, "MUCK! WHAT DO I DOOOOO?"

But there was no time. The referee was skating alongside him now, watching. The little Swedish goaltender was wiggling back into his crease and still had given Travis nothing to shoot at.

There's too much snow!

The ice is too bad!

I need to circle back and come in again!

It was too late. He was in too close. He decided, at the last moment, to go backhand, and flicked the puck over from his forehand.

The puck slid away from him!

Travis jabbed at it. He hit the puck badly with the blade of his stick. It skipped towards the corner. He lunged, swinging madly at the puck and catching it with the heel of his stick.

The puck shot towards the net, narrowly missing the post – but on the wrong side!

The whistle blew, the Djurgården bench erupted – Travis started to turn away from the net, lost his edge, and fell, sliding into the boards.

He could hear people in the crowd laughing.

He got up, knocked the snow off – *See*, he wanted to yell, *look at the snow!* – and headed back to a bench where no one was cheering, where hardly anyone was even looking at him.

He had failed the Owls.

Sarah gave him a sympathetic smile, but it wasn't what Travis needed. He needed a second chance.

Muck had his big fists jammed deep in the pockets of his old windbreaker. He was half smiling, half shaking his head.

"Shoot next time," Muck said in his very quiet voice.

Travis nodded. Inside, he was bawling.

8

ravis had no idea how long he'd been standing at the urinal. He'd come off the ice with
the rest of the Owls – the silence crushing as
they slouched their way back to the dressing room – and he'd
set his stick against the wall, lopped off his helmet, dropped his
gloves, and hurried off to the little washroom. He didn't need to
go. He'd just wanted to get away.

He stood there, waiting, all through the low rumble of
Muck's short post-game speech. He knew what Muck would be
saying: *Good effort, good work, lucky to come out of it with a tie, we'll
just have to be a little sharper next game* . . . He could hear Mr.
Dillinger putting away the skate sharpener and bundling up the
sticks, lightly whistling as he worked, the way he always did
when there was a bit of tension in the dressing room.

Travis felt terrible. He felt he'd failed the team. He felt he
should rip the "C" off his sweater and hand it back. A captain
was supposed to lead by example, or so Muck always said, and
what an example Travis had set:

Blow the penalty shot.

Give up the win when it is yours for the taking.

Choke under pressure.

Travis stood there until he knew he could put it off no longer. He buckled up and headed back in to face the jury.

As he came through the door, he pretended to be absorbed in lacing up his hockey pants. The Owls were all busy shedding their gear. There was the familiar smell of *hockey* in the air, a steely, damp, and sweaty smell found nowhere else on earth but a dressing room in the minutes following a hard-fought game.

Fahd looked up first, one of his ridiculous questions rising.

"Where were *you*?" Fahd asked accusingly.

"Going to the bathroom," Travis said, trying to sound matter-of-fact.

Nish looked up, grinning like a red tomato.

"Did you miss *that*, too?" Nish giggled.

The dressing room exploded with laughter.

"Nish is a goof," Fahd said to Travis as they backed out through the door with their equipment.

"You're just realizing that?" Travis said. His voice made him sound angrier than he was. He wasn't upset with Nish – at least, not as much as he was with himself.

The bus was parked behind the MCI Center, and the fastest way out was through the Zamboni chute. They pushed through a second door, neither one saying a word, and began to walk across the drainage grating alongside the Zamboni.

"DON'T MOVE!"

Travis and Fahd froze in their tracks. It was like being in a movie. Someone they couldn't see had barked a command. *What was next? Gunfire?*

A shadow emerged from the far side of the Zamboni.

Earplug!

He was snapping his gum and had one hand just inside his jacket as if prepared to pull out his .38 snubnose Smith & Wesson and blow the two Screech Owls away.

"What're you two doing here?" Earplug snapped.

"We just played a game," said Fahd. "We're leaving."

"Door's that way, smart fellow!" Earplug barked, nodding in the opposite direction.

"Our bus's out back," said Fahd.

Earplug seemed to think about that a moment. There was no sound at all in the room but the grind of his teeth and the periodic little *snap-snap-snap* as he flicked his tongue through the gum.

Like a snake! Travis thought. A gum-chewing snake!

Finally, it seemed to register on Earplug. The bus *could* be out back. The shortest route between dressing room and back parking lot was indeed through the Zamboni chute and out the back door.

He nodded to himself and stepped back for them to pass. He waved them along with his one free hand, as if directing traffic.

Travis could hardly believe how jumpy Earplug was. He seemed almost out of control – one hand waving two peewee hockey players through to the parking lot, the other hand on his concealed weapon as if, any second now, he'd be forced to blow them away.

"Th-thanks," said Fahd.

The two Owls squeezed by. The Zamboni had been opened up so Earplug and his security force could check the insides. Travis could see the blades that sent the shaved ice up into the holding tank and the hydraulic pistons that dumped the snow out. What did he think? Travis wondered. That one of the Zamboni drivers might sneak out with the machine during play, slip up behind the President's son during a faceoff, gobble him up, and then race out the back doors to hold him for ransom? Travis giggled to himself at the thought of the chase: police cars, fire engines, helicopters all chasing the chugging Zamboni down Pennsylvania Avenue.

Ludicrous, he thought.

But still, he had to give Earplug credit. He was thorough.

 ahd turned the television on. He wanted to
play the hotel's in-house Nintendo, but Travis
caught him before he switched it over.

"There's the White House!" Travis almost shouted.

"So?" Fahd said. "It's CNN. It's always got the stupid news
on."

"Yeah, but that's live – and it's just around the corner."

Fahd paused. "Yeah, weird."

They watched for a few moments. It was a report of a big
summit on the Middle East Peace Accord, and there were shots
of limousines arriving and world leaders getting in and out.
There was a clip of the President talking to the media out in the
garden, the White House huge behind him.

Travis wondered what it must be like to live there – especially for a kid. Could the President's son have friends over after
school? Did he have a net set up in the basement like Nish did,
and could he just jump up from his homework at the kitchen
table – *would he even have a kitchen table?* – and run down and

take shots until, as Nish's mom always said, he'd "worked the heebie-jeebies out of his system"?

Travis knew he wouldn't trade places for anything. His father might never be on the news, people outside of Tamarack might not know his name, but he liked his quiet little house and the fact that his father worried more about things like the lawn than whether he could stop bombs from going off in the Middle East.

"You can switch it," Travis said.

Fahd fiddled with the control and the familiar Super Mario music came on. He would be lost for the next hour or so.

The telephone rang.

Travis rolled on his shoulders across the bed and dropped off the side, scooping up the phone as he fell. It was Mr. Dillinger.

"Muck wants the team down in the lobby," Mr. Dillinger said. "Round up your roomies and get everyone down here."

"Now?" Travis asked. He could see Fahd's questioning stare. "Right now."

Muck was waiting for them, standing in the middle of the lobby with his fists jammed into his old windbreaker. He didn't seem upset, but he did look serious.

Once everyone was there, Muck began.

"The Screech Owls have been asked if they'd do a favour for our hosts," he told them. "I said I'd put it to a vote."

"What is it?" Fahd asked unnecessarily.

Muck didn't want to get to the point right away. "You know," he said, "believe it or not, Wayne Gretzky was also a peewee player much like you guys."

Travis blinked. Was Wayne Gretzky here? Was the all-time leading goal scorer in the National Hockey League coming to the tournament? Was his kid playing in it?

"Wayne Gretzky was so famous even as a peewee, he couldn't live a normal life," Muck went on. "One of the things his teammates used to do was swap jackets with him at the end of the games so he could sneak out without the other team's parents screaming at him. Did you know that?"

"Yes," said Willie Granger, the team trivia expert. No one else seemed to know.

"Mr. Dillinger and I have discussed helping out a youngster in this tournament. His team has asked us if we might consider including him in our tour plans – so he can fit in just like any other player and not be bothered by anyone."

Mr. Dillinger held out a team jacket. He'd already stitched a number on the sleeve, 17, that no one else on the team wore.

Travis felt a shiver of understanding go up and down his spine.

"Who is it?" Fahd asked.

Muck cleared his throat.

"Chase Jordan. The President's son."

"*Why us?*" Nish squeaked from the back of the gathering.

"Why not us?" Muck asked. "We're not even an American team. We're from Canada. We plan on visiting the sights. We have our own bus –"

"Even if it is only running on five cylinders," Mr. Dillinger added.

"– and, most important of all," Muck continued, "we already

have a player who has to be the centre of attention everywhere he goes."

"*Who's that?*" Nish squeaked.

Muck closed his eyes and, very slightly, shook his head.

"Well?" Mr. Dillinger said. "What do we say? Do the Owls take on a temporary player or what?"

"*Yes!*" shouted Sarah.

"*Absolutely!*" yelled Sam.

"*Yes!*"

"*Yes!*"

"*Yes!*"

10

"You might not believe this," Chase Jordan was saying, "but I've lived here nearly two years and I've never seen the sights of Washington."

A group of the Owls were walking away from the building holding the Smithsonian space travel exhibits and back toward the park and the Washington Monument. They looked the same as always: peewee hockey players in team jackets, all of them bobbing along with their fists rammed into their windbreaker pockets.

Travis wished he could step back a moment and see if he could notice anything different about them. They were boys and girls, all around twelve years of age, some a bit bigger than others, and some standing out for other reasons – Sam's flame-coloured hair in a ponytail, Nish swaggering like he owned Washington. No one, however, would ever have noticed number 17 for anything other than the curly red hair that bounced out the back and sides of his Screech Owls ball cap.

That this was the son of the President of the United States

would never have seemed possible. Wilson even wore a red maple leaf cap instead of his usual Screech Owls one so people would know this was a team from Canada. And they were sight-seeing like tourists. Who would ever expect a member of the First Family, who *lived* there, to be walking around Washington gawking at the sights like he'd never been here before?

But that's how it was. The Jordans had a dog, Nixon, but even it was walked by the Secret Service. "I was surprised they didn't hook Nixon up with a plastic earplug," Chase said at one point. Travis liked him at once. He was funny. He made fun of himself. And he seemed grateful to be included as part of the gang.

Travis knew they were being watched. It made no sense just to let Chase go out wherever he wished with the Owls. Once, Travis even thought he saw Earplug himself, walking along the souvenir stands, drinking out of a water bottle and seeming to talk into his wrist as he did so. But still, they were giving Chase a little space. Fahd bought a couple of Stars-and-Stripes Frisbees and they kicked off their shoes and played on the grass in their bare feet. Willie and Fahd and Data even came up with a new game called "Frisbee hockey," and they divided up into teams, put out some runners for goal posts, and played for a good half-hour.

Chase Jordan was a good athlete. He could run almost as fast as Sarah, and he had a natural gift for throwing the Frisbee so it shot down, skimmed the ground, and then up again perfectly into another player's hands. He ran and laughed and shouted for passes, and after the first few minutes of play, it was like he'd always been an Owl.

Out of breath and damp with sweat, they broke for drinks from a little stand at the side of the road. Travis was chugging an ice-cold Snapple when he noticed Mr. Dillinger and Muck coming along from the opposite direction.

"Time you kids saw The Wall," Muck said.

"Been there, done that!" called out Nish, causing the rest of the Owls to laugh and Muck and Mr. Dillinger to look baffled. They didn't know that in Lord Stanley Public School back in Tamarack, kids who talked too much or acted up were sent to stand and face a wall to get a grip on themselves before returning to class. Some even called it "Nish's Wall" in honour of its most frequent user.

"I want you to show a little respect, Nishikawa," Muck said. "Hard as it might be for you to think about anyone but yourself, this is where you need to do it."

They began walking across the grass. Travis felt a presence at his side. He glanced over. Chase Jordan, the President's son.

"I've been a couple of times," Chase said. "But always formal things – my father speaking, that sort of thing. I always wanted to come myself but never got the chance."

Travis wasn't sure what Chase Jordan was talking about. He knew enough about Washington to know that the wall Muck was taking them to was the memorial to the Americans who had been killed in the Vietnam War. He'd seen a picture of it – rectangular black granite slabs sitting on the grass – and, to tell the truth, he hadn't been much impressed.

They could see The Wall now. It looked, from the distance, much as Travis remembered. Vertical black granite slabs banked into the grass. There was a walkway alongside it for visitors, and it was dug down so that, as the tourists walked along, the slabs rose above them and they seemed to disappear into the earth.

"*Bor-ring!*" a familiar voice hissed in Travis's ear.

"*What do we see next?*" Nish whined. "*A tree? A stick? A real, genuine stone? I can hardly wait.*"

Travis said nothing. He was afraid of being overheard by Muck or Mr. Dillinger, who were walking ahead of them each with his hands clasped in front like he was walking up the aisle in church.

Like the rest of the Owls, Travis just followed along. He let his mind drift as he began heading down the walkway.

It took a while for Travis to realize what he was passing by. First, there were just short granite slabs with a few names on them, and every now and then a date. It seemed so long ago. Nineteen fifty-eight. Nineteen sixty.

But as he began moving through the 1960s, he began to understand why it was that the walkway seemed to go down deeper into the ground. The granite slabs were rising high above him – and the number of names began growing and growing until, by the mid-1960s, he could no longer see where one year ended and the next began. There were names by the thousands. By the tens of thousands.

And then he began noticing the tributes. A small withered rose was the first that caught his attention. Someone had laid it at the foot of a slab, and he saw that there was a note attached. Travis looked in both directions. Farther along the walkway there were more flowers, some quite fresh, and more notes, and people were reading them and even photographing them. He leaned down and opened the note. It was from a woman. Her handwriting was beautiful. She had attached a picture of herself smiling and holding a small baby, a new photograph. The note was to her father. She wanted him to know that he had become a grandfather.

"I'm thirty-two now, Daddy," the note read. "Ten years older than you were when you went away forever. I would give anything to see you again for even a moment. There's someone here you should meet – Mom says he's just like you."

Travis dropped the note. He felt as if he had invaded someone's privacy. The smiling woman and the little boy who wouldn't know his grandfather. But then, why would this woman have put this note here if she didn't want people to know?

Travis swallowed hard and moved on. There were dozens of notes. There were bouquets of flowers. He came upon an entire family – children, parents, grandparents – taking pictures of each other as they stood, in turn, and touched one of the names that had been carved into the black granite. The older people were crying, the younger ones seemed uncertain how to react.

It was here where Travis first saw a person take a rubbing. A woman had something that looked like wax paper laid over one of the names and she was rubbing furiously with what seemed to be a thick crayon. The name was coming through onto the paper exactly as it appeared on the granite.

He now saw that there were many people taking rubbings. There was even a stand where paper and crayons were being given out to anyone who wanted them.

He was walking backwards, watching these people, when he backed into the wheelchair. At first, when he heard the clang and felt the handle as he turned, he figured it would be Data. He was already apologizing when he saw that it wasn't Data at all. It was an old man. He had a scraggly beard and was wearing a military shirt with decorations over the heart. His sleeves were rolled up to reveal dark blue tattoos.

Travis knew he should have been frightened, but he wasn't. He knew the person he'd just slammed into should have been upset, but he wasn't.

"Help me out, dude?" the man asked.

Travis thought he must want to be pushed somewhere. "S-sure," he said.

The man fumbled in a bag slung from the side of his wheelchair. He pulled out some wax paper and a crayon. "I can't reach it," he said.

Travis looked into his eyes. They were clear and blue and full of pain. It took some effort to look away. The man's stare was hypnotic.

"What do you want?" Travis said.

"I need a rub to take home to Alabama," the man said in a drawl that sounded, at first, made up. "And I can't reach it, dude. You'll have to do it for me. Okay, soldier?"

Travis felt foolish being called "soldier." He was no soldier. Soldiers were tall and stood at attention like they did up at Arlington Cemetery guarding the Tomb of the Unknown Soldier. And they wore perfectly pressed uniforms, not Screech Owls jackets. And not torn and scraggly uniforms like this man wore. If he wasn't in a wheelchair, and if Travis hadn't felt sorry for him, he would have thought the man was a . . . *bum*. That's it, a bum.

"I don't know how," Travis said.

"It's not rocket science, dude," the man laughed. His teeth were black, some of them missing. "Just put the paper over the name and rub."

Travis looked up. The names seemed to stretch into the sky. "Which one?"

"Dougherty, C. A." the man said. "Private Charlie Dougherty."

Travis looked along the list of D's rising before him. Doyons, D. F. . . . Dover, P. L. . . . Dougherty, C. A.

"There," Travis said, pointing.

The man nodded. "My brother," he said in his deep drawl. "Not my brother in a court of law, dude, but my brother in 'Nam. We served together. I just lost my legs. He lost everything."

The man said it all so matter-of-factly it seemed unreal. Travis couldn't ask him anything more. He stretched up and started rubbing. He started with the "D" and marvelled at how it soon seemed to move off the wall and onto the paper. No wonder people wanted to take the names home with them.

Travis stretched and rubbed and the man kept talking.

"Charlie was the funniest dude you ever could imagine," he said. "They shoulda made a TV show of the things he did over there. Twice as funny as anything you ever saw on *M.A.S.H.*, I'm telling you."

Travis had to know. "What happened?"

"Charlie 'n' me and our platoon were on patrol. I stepped on a mine – last step I ever took, dude – and Charlie was the one who came back to drag me away. Carried me on his shoulders, dropped me in the medics tent and dropped dead himself. Sniper'd shot him while he was carrying me and he never even flinched. Charlie saved my life, dude – with his."

All Travis could do was nod and continue rubbing at the letters. His mind was swimming with the images this old ragged-looking man had put there: the exploding land mine, the friend running through the smoke and gunfire to rescue his buddy, knowing he'd been shot but knowing, too, he had to get back or they were both dead . . .

Travis knew nothing of war and what it could do to people. Suddenly it seemed absurd to him that, during the Stanley Cup playoffs, the announcers would talk about hockey games as though they were wars and battles. No one ever had their legs blown off in a hockey game. No one ever sacrificed his life for a teammate. There were no whistles or horns to make a war stop. War had no scoreboard.

But it did, too. It suddenly hit Travis that this was what the Vietnam memorial was all about. It was the home-side score from a terrible war, each name a permanent loss.

He could no longer think of it as granite slabs. It was the place where this scraggly old man in the wheelchair could once again be with his buddy and thank him for what he did.

"Eighteen years old, dude – never even had a damned chance."

Travis shivered. Eighteen years old was "draft age" in hockey, an age Travis and Nish and the others sometimes dreamed they were, with their lives as NHL players just about to begin. But for Charlie Dougherty it was already over.

Travis's arms were killing him. He felt ashamed of himself. He wanted to quit because his arms hurt. Charlie Dougherty hadn't quit even after being hit by a sniper's bullet.

A big thick hand came over the top of his head and pushed against the wax paper. A second big hand reached in and took the crayon from Travis.

It was Muck.

Muck saying nothing, just reaching to take over from Travis.

Muck staring straight ahead, refusing to look down.

His big hands shaking, although he had not yet begun to rub.

11

ravis was amazed at how quickly Chase Jordan seemed to have become best friends with Nish. To Travis, they were direct opposites: one red-headed, one dark; one slim, one a bit heavy; one quiet, one loud; one seeking to escape the spotlight, one willing to do anything for attention. But then, had he not read somewhere that opposites attract?

By day's end, the two very different peewee hockey players seemed lifelong buddies. They had toured The Wall together, had played Frisbee hockey together, and had even stuck together when Mr. Dillinger took them all off to Dave & Buster's, a special, three-storey extravaganza of video games, sports fun, and restaurants. Mr. Dillinger called it "A Special, Once-in-a-Lifetime Stupid Stop."

They had virtual reality battles and played all the latest video games. They ate hot dogs and hamburgers and fries, and Nish taught Chase how to regulate his belches after chugging an entire Coke so he could walk along and burp loudly every third

step. During lunch, Nish told Chase about his many adven-
tures with plastic puke and X-ray glasses and nude beaches,
and then he and Wilson taught Chase a trick they claimed they'd
invented in Tamarack: cupping their palms together, squeezing
out the air, and then flexing their hands to produce quick little
farting sounds.

"Works great in class," Nish said as if he were giving a university lecture on the art of hand-farting. "Teachers never know
who's doing it. Drives them crazy."

Chase Jordan listened intently, his eyes wide and his mouth
hanging open. He mastered the "art" of hand-farting and was
soon belching and burping and snorting like a Nish understudy
in a play called *The Most Ignorant Twelve-Year-Old on the Face of
the Earth*.

What would the President think? Travis wondered. Never
mind that, he told himself. What would poor Mrs. Nishikawa
think, her son corrupting the son of the President of the
United States?

But he knew the truth. Mrs. Nishikawa would think it only
natural that a member of the First Family would fall for the
charm of her one and only darling son. And if there was trouble,
she'd think it was the President's kid who had corrupted her
little angel.

It hardly surprised Travis at all when Nish announced, just
before the Owls all tucked in for the night, that he had struck a
special deal with Chase Jordan.

"Chase's gonna pay me back for all I've done for him," Nish
announced after the light was out.

Travis bit his tongue. *"All I've done for him?"* Travis repeated to himself. Where did Nish get off thinking this was all his idea?

Fahd, however, couldn't resist. "How?" he asked.

Nish lay in the dark snickering to himself.

Finally, Travis was caught. He had to know. "*How?*" he said, slightly annoyed.

Nish sighed deeply, immensely satisfied with himself.

"The Old Nisherama's gonna streak the White House."

12

The Screech Owls were playing again at the MCI Center, but this time it was not a Swedish team from Stockholm, it was the hometown favourite, the one team that was getting all the news coverage: the Washington Wall.

"Will the President be there?" Fahd had asked on the drive over to the rink.

Mr. Dillinger had shaken his head. "He won't be there. If *I* had to choose between a hockey game and leading the Western world, I'd probably pick the hockey game – but that's why I'm not President."

"But what about the final?" Fahd persisted.

"He's supposed to come," Mr. Dillinger said, "but I doubt there's billboards up all over the world telling people not to kill each other on Sunday because the President's got to go to his kid's hockey game. If he can be there, I imagine he will. If he can't, it's no big deal."

But everything seemed like a big deal anyway. They got to

the back of the rink and, again, security was everywhere, just
like when they first arrived. Their bags had to be checked by the
sniffer dogs, and they discovered that a strange arch had been
erected just inside the door, with police tape funnelling everyone through it.

"What's that?" Lars had asked.

"Metal detector," said Data. "Same as at the airport."

One by one the Owls and their equipment went through.
The players had to empty their pockets of metal and even take
off their windbreakers so the zippers wouldn't set off the alarms.

Travis and Sarah were right behind Nish as he started
through.

Nish was barely halfway through the detector when red
lights began flashing and an alarm went off.

Instantly, there were guards everywhere.

"*Looks like it won't let a tin brain pass*," Sarah giggled into
Travis's ear.

"*Or a lead butt!*" Travis added.

But none of the security force was laughing. A stern-
looking woman stepped forward. "Empty your pockets!" she
ordered Nish.

Nish complied, his face reddening the deeper he dug.
Candy, licorice, new gum in wrappers, old gum in Kleenex, a
pen, a golf tee, coins, keys. He laid it all out in a plastic box and
then the woman told him to turn around and go through again.

Again the alarm went off.

"What's in your back pocket?" the woman commanded.

"Nothin'," Nish whispered.

"There's *something* there," she snapped. "What is it?"

Nish slowly removed a long object from the back pocket of his droopy jeans.

"*What's this, then?*" she snapped.

"Remote control," Nish mumbled.

"*A what?*"

"Remote control," Nish repeated. "For a TV."

"You steal this from your hotel room, young man?"

Nish shook his head violently. "No."

"Where did you get it? Shoplifting?"

Again he shook his head. "It's mine from home."

The woman blinked several times, not comprehending. "You brought it from home," she said, a smile cracking her stern face. "What is it, your security blanket? Can't you go anywhere without television?"

"I guess," Nish said.

Travis guessed better. He remembered a conversation from the last practice before they left Tamarack. Nish had a new theory. The reason they couldn't get the adult channels in hotels, he said, was because the pay channels were all blocked through the converters.

"All I have to do is bring my own along," he had claimed. "And we'll be watching all the disgusting filth a young man needs."

"You're sick," said Wilson.

"Why, thank you," Nish answered.

"It won't work," predicted Travis.

Nish had laughed it off, convinced he had finally solved his lifelong quest to watch restricted movies.

They finally got through the check and were on their way to the dressing room. Sarah and Travis hurried to catch up to Nish, still red-faced and sweating from the grilling he had taken.

"Well?" Travis asked. "Did it work?"

"Did what work?" Nish said, pretending not to follow.

"The remote."

Nish only shook his head angrily and hurried on, leaving Travis and Sarah to laugh at their goofy friend and try to imagine poor Mrs. Nishikawa back in Tamarack, with a solid week of searching through their little house wondering where on earth she had mislaid the television remote.

"He is a mental case," said Sarah.

"If the President only knew who his son's been hanging out with," said Travis.

13

"I've been doing some calculations," Mr. Dillinger was saying as he stood in the centre of the dressing room.

The Owls were all dressed for the game against the Washington Wall. Nish was in his usual pre-game pose: helmet on, head bowed down to the top of his shin pads so it looked like he was sleeping. He couldn't be, though. He was still doing that obnoxious tapping very lightly with the blade tip of his stick. *Tap-tap . . . tap-tap-tap . . . tap-tap.*

It was unusual for Mr. Dillinger to make any kind of a speech. He had a piece of paper in his hand and was checking some scribblings on it.

"Take this tournament so far," Mr. Dillinger continued. "Go back two weeks in our regular season play. Add in the tournament we played over in Parry Sound, and we're on a twelve-game unbeaten streak. Nine wins, three ties, and *zero* losses. A dozen games without a loss, Owls. That's our best streak ever!"

"Not quite," a muffled voice said from the corner.

Mr. Dillinger spun around to look at Nish, whose head was seemingly glued to his shin pads.

"*What did you say?*" Mr. Dillinger said, surprise in his voice. He began checking his figures.

"Nuthin'," the voice barely mumbled.

"No, Nish – you had something to say," Mr. Dillinger persisted.

Slowly Nish's head came up. Even through Nish's face shield Travis could see that his pal was turning beet-red.

"What was it you said?" Mr. Dillinger pressed.

Nish cleared his throat. "It's just that the *best* streak is about to come," he said in a sheepish voice.

Mr. Dillinger nodded, satisfied. "Attaboy, Nish! Thinking ahead as always. That's my boy! Win this one, and it's thirteen without a loss. Then fourteen, fifteen, sixteen . . . !"

Nish nodded happily in agreement.

Sarah and Travis looked at each other, shaking their heads in amazement.

Nish didn't mean hockey.

He was thinking of the White House.

Nish the Bubble Butt, streaking the White House.

Muck told them the tournament was running a bit late. They should keep their legs loose, the coach advised them. Loosen their skates if they liked. The delay would be at least fifteen minutes.

Some of the Owls lay flat on their backs on the floor and raised their skates up on the bench. Mr. Dillinger was a great believer in keeping the blood flowing to the brain before a big game. No one knew if this were true or not, but most of the Owls didn't want to take a chance.

Travis got up and shuffled out the door. He was too nervous to sit still. He hated delays. He always tried to finish dressing – with the sweater going over his head, him kissing the inside of it as it passed – just as Muck was coming in the door for one of his little speeches – if you could even call them that. Then they'd be up and away out the door almost immediately.

He walked along the rubber carpeting to the maintenance area. There was a swinging door there with a small window in it. On his skates, he was tall enough to look through it.

The Zamboni was already running. The driver had moved it to the entrance chute, and another worker was waiting with his hands on the lever that would open up the doors onto the chute the moment the buzzer sounded.

Travis heard the buzzer sound in the rink and a cheer from the small crowd for whichever was the winning side. Almost instantly, the worker jacked open the big doors, pushed them clear, and the Zamboni driver all but bucked the huge machine out onto the ice surface.

It had all happened in an instant. Travis was now looking at an empty Zamboni chute.

But only empty for a moment.

As soon as the machine left, another person came in and brushed right in front of the small window Travis was staring through. It wasn't an arena worker – this was someone in a grey suit.

As Travis tried to get a second look, the grey suit shot across to the other side.

Travis jumped back.

Earplug!

He was moving quickly. He yanked open the door leading to the compressor and the cooling pipes, and darted in. In a moment, he was back out. He checked in closets and equipment docks and pushed aside cabinets to look behind them.

Travis shook his head. A special security sweep before a peewee hockey game when they'd already checked everyone at the entrances? The President wasn't even coming to this game.

Earplug checked to see where the Zamboni was on the ice, then pushed one of the cabinets up against the far wall, just beyond the drainage dock where the Zamboni sat when not in use.

He jumped up on the cabinet and reached above him.

Travis shook his head in amazement. Earplug was even checking the security video camera. Travis had noticed them earlier; little cameras in every corridor, panning from side to side, even outside the dressing rooms.

Earplug waited while the camera lens slowly panned away from him. Then he pulled a square block out of his jacket pocket, peeled off a paper covering that Travis realized was over sticky glue, and quickly set the block neatly into the corner of the wall so that it fit snugly and stayed there.

Travis was amazed at Earplug's thoroughness – the small block was even painted the same blue-grey colour as the walls. It was barely noticeable.

Earplug watched as the camera lens panned back towards the block, struck against it, stayed there a moment, and then reversed direction.

Earplug watched the camera move, obviously satisfied. He hopped down, quickly moving the cabinet back to its original position, and checked the camera action again. It swept across the far side of the chute, hit against the painted block, shuddered slightly, then swept back.

What was with Earplug? Travis wondered. Was he so certain something bad was going to happen in the far corner of the Zamboni chute that the camera had to do double time over that spot? A bit much, Travis figured. But then, everything to do with security and the President, and even the President's son, seemed a bit much to Travis.

He headed back to the dressing room for his stick. Earplug was already gone and the Zamboni was heading back towards the chute, the fresh new ice gleaming in the background.

14

ravis hit the crossbar during the warm-up. He would have a good game. The Owls were pumped for the match. Two of the local television stations were here to film the President's son playing for the Wall.

"He comes one-on-one against me," Nish said as they lined up for shots on Jenny, "I'm gonna let him beat me."

"Is that your deal?" Sam called from the other side of Travis. "He gets to beat you, you get to streak his living room?"

Nish made like he was about to hurl on her.

"*Get a life!*" Sam shouted back as she jumped up to take a shot.

"She's just jealous," Nish hissed in Travis's ear, "'cause I'll be on TV and she won't."

The Wall were a fine team. They were coached by a former Washington Capitals player who'd stayed on in the area after he'd retired, and the team played excellent positional hockey.

They did not, however, have a playmaker to match Sarah, or anyone with quite the speed of Dmitri. The Owls quickly went up 2–0 on a goal by Dmitri on a breakaway, and by Travis on a nice tip off a shot from the point from Sam.

Travis was impressed with Chase Jordan. He had good speed and fair skills, but more than anything else he had unbelievable determination. He was the kind of player Muck liked best, the player who can deliver a better game than his skills would suggest, simply out of sheer will.

It took a while for the Washington Wall to find their game. They seemed intimidated by the Owls at first, but by the second period they had come to realize if they put a special checker – Chase Jordan – on Sarah, they could do much to neutralize the Owls.

"He's good," Sarah puffed as their line came off for a break.

Travis nodded. He heard the admiration in Sarah's voice. She was different from most other good players, who showed their frustration at being checked. Sarah never got angry. She got even. She would figure out Chase Jordan.

The Wall tied the game at 3–3 and then went ahead 4–3 on a fluke goal that went in off Fahd's skate.

Chase Jordan went off for tripping on the next shift, however, after hauling down Sarah when she gave him the slip. The cameras were right on him during the play and followed him into the penalty box. Travis was certain this would be the clip they'd be playing on the evening news.

"She shoulda got a penalty herself for diving," Nish hissed as he and Travis circled, killing time before the faceoff.

Travis couldn't believe what he was hearing. Nish was

blaming Sarah for faking the trip, just so she could get on television instead of him.

Travis could sense what was coming. Nish was going "coast-to-coast" the second he got the puck. Nish knew that if the Owls scored while the President's son was in the penalty box, it would become part of the story.

Sarah won the faceoff and sent the puck over to Travis, who chipped it back to Nish.

Nish turned back, leaving the checkers waiting. He went behind his own net, stickhandling slowly, and stopped.

Ridiculous, Travis thought. It looked to the crowd like Nish was figuring out the lay of the ice, but in fact all he was doing was waiting for the cameras to find him.

Satisfied, Nish began stickhandling out of his own end. Up to the blueline and over, where the first checker tried for him.

Nish faked a pass to Travis. The checker fell for it, and Nish stepped around him, moving to centre.

A second checker charged, but Nish deftly slipped the puck between the Wall player's skates and picked it up on the other side.

Dmitri was breaking fast, pounding the ice for the pass that should have come.

But Nish wasn't passing.

Dmitri broke over the line offside, braked so hard snow flew up towards the glass, and he cut back hard, straddling the blueline with one leg while he waited to see what Nish would do.

Nish changed speeds, moving quickly toward the blueline. The Wall defence backpedalled, moving in towards him to pinch him off if necessary.

Sarah was clear on the other side, but Nish ignored her.

Travis looped back, coming in behind Nish for the drop pass, but Nish ignored him.

Nish let the puck go, raised his arms, and drove like a bulldozer into the two defenders as all three came together. Both Wall defence went down, leaving Nish staggering slightly but still moving.

He raced for the puck just as the Wall goaltender decided to lunge for it with his stick.

Nish reached out at the same moment, and the puck popped between the two stick blades, rising high and spinning until it came down on the far side of the net.

Sarah was there, waiting.

The goalie sprawled helplessly as Sarah came in on the empty net. She tapped the puck in and spun into Dmitri's arms.

Tie game, 4–4!

All the Owls on the ice converged on Sarah, slapping her helmet and pounding her on the back. All but Nish, who lightly tapped her shin pads and spun away.

"Glory hog!" he hissed back.

The Owls moved ahead to stay on a sweet goal by Simon, a hard blast by Andy, and a weird "knuckler" from the blueline by Wilson.

The clock was ticking down fast, with the Owls ahead 7–4, when, in the dying moments, Chase Jordan swept the puck away from Sarah and ended up all alone with it at centre ice.

Sarah had fallen when Chase Jordan checked her, so she was out of the play. Dmitri and Travis were too far down the ice to get back in time. Fahd, the other Owls defence, was out of position and scrambling to get back.

It was Chase Jordan against Nish. One on one.

Chase Jordan came over the blueline, with only Nish between him and the net. He set to shoot, no doubt hoping to blast a screen shot that Jenny wouldn't see until too late.

Nish fell to block the shot, spinning towards Chase.

Chase seemed surprised – Nish had gone down too soon.

He checked his swing and drew the puck back again with his blade, out of Nish's reach.

Nish spun helplessly towards the boards.

Chase moved in quickly. Forehand, backhand, forehand, backhand again.

Jenny went for the fake, guessing.

Chase held, the side of the net opening up.

He looped a high backhand in under the crossbar, sending the water bottle sailing as high as if Dmitri himself had taken the shot.

The horn blew. The whistle blew. The Wall bench emptied, every player charging Chase Jordan for his spectacular goal.

The cameras were racing out onto the ice.

Forget the penalty, forget the girl the President's son had tripped – *this* was the shot for the evening news! The Owls had won 7–5, but anyone who walked into the building at that moment would think the Wall had won the Stanley Cup.

The Owls each rapped Jenny's pads and then lined up to shake hands with the Wall who were still celebrating.

Travis found himself lining up right behind Nish. He couldn't help but ask. "You *didn't*, did you?"

Nish turned, face red, eyes wide. "*What?*" Nish asked, as if he had no clue what Travis meant.

"Let him do that?"

Nish grinned, ear to ear. "What do you take me for?"

Travis couldn't be bothered answering.

It would take forever.

15

ravis woke to the sound of Fahd clicking
through the television channels in search of
cartoons.

Click.

"Shoot!"

Click.

"Bor-ring!"

Click.

"Dumb!"

Click.

"It should be illegal to run news on Saturday mornings!"

Travis rolled over, rubbing the sleep out of his eyes and
trying to focus on the rapidly flipping television screen. Fahd
was right. Saturday morning in Washington, D.C., and it seemed
every television station was talking about the big crisis they
were trying to solve at the White House. Channel after channel
showed nothing but men in blue suits talking. A spokesman
from the White House was saying they were this close – and he .

held out his thumb and forefinger with a tiny gap between them – from reaching a breakthrough agreement. No one knew what would happen, but that wasn't stopping every expert on television from giving an opinion.

Travis agreed with Fahd. He'd rather watch cartoons.

"This is *ridiculous!*" said Fahd, slamming down the remote.

Travis was about to suggest they pass on cartoons and play a round of Nintendo instead, when the telephone rang beside Nish's bed.

A huge pillow looped over from the other side and smothered the phone. Nish's way of answering.

Lars dug out the phone and answered it. "Johanssen."

Travis shook his head. He'd never heard anyone answer a telephone that way until Lars came over from Sweden. Lars said he couldn't understand why people in North America just answered "Hello," and he refused to change.

"Uh huh . . . yeah . . . uh huh . . . okay . . . thanks." He hung up.

Travis waited, but Lars wasn't quick enough. "*What?*" Travis and Fahd said at once.

"Mr. Dillinger. Chase Jordan's pulled a few strings, it seems."

"*Meaning?*" Fahd said, again not waiting for Lars to finish.

"*Our White House tour starts in forty-five minutes!*"

Fahd pumped a fist. "*Yes!*"

On Nish's bed, several pillows shifted. A huge, puzzled face emerged, like a bear shaking off a cover of snow.

"*Huh?*" Nish grunted.

"*The tour! Nish! We got the tour!*"

"*Whazzat?*" Nish mumbled.

"*We're going to the White House!*"

Nish shook his head again, rubbed a hand through his flyaway hair, then began nodding and smiling.

"You gotta get ready," Fahd said, scrambling to put on his Owls track pants.

"We've only got forty-five minutes," added Lars.

With a big arm, Nish swept away the remaining pillows and sheets that were covering him.

He was buck-naked, not a stitch on.

"*I'm already ready!*"

They made it easily. Mr. Dillinger had the bus rolled up to the hotel entrance and the Owls hurried out and into their seats for the short ride over to the White House. They were all in their team windbreakers, Nish included. They had on their Owls track pants, Nish included. He'd even taken time to comb his unruly hair. They looked like a perfect, well-behaved peewee hockey team, which is exactly what they were – with one possible exception. But Travis wasn't that worried about Nish. He wouldn't have the nerve to try anything stupid here.

Chase Jordan had made wonderful arrangements. A tour guide met their bus and took them in through a special entrance. With the Summit underway, most of the White House had been cordoned off to the usual tour groups, but there were still parts of the enormous building open to the public, and the Owls were going to see other rooms in the White House that visitors rarely see.

Chase Jordan high-fived the Owls as he joined them for the tour. He was wearing his Washington Wall track pants and a Capitals T-shirt.

The guide was great. She told stories about the history of the White House, and even one wild story about a child ghost – a young son of Abraham Lincoln who had died there – who people claimed to have seen over the past century and more. She took them through the portrait gallery and showed them various rooms – including the Lincoln bedroom, where rich tourists were allowed to pay to stay over. No one seemed more pleased with the tour than Muck, the history lover. Chase Jordan added the odd story from the present. He even showed them his secret hall, where he and his brother sometimes played hockey mini-sticks below the glowering portraits of Herbert Hoover and George Washington.

"We're going now to see the Oval Office," the guide told them. "That's where the President does most of his work."

"Is he there now?" Fahd asked.

The guide shook her head, smiling. "No. I'm afraid not. There are special meetings going on in the West Wing, where we won't be allowed today. They might prove to be the most important meetings in the world this year. So you're lucky to be here on such a historic occasion."

"Fantastic!" Sam said. "We get to be a part of history!"

Travis felt Sarah nudging his arm. She had a worried look on her face.

"What is it?" he whispered.

"Have you seen Nish?"

Travis looked around.

No Nish, anywhere.

"I think I saw him and Chase slip through that door back there," Sarah whispered as quietly as she could.

Travis squeezed his eyes shut and shook his head violently. Surely not.

Anything but that.

16

Muck and Mr. Dillinger were so wrapped up in the tour of the White House that neither was aware that a Screech Owl had gone missing.

Travis felt sick to his stomach. Normally, if one of the players was missing, there would be an instant alert and they would all go off and try to find the straggler. But this wasn't normal. This was Nish, and he was with the President's son. They were in the White House, Chase Jordan's own home. So it was hardly as if Nish was *lost*.

Maybe Nish had just gone to the bathroom or something. That would be perfectly normal: Chase taking Nish off to a washroom in another part of the White House.

But he didn't believe it. And he knew, as captain, he should let Muck or Mr. Dillinger know if something was wrong.

They spent about fifteen minutes in the spectacular Oval Office. They saw the chair where President Kennedy had sat. They were told that here was where the critical decisions had been made for every war America had fought – including both world wars and the Vietnam War – and here was where the famous tapes had been made that caught President Nixon in a lie and led to his resignation in disgrace.

The tour of the Oval Office over, they headed out through a corridor towards the garden, where the President held so many of his press conferences. Just as Travis decided now was the time to tell Muck and Mr. Dillinger, a door swung open and Nish and Chase Jordan spilled through.

Both looked like they'd seen a ghost.

"Where *were* you guys?" Fahd asked.

"Nowhere," Nish said quickly.

"Washroom," Chase Jordan said. "Nish isn't feeling well."

That explains Nish's look, Travis thought. But what about Chase? He looked just as shocked. They couldn't both have been ill, could they?

"Something's happened," Sarah whispered to Travis.

Nish was uncommonly quiet on the bus ride back to the hotel. No farting noises, no burping or belching or screaming at the top of his lungs. No irritating *tap-tap . . . tap-tap-tap . . . tap-tap* on the window. Just Nish sitting quietly near the front of the bus, his hands folded in his lap as he stared out like an elderly tourist interested in the architecture of downtown Washington.

Something *had* happened. Travis just wasn't sure he wanted to know what.

17

They had two hours to kill before heading off for the next game, this one against the Portland Panthers, the team the Owls had come up against in so many other tournaments.

Muck told them they could take a nap in their rooms or go for a walk around the block, but nothing energetic and no straying too far.

Travis tried to doze off a while. Fahd began flipping once again through the TV channels.

Click.

"Darn!"

Click.

"Stupid!"

Click.

"*Gimmee that!*" someone screamed out.

It was Nish, his hand shaking as he reached out and demanded the remote from Fahd.

"GIVE IT TO ME!" Nish shouted.

"Okay, okay," Fahd said, flipping it to him.

Nish jammed it into his belt. "You watch way too much television, you know," he said angrily.

"And *you* don't?" Fahd asked.

"Muck wants you to get ready for the game," Nish said, his face beaming red. "Think about that, not some stupid cartoons."

With the remote control still jammed in his belt, Nish walked out and slammed the door.

Nish had never gone for a walk in his life. He adored cartoons. And since when had noise ever bothered him?

"I don't understand," said Lars.

"There's something he doesn't want us to know," suggested Travis.

"Or *see*," added Fahd.

"What do you mean?" Travis asked.

"He took the remote," Fahd said. "It can't be just to stop me watching cartoons."

"Then why?" asked Lars.

"So *we* couldn't watch," said Travis. "There's something on TV that's bothering him."

"Let's check it out," said Fahd.

"We *can't*!" Lars said, shaking his head in disbelief. "He took the control – remember?"

Fahd giggled. "I know he took it," he said. "But don't forget he also *brought* one."

The TV remote from home! The one that was supposed to get Nish access to those movies he was always trying to see.

"Where is it?" Lars demanded.

"In his equipment bag," Fahd said.

All three looked at each other.

"I'm not sticking my hand in there!" said Fahd.

"We need one of those dogs!" laughed Lars.

"C'mon," said Travis. "Somebody's got to do it."

They gathered over Nish's hockey bag like they were about to defuse a bomb. Travis quickly unzipped the bag.

"*Open the window!*" Fahd called.

"I'll get it!" Lars said, glad for an excuse to back away.

Travis held his nose and reached his free hand in, moving it about quickly. His imagination raced with wild ideas: tarantulas, lizards, rattlesnakes, rotting corpses, slugs, horse droppings . . .

"It might not be so bad," Fahd said in a calm voice. "Everything's fairly fresh since they blew up his other bag."

Travis groped around, then felt something that was either a rock-hard chocolate bar or the remote. He pulled it out.

Mrs. Nishikawa's missing remote!

"I'm surprised the plastic didn't melt," said Lars.

Travis aimed Mrs. Nishikawa's remote at the television and pushed "power." The television clicked, hissed, then brightened. He pushed the channel button.

Click.

A nature show.

Click.

News.

Click.

More news.

"It's the same old junk!" Fahd whined. "There's nothing here about the hockey team."

Lars seemed unconvinced. "If there's nothing on but news," he said, "maybe it's the news he doesn't want us watching."

Travis clicked over to CNN, the all-news channel. There were more reports from the White House. Then more political experts. Then reports from the countries involved in the Summit.

"*Bor-ring!*" Fahd called out every so often.

"A few more minutes," said Lars. He seemed to be losing hope himself.

The news anchor was smiling now.

"A most unusual development today at the White House Summit," she said. "We go now to Andrew Carter for a report."

The three boys watched as the picture turned to a CNN reporter standing just in front of the White House.

"White House staff have been scrambling since before noon to explain the circumstances behind today's bizarre developments at the Summit . . ."

The screen switched to stock shots of the Summit: mostly men talking to other men, men meeting in corridors, men gathered around a long table.

"Around 10:45, according to witnesses, a door to the boardroom where the main Summit participants had gathered burst open, and what appeared to be a naked young man wearing only a hockey goaltender's mask ran into the room, stopped sharply, and ran right back out . . .

"Both sides have accused the other of deliberately trying to sabotage the Summit with this unusual incident . . .

"CNN has obtained amateur videotape of the incident taken by one of the participating officials. We apologize for the poor quality, but it does give some sense of what occurred late this morning at the White House . . ."

The screen went fuzzy, a lens moved in and out of focus. The video was of poor quality, as warned, but clearly showed men gathering in a room and sitting down. Then the picture jumped and blurred across the room to catch only the hasty exit of the young man.

A young man wearing nothing but a goalie mask, his big, naked bum churning out the door.

"I'd recognize that butt anywhere," said Lars, shaking his head.

Travis closed his eyes, hoping it would go away. When he opened them the film was being run again. Nish's naked butt, *on instant replay!*

CNN switched back to the reporter, who was doing his best not to smile.

"Early reports were that this was a prank pulled off by the President's hockey-loving son, Chase, but the White House has strongly denied that the naked youngster is Chase Jordan . . .

"The White House has assured Summit participants that an immediate investigation will be carried out and, once identified, the guilty party will issue an apology. The incident is being treated as a scandal in parts of the Middle East, where public streaking is not considered quite as humorous as it might be here in North America. The President, according to sources, is furious over the incident and fearful that it may derail the agreement he had hoped could be reached today."

Travis flicked the channel.

More news on the White House streaker. More videotape replay.

Another channel, one more shot of the streaker.

"That's our teammate," Lars said.

"Internationally famous," added Fahd, "just like he always wanted."

18

"*Very funny!*"

Jeremy Weathers's goal mask went flying across the room and slammed into the far wall.

There wasn't a Screech Owl in the room not howling with laughter. Well, there was one. Wayne Nishikawa, CNN headline news, the "butt" of every joke in America.

"I just wanted you to know where you were sitting," Jeremy called back to Nish as he scrambled to pick up his goalie mask.

"I *know* where I'm sitting!" Nish snarled.

"*Right on the most famous big butt in America!*" Sam roared, and the dressing room howled once more with laughter.

The President had issued immediate apologies to each participant in the Summit, and they had been accepted. The Summit was once again underway.

The President had even answered questions about the incident at his daily press conference, but most of the questions ended in giggles, and even the President couldn't help but laugh a few times.

"When I declared my candidacy for President," he said with a straight face, "there were people on the other side who said they didn't want a bum in the White House."

The White House press gallery groaned at the bad joke, and that appeared to be it for the infamous "White House Streaker," as Nish had become known all over the world.

Only no one knew it was Nish. The Owls knew, and probably Muck and Mr. Dillinger knew, but all the reports had blamed it on one of the President's rambunctious kids, and Chase, to his great credit, had said nothing to set the record straight.

Nish would neither confirm nor deny that he was the White House Streaker.

"You really think there's another butt like that in the world?" Sam had asked.

"He had a mask on!" Nish protested.

"His face," Sarah said, "is not important. Put that butt of yours in a police lineup and anybody would pick you out."

"Sit on it!" Nish snapped.

Mr. Dillinger came whistling through the door, carrying his portable skate sharpener. He set it up in a corner, plugged it in, and began work on some skates.

No one spoke above the grinding whine of the machine as Mr. Dillinger expertly drew skates back and forth over the stone, the sparks shooting out behind like a miniature comet's tail.

Muck came in just as the last Owls were fastening their helmets tight. He stood in the middle of the room and stared hard at Nish.

Nish looked up once, then went back to his pre-game ritual of laying his head down over the tops of his shin pads. Travis could still see that his friend was redder than usual.

Muck said nothing. He turned and looked at all the players, one after the other.

"You know this team," he said. "Portland's a great side. They have size and speed. Look out for the big centre, Sarah. They're hurting, though. The little defenceman – I forget his name –"

"Billings," Travis said. He still had the signed card he'd exchanged with the little defenceman back in Lake Placid.

"Billings," Muck continued. "He's out with an ankle sprain. He won't be dressing."

Travis felt a twinge of regret. He knew what Billings meant to the Panthers. He also knew that not having him on the ice would help the Owls considerably, but he considered the little Portland defender a friend even though they barely knew each other.

"One more thing," Muck said. "We win this game, we're in the finals."

It was all Muck needed to say. The Screech Owls played as if possessed. Sarah was exceptional, shutting down Yantha, the big Portland centre, and scoring twice herself. Dmitri scored one of his "flying water bottle" specials, and Nish scored a beauty on an end-to-end rush.

The Panthers clearly missed Billings. With no one to get the puck out of their end or make the long pass, they weren't nearly the team they should have been, and the Owls won easily, 6–2, with Sam and Derek scoring late in the game.

Travis had three assists and felt terrific. He knew, however, that all the glory went to the goal scorers. Perhaps he and Muck would be the only two who had noticed how well he had played.

They lined up to shake hands. The Panthers were on the verge of elimination. Either they won their next game or they were headed home.

Travis went down the line, bumping gloves with the various Panthers, including big Yantha.

He was about to turn away and head for the exit when he noticed one more player coming to shake hands. It was Billings, limping badly, an upturned hockey stick for a crutch as he made his way across the ice.

He was smiling. "I gave you first star, Travis."

Travis high-fived the open hand presented to him.

"Thanks," Travis said.

"See you next tournament."

Travis nodded.

Someone else had noticed.

19

Most of the other Owls had already headed for the team bus for the ride back to the hotel when Travis, Fahd, Lars, and Nish decided to take the shortcut out the Zamboni chute and through the back door.

They were just moving into the Zamboni chute when a familiar voice barked, "*Halt! Who goes there?*"

Earplug!

They couldn't see him, but they could hear him. "What is this?" Nish said. "A *pirate* movie?"

Travis cringed. The old Nish was back – but this was hardly the time to kid around.

"*Identify yourselves immediately!*" Earplug barked.

"T-Travis Lindsay," Travis said.

"Fahd Noorizadeh."

"Lars Johanssen."

"Paul Kariya."

Travis winced.

"*Drop the bags!*" the voice ordered.

The four Owls dropped their equipment bags.

"*Up against the wall!*"

The four boys moved towards the wall. Nish, having seen it so many times on television, automatically faced the wall and leaned against it, his hands high, as if he were about to be frisked.

Earplug came around the doorway, his hand tucked inside his jacket like it was petting his revolver.

"*That's the idea, Kariya!*" he called out. "*You others do the same!*"

The three followed Nish's lead, Fahd letting a giggle slip out as he did so. *Kariya?*

"*What's so funny, you?*" Earplug snapped.

"Nothing," Fahd said in a quick, small voice.

"*What are you boys doing here? This is a restricted zone!*"

"*We're taking a shortcut, sir!*" Nish barked back, as if he were a marine recruit.

This time both Fahd and Lars giggled. Let it alone, Nish, Travis thought. Let it alone.

"Shortcut?" Earplug said, for the first time speaking in a nearly normal voice.

"The team bus is out back," Travis said. "We always go through this way. It's shorter."

"You'll go through this way no more, young man," Earplug said. "The FBI and Secret Service have declared this off limits to the end of the tournament. *Understand?*"

"*Yessss, sirrrrr!*" Nish snapped back over his shoulder.

"You other boys act more like Kariya, here," said Earplug. "And we'll understand each other just fine. Now get out of here, the *long* way!"

"*Yessss, sirrrrr!*" Nish snapped again.

The four Owls gathered up their equipment bags and sticks and turned back the way they'd come, heading the long way around for the bus. Mr. Dillinger and Muck would be wondering what had happened to them.

"What's with the 'Paul Kariya'?" Lars asked Nish as they went through a door into the corridor heading toward the front entrance.

"First thing that came into my mind," Nish said.

Travis shook his head. Life would certainly be a lot easier if only his friend would wait for the second, third, fourth – *or two hundredth* – thing that came into his twisted mind.

hase's team beat the Panthers!" Lars shouted. Travis couldn't believe it. The Washington Wall beat the Portland Panthers? *Impossible.* But then he remembered – Billings still hadn't been able to play. Without him, the Panthers were just another team. And now they were out of the tournament.

"*The final's at six o'clock!*" Fahd yelled. "*We're playing the Washington Wall for the championship!*"

"And they've just announced that the President *can* come!" added Lars.

There'd be more television coverage than the Owls had ever experienced.

All the Owls but one, that is.

One of them – or at least a significant *part* of one of them – was already a television star around the world.

Entering the MCI Center later in the afternoon was like entering an armed camp. The Owls had been amazed before by the
security when Chase Jordan was playing, but that was nothing
compared to this.

There were Secret Service men everywhere. There were
metal detectors and X-ray machines and guards at every entrance
and, once again, dogs to check every equipment bag.

"Good thing they don't have sniffer dogs for streakers'
bums!" Sam yelled out.

"*Shut up!*" Nish snapped, his face glowing like the burner
on a stove.

They're going too far with Nish, Travis thought. I've got to
put a stop to this.

But there was no time. The delay getting into the rink
meant that they had to hurry into their hockey equipment, and
Mr. Dillinger was in the dressing room sharpening a few of the
Owls' skates. There was no use trying to talk over the noise.

Nish had dressed in silence and was sitting in his usual
corner in his usual fashion: head down on the tops of his shin
pads, his eyes closed. Normally, Travis would have thought his
friend was trying to "envision" the upcoming match, but this
time he had the feeling that Nish was trying to escape.

The machine shut off.

I should say something, Travis thought. I should do it now.

But he was too late. Willie and Andy and Wilson were
already back at it.

"Can you imagine if they *did* have a sniffer dog for streakers!" Wilson shrieked, still laughing at Sam's joke.

"*No dog'd take the job!*" giggled Willie.

"*It'd be worse than getting skunked!*" laughed Andy.

Nish's head was up. He looked furious.

He stood up, and with a swift kick of one skate, sent all the sticks flying off the wall in Andy's direction.

"*Hey!*" Mr. Dillinger shouted.

But Nish was already at the door and out, slamming it hard behind him.

Should I go after him? Travis wondered. No. Give him a minute or two by himself. Deal with the team first.

"Lay off him, okay?" Travis said.

"It's just a little fun," Andy said weakly.

"I know," Travis said. "But fun's over. Can't you see he's had enough?"

No one said anything. Travis was afraid they thought he was being too pushy, that he was overreacting.

"He's right," Sarah said. "Let's just let it go."

Travis felt the air come out of his lungs. He hadn't realized how tightly he'd been holding his breath. Thank heavens for Sarah.

"He's still a butt brain," Sam said.

I can't argue with that, Travis thought. But he wisely said nothing.

21

Nish burst through the dressing-room door, slammed it behind him, and instantly wondered why he'd done it. He didn't know which way to go. *Back into the dressing room? Take off somewhere? Wait where he was until Muck came along?*

He had that old out-of-control feeling inside him, almost as if his blood was boiling and steaming through his veins. He could still remember how, whenever he got this way when he was small – frustrated, angry, upset, his brain spinning, racing – his mother would simply pick him up, hold his arms tight to his body, and move somewhere quiet with him until he calmed down. He wished his mother was here right now. But she wouldn't be able to pick him up any more. And she might find out he'd run off with the television remote . . .

He tried counting to ten. He tried holding his breath. He tried counting back from ten. He needed to move. He needed to shake the hot blood out of his veins and the spiders out of his stomach and the squirrels out of his head. If he didn't move, he thought he'd explode.

Careful not to scrape his skates, Nish shuffled down the corridor towards the Zamboni chute just as Muck came around the far corner from the opposite direction.

Muck stared curiously at Nish. No one, not even Mrs. Nishikawa, understood Wayne Nishikawa better than Muck Munro, the coach of the Screech Owls. He'd known Nish for too long now. He'd seen him in every imaginable state of mind, including the one where he just had to get away and be on his own.

Muck decided to let him go, for the time being.

Travis had his head down, thinking about the game, when Muck came into the dressing room. Muck looked his usual self: casual, relaxed, more like he was about to go fishing than coach a team in a championship game. A championship game before the President of the United States.

Travis couldn't stop a small smile from flickering across his face. Most coaches would have worn a suit under the circumstances. Most would be carrying a clipboard filled with nonsense, or chewing ice like they do in the NHL. But not Muck. Never Muck. Same old windbreaker. Same old pants. Same old boots.

"Nishikawa needs some private time," Muck said matter-of-factly.

"We kidded a bit too much," Sarah said.

Good for Sarah, Travis thought. If he had said it, it would have sounded more like "telling."

"He'll be fine," Muck said.

"When're we on?" Fahd asked.

"Zamboni's finished," Muck said. "We can go out any time."

The Screech Owls started moving, but Muck held up his hand, palm out, and they stopped dead.

"A couple of things."

Travis sat back, slightly surprised. Muck rarely talked to them before games, and most assuredly *never* gave anything like a "coach's speech."

"They're a good team," Muck said. "You already know that. They tied you in the early round. They're very well coached and play exceptional positional hockey. But they do make mistakes. We stay in our positions and trust in their mistakes. When they make one, we pounce with our speed. Okay?"

"Okay," Fahd said unnecessarily.

"Now there's a lot of attention out there. Cameras. Reporters. Lots of people. They're not here to see you. They're here because the President's coming later and the President's kid is playing. I don't want anybody thinking outside the ice surface, okay?"

"Okay," Fahd said.

"I don't know why I'm telling you all this," Muck smiled. "The only one I really need to speak to isn't even here."

Nish could feel himself calming down. The squirrels were slowing in his head. The spiders were quiet in his gut. His blood was flowing rather than boiling over. Even his thoughts were back as close to normal as they ever got.

He just needed some space. Just a little time to himself and he could go back and join the team like everything was back to the way it used to be. If they said nothing, he'd say nothing. They could all just forget any of this stupid stuff ever happened.

Nish figured he needed something to distract himself. Something else to think about apart from Sam's constant cracks and what might happen if the authorities found out he was the one who streaked the President.

The Zamboni room. He'd go in and check it out. Maybe talk to the driver about keeping ice down here in Washington where it could get so hot at this time of year. Something to take his mind off everything.

Nish stood at the door and tried to see into the Zamboni chute area, but the window in the door was papered over for some reason, as if they were trying to keep people out. Or at least from seeing in.

Nish knew the Zamboni driver wouldn't mind. He was a happy old guy, always laughing and joking with the kids. Nish would just walk in and start talking to him. He leaned into the door.

The door opened too fast – almost as if someone had yanked it from the other side. Nish fell through the doorway, his skates scraping horribly across the concrete floor.

He felt something being slapped over his mouth just as he opened it to cry out. Something sticky – and terrible-tasting!

Duct tape!

And then pain – followed by darkness.

There was a quick knock on the dressing-room door and a man's voice called out. "*Ice's ready! You're on, Screech Owls!*"

Muck checked his watch and shrugged. "I guess Nish is having a longer talk with himself than I thought," he said. "He'll just have to catch up to us. *Let's go!*"

"*Yesss!*" shouted Sam.

"*Go Owls!*" called Sarah.

"*Be smart!*" Travis yelled.

"*Go Can-a-da!!*" shouted Fahd.

22

ravis hit the crossbar first shot in the warm-up. He felt good. The ice was in perfect shape. The rink was filled with far more fans than the usual crowd of parents and relatives. There were several TV crews as well, but none of the cameras was pointed in the direction of the Owls. All media attention was on the Washington Wall, Chase Jordan's team.

Mr. Dillinger had found out that the President would be arriving around the third period. It was all he could manage with his busy schedule, especially with the White House Summit about to wind up. He'd watch the final period and then make the presentation.

Travis didn't doubt for a moment that the crowd would be cheering for the Wall. Especially the television people. Footage of the President handing the trophy to his own son would be far more valuable than shots of the President of the United States shaking hands with some little kid from Canada.

It made Travis want to win all the more.

The officials were calling the teams to get ready for the faceoff. Travis looked desperately towards the door leading to the dressing rooms.

Still no sign of Nish.

Muck seemed equally concerned. He whispered something to Mr. Dillinger just before the opening faceoff, and Mr. Dillinger hopped over the boards at the visitors' bench and headed back through the seats towards the exit.

He would be going to get Nish.

Everything would be all right.

The squirrels in Nish's head and the spiders in his gut were gone, but now that he had come to, he had howling hyenas up top and crocodiles below. He was terrified he would throw up. With duct tape covering his mouth, he'd choke himself and *die*!

He couldn't see. He couldn't yell.

He couldn't move his hands. They must be wrapped in duct tape, too.

He had no idea where he was. It was cold and hard and damp, that was all he knew.

Perhaps it was the cameras, perhaps it was knowing the President of the United States was going to be there – whatever it was, the Owls were off their game and the Wall were on theirs.

The Washington team seemed driven to play hard. Maybe it was the idea of beating the Canadians at their national game. Or maybe they were just more used to all the attention that came from having Chase Jordan on their team.

Chase scored the first goal on a beautiful passing play with one of his wingers. They forced a turnover on Andy's line and came in so fast that Willie Granger failed to get back in time, stranding Fahd to deal with the attack.

Chase hit his left wing early with a pass, Fahd went for the puck carrier, the winger flipped the puck back, and Chase one-timed it behind Jeremy.

Travis cringed on the bench. Fahd should never have fallen for it. Nish would have stayed to the middle, taking away the pass and letting them have the long shot if they wanted.

Where was he?

23

M etal, Nish thought.

Whatever he was on, it was metal. And *tight*, an enclosed space.

He tapped one skate against the wall to make sure. Hard, cold, wet metal. But what was it, and where was it, and why was he there?

Nish tried to piece together what little he knew.

What had he heard? *Nothing.* He'd pushed through the door, and the door had seemed to fall away. In an instant, he'd been down on the floor and the tape was ripping and then it was over his mouth and then everything went dark.

What had he seen?

Nothing.

Chase Jordan was having the game of his life. He'd scored twice and set up another by the time the first period was over. The Washington Wall were ahead 4–2. Only Sarah, on a backhand as she'd been tripped, and Jesse, on a wraparound that caught the

Wall goaltender off guard, had been able to score for the Owls.

Travis knew what was wrong. The Wall were sending two forecheckers in hard to try to panic the Owls' defence, while the third forward, usually the centre, stayed back around the blue-line ready to pounce on any long passes the panicking Owls defence might try.

Travis also knew what was missing.

If Nish were on the ice, the Wall wouldn't have been getting nearly so many chances. Nish knew how to get a puck out of his own end. He could carry a puck better than anyone but Sarah, and he had a good eye for the long breakaway pass to Dmitri or Travis on the wings. He also knew how to defend in his own end.

Travis had already seen Mr. Dillinger come back shaking his head, and he had caught the look on Muck's face as the coach realized Nish was nowhere to be found.

So where was he? Travis asked himself. How badly had they hurt Nish's feelings? Could he have left the rink?

No. He'd left his clothes and runners in the dressing room when he stomped out. Travis tried to imagine Nish, in full equipment, scraping along Pennsylvania Avenue, in his skates, around the Washington Monument and the long reflecting pool while office workers sat about in the sun.

Travis knew Nish had to be in the MCI Center.

But where?

24

The third period was underway, with the Wall ahead 5–4. Chase Jordan had scored his third goal of the game, and there had been a delay while a couple of dozen hats soared out of the stands and onto the ice to celebrate the hat-trick. The cameras had recorded every moment of it, even coming down onto the ice to film the workers piling the hats into a large garbage bag.

It seemed to Travis that nothing could stop the Washington Wall. Everything seemed to be working out for everyone: Chase was having the game of his life; the Wall were leading in the championship game; and the television crews were delighted with their story. All that was needed to complete the perfect day was for the President to arrive and present the trophy to his own son.

Perfect, Travis thought, for everyone but the Screech Owls. They weren't on their game. He liked Chase Jordan enough to appreciate what this must mean to him, but he couldn't help but feel that this was not a true measure of the Owls.

They needed their top defenceman. Desperately.

But there was no sign of Nish. No word. Nothing.

Nish had never tasted anything so horrible. He was chewing the duct tape from the inside. His mouth must have been opened to scream when the tape was slapped over it. He could move his jaw just enough to bite into the tape and grind at it.

It tasted bad. But it was working. He had chewed a small hole in the cover, but not enough yet to call for help. All he could manage was a tiny squeak.

He thought he could hear something now, but the sounds were terribly muffled. He felt like he was inside a cookie tin. Some container of some kind. And somewhere beyond the cold metal walls was the sound of a crowd calling and cheering. He also thought he heard a buzzer.

He must still be inside the rink!

He chewed faster and harder.

Two minutes to go, and the Owls were still down by a goal. Muck called Sarah's line out for the faceoff, and Travis leapt the boards, tapping Andy's and Jesse's shin pads as they puffed by to take their rest on the bench. All the Owls were giving everything they had, but it was doing no good. They needed someone to move that puck up.

They circled for the faceoff, Sarah choking up on her stick as she began to glide in for the puck drop. Suddenly there was a huge commotion in the crowd, and the linesman backed off, waiting.

Everyone in the rink, players included, turned their attention to an entrance to the stands.

An army of Secret Service men, led by Earplug, were moving down the aisle towards a seat just behind the Wall's bench.

Earplug seemed even more nervous than usual. His eyes were darting every which way. His hand was tucked inside his jacket, ready at any moment to pull out his gun.

To Travis, it seemed unbelievable. More like a movie than real life. But then the stands broke into applause and cheers. Behind the first wave of Secret Service men, a tall grey-haired man in a dark blue suit moved athletically down the steps, waving and smiling.

Anthony Jordan, the President of the United States.

Some people were getting to their feet.

Travis didn't know what do to. Stand at attention?

Without thinking, he began tapping his stick on the ice in salute. The rest of the Owls on the ice followed suit. The Owls on the bench stood and leaned over and rapped their sticks on the boards.

It was a wonderful moment. The cameras turned on the Owls and then on the Wall, all of whom began doing the same thing.

The President noticed and gave the Owls' bench the thumbs-up, which Mr. Dillinger returned. Muck didn't even notice. The puck was about to drop, and Muck was already lost in the play.

The President took his seat and the linesman moved back into position for the faceoff.

Travis looked up.

Chase Jordan was staring at him.

Chase winked.

Travis winked back.

The puck dropped.

"*H-h-h-helpppp!*" Nish called.

He could hear it well enough himself. But was the sound getting out?

He had chewed through and spat out enough of the foul-tasting tape to be able to call out. But any noise he made seemed to bounce right back at him.

Was there any air getting in? he suddenly wondered.

What if he died in here?

25

Sam did her best to work the puck out. She rapped it off the boards, stepped around the first forechecker, and moved as quickly as she could up towards the blueline before flipping the puck ahead to Sarah.

Sarah spun just as she gathered in the pass, her sudden movement to the side throwing off her check. She had enough space to move and dug in hard, moving up over centre, stick-handling and looking for a play.

Dmitri broke hard, cutting from the boards towards the centre of the Wall's blueline, and Sarah hit him with a perfect pass. Travis knew the play. If Dmitri was coming his way, he should go Dmitri's way. The criss-cross, a play to throw off the other team if they were trying to cover each player.

Dmitri carried the puck in, and both Wall defence, momentarily confused, moved to check him at the same time.

Dmitri saw them coming and dropped the puck. But he kept going, "accidentally" ploughing into the two defence. One went down with Dmitri, the other lost his stick.

Travis was in free, with nothing between him and the Washington goal but a stickless defenceman.

The defender lunged and fell, hoping to gather the puck into his body. Travis tucked the puck and stepped around the spinning defenceman.

Completely free!

He looked up. The Wall goalie was skittering out to cut off the angle. Travis knew exactly what he would do: fake the slapper, maybe draw the goalie out even more, then hold and cut for an angle shot, hoping the goalie wouldn't be able to recover and get back in time.

He raised his stick to fake the slapper.

The goalie went for it, driving hard towards Travis and going down to cut off the angles.

Travis held and swept around the goalie.

Empty net!

He had the tying goal. He aimed dead centre.

And suddenly his feet went out from under him.

"H–H–H–ELLLP!!!"

Nish could really yell now. He had chewed off and spat away most of the duct tape. He was yelling and screaming.

"H–H–HELP! . . . SAVE MEEEEE! . . . HHHELLLP MMMEEEEEE!!!!"

But nothing.

Nothing save his own desperate voice bouncing back at him.

He began to cry.

"PENALTY SHOT!"

Travis, still down on the ice, could hardly believe it. He had turned enough to see who had tripped him, and he had heard the referee's whistle. But he hadn't expected this. It was a penalty shot! His second of the tournament! And the player who had tripped him was *Chase Jordan*!

Sarah was tapping his pads as he got to his skates.

"It's up to you, Trav," she said. "We need you here."

The Owls needed the goal to tie. There were only forty-five seconds left on the clock. It was up to him.

Muck called them over to the bench. The other Owls would all have to be on the bench for the shot. Only Travis and the Wall goaltender would be on the ice.

The camera crews were all down at ice level now. They were acting like they were in charge, ignoring the referee and jumping over onto the ice to get the best shots. One crew was over at the Wall bench, the camera in the face of Chase Jordan, who was trying to ignore them.

Travis wished they would all go away. Why him? Why couldn't it be Sarah or Dmitri taking the shot? Or Nish? No one would enjoy all the attention more than Nish.

Everyone was on their feet, even the President.

Travis looked up, trying to clear his mind.

All he could focus on was Earplug, chewing his gum so fast it was a wonder smoke wasn't coming out his mouth.

"Lindsay," Muck said in a quiet voice. He was smiling. "Just remember to shoot this time, okay?"

The linesman placed the puck at centre ice, and the referee blew his whistle, the signal for Travis to start skating.

It all felt so dreadfully familiar: too much snow on the ice, a forty-pound puck, legs like wet spaghetti, arms of lead, brain of marshmallow.

Travis picked up the puck and bore down.

Muck had said it all: *just shoot the puck.*

Travis felt instantly better. His speed picked up. The puck lightened on his stick.

He reviewed what had happened just before the foul. The goalie had fallen for his fake slapshot and Travis had tried to go around him. He'd be expecting Travis to try the same thing.

Travis pushed the puck over the blueline. High in the slot, he went into the same slapper motion.

This time the goalie stayed back, sure Travis would try to pull him out and get the angle on him.

It was one of Travis's better slappers. The heel of his stick caught the puck flush, and he was certain he could feel the puck roll along the length of his blade and spring off the slight curve at the end. The puck rose about a foot off the ground and smashed – *hard* – into the pads of the goalie.

"*No!*" Travis shouted to himself, spinning away and raising his eyes to the rafters.

Failed, again.

But then he saw the cheers go up from the Owls' bench.

Sarah threw her stick in the air.

Sam leapt up, screaming.

Fahd pumped his fists.

Travis turned back.

The puck had trickled through the goalie's pads!

Tie game, 5–5.

They played out the final few seconds and the horn blew. The Presidential party was already headed for the Zamboni chute. But the championship game was tied. There would have to be sudden-death overtime.

The referee blew his whistle, consulted with the linesmen and then the off-ice officials.

He went over to both benches. "I'm ordering a flood," he told Muck. "There's too much snow on the ice to play."

"Good," Muck said. The Wall coach agreed.

All the players leapt over the boards onto their benches to wait out the quick flood.

"WHAT THE HELL DO YOU THINK YOU'RE DOING?" It was Earplug. He was screaming, hammering on the glass behind the off-ice officials' bench. He looked like he was about to burst.

"We can't play on this," the referee calmly explained. "I've ordered a fresh flood."

"YOU CAN'T DO THAT!" Earplug roared. "THIS IS THE PRES-IDENT OF THE UNITED STATES. HE HAS A STRICT SCHEDULE TO STICK TO!"

"It's *my* call," the referee said, clearly fed up. "It's for safety reasons. These are peewee hockey players, not soldiers."

"I'M ORDERING YOU RIGHT NOW TO PROCEED WITH THE GAME INSTANTLY!" Earplug screamed.

The referee shook his head. "You're in charge of nothing here, pal, so relax. Five minutes, that's all it takes."

Earplug slammed his fist so hard against the glass Travis thought it would shatter. He stomped away towards the Presidential party. The President himself was busy talking to people in the crowd and shaking hands. He didn't seem in the slightest concerned about a five-minute delay for a flood. If anything, he was welcoming the opportunity to do a little campaigning.

Earplug needs a vacation, Travis thought to himself.

26

Nish was already screaming when he heard the roar.

He was screaming and crying, convinced he was going to smother in this airtight box, when, suddenly, there was a slight whining noise, then the sound of something catching, coughing, then an enormous roar.

Mr. Dillinger took the opportunity to race back to the dressing room. He had five minutes to check the room and around most of the rest of the lower arena for Nish.

Mr. Dillinger was getting worried. He was responsible for the kids off the ice. He prided himself on taking great care of the team, without being *too* protective. But right now he felt terrible. *He had lost Nish.*

He checked the Screech Owls' dressing room, and the equipment rooms, and even the other dressing rooms. He checked the washrooms and corridors. He asked Secret Service guards at two rear doors and at the Zamboni main doors if they'd seen a chubby little kid in full hockey uniform, but no one had seen him.

That smell. What was that smell?

Nish knew it from somewhere. It was like . . . like . . . like *rotten eggs*! Yes, that was it. Rotten eggs.

Had he smelled it in science class? Fahd's old egg salad sandwiches he kept forgetting in his locker?

He felt a motion. Whatever he was in seemed to jump and chug and roll. And then the roar again – a huge roar.

His nose filled once more with a fresh burst of the rotten-egg smell.

But now he knew what it was.

Not rotten eggs, but *propane fuel*!

He felt his little prison cell moving now, smooth and fast. He heard all kinds of new sounds: valves turning, water running, something twisting, something grinding.

He felt something being sprayed onto him. Something cold, very cold.

Something like ground-up ice, or *snow*!

He knew now. He knew exactly where he was.

Inside the Zamboni!

27

Muck looked up as Mr. Dillinger climbed back onto the bench. Mr. Dillinger looked crushed. He shook his head at Muck, but it was already obvious. Everything Mr. Dillinger had to say was on his face. No Nish.

"We could use that crazy idiot right about now," said Sam.

Travis saw that Sam was beyond worry. She was afraid for Nish. He realized how much Sam liked Nish, even if she never let on for a moment. The same for Sarah, who was biting her lip and staring out at the Zamboni as if it, somehow, held the answer.

"HHHHELLLPPPPPP!"

"I'M HERE – INSIDE THE ZAMBONI!"

The louder Nish screamed, the more his voice seemed to be lost in the roar of the machine.

The smell of the propane was much stronger now. He was breathing in fumes. His head was throbbing. His eyes stung. He was gagging. The snow was churning in on him. He didn't know how much longer he could hold out.

The thought came to him in a flash. He'd use his skates! His hands were tied in duct tape, but whoever had tossed him in here had done nothing to his legs. He could bang his skate blades against the metal sides of the Zamboni.

He kicked hard.

Bang! Bang! . . . Bang! Bang! Bang! . . . Bang! Bang!

"*Do you hear that?*" Sarah turned her head.

"Hear what?"

"Something's banging in the Zamboni!"

Travis listened hard. "Yeah," he said, "I do hear something."

"So do I," said Sam.

"Wait'll it comes around again," said Sarah.

The Zamboni made a wide turn, the ice glistening wet behind it, and headed back up-ice, drawing closer to the Screech Owls' bench.

At first the sound was faint. But then, as the big ice-surfacing machine drew alongside the bench, the sound grew considerably louder.

Bang! Bang! . . . Bang! Bang! Bang! . . . Bang! Bang!

That familiar rhythm . . . *It was Nish!*

Sarah stood up, screaming at the Zamboni driver. "*Stop!* STOPPPPP!"

Sam was already over the boards.

"STOPPPPP!"

28

nother few circles and we might have lost
him."

Nish was under the care of the Presi-
dent's own personal doctor. He had come running down onto
the ice immediately after Travis and Sam and Sarah had forced
the Zamboni driver to stop.

The driver had been furious. No one was to come onto the
ice when the machine was resurfacing, he yelled at them. It was
dangerous.

And then he, too, had heard the banging.

He had reached up and pulled a lever. There was the sound
of valves moving and gears shifting, and slowly, like some
yawning prehistoric monster, the Zamboni had opened up.
Inside, half covered in snow and ice chips, was Nish, still
screaming and pounding his skates against the insides of the
huge machine.

"Either the snow would have smothered him," the doctor
was saying, "or the fumes would have killed him."

"He's used to fumes," said Sam. The doctor looked at her, but he didn't get it.

The Screech Owls were all in the dressing room, waiting. Nish was in the corner, his skates kicked off and his face beaming red, but he hardly looked ill. He had two Cokes going at once and seemed, once again, delighted with all the attention.

But the big news story was unfolding outside the dressing room. The television crews that had come to get some footage of the President at a hockey game were now going live with a much different story.

A threat on the life of the President!

Travis was stunned by how quickly the Secret Service had moved. The building had been cleared at once. Both teams dispatched to their dressing rooms with guards on the doors. A complete investigation had taken place in less than an hour.

Two older men, one Secret Service, the other a presidential aide, had come around to the Owls' dressing room to explain.

Nish had come across an act of sabotage. The plan had been to assassinate the President as he was stationed in the Zamboni chute waiting to present the championship trophy – presumably to his son, Chase.

High-tech plastic explosives had been smuggled in past security and wired to explode when a signal was transmitted from a hand-held device by the assassin, who was also in the building.

The security camera in the Zamboni area had been tampered with so that it failed to cover that small space in the corner where the explosive had been planted.

The worst part, the Secret Service man said, was that the suspect in custody was "one of our own."

But Travis already knew that. He knew now why that little block of wood had been placed next to the security camera in the Zamboni chute.

He knew now why a certain person had seemed so nervous.

He knew now why there had been such yelling and screaming about a silly flood.

Only one person knew that Nish had been bundled into the Zamboni, and that once the Zamboni was back on the ice it was only a matter of time before Nish would be discovered, alive or dead, and the opportunity to kill the President would be lost.

The assassin was Earplug.

"Why would he?" Fahd asked the men.

The answers were shrugs. "We have no idea," the Secret Service man said. "We hope to find out. He might well have been acting alone. Obviously, he had become a very sick person without us noticing. And it's our job to notice."

There was a knock at the door and a man walked in, another of the President's aides. He smiled at the Screech Owls and nodded appreciatively to Nish, who had helped avert a terrible disaster. Had they not discovered him and then checked the chute, they would never have found the explosives.

"President Jordan has asked that the game continue," the man said. "The ice is ready."

The Owls cheered.

Nish reached down and picked up his skates. He handed them to Mr. Dillinger.

"Can I get a quick sharp," he said. "I think I took a bit of the edge off them."

Mr. Dillinger took the skates, his eyes wide in shock. Nish was going to play? Not even an hour ago he had been facing death!

Mr. Dillinger looked questioningly at the doctor, who smiled back.

"Probably the best thing for him," he said.

"Can I play?" Nish said to Muck.

Muck seemed to think about it awhile. Then he nodded. "You were on the game score sheet. Nothing says you have to see ice before overtime, I guess."

"LET'S GO!" shouted Sam, who slammed her stick into Nish's pads as she jumped up.

29

he ice was perfect.

Travis took a few easy loops around the rink before the officials came out to start the overtime. He was glad to get back to the game. He tried not to think about what had almost happened. Earplug, for whatever reason, had wanted to kill his President. Maybe he was a double agent, or maybe simply insane. He hadn't even given a thought to all the other deaths and injuries the explosion might have caused. Earplug could have been killed himself.

Nish made it out just before the game got underway again. He seemed a bit wobbly as he checked out Mr. Dillinger's sharp on his skates, but he also seemed keen to play.

The overtime started and the Owls got an early chance. Sarah hit Travis with a quick pass and he managed to squeeze between the boards and the Wall defenceman, popping free with the puck along the left side and no one between him and the goalie.

He wished he'd shot. Muck always said, "You can't go wrong with a shot." But he'd seen Dmitri swooping in from the far side and tried to hit him with a pass, only to have the other Wall defender dive onto his stomach and reach his stick out to jab the puck away.

The Owls had other chances. Little Simon broke in but hit the post. Fahd almost scored from the point, but the Wall goaltender stacked his pads and just got enough of the puck to deflect it clear. Sam had a clear shot and put it right into the goalie's chest.

Nish began slowly, but he was regaining his form. Once, he carried end to end, only to have a good slapper go off the outside of the far post.

The Washington Wall had chances too, but Jeremy was spectacular in net.

Up and down the game went. Shift after shift, Travis tried to create something, but nothing was happening for his line. Sarah couldn't break through. Dmitri couldn't use his speed to get clear. The line they were on against couldn't get anything going, either. It was that tight a match.

Travis was on the bench when Fahd pinched up and lost the puck. A Wall winger plucked it off the boards and sent a high sailing pass out over centre. He hadn't even meant it as a pass, just a clearing shot, but Chase Jordan had anticipated perfectly.

Chase caught up to the puck around centre. Wilson was chasing, but he lacked the speed to make up the gap. Chase moved in fast on Jeremy, who came out to cut out the angle. He shot hard. Jeremy caught it with his blocker – a fabulous save! –

but the puck bounced right back into Chase Jordan's chest, fell
to the ice, and Chase rapped it in on the rebound.

The Wall were champions!

The President's son was the hero!

Travis felt the sag on the Owls' bench. It was as if the air had
gone out of the entire team. He turned and looked at Muck,
who was already walking up the bench lightly touching each
and every Owl on the back of the neck – his little message that
they'd done their best, that there was no shame in losing such a
great game. And in fact Travis felt good for Chase Jordan. In a
way, this was how it *had* to end after all that had happened.

It was Travis who began the salute. He stood up, leaned over
with his stick, and began pounding the boards with it. Sam and
Sarah joined in, and soon all the Owls on the bench were doing
it. The six Owls on the ice, Jeremy included, began slamming
their sticks on the ice.

The crowd took up the chant. They clapped in time with
the pounding sticks.

Chase Jordan broke out of the backslapping scrum of
Washington Wall players and circled towards the Screech Owls'
bench, raising his own stick to return the Owls' salute.

The rest of the Wall followed suit.

The Zamboni chute was opening. Two men were wheeling
out a table, and on the table was the championship trophy. Right
behind came the President of the United States, his shoes sliding
on the still-clean ice.

The teams lined up on their bluelines for the presentation.
The TV cameras were all back on the ice to record it on video.

The President made a little speech, only parts of which Travis could catch in the echoey arena, and then Chase Jordan, his helmet and gloves off, skated over to accept the trophy from his father.

It was a wonderful moment. So close to being a disaster.

Travis felt a chill run up and down his spine. He didn't think he'd want to live life the way Chase Jordan and his father lived it. Better to be safe in Tamarack, with only practice and homework to worry about.

Chase handed the trophy to his assistant captain, who raised it high over his head and began a Stanley Cup parade around the rink, while the crowd cheered them.

Chase left the group and skated back to the Owls. He high-fived the Owls until he came to Nish. "My father wants to speak to you."

"You *told!*" Nish shrieked, his eyes widening.

Chase Jordan laughed. "No – don't be silly. He wants to say something to you."

With the cameras following, and the colour in Nish's face rising, Chase Jordan and Nish skated over to where the President stood, smiling.

Travis watched the President lean over, say something to Nish as they shook hands, and then, with his other hand, give him something in a small blue box. Nish looked at it as they continued talking. Travis could swear Nish was glowing ever redder.

Nish skated back to the cheers of the crowd and the pounding sticks of the players. He was staring with an odd expression at the tiny blue box he held in his hands.

"*What is it?*" Fahd shouted.

"*What did he give you?*" Sam yelled down the line.

Nish held the box out and opened it for his teammates to see: tiny silver buttons with the Presidential seal on them.

"*Cufflinks!*" Andy shouted, laughing. "*You don't even own a suit!*"

Nish was now a deep, deep crimson. "That's what *I* said."

"Well," said Sarah, "what did he say back to you?"

Nish's face looked like it was about to burst.

"He said maybe I could wear them with my birthday suit."

THE END